PRAISE FOR
JOEL C. ROSENBERG

"His penetrating knowledge of all things Mideastern—coupled with his intuitive knack for high-stakes intrigue—demand attention."

PORTER GOSS
Former director of the Central Intelligence Agency

"If there were a *Forbes* 400 list of great current novelists, Joel Rosenberg would be among the top ten. . . . One of the most entertaining and intriguing authors of international political thrillers in the country. . . . His novels are un-put-downable."

STEVE FORBES
Editor in chief, *Forbes* magazine

"One of my favorite things: An incredible thriller—it's called *The Third Target* by Joel C. Rosenberg. . . . He's amazing. . . . He writes the greatest thrillers set in the Middle East, with so much knowledge of that part of the world. . . . Fabulous! I've read every book he's ever written!"

KATHIE LEE GIFFORD
NBC's *Today Show*

"Fascinating and compelling . . . way too close to reality for a novel."

MIKE HUCKABEE
Former Arkansas governor

★ ★ ★

JOEL C. ROSENBERG

A J.B. COLLINS NOVEL

WITHOUT WARNING

TYNDALE HOUSE PUBLISHERS, INC., CAROL STREAM, ILLINOIS

Visit Tyndale online at www.tyndale.com.

Visit Joel C. Rosenberg's website at www.joelrosenberg.com.

TYNDALE and Tyndale's quill logo are registered trademarks of Tyndale House Publishers, Inc.

Without Warning

Designed by Dean H. Renninger

Unless otherwise indicated, all Scripture quotations are taken from the New American Standard Bible,® copyright © 1960, 1962, 1963, 1968, 1971, 1972, 1973, 1975, 1977, 1995 by The Lockman Foundation. Used by permission.

2 Corinthians 5:8 and Luke 23:43 in chapter 49 are taken from the New King James Version,® copyright © 1982 by Thomas Nelson, Inc. Used by permission. All rights reserved.

Jeremiah 29:11 in the dedication and Psalm 9:3-6 in chapter 86 are taken from the *Holy Bible*, New Living Translation, copyright © 1996, 2004, 2015 by Tyndale House Foundation. Used by permission of Tyndale House Publishers, Inc., Carol Stream, Illinois 60188. All rights reserved.

Without Warning is a work of fiction. Where real people, events, establishments, organizations, or locales appear, they are used fictitiously. All other elements of the novel are drawn from the author's imagination.

For information about special discounts for bulk purchases, please contact Tyndale House Publishers at csresponse@tyndale.com, or call 1-800-323-9400.

Library of Congress Cataloging-in-Publication Data

Names: Rosenberg, Joel C., date, author.
Title: Without warning : a J. B. Collins novel / Joel C. Rosenberg.
Description: Carol Stream, Illinois : Tyndale House Publishers, Inc., [2017]
Identifiers: LCCN 2016043153 | ISBN 9781496406163 (hc)
Subjects: LCSH: Journalists—Fiction. | IS (Organization)—Fiction. | GSAFD: Christian fiction. | Suspense fiction.
Classification: LCC PS3618.O832 W58 2017 | DDC 813/.6—dc23 LC record available at https://lccn.loc.gov/2016043153

ISBN 978-1-4964-0629-3 (International Trade Paper Edition)
ISBN 978-1-4964-0620-0 (sc)
ISBN 978-1-4964-2329-0 (mass paper)

Printed in the United States of America

23 22 21 20 19 18 17
7   6   5   4   3   2   1

To our youngest son, Noah—you have such an inquisitive and creative mind and, oh, what a storyteller you are! Your mom and I cannot wait to see the great things the Lord will do in and through you, young man, as you follow him with all your heart.

"'For I know the plans I have for you,' says the Lord. 'They are plans for good and not for disaster, to give you a future and a hope.'"

JEREMIAH 29:11

★ ★ ★

CAST OF CHARACTERS

★ ★ ★

JOURNALISTS

James Bradley "J. B." Collins—national security correspondent
for the *New York Times*
Allen MacDonald—D.C. bureau chief for the *New York Times*
Bill Sanders—Cairo bureau chief for the *New York Times*

AMERICANS

Harrison Taylor—president of the United States
Martin Holbrooke—vice president of the United States
Margaret Taylor—First Lady of the United States
Carl Hughes—acting director of the Central Intelligence Agency
Robert Khachigian—former director of the Central Intelligence
Agency
Paul Pritchard—former Damascus station chief for the Central
Intelligence Agency
Lawrence Beck—director of the Federal Bureau of Investigation
Arthur Harris—special agent with the Federal Bureau of
Investigation
Matthew Collins—J. B.'s older brother
Lincoln Sullivan—attorney
Steve Sullivan—attorney, grandson of Lincoln

JORDANIANS

King Abdullah II—the monarch of the Hashemite Kingdom
of Jordan

ISRAELIS

Yuval Eitan—Israeli prime minister

Ari Shalit—acting director of the Mossad

Yael Katzir—Mossad agent

EGYPTIANS

Wahid Mahfouz—president of Egypt

Amr El-Badawy—general, commander of Egypt's special forces

Walid Hussam—former chief of Egyptian intelligence

TERRORISTS

Abu Khalif—leader of the Islamic State in Iraq and al-Sham (ISIS)

Tariq Baqouba—commander of ISIS forces in Syria

OTHERS

Prince Mohammed bin Zayed—head of intelligence for the
    United Arab Emirates

Dr. Abdul Aziz Al-Siddiq—onetime professor and mentor
    of Abu Khalif

PREFACE

★ ★ ★

From *The First Hostage*

The camera zoomed in on the president.

And then, on cue, Taylor spoke directly to the camera.

"My name is Harrison Beresford Taylor," he said slowly, methodically, wincing several times as if in pain. As he spoke, Arabic subtitles scrolled across the bottom of the screen. "I am the forty-fifth president of the United States. I was captured by the Islamic State in Amman on December 5. I am being held by the Islamic State in a location that has not been disclosed to me, but I can say . . . I can say honestly . . . I can say honestly that I am being treated well and have been given the opportunity to give *ba'yah*—that is to say, to pledge allegiance . . . to the Islamic State. I ask my fellow Americans, including all my colleagues in Washington, to listen . . . to listen carefully . . . that is, to listen carefully and respectfully to the emir, and to follow the instructions . . . he is about to set forth for my safe and expeditious return."

When Taylor was finished, the camera panned back to Abu Khalif, emir of the Islamic State.

"Allah has given this infidel into our hands," Khalif said in Arabic. "O Muslims everywhere, glad tidings to you! Raise your heads high, for today—by Allah's grace—you have a sign of his favor upon you. You also have a state and caliphate, which will return your dignity, might, rights, and leadership. All praise and thanks are due to Allah. Therefore, rush, O Muslims, to your state. Yes, it is your state. Rush, because Syria is not for the Syrians, and Iraq is not for the Iraqis, and Jordan is not for the Jordanians. The earth belongs to Allah.

"I make a special call to you, O soldiers of the Islamic State—do not be awestruck by the great numbers of your enemy, for Allah is with you. I do not fear the numbers of your opponents, nor do I fear your neediness and poverty, for Allah has promised your Prophet— peace be upon him—that you will not be wiped out by famine, and your enemy will not conquer you or continue to violate and control your land. I promised you that in the name of Allah we would cap- ture the American president, and I have kept my word. The king of Jordan will soon be in our hands. So will all the infidel leaders in this region. So will all the dogs in Rome. The ancient prophecies tell us the End of Days is upon us and with it the judgment of all who will not bow the knee and submit to Allah and his commanders on the earth."

Khalif now turned to his right and faced a new camera angle. Behind him was a shadowy stone wall. When he resumed speaking, it was in English.

"Now I speak directly to Vice President Holbrooke. Fearful and trembling, weak and unsteady, you and the infidels you lead have lost your way. Now you have three choices—convert to Islam, pay the *jizyah*, or die. You must choose your fate and choose it quickly.

If you and your country choose to convert, you must give a speech to the world doing so under the precise language and conditions of Sharia law, and you will be blessed by Allah and have peace with the caliphate. If you choose to pay the *jizyah*, you must pay $1,000 U.S. for every man, woman, and child living in the United States of America. If you do not, or if you act with aggression in any matter against me or against the caliphate, the next video you see will be your beloved president beheaded or burned alive. From the time of this broadcast, you have forty-eight hours, and not a minute more."

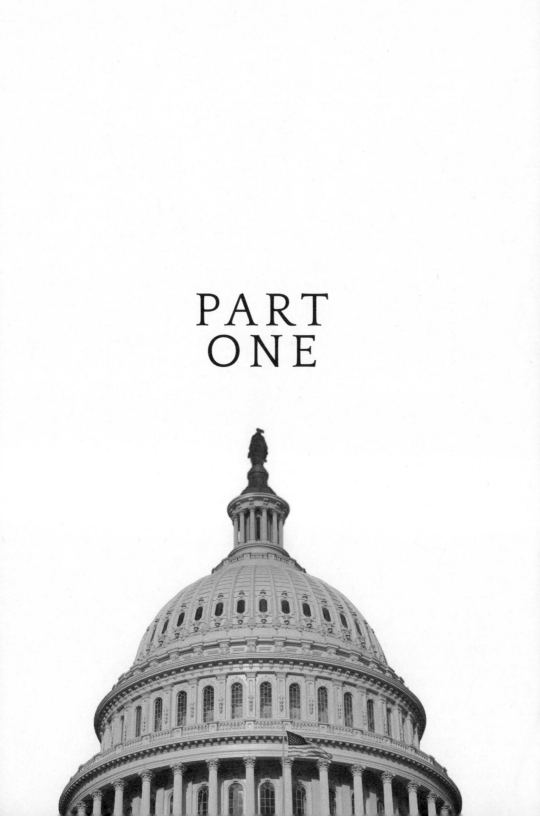

PART
ONE

1

★ ★ ★

I had never been in the Oval Office before.

But I'd always imagined my first time going differently.

The tension wasn't immediately apparent as I stepped into the most coveted executive suite on the planet. But it would come. It had to. I would force it. And when it did, my fate would be sealed.

At first, the president and I were both on our best behavior. As far as he was concerned, our past battles were water under the bridge. Yes, in Amman he had been blindsided by an enemy he neither truly understood nor saw coming. But in his eyes, the successful rescue effort had been enough to shift the balance of power, and he had adapted quickly. Tonight, as he addressed the nation and the world in a live televised speech to a joint session of Congress, he was at the top of his game. Soaring in the polls. Confounding his critics. Seemingly destined to leave the American people the legacy of peace, prosperity, and security they so desperately longed for.

The president beckoned for me to be seated, then took a seat himself behind the *Resolute* desk, built from the timbers of a British naval vessel abandoned in a storm in 1854. As he did, he opened a black

3

leather binder embossed with the presidential seal. He picked up a Montblanc fountain pen and excused himself for a moment to make a few final edits to his speech before we loaded into the motorcade to head up to Capitol Hill together.

With every passing moment, my anxiety grew. In less than an hour, Harrison Beresford Taylor, the nation's forty-fifth president, would deliver his annual report to the legislature. He would assert unequivocally, as he had on every other such occasion, that "the state of the union is strong."

Yet nothing could be further from the truth.

I could take it no longer. It was time to say what I had come to say.

"Mr. President, I very much appreciate you inviting me here. I know you have a great deal on your plate right now. But I have to ask you, not as a reporter, just as me. Do you have a plan to kill Abu Khalif or not?"

It was a simple, direct question. But it immediately became apparent that Taylor was going to avoid giving me a simple, direct response.

"I think you're going to be very pleased with my speech tonight, Collins," he said, leaning back in his black leather chair.

"Why?" I asked.

"Trust me," he said with a smile.

"That's not exactly in my nature, sir."

"Well, do your best."

"Mr. President, are you going to lay out for the American people a plan to take down the ISIS emir?"

"Look, Collins, in case you haven't noticed, in the last two months we've ripped ISIL to shreds. We're targeting all of their leaders, including the emir. We've stepped up our drone strikes. We've taken out twenty-three high-value targets in the last six weeks alone. Is it going as fast as I'd like? No, and I'm pushing the Joint Chiefs. But you need to have patience. We're making great progress, and we're going to get this thing done. You'll see."

"Mr. President, with all due respect, how can you say we're making progress?" I shot back. "Abu Khalif is on a genocidal rampage. As we speak, he's slaughtering Muslims, Christians, Yazidis, and anyone who gets in his way: beheading them, crucifying them, enslaving them—men, women, and children. We're getting reports of unspeakable acts of cruelty, worse every day. He's murdered your friends and mine. This is the guy who held you captive. If we hadn't gotten there when we did, he would have taken a knife and personally sawed off your head—or put you in a cage and burned you alive—and uploaded the video to YouTube for the entire world to see."

"And now we have them on the run," Taylor countered. "We're blowing up their oil fields. We're seizing their assets. We're blocking their ability to move money around the world. We're shutting down their social media accounts and cutting off their communications."

"It's not enough, Mr. President," I insisted. "Not unless you're going after the emir directly. You're hitting his men and his money, but, sir, you can't kill the snake unless you cut off its head. So I must ask you again: have you signed a presidential directive to take Abu Khalif out, or not?"

2

★ ★ ★

The president leaned forward and glared at me.

"I was *there*, Collins. I was *in* that cell. I was *with* those children. Every night their faces haunt me. Every morning I hear their shrieks echoing down these hallways. Don't stand there and make it sound like I'm doing nothing. You know full well that's not true. I'm not sitting on my hands. I put American boots back on the ground in Iraq. I sent America back to war in Iraq—against the will of my party and much of my cabinet. My base went ballistic, but I did it. Because it was the right thing to do. And we're winning. We're taking out ISIL's forces. We're cutting off their supply lines. We're taking back land. We've got them on the run. What more do you want?"

"Simple. I want Abu Khalif's head."

"It's *not* that simple, Collins."

"Mr. President, do you really understand who this man is, what he wants, how far he's willing to go?"

"*Me? Do I* understand?" Taylor bellowed, suddenly rising to his feet. "You're honestly asking if *I* understand who we're up against?"

"Sir, this is not Saddam Hussein. It's not bin Laden. It's not Zawahiri or Zarqawi. Abu Khalif is not like any enemy we've ever faced before. This is a man who thinks he was chosen by Allah to bring about the end of the world, a man willing to use genocide to hasten the coming of his messiah and establish a global caliphate."

Taylor was seething. But I didn't stop.

"And he's coming here, Mr. President. *Here.* To America. To our streets. He's said so. He's promised to kill you and as many Americans as he possibly can, and he will—unless you take him down."

Taylor shook his head in disgust and walked over to the windows. As he looked out at the snow falling on the Rose Garden, I stood as well.

"You're a real piece of work, Collins, you know that? You need to take a deep breath and calm down and show a little trust in the armed forces of the United States and their commander in chief. We're winning. We have the enemy on the run, and we're not going to let up."

"Mr. President, I watched Abu Khalif behead two men. I saw him test sarin gas on prisoners who died a grisly, gruesome, horrifying death. I've looked in his eyes. I know who he is. And he told me exactly what he was going to do."

Taylor didn't say anything. He just glanced at his watch and then again stared out the window into the icy darkness that had descended on the capital.

"Look, Mr. President, I know you've gone against your party, your cabinet, even your own campaign promises by putting U.S. forces back into Iraq. I'm not saying you're sitting on your hands. You want to win. I see it. But, sir, don't underestimate this man. Abu Khalif has kept every threat he's made so far. How many times has he bragged how his experienced, trained, battle-hardened jihadists are coming here carrying American passports, fighters who will easily slip across our border and blend into society until they're ready to strike? He's coming here, Mr. President, and unless you stop him, it's going to be a bloodbath."

At this, Taylor turned to face me. "You think I don't know that, Collins? Are you really that arrogant?"

"Then tell me you've signed a presidential directive to hunt down the emir of the Islamic State, wherever he is, whatever it takes. Give me that, and I'll back off."

"I'm not going to get into operational matters, Collins—not with you. Not with any reporter from the *New York Times*."

"So I'll take that as a no."

"Don't play games with me, Collins. Don't twist my words. I didn't say no. I said I'm not going to discuss it—not with you."

"Off the record," I said.

"Nice try. This entire conversation is off the record."

"But—"

"How many ways can I put it to you, Collins? I get it. Abu Khalif is a thug, a cold-blooded killer. He's the face of ISIL, I grant you. But you're making too much of him. He's just one man. We'll find him. We'll take him out. But don't kid yourself. That won't be the end of it. There's going to be another thug after him, and another after that, and another after that. And we'll find them and neutralize them as well. But I'm not going to paralyze my administration in the hunt for just one guy. We're going to go after the entire ISIL leadership and their infrastructure and their money—systematically, step-by-step, until we're done, until it's over. But you've got to understand something, Collins. ISIL is a threat, but it's not an existential threat to America. They can't destroy us. They can't annihilate us. I don't care about all their talk of building a global caliphate. It's never going to happen. You want to talk about a potential existential threat? Then let's discuss climate change, not ISIL."

What in the world is he talking about? I asked myself. I hadn't called ISIS an existential threat. And how on earth did this compare to climate change? "Mr. President, Abu Khalif is not *just one guy*. He's different—brilliant, savvy, charismatic, irreplaceable."

"Nobody's irreplaceable."

"This guy is. He's not some back-alley street tough like Zarqawi.

8

This is one of the smartest foes we've ever been up against. He's got a doctorate in Islamic theology and another one in Islamic eschatology. He's fluent in seven languages. He's a genius with social media. He's casting a spell over the entire Islamic world. He's a magnet, attracting jihadists from 140 different countries. He's mobilizing and training and deploying foreign fighters on a scale unlike anything we've ever seen. This is no longer just a terrorist movement. Abu Khalif has built himself a full-scale jihadist army—a hundred thousand men consumed by the notion that Allah has raised them up to conquer the world. His forces may be in retreat in Iraq, Mr. President, but they're spreading like a cancer across the Middle East and North Africa, they're penetrating into Central Asia and Europe and Latin America—and they're coming here next."

3

★ ★ ★

A Secret Service agent entered the Oval Office.

"Mr. President, it's time. The motorcade is ready."

Taylor, the hard-charging former governor of North Carolina and onetime founder and CEO of an enormously successful tech company in the Research Triangle near Raleigh, was not a man accustomed to being challenged to his face. He kept his eyes locked on mine for a few more moments.

"Mr. Collins, I invited you here to thank you for all you did to save my life. I asked you to be my honored guest tonight at the State of the Union. Tomorrow you will receive the Presidential Medal of Freedom in the ceremony we have planned, and this is how you thank me, by telling me I'm not doing enough to keep Americans safe? We're on the verge of a great and historic victory against the Islamic State, and you're standing here in the Oval Office asking me for vengeance."

"No, sir—I'm not asking for vengeance. I'm asking for justice."

The president shook his head. "I'm an antiwar Democrat, Collins, yet I went to Congress and demanded they pass a formal declaration of war against ISIL. I'm the man who pulled the last of our forces out of Afghanistan, yet I just sent thousands of American ground forces back into Iraq. Why? To crush ISIL once and for all. And that's precisely what we're doing. Did we find Abu Khalif in Alqosh? No. Did we find him in Mosul? No. But are we going to keep hunting him? Absolutely. And for you to suggest I'm not serious about getting this guy is not just crazy. It's downright offensive."

"Are you going to attack Raqqa?" I asked, speaking of the ISIS capital in Syria.

"We're focused on Iraq right now, and you know it."

"Are you going to take Homs? Aleppo? Dabiq?"

At this, the president's entire demeanor shifted. Instead of fuming at me, he laughed out loud. "Collins, have you completely lost your mind? I'm trying to put *out* the forest fire in Syria, not pour gasoline on it. I'm working night and day with the Russians and the Iranians and the Turks and the U.N. to try to nail down a cease-fire that will hold, something that'll actually stop all the killing, not increase it."

"But, sir, don't you see? Agreeing to a cease-fire before destroying Khalif would be a disaster. You'd be giving him a safe haven. You'd be effectively handing him enormous swaths of territory he alone would control, territory he could use as a base camp to launch attacks against the U.S. and our allies."

"So what would you have me do, exactly?" Taylor asked as he took his suit jacket from a hanger in the corner. "You want us to get sucked into a bloody ground war in Syria? Because that's exactly what Abu Khalif wants. He's practically begging me to put a quarter million American troops smack-dab in the middle of Syria's civil war. He *wants* me to attack Dabiq. He *wants* me to get caught in a quagmire. And why? To bring about the end of the world, right? You said it yourself. He's consumed with establishing his global caliphate. He's transfixed on slaughtering the 'forces of Rome' and ushering in the End of Days. And now you really want me to play into his sick, twisted game? I took you as smarter than that."

This was going nowhere. But I took a deep breath, and one last shot. "Mr. President, I'm asking you a simple, straightforward question. And you still haven't given me a simple, straightforward answer. So let me ask you one more time: Do you have a plan to hunt down and kill Abu Khalif, wherever he is, whatever it takes, or do you not?"

The president didn't say anything. Instead, he buttoned his suit coat, walked back to his desk, and picked up the loose pages of his speech. He scanned several of them closely, as if looking for a particular section. Then he scribbled a few notes in the margin.

"Sir?" I asked after several moments of silence.

Taylor ignored me for a while longer, making more changes before putting all the pages into the binder.

"Yes, we have a plan," he said finally, quietly, closing the binder and looking back at me. His voice was once again calm, collected, and presidential.

He pushed a button on his phone, then turned back to me and kept talking. "Abu Khalif came after me personally. Why? Because we'd actually hammered out a comprehensive peace treaty between the Israelis and the Palestinians. My predecessors tried to get it done, and they failed. I was *this* close. And then Khalif and his thugs came along and blew it all to kingdom come. I won't forget that, Collins. Not ever. And as long as I am the commander in chief, I won't rest until we take these guys down—all of them. On that, you have my word."

He looked sincere. He sounded sincere. But I wasn't convinced. Harrison Taylor was a consummate politician, and the simple fact was I didn't trust him. It had been two months since the forces of the Islamic State had blown up his peace summit in Amman. Two months since ISIS forces had launched a chemical weapons attack in the Jordanian capital and captured the leader of the free world. Two weeks later, Congress had declared war and a coalition of U.S. and allied forces had "reinvaded" Iraq—albeit this time at the invitation of Baghdad—and made a big show of it on worldwide television.

But ISIS was still slaughtering thousands of innocents. Its leader was still a free man. And it was now increasingly clear to me that this president had neither a plan to bring him to justice nor the will to see one through.

For years, the Taylor administration's approach to the Middle East and North Africa had been a disaster. Foreign policy was driven by press releases and photo ops. Taylor had been repeatedly warned about the magnitude of the threat posed by the Islamic State, yet he'd been caught off guard by the ISIS onslaught in Amman. Now much of the region was on fire. The cost in human lives had been catastrophic. Yet there had been no political cost whatsoever. To the contrary, Taylor was more popular than he'd ever been.

The president loved to say that ISIL was on the run and that the caliphate had been cut in half. But he hadn't asked Congress to authorize the use of force in Syria. He refused to conduct bombing raids there or send Special Forces to find Abu Khalif or any of the rest of the ISIS psychopaths. And yet, for now, at least, the public was giving Taylor and his administration tremendous credit for freeing Iraq and returning millions of refugees to their homes. The homecoming Iraqis cheering the American and allied forces and even bowing down before the cameras and kissing the land that had been returned to them made for great television, I admit, and I'm not saying it wasn't a victory. It was. But it was a Band-Aid on a severed artery.

The region was bleeding to death, and ISIS was causing the bleeding. This wasn't the Cold War. The jihadists couldn't simply be driven out of Iraq and back into Syria and "contained" there. They were bloodthirsty lunatics, driven by an apocalyptic, murderous brand of Islam unlike anything the world had ever seen before. Abu Khalif and his men chilled me to my core. They were a lethal virus that had to be eradicated before they spread to every part of the planet, leaving a trail of death and heartbreak in their wake.

I had braved a mounting winter storm to come here to the Oval

Office to see the president of the United States in person for the first time since we'd been airlifted together out of Erbīl at the beginning of December. I had come at the president's personal request. I had hoped to find a man sobered by reality, a leader who had truly learned and absorbed hard lessons from all that had transpired. Instead I saw a risk-averse politician basking in the glory of an adoring nation, disturbingly unaware of the catastrophe I sensed was coming next.

4

★ ★ ★

"Why, James, what a pleasure to see you again," the First Lady said in her typically warm and gracious manner as she entered the Oval Office and eased the mounting tension.

"Thank you, Mrs. Taylor," I replied as she gave me a quick hug and a kiss on the cheek, leaving behind a smudge of pale-pink lipstick in the process. "It's an honor to see you as well."

"Please, James, it's Meg," she said as she drew a white cotton handkerchief from her purse and dabbed it on my cheek until the lipstick was gone. "How many times must I ask you to call me Meg?"

"Sorry, ma'am," I said. "Guess I'm just not used to being on a first-name basis with a First Lady."

"Hush—you're practically family now, James," she said in her distinctive Southern lilt. "Harrison and I can never repay all you've done for us, and we want you to feel welcome and at home in this house. Now, how's your mother? Did her surgery go well?"

Whatever her husband lacked in Tar Heel charm, Margaret Reed Taylor made up for in spades. Now fifty-eight, the eldest daughter of a former North Carolina senator—and the granddaughter of a onetime president of UNC Chapel Hill—was as politically savvy as she was lovely. She'd earned her MBA from Wharton and her law

15

degree from Harvard, and my colleagues on the White House beat swore she was the administration's chief strategist, though she was far too clever to let anyone get a clear look at her maneuverings. Tonight, she wore a modest but elegant robin's-egg-blue suit and a gorgeous string of pearls, and clearly she knew how to extricate her husband of thirty-two years from a delicate moment like a seasoned professional.

"It did, ma'am," I said, impressed that she was aware of my mom's hip surgery less than two weeks earlier. "Thanks for asking."

"Is she up and about yet?"

"Not quite yet, but it could be worse."

"I hear she's one tough cookie."

"She'd be glad to hear you say it, ma'am. She sure wishes she could be here tonight, and not so much to be with me as to meet you."

"Well, bless her heart. Tell her I'd love to give her a call in a few days, and I'd certainly love to have you both come for a meal when she's up to it."

"That's very kind, ma'am. She'll be tickled pink."

"Good. Now have your brother and his family come to Washington for all the festivities? Will they be in the chamber tonight?"

"Matt came, and I'll meet him over there. He was having dinner with Senator Barrows," I said.

"And his wife?"

I shook my head. "Annie felt she needed to stay with Mom and the kids. But she also would have loved to meet you."

"You bring her with your mother and we'll all do lunch. They'll be watching you on television tonight, I'm sure?"

"Absolutely—and tomorrow, too," I said. "It's the biggest thing that's ever happened in Bar Harbor. I can tell you that much."

"We hear you've become quite a hero up there." She smiled, then turned to brush a few pieces of lint off her husband's freshly pressed navy-blue suit and adjust the Windsor knot in his red power tie.

Just then, another Secret Service agent stepped into the room. He said nothing. But he didn't have to.

"It's time, sweetheart," the First Lady said. "We mustn't keep all your fans waiting." At that, she turned to me and smiled. "The American people just *luuuv* my husband, James," she said with a wink. "Don't forget that now, you hear?"

She held my gaze until I nodded. She didn't say another word, but she'd made her point. *My husband is beloved and thus more powerful than ever. You're just a reporter. Don't ever forget that, James—ever.*

It was true that the president's approval ratings were soaring. But on the issue of Abu Khalif, the American people were with me. It was a small comfort at the moment, but it was true. Earlier in the day, Allen MacDonald, my boss at the *Times* who had recently been promoted to D.C. bureau chief, had e-mailed me an advance look at the latest numbers from a *New York Times*/CBS News poll fresh out of the field. The survey found that 86 percent of the American people wanted the president to "use all means necessary" to bring the leader of the world's most dangerous terrorist movement to justice, and 62 percent said they would be "satisfied" if the ISIS emir was captured, convicted, and sent to Guantánamo. But fully nine in ten Americans said they wanted Abu Khalif hunted down and killed in retribution for what he had tried to do to our country.

I was sure Taylor was aware of the numbers. Yet they'd apparently had no impact at all. Did the president really think the American people were going to believe him when he looked them in the eye tonight and told them he was doing all he could, even if he was clearly dead set against sending U.S. and allied forces into Syria under any circumstances? Did Taylor really think Abu Khalif was going to abandon his very public—and oft-repeated—pledge to assassinate him and raise the black flag of the Islamic State over the White House?

For nearly two months, I had lain in a hospital bed, endured multiple operations, struggled through rehab, and tried to recover physically and emotionally from all that I had witnessed in Alqosh. Almost seven hundred ISIS jihadists had been killed, but two Delta squads had also been wiped out in one of the deadliest battles in the history of Delta Force. And I had been right in the middle of it.

The one thing that kept me going every day—despite wrenching pain and utter exhaustion—was the certainty of hearing one day soon that Abu Khalif had been captured or killed.

Now, it seemed, that hope was all but gone.

As the president and First Lady stepped out of the Oval Office and headed through the West Wing to the foyer on the north side of the White House, I pulled out my gold pocket watch, a gift from my grandfather, and glanced at it as I followed close behind. It was 8:27 on a dark and snowy night in February. I was going to my first joint session of Congress. I was about to be a guest of the president during his State of the Union address, one in which I was going to be prominently mentioned. I completely disagreed with the president about his policies toward the Islamic State. I was increasingly fearful that Abu Khalif was preparing to strike again, perhaps even here inside the United States. But for now, I had a genuine sense of excitement about what lay ahead.

This was going to be an evening to remember.

5

★ ★ ★

This was my first time in a presidential motorcade.

It was a sight to behold. Amid the gusting winds and blowing snow and unusually bitter temperatures—hovering at a mere eight degrees, at last check—seven D.C. Metro police motorcycles gunned their engines at the head of the pack, preparing to exit the northeast gate of the White House complex for the two-mile journey to the Capitol. Next in line was the lead car, a police cruiser with its red-and-blue lights flashing, and its two officers—wearing thick winter coats and sipping what I assumed was strong black coffee from a thermos—ready to clear the way for the rest of the team.

Behind these were two identical black stretch Cadillacs, covered in white powder and a bit of ice. The first, in this case, served as the presidential limousine. The second served as the decoy car to confuse any would-be attackers as to which vehicle actually carried the chief executive.

Given my little contretemps with the president in the Oval Office, I suspected I was no longer going to be invited to join the First Couple, and I quickly learned my instincts were right on the money. As I came through the North Portico, I watched as three-star General Marco Ramirez, the commander of Delta Force, wearing his full dress uniform under a thick wool overcoat, got into the president's limousine with the commander in chief and First Lady.

As an agent closed the door behind them, I have to admit I found myself a bit jealous. It wasn't that I wanted more time with the president. He wasn't going to say anything more to me tonight on or off the record, and that was okay. I'd said what I'd come to say. Still, I would have loved an inside look at the car they called "the Beast." The specially built Cadillac clocked in at about a million and a half dollars. Each door had eight inches of armor plating capable of surviving a direct assault by a rocket-propelled grenade or an antitank missile. The windows were capable of taking direct fire from automatic machine guns without shattering. The chassis was fitted underneath with a massive steel plate designed to withstand the blast of a roadside bomb. The vehicle was even hermetically sealed to protect against biochemical attacks.

Or so I'd been told. I wasn't going to get to see it for myself tonight. But that was fine. I was at ease with my conscience, and for the moment that was all that mattered to me.

Behind the two limousines were five black Chevy Suburbans, all awash in red-and-blue flashing lights, all being constantly brushed off by agents trying to keep their windows as clear from the elements as they possibly could. I knew from my research that the first Suburban was known as "Halfback" and was filled with a heavily armed counterassault team. The next carried classified electronic countermeasure equipment. The rest I wasn't entirely sure about, though I knew they carried more agents, a medical team, and a hazmat countermeasures team. These were followed by a vehicle known as "Roadrunner," which carried the White House communications team, and an ambulance.

I donned my black leather overcoat and matching leather gloves and pulled a black wool cap over my bald and freezing head. Not three steps out the door of the White House, I could see my breath, and my glasses were fogging up. A deputy press secretary directed me into one of several black Lincoln Town Cars that would carry White House staff. Behind these were a number of white vans for the White House press corps, more Secret Service Chevy Suburbans, three or four additional police cars, and more motorcycles.

Fortunately, the driver of my Town Car already had the heat running. It felt good to get inside, shut the door behind me, and take shelter from the storm. I'd expected that. What I hadn't expected was to see anyone I knew waiting for me.

"Good evening, Collins," said the man in the backseat. "Good to see you again, and good to see you getting out for a change. How are you feeling?"

"Agent Harris, what a pleasant surprise," I said, genuinely happy to see him once I'd cleaned the lenses of my glasses and put them back on. "To what do I owe this pleasure?"

Arthur Harris was a thirty-year veteran with the FBI and part of a rapidly growing unit of special agents hunting ISIS operatives in the U.S. and abroad. We'd first met in Istanbul when he was investigating the car bombing that had taken the life of one of my colleagues at the *Times*. Later, he'd been involved in the mole hunt that had led to the stunning arrest of CIA director Jack Vaughn, his mistress, and a top intelligence analyst at the NSA back in December. It was Harris who had come to find me at the Marka air base in Amman, and it was Harris who had cleared me for release from Jordanian custody when I had been briefly suspected of being complicit in the attack on the royal palace. As such, Harris and I had spent quite a bit of time together in recent months. We were among the few Americans who had survived all that had happened in Jordan and Iraq, and I was honestly glad to see him again.

Harris smiled. "Between us, I believe the president would like you arrested and beaten. That's off the record, of course."

I laughed as the motorcade rolled, but I wasn't entirely sure he was kidding.

6

★ ★ ★

Almost immediately Harris's mobile phone rang.

As he took the call, we exited the White House grounds through the northeast gate, turned right on Pennsylvania Avenue, then immediately took another right onto Fifteenth Street just past the Treasury Department. Moments later, we turned left, rejoining Pennsylvania Avenue, and from there it was a straight shot to the Capitol building.

Looking out the window at all the snowplows working feverishly to keep the president's route clear, I resisted the impulse to check the latest headlines on Twitter. I already knew the news was grim. Turkish military forces were bombing Kurdish rebels in northern Syria. A series of suicide bombings had just ripped through Istanbul, Ankara, and Antalya, mostly targeting government offices and hotels frequented by foreigners. A petrochemical plant in Alexandria, Egypt, had just come under attack by as-of-yet unknown militants. Rather than be reminded of all that was going wrong in the world, however, I simply wanted to enjoy this moment.

Against all odds, I was actually heading to the U.S. Capitol building to be the president's guest at the State of the Union address. I was under no illusions. I didn't deserve to be there. In fact, given all that had happened in the past several months, I should probably be dead, not still working as a journalist and winning awards. For the first month and a half of my recovery, I'd been certain I'd never go back to my life as a foreign correspondent, and even if I did, I had no desire to cover wars and terrorism. I'd seen too many friends get killed and wounded. I'd seen too much horror.

The bitter truth was I'd given my entire career to being part of an elite tribe of war correspondents, and it had cost me nearly everything. Now in my early forties, I was divorced. I had no kids. I barely saw my mom or my brother and his family. I was a recovering alcoholic. My neighbors didn't know me. The doorman at my apartment building across the Potomac barely even recognized me. Wasn't it time for a change?

But a change to what? I had no idea what I'd do if not write for the Gray Lady. Teach journalism to a bunch of lazy, spoiled twenty-somethings who had no idea how the world worked? Cash in with some Wall Street gig—VP of public affairs for some multinational bank or investment firm? I'd rather drink poison. In theory, a change sounded great. But what exactly would I do next? What *could* I do that I would actually enjoy?

Unbidden, my thoughts abruptly turned to Yael Katzir, the beautiful Israeli agent I had met in Istanbul and with whom I had survived the grueling events in Jordan and northern Iraq. I'd barely seen her since we'd been evacuated together on Air Force One after the attack in Alqosh. Yet I had to admit she was never far from my mind.

As a senior chemical weapons expert for the Mossad, Yael had been at the top of her game. She'd been right about ISIS capturing chemical weapons in Syria. She'd been right to warn then–Prime Minister Daniel Lavi that ISIS was planning a coup d'état in Amman. He hadn't listened, and now he was dead. What's more, she'd been spot-on in her analysis that President Taylor was being held by ISIS forces not in Mosul or Homs or Dabiq as many U.S. intelligence analysts had believed at first, but in the little Iraqi town of Alqosh, on the plains of Nineveh. She'd nearly paid with her life. But she'd been right, and now she was a rock star at the highest levels of the Israeli government. The last text she'd sent me, almost three weeks before, was that the new prime minister, Yuval Eitan, had asked her to serve as his deputy national security advisor. It was a big job, a heady promotion. She wasn't sure she wanted to take it. But it was evidence of the enormous respect and influence she held in Jerusalem.

She had sent me a note asking me what she should do. I'd written back immediately and told her to take it and to make sure she got a big raise to go with it. I couldn't have been more proud of her, I told her. She deserved every accolade and more.

Selfishly, however, it was hard not to think of her promotion as my loss. I knew there was likely no future for us. She had a job, and she wasn't going to leave it for me. And honestly, what was I going to do? Move to Israel? Learn Hebrew? Convert to Judaism? The fact was, I'd only known her for a few months. We had only just begun to be friends. Still, I missed her. But with her new responsibilities, I had no idea when I would even see her again.

Harris finally finished his phone call and turned back to me. He didn't look well.

"What was that all about?" I asked.

"Want a scoop?"

"You kidding?" I asked.

"No," he said, dead serious.

"Sure. What've you got?"

"State police in Alabama just took down an ISIS sleeper cell near Birmingham."

"Seriously?" I asked, pulling a notebook and pen from my pocket.

"Four males, all Iraqi nationals, and a woman from Syria."

"What were they doing in Birmingham?"

"Weird, right?"

"Very," I concurred.

"That's not the half of it," Harris said. "When the troopers got a search warrant for their apartment, what do you think they found?"

I shrugged.

"Almost five hundred mortar shells—not active ones, mind you, just dummies, the kind the military uses for target practice."

"What would they need those for?" I asked. "And where would they get them in the first place?"

"Well, that's the thing," Harris said. "We have no idea."

"Does the president know?" I asked.

"No, not yet—I don't think so," he replied. "We're just getting this ourselves."

"Well, somebody better tell him before he starts speaking."

The motorcade soon pulled up to the parking plaza on the north side of the Capitol and came to a halt. Photographers and news camera operators recorded the president and First Lady and General Ramirez being greeted by the Speaker of the House and led inside. I glanced at my grandfather's pocket watch. It was almost 9 p.m. The networks would go live in six minutes.

7

★ ★ ★

THE U.S. CAPITOL BUILDING

"Mr. Speaker, the president of the United States!"

The sergeant at arms of the United States House of Representatives shouted the words at the top of his lungs. When he finished, the room erupted. Everyone in the House Chamber jumped to their feet and launched into deafening and sustained applause. Members of both parties from the House and the Senate were whooping and hollering and cheering the leader of the free world, and they did not stop. Indeed, by my reckoning, Taylor received the longest recorded standing ovation in the history of any State of the Union address.

No wonder the man wasn't listening to me. Why should he? The president's approval ratings were now in the mideighties. It was a stunning, neck-wrenching turn of events, given that two months earlier—just before the ISIS attack on the peace summit in Jordan— his approval ratings had been drifting down into the midthirties, imperiling the administration's entire agenda and threatening to bury dozens of House and Senate Democrats in a political avalanche in the next elections. But since then, the world had dramatically changed. No longer was Taylor politically dead and buried. He had been resurrected, and tonight he was taking a victory lap.

I watched it all unfold from the section of the second-floor gallery reserved for the First Lady and the guests of the First Family. General Ramirez stood directly beside Mrs. Taylor, two rows ahead of me. To their right were the fifteen Iraqi children we had rescued from Abu Khalif's underground prison in Alqosh, all cheering the president, along with several of the social workers who were caring for them after their traumatic ordeal and helping them get adjusted to their new lives in America. In the row behind the First Lady stood members of her Secret Service protective detail, and beside them stood the wounded but surviving members of the Delta squad who had rescued the president in Alqosh.

Standing beside me was my brother, Matt, also cheering enthusiastically. I was glad he could be here. He'd been with me every step of the way since this ordeal had begun. He had come down from Maine every week, sometimes for two or three days at a time, to spend time with me at Walter Reed. He'd sat with me for hours and let me talk about what I'd been through, what I'd seen and heard in Alqosh and Mosul and Abu Ghraib. Together we'd theorized about where Abu Khalif could be holed up. I thought Khalif was probably in Raqqa. Matt was convinced he was now somewhere in Libya. We'd argued about where Khalif might strike next and how the Taylor administration might respond. He'd read me every newspaper and magazine article he could get his hands on about the allied offensive in northern Iraq. He always prayed with me when he arrived and before he left, and whenever I let him, he read the Bible to me too, working his way through the Gospel according to John. I listened politely. Sometimes I asked questions. Matt always had answers—good ones, interesting ones, compelling ones—but he hadn't pushed me, and for that I was grateful.

Matt clapped and hollered for the president like just about everyone else in the room, and I understood why. He was a patriot, and he was being swept up in the moment. We'd all thought this president was dead in Jordan, and then in Syria or Iraq, and then—almost miraculously—he'd been rescued, and these dear, precious children had been liberated from the clutches of those ISIS monsters. What's more, millions of Muslims and Christians and Yazidis in northern Iraq had been liberated from a dark, oppressive force. It was a great story, one for the ages. From most of the country's vantage point, it all looked like one giant success story. Why shouldn't they celebrate? They didn't see what was coming.

But I did.

Abu Khalif had promised he would come to the U.S. Brazenly, proudly, smugly, he'd told me he had American and Canadian jihadists fighting for him in Syria and Iraq. He'd bragged to me that such men would be able to enter the United States undetected. And now they were here. In Alabama, anyway. Sure, some in Birmingham had been caught. But there were others. Many. I was sure of it. When and how and where they would strike, I had no idea. But I had my guesses. It wasn't going to be a workplace shooting like in San Bernardino. It wasn't going to be the attempted assassination of a lone police officer sitting in his patrol car on the streets of Philadelphia. I doubted it was going to be an attack on a satirical newspaper office like *Charlie Hebdo* in Paris or even an international airport like in Brussels or Istanbul. No, this was going to be bigger. Much bigger. And I suspected Abu Khalif had set his next action into motion even before the attack on the peace summit in Amman.

That's why he'd gone on the record with me. That's why he had laid out his entire wicked strategy when I interviewed him in the Abu Ghraib prison outside of Baghdad. That's why in Mosul he had demonstrated for me that he was fully capable of carrying out his threats. The attacks in Jordan were just a trailer. The coming attacks in America were the main attraction.

So I clapped politely. I knew I was on live worldwide television. I needed to be respectful. I would give Taylor his due. But I could not bring myself to do more. I was deeply grateful we'd found the president alive and gotten him out safe. At the same time, I was more convinced than ever that he didn't truly understand the nature and threat of the evil that was coming. Unless the FBI and the CIA were at the top of their game, the president was about to be blindsided again. We all were.

I discreetly glanced over to Matt's right. Agent Harris stood politely but did not clap. Perhaps he couldn't, I thought. Perhaps that was part of the bureau's code of conduct, like that of the Secret Service. The agents protecting the First Lady weren't clapping either. They weren't showing emotion of any kind. I wasn't sure why, exactly. I didn't spend much time in such circles. But I must say, I was a bit envious.

Grinning broadly, the president shook hands and posed for selfies with congressmen and senators of both parties as he worked his way down the center aisle, clearly enjoying every moment. Had he been briefed on the takedown of an ISIS cell on American soil? If so, I wondered whether it would affect anything he was about to say.

Eventually Taylor reached the well of the House—the open area in front of the rostrum—where he greeted the assembled Supreme Court justices, all of them seated, and embraced each of the members of his cabinet, all of them standing. From there, he shook hands with each of the Joint Chiefs before finally making the turn and climbing the rostrum, where he was reintroduced by the Speaker of the House and greeted by even more tumultuous applause.

8

★ ★ ★

Finally the chamber settled down and people again took their seats.

The president looked at the teleprompter screen to his left and at the other on his right. Then he glanced down at the printed pages of his remarks in the three-ring binder on the podium—the one I'd seen him making notes on in the Oval Office less than an hour earlier—and his broad smile faded somewhat. I tried to imagine what he was thinking. I wanted to believe that the argument I'd made to him—and what he'd hopefully just heard from his national security advisor—was weighing heavily on his mind. But I couldn't read him. Not from where I was sitting.

When he looked up, he surveyed the audience, all four hundred thirty-five members of the House, all one hundred members of the Senate, ambassadors from nearly every nation, members of his administration, official guests, and of course, the members of the Fourth Estate. For almost a full minute, he said nothing. But then he cleared his throat as he took out a handkerchief and dabbed his eyes.

"Mr. Speaker, Mr. Vice President, members of Congress, distinguished guests, and my fellow Americans," he finally said, his voice shaky at first but gradually gaining strength. "Over the course of this past year, the American people and our government and our military have been tested as at few other times in our history. The forces of freedom have come under a vicious assault by the forces of violent extremism. Our enemies have tried to murder our leaders. They have sought to terrorize and blackmail our people and force us into submission to their perverted vision of global domination. They have done so at the point of a gun, at the tip of a sword."

The room was deathly quiet. Taylor reached for a glass of water. He took a sip. He cleared his throat once more. And then he turned back to the teleprompters.

"When I was seized by the forces of ISIL, it wasn't just I who was taken hostage. We all were. America was held hostage. But America did not surrender. You did not surrender. You did not give in. No, you came together. You united as one people. You fought back against the terrorists. You fought back against the forces of darkness, and you won—America won—and if we stay united, America will keep on winning!"

This brought the house down. What ensued was a two-minute-and-twelve-second standing ovation.

I timed it.

"You did *not* surrender," the president continued when the audience had just barely settled back in their seats. "You stood tall and true, and the forces of freedom prevailed. The American armed forces prevailed. The American people prevailed, and the state of our union has *never* been stronger."

Back to their feet they jumped. They whooped and hollered. Some stamped their feet. It was a good old-fashioned political revival meeting, and it struck me that Taylor should probably just say thank you and good-night. No good could come of trying to go on any further. Then again, the man was a politician, and what politician had ever quit while he was ahead?

"In my capacity as commander in chief, I asked Congress—the people's representatives—to formally declare war on ISIL, and you agreed," the president said when everyone was seated. "With your full support and approval, I sent fifty thousand of America's finest soldiers, sailors, airmen, and Marines back into Iraq."

I couldn't help but be impressed. Taylor was skillfully tying Congress's fate in the Middle East to his own. They loved him now. They were with him now. But if things went bad, the president was making sure they couldn't throw him under the bus. They had made these decisions together, he told the country, Republicans and Democrats. The election breezes were already blowing.

"Together we sent five hundred tanks and more than two hundred aircraft to the region. Together with our Sunni Arab allies—the Iraqis, the Jordanians, the Egyptians, the Saudis, the Gulf Emiratis, and the Kurds—we built a powerful military, diplomatic, and economic coalition. And tonight I can report that together we have achieved impressive results. We have liberated the city and people of Mosul."

Applause erupted again.

"We have liberated Alqosh."

More applause.

"We have liberated the province of Nineveh—indeed, the entire nation of Iraq is now free from the black flags of ISIL."

Still more applause—and then came the coup de grâce.

"We have accomplished what our critics said was impossible," the president declared. "We have cut the caliphate in half, and now ISIL's days are numbered."

Another standing ovation.

"He's crushing it," Matt shouted to me as we both rose to our feet.

I said nothing, just made a perfunctory smile for the cameras. Apparently the president hadn't been told, or he didn't care. Either way, I knew at that moment he wasn't going to mention the capture of an ISIS cell on American soil. He had a narrative: Victory. Success. Glory. And what had unfolded in Alabama didn't fit it. It raised too many questions. *If America was truly winning against the forces of Abu Khalif in the Middle East, what was ISIS doing here, in the South, so deep inside the homeland? Were there more of them? How many? Where were they? What were they planning? And what were they doing stockpiling empty mortar shells?*

As I scanned the audience, another line of questions came to mind. Where was King Abdullah II? Why wasn't the Jordanian monarch—our most faithful Sunni Arab ally—here as an honored guest of the president? Where were Palestinian president Salim Mansour and Egyptian president Wahid Mahfouz and the Saudi king and the Gulf emirs? If I was here, why weren't they? Why weren't we honoring our Arab allies who had done so much of the heavy lifting in the fight against the forces of darkness? And where was Yuval Eitan, Israel's new prime minister? Was the president going to acknowledge his late friend and ally Daniel Lavi? No country had stood with the U.S. more faithfully during the current crisis than Israel. So why weren't the Israelis being honored? Why was the president taking all the credit for himself?

Just then, however, Taylor asked everyone to be seated while he honored every American who had fallen in Amman and Alqosh. He read the list slowly and respectfully, giving not just the names but several sentences of description about each. And he paused after each one, offering the audience and the nation time to absorb the details and remember their sacrifice. Still, why hadn't he invited our allies? Wouldn't that have been a powerful demonstration of solidarity in a time of great darkness and turmoil?

When he had finished reading every name, the president called for a moment of silence. Most people bowed their heads. I'm sure Matt prayed for the families and friends of the slain. I just stared blankly as the horrific images from Amman and Alqosh came flooding back.

After a few quiet moments, the president turned and looked up to the gallery. He asked General Ramirez and his Delta commandos to stand. He recounted what they had done in Alqosh. He thanked them for their loyal, sacrificial service. Then he asked the nation to join him in honoring "these unsung but unmatched American heroes." The tall, burly, freshly shaven men—all dressed in new suits with crisp white shirts and neckties—looked uncomfortable as they received such a sustained standing ovation that I actually forgot to check my watch and see how long it lasted. These were rough men. They were used to operating in the shadows, in faraway places. They had no experience in the spotlight. They had no desire to walk the corridors of power. Yet they were being celebrated tonight, and as the applause went on and on, each of them seemed deeply moved. And I have to admit that even as a cynical war correspondent, I found my eyes welling up with tears. These guys had saved my life, and I would be forever grateful.

The president turned next to the Iraqi children. He briefly explained who they were, though he omitted the details of the cruelest things that had been done to them. But he made it clear enough how much they had suffered. He did not ask them to stand, but everyone in the room stood for them. We all cheered them, me included, as if hoping that the applause might somehow wash away the more nightmarish moments from their memories.

As much as I didn't want to, I had to concede Taylor was a master at this. Yes, there were still threats out there. Yes, ISIS was still a clear and present danger. But the president wasn't entirely wrong. America had won some real successes on the battlefield. We were doing some things right. These were all bona fide heroes, and they deserved the president's attention and respect and the respect of the nation. I could hardly fault Taylor for the address he was delivering. It was beautifully crafted and touchingly delivered. I hoped he would still lay out the enormous challenges ahead of us. But the American people had been through a terrible ordeal. There was a time and a place to come together and celebrate what was going right. This was that time. This was that place. Even I was moved by it all.

When we all sat down again and the room had settled, the president surprised me by asking me to stand. I wasn't sure exactly why I was caught off guard. I should have known it was coming. It's why he had invited me. It's not that I thought he'd cut me out of the speech given the dustup we'd just had in the Oval Office. But my thoughts were elsewhere. I'd been caught up in the moment, in the tributes to the others, in my emotions, and I had temporarily forgotten that I, too, was going to be singled out.

The president began to explain the role I had played in the hunt to find him and in saving his life and the lives of these children. His words were simple and direct but exceedingly generous and kind, especially given the history between us.

But as he spoke, something happened that I did not expect. I heard a boom. We all heard it. It shook the House chamber. Then we heard another and a third.

At first it sounded like thunder. But as the shaking intensified, I knew exactly what was happening. I shot a look to Harris, and it was clear he knew too.

The Capitol was under attack.

9

★ ★ ★

It took Harris only a fraction of a second to react.

"Get them out—all of them—now!" he ordered the head of the First Lady's detail.

For a moment, the agent hesitated. Technically, this wasn't Harris's call to make. The agent looked at me, then down at the president. I was still on my feet, not sure what to do. When the booms had begun, the president had briefly paused, midsentence, distracted by the sounds and the vibrations. But then—perhaps assuming he was merely hearing thunder—he had once again found his place on the teleprompter and continued delivering his speech.

Now, however, hearing the commotion in the gallery, he stopped again and looked back up at me and those around me. He could see Harris—whom he knew personally—talking to the agent in charge of his wife's safety. From that distance, he couldn't have heard what Harris was saying. But he didn't have to hear the words. He could see the look in Harris's eyes. This wasn't thunder. Washington was under fire.

It all seemed to be happening in slow motion. I saw the First Lady's lead agent talking into his wrist-mounted radio. Then he was on his feet. I turned and saw two enormous Secret Service agents bound up the stairs of the rostrum. They grabbed the president and pulled him away from the podium. I stared as they literally lifted him off his feet by several inches, carried him down the stairs, and whisked him out a side door. The First Lady's detail started moving as well. They pulled her out of her seat and raced her past us, up the stairs and out of the gallery. As I watched them go, I just stood there, frozen in place, paralyzed with fear and shock and disbelief. Then I saw more Secret Service agents race to Vice President Holbrooke and pull him out of the chamber, even as the Capitol police detail assigned to protect the Speaker of the House moved to evacuate him as well.

I was still standing there, not moving, not running, not reacting at all. And it wasn't only me. In those few seconds, no one in the chamber except the Secret Service and the Capitol police was reacting. Not yet. We were all too stunned by what we were seeing and hearing around us.

Suddenly I could hear Harris shouting my name.

"Collins—Collins—do you hear me? We need to go, now!"

I heard the words but couldn't think, couldn't move. Harris's voice seemed distant and hollow. But then I saw my brother jump up. He grabbed me by my suit jacket and pulled me into the aisle. At the same time, I saw General Ramirez and his men jump to their feet. And then everything snapped back. It was as if I had suddenly reconnected to time and space—to reality.

"Move, J. B.—go!" Matt shouted.

But I couldn't leave—not yet—and it wasn't because I was in shock. *"The children!"* I shouted back. *"We need to get them out!"*

Harris hesitated. He was trying to get me to the door and back to the motorcade. But Matt and the Delta guys were already moving toward the kids, and I was right behind them. I could see the fear in the children's eyes, but they responded quickly and obediently as Matt and I motioned to them to get up and follow us out of the gallery.

Just then, an immense explosion rocked the chamber. Chunks of plaster and Sheetrock came raining down on the House and Senate members below.

We burst into the hallway, where we met a team of Capitol police officers rushing toward us. They assured us they would take the children and their chaperones to a secure location. A moment later, they were moving the Iraqi kids and their handlers down the hallway and soon they had all disappeared around a corner.

Another explosion rocked the building. The hallway lights flickered. More plaster fell from the ceiling. People were screaming and scrambling to get out of the building. Harris ordered us to follow him, and Matt and I raced for a nearby stairwell. When we reached the ground floor, we slammed through the doors and followed Harris down another long hallway.

Now we were hearing one explosion after another in rapid succession. The entire building was shaking. The Capitol was taking direct hit after direct hit, and I suddenly had flashbacks to the ISIS onslaught against the Al-Hummar Palace in Amman.

How many attackers were coming? How soon would they be here? Were the mortar rounds raining down on us filled with chemical weapons, as they had been in Amman? If so, was there sarin gas pouring through the halls of the Capitol? We'd never be able to see it or smell it. Had we already inhaled it? If so, how much longer did we have?

As we rounded a corner, we were halted by Capitol police and Secret Service agents brandishing automatic weapons. Some of them were donning full chem-bio suits, blocking our path back to the motorcade. A chill ran down my spine. We had no protection from poison gas, and I had no idea how we were going to find any. Harris flashed his FBI badge and credentials. He was cleared to pass, but Matt and I weren't.

"They're with me," Harris shouted.

"I don't care," a lieutenant shouted back. "I can't let them through."

"They're guests of the president," Harris insisted. "We're supposed to be in the motorcade."

"I have my orders," came the reply. "No civilians in or out of this checkpoint."

Harris was enraged. I could see it in his eyes. But he was a government man, first and foremost. Moreover, he wasn't an idiot. He wasn't about to storm through a checkpoint in a crisis. Instead, he turned and motioned for Matt and me to follow. We backtracked down the hallway, took a left at the next corridor, then a right and another left, running at full speed. Still recovering from my injuries, I wasn't entirely able to keep up with either him or Matt, but I wasn't too far behind. I'd been faithful in doing my rehab exercises, and fortunately it was paying off.

A moment later we reached another exit. Two heavily armed Capitol police officers—also in chem-bio suits—were guarding the door. They checked Harris's credentials, then urged him to stay inside.

"No, we have a car!" Harris shouted over the deafening, nonstop explosions. *"We're supposed to be in the motorcade!"*

"The motorcade's gone, sir!" one of the officers yelled.

"Gone?"

"Most of it. They had to get POTUS out."

"Fine—but I need to get back to the bureau immediately. I'm part of the ISIS unit. And I suspect that's who's hitting us."

"Maybe, but it's not safe out there, sir," the officer shouted back.

"We'll take our chances," Harris insisted. *"Now move aside—that's an order."*

I wasn't sure Harris was making the right move. Yes, the Capitol was under a withering assault. But weren't we safer here than dashing out into a massive winter storm with mortars raining down death and sarin gas possibly blanketing the Capitol grounds?

Before I could say anything, though, both officers stepped aside and Harris bolted out the door. Matt dashed out after him. For a moment, I couldn't move, once again paralyzed with fear. I'd seen this film—twice—and I hadn't liked it either time. But as I watched Harris and my brother reach the sedan we'd arrived in, I didn't want to be left behind. If I was going to die, it was going to be with them. So into the storm I went, bolting across the plaza.

10

* * *

Our driver hit the gas.

We peeled out, fishtailing on the ice. Harris was in the front passenger seat, on his phone and already briefing someone back at the bureau on the nightmare unfolding around us. Matt was sitting to my right, staring out the window as round after round of mortars smashed into the roof and the walls of the north wing of the Capitol, where the Senate offices were located. I had my phone out. I was speed-dialing my bureau chief, Allen MacDonald, over and over again but kept being directed to voice mail.

Unable to complete a call, I opened Twitter instead and started writing dispatches, 140 characters at a time. I quickly described the scene I'd witnessed inside the Capitol moments before and what was unfolding outside as well, putting specific focus on the fact that the attack was being waged by mortar fire, something I couldn't remember ever happening inside the continental United States. Then I tweeted out my "breaking news" exclusive: authorities had arrested members of an alleged ISIS sleeper cell in Alabama that was stockpiling hundreds of mortar shells. I didn't say where I'd gotten the information. Nor did I add other details. I hadn't, after all, had the opportunity to find a second source. But I trusted Harris; he hadn't steered me wrong yet. Given that the site of the State of the Union address was now under mortar attack for the first time in U.S. history, it seemed imperative to me to get the word out there that the U.S. government knew for a fact that ISIS operatives had apparently been in possession of—and thus had presumably been experimenting with—mortar rounds on American soil.

Those were all the facts I had at the moment. But I hoped that by my getting them out there, other enterprising reporters would pick up the trail and hunt down more.

Suddenly the driver stomped on the brakes and turned hard. We found ourselves twisting, turning, sliding twenty or thirty yards across the ice- and snow-covered pavement, barely coming to a halt in front of a Capitol police cruiser. Our driver put his window down and demanded to be let through. But he was told this exit on the north side—leading to Constitution Avenue and from there to Pennsylvania Avenue—had been sealed off until the president's motorcade made it safely back to the White House. Harris flashed his badge and explained we urgently needed to get back to FBI headquarters, but the officer told us there was nothing he could do. The orders had come from the top. The only way out, he told us, was on the opposite side of the Capitol grounds.

Infuriated, Harris ordered the driver to backtrack. He did, slamming the sedan into reverse, spinning the car around, and racing for the southeast gate, swerving to avoid the craters caused by errant mortar rounds.

As we spilled onto Independence Avenue and headed west, lights flashing and siren blaring, I looked back at the Capitol. The scene was surreal, like something out of Hollywood. The entire north wing—the Senate side—was ablaze. Through the blowing, swirling snow, I could see additional mortar rounds arcing in from multiple directions. Several smashed into the great dome, which was soon engulfed in flames as well. Police cars, fire trucks, ambulances, and hazmat teams were racing to the scene from all directions, even as we raced away at ever-increasing speed.

Our driver took a hard right turn on Third Street and headed for the intersection with Pennsylvania Avenue just a few blocks ahead. Matt and I were riveted on the Capitol out the window to our right. But when we heard Harris gasp and drop his phone, we both turned to see what in the world he was reacting to.

Then I gasped as well. The president's motorcade—what was left of it, anyway—was straight ahead, trying to advance westward on Pennsylvania, back to the White House. But it was under attack from RPG and automatic-weapons fire. At least four of the police cruisers that had been in the lead had smashed into one another. Now they were a raging inferno piled up in a way that blocked the path forward for the rest of the team, including the Beast and the decoy car. Both limousine drivers were trying to back up, but they had at least a dozen Chevy Suburbans behind them, also trying to back up and creating a logjam.

Out of the corner of my eye, I saw a brilliant flash of light. It originated from a high window of a large office building to the right of the Labor Department. Next I saw the contrail, and then one of the Suburbans behind the Beast erupted in a massive explosion. The SUV was lifted into the air and then flipped over, landing on its roof. A fraction of a second later, there was another flash of light, another contrail, and another Suburban was blown sky-high.

Our driver slammed on the brakes and we went skidding for a good thirty or forty yards. Fortunately, with all the roads blocked off and cleared of traffic, there was no danger of smashing into anyone else. But we still were watching the president's motorcade come under assault, and we were horrified at the sight.

With a clear view of everything that was unfolding, I used my phone to take multiple pictures of both the motorcade and the Capitol and immediately tweeted them out. Just then I saw members of the Secret Service's tactical unit open fire on the office building. Two agents fired RPGs into the window from which the incoming fire was emanating. At the same time, another agent popped out of the roof of one of the remaining Suburbans. He was armed with a .50-caliber machine gun. He pivoted toward the office building and let her rip, though not before a final rocket-propelled grenade was launched at the Beast. Switching my iPhone to video mode, I was filming as an RPG hit the side of the lead limo and burst into a ball of fire, even as both that limousine and the one behind it maneuvered to get out of the kill box, onto a sidewalk, and around the burning wreckage of the lead cars in front of them.

Our driver started shouting into his wrist-mounted radio. He was explaining what he was seeing, and while I couldn't hear what he was being told in return, it soon became obvious. *We* were now supposed to act as the lead car, a blocking force to get the president back to the White House. Our driver gunned the engine, and we raced for the intersection, fishtailing when we got there but narrowly making the left onto Pennsylvania Avenue. We couldn't see anything but the snowstorm ahead of us. Luckily the boulevard was clear of traffic. D.C. Metro police cruisers blocked most of the access streets on either side of us, and several massive white-and-orange D.C. snowplows and salt-spreader trucks blocked the remaining ones. I figured we ought to be home free once the presidential limos worked their way around the burning vehicles currently blocking their path.

"Here they come," Matt said as the first limo found an opening and began to catch up with us.

Harris and I craned our necks to get a look. For a moment, I saw only one of the limousines, but soon the second emerged through the flames and billowing smoke as well.

"Floor it!" Harris shouted, and the driver did just that.

Soon we were racing west on Pennsylvania, past the Canadian embassy, past the Newseum on our right and the National Gallery of

Art on our left. But when we got to the Navy Memorial, all hell broke loose. I heard automatic gunfire erupting to our right. It seemed to be coming from one of the adjacent office buildings. But before I could pinpoint the exact location, one of the D.C. snowplows blocking a side street suddenly surged forward and pulled directly into our path. Our driver mashed the brakes and swerved left, but I knew instantly there was no way we were going to clear it, and I was right.

11

★ ★ ★

We slammed into the driver's side of the enormous truck.

There was a deafening crunch of metal on metal, and the windows in our car blew out. We all lurched forward. I saw the air bags deploy in the front seats, but in the back, neither Matt nor I wore seat belts. In the intensity of our exit from the Capitol, neither of us had even thought of it, and now we were being thrown around like rag dolls. The limousine behind us tried to swerve out of our way but couldn't turn fast enough. It clipped the rear of our Lincoln Town Car, sending us spinning out into the middle of the street, where we were then broadsided by the second limousine seconds later.

When we stopped moving, everything grew quiet. We were all choking on the smoke emanating from the explosive charge of the air bags, badly rattled by the crash. But we were still alive, and as best I could tell, I hadn't broken any bones.

"Everyone okay?" I asked, kicking open my door.

We were hit by a frigid blast, but at least we could breathe.

"I'm good," Matt said. "But my door—it's stuck."

I glanced over at him. Matt wasn't good. He'd cracked his head. Blood was pouring down his face. I offered to help him, but he waved

46

me off. He insisted he must look worse than he felt. He pulled out a handkerchief and applied pressure to the gash across his forehead.

"Get out on my side," I said, gritting my teeth against the bitter wind and snow.

As my brother scrambled across the broken glass covering the backseat and exited through my side, I checked on Harris. He said he was fine and focused on our driver.

"He's not moving," Harris said.

"Does he have a pulse?" I asked.

Harris checked, then shook his head. "No, he's gone."

Just then I heard gunfire erupt again. It wasn't close, but it wasn't far enough away for comfort either. I scanned the sidewalks and the buildings around us but couldn't find the source. Harris drew his service weapon, a Glock 9mm handgun. That wasn't going to provide much protection if our attackers stormed into the street with automatic weapons, but it was better than nothing.

Suddenly a pistol fired. This *was* close, directly to my left. I turned quickly and stared in horror as the driver of the snowplow—clad in a black parka and black ski mask—climbed out of his cab and fired twice more, aiming at Harris. The FBI agent wheeled around and fired once but then went down.

The snowplow driver had also been hit by Harris's return fire. He landed with a crash on the crumpled hood of the sedan. He was groaning in pain, but he was alive and began pulling himself to his feet. To my right, I saw Matt hit the deck. I knew I should have done the same. The gunfire to our right was getting louder by the second, and the snowplow driver with the pistol was no more than ten feet away. But with Harris down and in mortal danger, I instinctively climbed back into the car. I reached for our driver's service weapon and yanked it from its holster under his jacket. The assailant was on his feet again and stumbling toward Harris. I didn't know if Harris was dead or alive, but there was no time to hesitate. I fumbled for the safety, flicked it off, aimed through the shattered windshield, and fired four times. At least one and maybe two of the rounds hit their mark. The man snapped back violently, then went crashing to the snow-covered pavement.

I immediately got out of the car and raced around the rear, the pistol in front of me, ready to fire again. But before I could, I saw Harris—on his back, on the freezing pavement—firing three more rounds into the hooded man.

"*Clear on this side!*" he shouted.

"*Clear on this side too!*" I shouted back.

Harris scrambled to his feet. He grabbed the gun from the man. There was no doubt he was dead. A crimson pool was now growing around him.

Harris tossed the terrorist's gun to me. Harris himself was covered in snow and ice, but he was moving with ease. He didn't look injured. It took me a moment, but then I realized he hadn't been shot; he'd merely slipped on the ice while whirling around. The fall had probably saved his life. He urgently signaled for me to double back and move around the front side of the snowplow while he went around the other side, just in case the driver had a wingman. I quickly did as I was told. I motioned for Matt to stay down and gave him the extra pistol, just in case someone got by me.

Then, as I peered around the front of the truck and the giant orange plow, Harris's instincts proved right. There was a wingman. Standing no more than two yards from me was an enormous figure— at least six-foot-five—also wearing a black parka and a black hood and holding a submachine gun.

He opened fire. I was able to duck just in time, but I could hear the rounds pinging off the cab and engine block. I could also hear the man running toward me, his heavy boots crunching in the snow. I crouched down and aimed around the corner, my hands trembling in fear as much as from the cold.

But just as the man approached, I heard Harris shout into the night. *"FBI—freeze!"*

The man didn't comply. A split second later I heard three shots ring out and a body crashing to the ground.

Again Harris yelled, *"Clear!"*

My heart racing, adrenaline coursing through my system, I forced myself to stand. Then I cautiously stepped out around the front of the plow to find Harris standing over the corpse. He kicked the machine gun in my direction and pulled the hood off the dead man. He looked Libyan to me, or perhaps Algerian. Either way, with the dark eyes and the oversize beard, it was obvious he was either from North Africa or the Middle East, and I had no doubt he was ISIS, working for Abu Khalif.

Two black Suburbans quickly arrived on the scene. In the distance, I could hear sirens coming from every direction. At first, I assumed the FBI had sent a team to help us. But the Suburbans didn't come to a stop. They weren't from the bureau. They were from the Secret Service. They'd come to rescue the president and get him and the First Lady back to the White House safe and sound.

But no sooner had they arrived than automatic gunfire erupted again. This time the source was clear: an upper floor in a nearby office building. Again I could hear rounds pinging off the snowplow and the Suburbans. Harris and I ran for cover, but just then I heard the sizzle of another RPG streaking through the air. The force of the explosion sent Harris and me flying. I landed flat on my back and hard, in the middle of Pennsylvania Avenue.

The wind had been knocked out of me. Burning pain shot through my back and legs. Wincing, I forced myself onto my right side. I looked back at the Capitol, now completely engulfed in flames. I could see Harris several yards away, closer to the plow, dazed and trying to get to his feet.

Then suddenly I found myself blinded by headlights. One of

the limousines was headed right for me, but I was in too much pain to move. With bullets whizzing by us, I felt someone grab me and pull me aside just as the first of the two limos whooshed by. When I looked up, I found Matt standing over me. But over his shoulder I saw another flash of light, another contrail, and another RPG streaking through the air.

"Matt, get down!" I yelled.

The second Suburban exploded on contact. It flipped through the air, landing not more than twenty feet from us and directly in the path of the second limo as it was roaring by. This time it was I who grabbed Matt and pulled him toward me as the second limo rushed past, missing Matt's left foot by inches. The driver of the second limo then hit the brakes, fishtailing past us. Right behind them were the Secret Service tactical units. They were returning fire, engaging the terrorists in the building beside us. But the president and his team were boxed in. With the storm, there were no choppers in the air. There would be no air support. Sharpshooters were trying to suppress the RPG fire, but they weren't having much luck.

How was this possible? I wondered. We were just blocks from the White House. But that didn't really matter just now. All I knew for sure was that we had to get off this street, and fast.

12

★ ★ ★

These were not amateurs.

Someone had been planning this attack, likely for months.

I forced myself to get up, despite the pain. I could now see that Harris was, in fact, wounded. His trousers were shredded, and he was holding his leg. Matt rushed to his side and assessed his wounds. Then he took off his scarf and wrapped it around Harris's left leg as a tourniquet. They were both hunched down behind the smoking wreckage of the sedan as the bullets kept flying in all directions.

Clearly the sedan we had been riding in was undrivable. It had been totaled. It was also leaking gasoline, putting us in additional peril. Just as clear was that none of the other vehicles on this street were going to stop for us. They had one mission only—to protect the president of the United States—not to get us to safety.

I turned to the snowplow. The lights were on. The windshield wipers were still running. So was the engine. I scrambled across the icy pavement, opened the door of the cab, and then returned to Harris's side.

"Matt, let's get him in the truck," I shouted across the firefight. *"We ought to be able to punch our way through in that."*

Matt looked back at the snowplow. He said nothing. I could see the skepticism in his eyes. But he nodded. This was our only shot, and he knew it. He also knew there was no time to overthink it. We had to move fast. Harris was losing blood, and if another RPG was fired at this sedan, we'd all be finished.

Careful to stay low, out of the line of fire, we dragged Harris through the snow, then lifted him up and laid him along the bench-style front seat. Matt climbed over him, shielding Harris's body while at the same time taking care to keep his own head away from the passenger-side window. Once they were in, I climbed into the driver's seat, put my seat belt on, revved the engine, and threw the Western Star 4800 into reverse. We jolted forward rather violently. I'd never driven anything so big and lacked any finesse whatsoever. It was all Matt could do to keep Harris from sliding off the seat. When I hit the brakes, we were thrown back. Grinding the gears something fierce, I finally jammed the stick into first gear, and now we were lurching forward—slowly, but we were moving.

That said, my driving was the least of our worries. The bullets were coming hard and fast, as if we were heading into a rainstorm of gunfire. The longer we stayed on this street, the sooner we'd be dead. So I hit the gas, using the massive engine and the plow blade to push the fiery wreckage of the Suburbans out of our way. That, in turn, cleared a path for both limousines, and as I braked, the first limo shot forward immediately. To my surprise, however, the second limo pulled alongside us. I waited for it to catch up to its decoy. Instead, as I looked down through the blowing snow, I saw the agent in the front passenger seat frantically waving me to move forward. Baffled but in no position to ask questions, I depressed the accelerator and again we lurched ahead, heading west down Pennsylvania Avenue. Rather than drop in behind me, however, the Beast hugged my left flank, and then it became clear. This limo held the president, and the Secret Service driver was using us as a shield.

We were taking withering fire on our right side, but we pressed on. Suddenly the passenger window exploded. Glass flew everywhere and I tromped harder on the accelerator. Despite the snow and ice, I had no problems with traction in this massive truck. Likewise, the Beast had no problems keeping up. We soon passed Freedom Plaza on our right and the Ronald Reagan International Trade Building on our left.

Fifteenth Street was coming up fast. I had a decision to make. Should I be taking a hard right by the Willard Intercontinental hotel and the Treasury Department, heading eventually for the northwest gate of the White House? Or should I continue straight through the southeast checkpoint? The former was the classic route, the usual route, but for that very reason I suspected it was also the most perilous. It would snake us through a canyon of hotels and office buildings, any one of which might have more terrorists waiting for the president. I had no way to contact the Secret Service team in the presidential limo. But I did have Harris. I gave him both options, and he ordered me to go directly to the southeast checkpoint and then slam on the brakes, letting the Beast blow through the lowered gates, and then using the snowplow's bulk to seal off the checkpoint from anyone else who might try to crash through.

That was fine with me. The only problem was that I had now built up a head of steam and badly miscalculated how long it would take to stop.

"Hold on!" I shouted as I slammed on the brakes.

We all braced for impact, and the last thing I remembered seeing was Secret Service agents diving out of the gatehouse before we hit it directly, smashing it to smithereens.

PART
TWO

13

★ ★ ★

I awoke groggy and disoriented.

"Welcome back," said a kindly looking older gentleman.

I said nothing, and he didn't press me. I just stared at him and tried to figure out where I was. The man was probably in his mid- to late sixties. He was clearly a physician, wearing a white lab coat and a stethoscope around his neck. He was standing over me, holding a clipboard and checking my pulse.

"How are you feeling?" he asked.

Again I said nothing.

"Can you tell me your name?"

I tried to form words, but nothing came out. He handed me a cup of room-temperature water. I took a small sip, and he asked me again.

"Collins," I whispered.

"Is that your first name or last?"

"Last."

"And your first?"

"J. . . ."

"J. what?"

"J. B."

"What's that short for?"

I stared at him blankly.

"What's your full name, son?"

"James," I said finally. "James Bradley."

"Do you remember your birthday?"

"Yes."

There was a brief pause while the doctor waited for the answer, but I said nothing. A moment later, with great patience, he asked me again to tell him the exact date of my birth.

"Oh, uh . . . May—May 3."

"Good," he said, apparently checking my answers against whatever was written on his clipboard. "Where?"

"Where what?"

"Where were you born?"

"Maine," I said. "Bar Harbor." I was finally starting to feel more like myself, my head clearer and the answers to his questions coming more easily now.

"What's your mother's name?"

"Maggie."

"And your father?"

"Next question," I said tersely.

He raised his eyebrows. "I need it for the files."

"No, you don't," I said, then noticed his name badge. "I'm not a minor, Dr. Weisberg. My father hasn't been in the picture for over thirty years."

"Okay," he said, shifting gears. "Do you know what day this is?"

That took me a moment. "Tuesday—er, no, Wednesday, probably."

"Good," said the doctor. "What's your brother's name?"

"Matt—Matthew—where is he? Is he okay?"

"A few stitches, a slight concussion, but yes, he'll be fine," he said.

"Can I see him?" I asked.

"Of course," Weisberg said, nodding. "He's in the room next door. You can see him in a few hours. Now, the other man you came in with? Do you remember his name?"

"Harris?" I asked.

"You tell me."

"Yeah, Harris," I said. "Arthur Harris. Works for the FBI—and how is he?"

"He'll be fine."

"He was shot," I said.

"True, but he was lucky—only grazed," Weisberg said. "It was a bit messy, but we patched him up. He'll be good as new in no time." He shone a penlight in my eyes and checked to see if my pupils were properly dilating.

"So where exactly am I?" I asked.

"GW," he said, apparently knowing that I lived in the area and would understand that he meant George Washington University Hospital on Twenty-Third Street, just minutes from the White House. "It's been a tough night. Considering the rest of the folks I've seen tonight, I'd have to say you guys are pretty lucky."

It was all coming back to me.

"The president?" I asked. "Are he and the First Lady safe?"

The doctor said nothing.

"I'm not asking for anything confidential," I insisted. "I don't need to know where they are. I just want to know if they're okay."

"They are," he said. "Now, just a few more questions. Do you have any allergies?"

"No."

"Do you have a heart condition?"

"No."

"Diabetes?"

"No."

"Are you currently on any medications?"

I shook my head.

"Do you use any illegal narcotics?"

"No."

"What about alcohol?"

"What about it?"

"Do you drink?"

"I used to."

He waited.

I didn't want to say any more, but I knew he could already see where this was going. "A lot."

He said nothing.

"I'm a recovering alcoholic," I conceded.

Again he waited patiently. So finally I told him. There was no reason not to. "Two years, five months, and twenty-eight days."

"Good for you—one day at a time," he said. "Now look: you need to get some rest. There's a team of agents from the bureau outside your room, and your brother's room and Agent Harris's room, to make sure you're all safe. I'll check back on you in a few hours, when the sun comes up. In the meantime, if you need anything, press this button and the nurses will take care of you."

"Got it," I said. "And, Doc . . . I'm going to be okay, right? I didn't lose a limb or a lung or something?"

"Nothing so dramatic," Weisberg said, writing a few final notes on my chart. "You got banged up pretty good out there. You have a mild concussion—certainly understandable. Still, given the injuries you sustained in December in Iraq—bullet wound to the right shoulder, significant burns due to a hand grenade, significant loss of blood, dehydration, and the like—I'd like to keep you for the next twenty-four to forty-eight hours for observation, just to be safe."

There was no way that was going to happen. Too much was at stake. I had a story to chase and I couldn't do it from a bed at George Washington University Hospital. But I knew better than to get into an argument I was sure to lose with my attending physician. So I just nodded. "Can you at least bring me my phone and turn on the TV?"

"No, Mr. Collins," he replied. "Right now you really need to rest."

"I realize that, Doctor, but I'm a reporter. I need to know what's happening out there."

"The worst of it is over," he said. "But there's nothing you can do about it right now in any case. You don't work for the *Times* tonight. Tonight you're a patient. My patient. So get some sleep, and I'll see you in a few hours."

I glanced at the wall clock. It was 4:23 a.m. The sun would be coming up in about two and a half hours over a capital and a nation traumatized by the deadliest terror attack on American soil since September 11, 2001. But the question that kept haunting me was: What was coming next?

14

★ ★ ★

I was awakened by two investigators from the FBI just after 6 a.m.

They had come to get a complete statement from me as to what I had seen and heard as the terrorist attacks unfolded the previous evening at the Capitol building and along Pennsylvania Avenue. The "taciturn twins"—they were about the same age, nearly the same height, similar build, similar off-the-rack suits (ugly ones, at that), with equally dour demeanors—interviewed me for about thirty minutes. They took detailed notes. They covered every conceivable angle but refused to answer any of my questions in return.

"You sent out a Twitter message last night about an ISIS sleeper cell in Alabama," one said.

"*Alleged* ISIS sleeper cell," I clarified.

"Fine, alleged ISIS sleeper cell," he replied. "You reported that authorities found hundreds of mortar shells in the perps' apartment."

"And?" I asked, unclear where he was going.

"How did you know any of that?" the investigator asked. "The news wasn't public yet. No press release had been issued. You don't live in Alabama."

"That's my job, gentlemen," I said. "That's what I do—report things other reporters haven't yet."

"But where did you get the information?"

"Nice try," I said. "You're not really asking about my sources, are you?"

"Mr. Collins, we need you to cooperate."

"I am cooperating," I noted.

"We need you to cooperate *fully*. We're asking how you knew when so few people did at that point."

"Lots of people knew," I countered. "The state police knew. The local authorities knew. The bureau knew. So did the White House, the CIA, Homeland Security, and the Joint Terrorism Task Force." I was spitballing, trying to throw them off the trail. But I had no idea if it was working.

"So, Mr. Collins, does it ever seem odd to you?" the lead agent now asked, trying a different tack.

"What?" I asked.

"That you keep winding up in the middle of terrorist attacks?"

"No," I said calmly.

"Why not?" the agent asked, incredulous.

"I'm a national security correspondent for the *New York Times*," I responded. "I cover war and terrorism. I don't expect to live a simple, easy life. If I did, I'd be writing for *Travel + Leisure* or *Better Homes and Gardens*."

"And it doesn't worry you?" his partner pressed.

"Of course it worries me," I shot back. "It worries me that ISIS operatives are able to slip across our borders and make it to Washington and fire mortar shells at our Capitol, and nobody stops them. It worries me that you guys can't protect the seat of our government from an attack everyone knew was coming. It worries me that the president of the United States doesn't seem to have the will to crush ISIS once and for all even though they took the man captive, put him in a steel cage, threatened to douse him with kerosene and set him ablaze. It worries me that they tried to convert the entire country to their insane vision of Islam. It worries me that Abu Khalif is on a genocidal killing spree and the U.S. government doesn't seem to have a plan to hunt him down and put a bullet between his eyes. Should I go on? You got all that? Or am I going too fast for you guys?"

"We're guessing you're done talking?" said the lead agent.

"Oh yeah, I'm done," I snapped.

"Here's my card," he said. "Please let us know if you think of anything else."

I took the card and put it down on the bed without looking at it.

When they were gone, a nurse brought me a Styrofoam cup of black coffee. It wasn't the worst I'd ever had, but it was close. I drank it anyway. It was going to be a long day, and I needed all the fuel I could get.

Then came a knock on my door and my brother popped his head in. "You decent?" Matt asked.

He looked pretty banged up—scrapes and bruises all over his face and nine stitches on his forehead—but when I asked, he said he felt fine. I waved him over and gave him a hug, grateful we were both still alive.

When he asked about me, I was tempted to lie and say I was fine too. I didn't want to look weak. Least of all in front of my big brother. Instead, I told him the truth, what I hadn't even told Dr. Weisberg. I felt horrible. My neck was in wrenching pain from whiplash. One of the disks in my lower back was pinched and it was killing me. The muscles in both my legs were severely cramped. My backside was bruised. I wasn't trying to complain, I insisted. I was just answering his question.

Matt stared at me for a moment. I think my candor caught him off guard. Then he said, "Well, the good news is you don't really look like you've been through a major terrorist attack."

At first I thought he was being sarcastic. But that wasn't Matt's style. It was mine. I hadn't actually looked in a mirror yet. Now I did. I pulled myself out of bed, walked into the bathroom, and stared at my reflection. Behind my designer prescription glasses, my eyes were bloodshot. My salt-and-pepper goatee needed a trim. My bald head needed a fresh shave. But Matt was right. I had only the mildest of scrapes and contusions on my face. What injuries I'd sustained were real enough, to be sure, but my bruises and contusions weren't immediately visible. In a day without much to be grateful for, I would take it.

Harris came in just then. He was hobbling around on crutches, but as Dr. Weisberg had predicted, he was going to survive. The look on his face, however, told me immediately there was trouble.

"Turn on the television," he said without any pleasantries.

"Why?" I asked.

"The president is about to address the nation."

15

★ ★ ★

"This is CNN Breaking News."

I moved over to the bed and sat down and urged Harris to take the chair to the right of the bed, as it was the only one in the room. He hesitated, but when I insisted, he finally accepted. It was clear he was in more discomfort than he was letting on. Matt came over and stood in the corner to my left.

Soon we were transfixed as CNN showed a split screen. On one side was a live shot of the still-smoking U.S. Capitol; on the other was a view of the East Room of the White House and an empty podium bearing the presidential seal. On the lower portion of the screen, scrolling headlines noted various world leaders sending condolences to the American people. Moments later, Harrison Taylor—looking somber yet resolute—stepped to the podium and began to speak. It was surreal to think that I had been with him just a few hours earlier. How fast the world had changed.

"My fellow Americans," the president began, staring directly into the camera and looking like he hadn't gotten any sleep at all. "Last night, enemies of the United States unleashed a cruel and cowardly attack. The attack occurred without warning. The terrorists targeted the heart of our capital, intending to decapitate our national leadership. But I am pleased to report that they were completely unsuccessful."

I was shocked. *"Without warning"*? How could he say such a thing? How much more warning did he need? A blind man could have seen ISIS coming. Abu Khalif couldn't have been clearer. I'd published his words verbatim, for all the world to read. Surely the DNI and the directors of the CIA and DIA and FBI and Homeland Security and their tens of thousands of employees had read them. I knew the president had read them. Last night I'd practically taken a yellow highlighter and pushed them in his face in the Oval Office. Okay, so Khalif hadn't given us the exact place and time of the attack, but was Taylor really so naive as to think he would?

"Fortunately, I am safe and unharmed," the president continued. "As you can see, I am here in the White House, at my post, doing the work of the nation. The vice president is also safe and unharmed, as is the Speaker of the House. Neither are in Washington at the moment. Both are currently in secure, undisclosed locations, but I can assure you that they, too, are hard at work. Indeed, during the night, I conducted a secure video conference with both of them, as well as the National Security Council and the Joint Chiefs of Staff, assessing the damage and mapping out our response.

"Moments ago, I finished another video conference, this one with the secretary-general of the United Nations and the leaders of Canada, Great Britain, France, and Germany, as well as the supreme commander of NATO. Each of them have pledged their full support to me as I manage this crisis, and to the people of the United States as we recover from these attacks and plan our response.

"In less than an hour, I will be meeting with my full cabinet and will be conducting additional calls with the leaders of our allies around the world, all to make sure they have a clear and detailed understanding of what has been unfolding here and so that I can answer their questions and enlist their assistance.

"In a moment, I will brief you on the damage that was inflicted last night and what is being done to bring those responsible to justice.

But first I want to assure you that every step is being taken to prevent other attacks from happening on American soil.

"First, I have directed the secretary of Homeland Security to shut down all civilian aviation to and from the United States and within the U.S. and our territories for at least forty-eight hours. This should give federal, state, and local authorities time to make sure no terror threats are being plotted in our skies and to plug any potential holes in our air-defense systems.

"Second, I have ordered that our borders with Mexico and Canada be closed for the next forty-eight hours. All seaports will be closed to incoming vessels—cruise lines, commercial container ships, private yachts, and so forth—during the same period. This will give the Coast Guard time to make sure we are on top of any possible new threats.

"Third, I have directed the secretary of the Treasury to suspend trading on the New York Stock Exchange and NASDAQ for the remainder of the week. It is my hope and expectation that the markets will reopen on Monday morning. But for now I'm asking the Treasury Department and the SEC to take all measures necessary to safeguard our financial systems against the possibility of terrorists exploiting these attacks or trying to exacerbate their effect to bring harm to the American economy.

"Now I want to be crystal clear—there is no credible evidence that other attacks are coming by land, air, or sea. I am working very closely with the director of National Intelligence, our entire intelligence community, and our allies to review every conceivable threat and every possible lead that will guide us to those responsible. I assure you, we will bring them to justice. I have great confidence in the men and women of our law enforcement community and our military. They are working around the clock to keep us all safe. However, out of an abundance of caution, I am using my authority under the Constitution as your commander in chief to take the measures

I deem appropriate to defend every American—and all the visitors under our care—against all threats, foreign and domestic.

"That said, let me take a few moments to share with you some details of what happened last night. At approximately 9:36 p.m., as I delivered the State of the Union address, terrorists unleashed a bombing campaign against the Capitol building using mortar shells fired from artillery pieces positioned in various places around Washington, D.C. Some of the explosive devices were filled with chemical weapons, specifically sarin gas. The damage to the Capitol was extensive, and I regret to inform you that there was significant loss of life. According to the latest information I have been provided with by the secretary of Homeland Security, a total of 136 people died in last night's attacks. Another ninety-seven were wounded, some of them critically. Among the dead are forty-nine members of the House, nineteen members of the Senate, seventeen members of the press corps, twelve foreign ambassadors, thirty-three guests, three police officers, two D.C. firemen, and one member of my Secret Service detail."

The number hit me like a punch in the gut. *A hundred and thirty-six dead? Ninety-seven more injured? How in the world could this have happened in the most secure facility on the face of the planet, in the heart of the American seat of government?*

"Authorities are still notifying the next of kin for a number of these folks," the president noted. "At the appropriate time, we will post every name on the White House website. When the moment is right, we will hold a memorial service to honor these brave men and women, all of whom deserve our deepest respect. For now, would you join me in a moment of silence to remember these fallen heroes?"

The president bowed his head and closed his eyes. Matt and Agent Harris followed suit. I just stared at the television. *A hundred and thirty-six dead in Washington, D.C., at the hands of Abu Khalif.* My blood was boiling. I had no doubt every American felt the same.

But for me, this was personal.

16

★ ★ ★

I should have turned off the television right then.

For when the president began speaking again, what he said absolutely infuriated me.

"My fellow Americans, rest assured that as I speak, the FBI, the Department of Homeland Security, and other federal law enforcement agencies are engaged in a monumental investigation that spans multiple locations, including multiple states and even nations. While it is too early to say who is responsible for these attacks, you have my word that I will keep you updated on critical developments in the hours and days ahead."

Too early? What in the world was he talking about? There was no question in my mind this was the work of ISIS. I didn't have solid, incontrovertible proof yet—the kind I could publish, the kind someone could use to prosecute—but I'd bet everything I had this was the work of Abu Khalif. It had his fingerprints all over it. Surely the president had been briefed on the capture of the ISIS cell in Birmingham by now. Surely he knew far more than I did. Why was he hedging? Why not just tell the American people the truth?

"I urge every American to show restraint at this difficult hour," the president continued. "We must not make the mistake of jumping to conclusions that this was the work of a single organization. And even if it so proves to be, let us not make the mistake of concluding that there was a religious motive to these attacks, much less that this was the work of a single religion."

Again I recoiled in disgust. Restraint? Was he kidding? Why weren't we already carpet bombing Raqqa, the ISIS capital in Syria? And no religious motive? What did the president think the *I* in ISIL stood for anyway?

I bit my tongue, not wanting to explode in front of Harris. The FBI agent had become a valuable source. I didn't dare risk offending or alienating him. But the president's equivocation in the face of direct attacks on the American people, our leaders, and our honor made me physically ill.

What's more, I felt nauseated by his genuflections at the altar of political correctness.

No one in his right mind was accusing the *entire* Muslim world of trying to kill us. Not the Republicans. Nor the Democrats. So why was the president determined to set up such a straw man?

When the president insisted the vast majority of the Islamic world didn't want to kill us, that was true, and good—wonderful, even. But survey after survey showed that while some 90 percent of Muslims around the world did *not* subscribe to the philosophy of violent jihad, somewhere between 7 and 10 percent of Muslims did. I was very glad that nine out of ten Muslims had little or no inclination to violence. But in a world of 1.6 billion Muslims, 10 percent represented some 160 million people. That was equal to half the population of the United States! A nation with a population that large would be the ninth most populous country in the world. This was a big deal. This was a real and serious threat, for it was precisely this pool of 160 million sympathizers and supporters of violence from which ISIS was recruiting.

Yes, Americans wished it could all be over. Taylor certainly did.

So did I. We were all exhausted by the conflicts in the Middle East. But the problem wasn't going away. It was actually getting worse. The last twelve hours proved it. To stick our heads in the sand and pretend we weren't engaged in a global war of guns and bombs and ideas was as foolish as it was dangerous.

Not once during his State of the Union address—nor during his address to the nation this morning—had Taylor mentioned the Islamic State by name. Rather, last night, as always, he had used the abbreviation ISIL. The acronym was accurate enough. It stood for the "Islamic State of Iraq and the Levant." But by only using the term ISIL and avoiding the full name, the president was purposefully avoiding using the words *Islam* and *Islamic* and *Muslim*. He was specifically avoiding any mention of the caliphate or any discussion of the theological and eschatological precepts driving Abu Khalif.

In one speech several months earlier, he had actually explained why he refused to say the full name of Khalif's emerging empire. "The Islamic State is neither Islamic nor a state," he had argued.

Such nonsense made my blood boil.

How could the president defeat an enemy he refused to define?

17

★ ★ ★

Then came the bombshell.

"The U.S. and our coalition allies have achieved remarkable victories in the Middle East in the last few months, and we must not allow what has just happened to drive us off target," the president continued. "As I said last night, we have liberated Mosul. In fact, we have liberated all of northern Iraq and made that entire country safe again. Our work there is nearly finished, and we can be proud of our success. We should be pleased with our progress, and we should stay the course. We must not change our strategy or weaken our resolve. We must not allow our enemies to force us to live in fear. Nor are we going to let them lure us into a quagmire that could bog us down for a generation. Our mission is nearly complete. We will bring to justice those who perpetrated this dastardly attack. But when our work is done, I won't delay for one moment bringing our troops home once again. I will not let terrorists dictate our national security policy. We will not become embroiled in the Middle East forever. We will do our job, and we will move on. To this end, you have my solemn pledge."

I couldn't believe what I was hearing, and as I glanced at Matt, it was clear he couldn't either. Harris was inscrutable, but my brother was livid.

The president's constitutional mandate was to protect us from all enemies, foreign and domestic. It was, therefore, the president's solemn responsibility to help the American people understand exactly what we were up against. For Taylor to pretend that ISIS wasn't involved in these new attacks—or that the fighters working for ISIS, or ISIL, or whatever he wanted to call it, weren't Muslims and weren't driven by their interpretation of Islamic theology—was just asinine.

As anyone who had studied their books and speeches and websites and videos could see, the leaders of the Islamic State professed over and over again to anyone who would listen that they didn't simply want to expel the infidels from the Mideast and North Africa. They wanted to either convert or exterminate the infidels, usher in the coming of their messiah known as the Mahdi, and establish the Islamic kingdom or caliphate that would rule over the entire globe. They weren't simply trying to conquer the "filthy Zionists" and the "ugly apostates" and "diabolical Crusaders." They wanted to force every person on the planet to bow down and submit to their version of Islam or be slaughtered. They were diabolically obsessed with bringing to fulfillment the Islamic prophecies supposedly uttered by Muhammad fourteen centuries ago, and they believed they could accelerate the End of Days by engaging in all-out genocide. And not only were they trying to hasten the end of the world through their own violent actions, they were absolutely convinced that Allah required this of them and that they would burn in hell if they did not destroy their enemies.

This was what Abu Khalif and his inner circle believed. This was what drove them. This was what they preached, what they talked about, prayed about, wrote about. This was what they studied, what they thought about, what they rallied their forces around and indoctrinated into their children and their newest recruits. This was what energized and enthused and enraged them. And this was what made Abu Khalif so much more dangerous than Osama bin Laden or any of his colleagues or predecessors. Khalif was not simply a terrorist. He was the head of an apocalyptic, messianic, genocidal death cult, and in his head was a ticking clock counting down to doomsday.

With a plethora of Islamic texts in hand—real or otherwise—Khalif was explaining to his followers and the whole of the Muslim world his view of Allah, his view of mankind, his approach to the End Times, and why it was urgent for all Muslims to get off the sidelines and come join the caliphate.

And it was working. Abu Khalif was winning Muslim recruits in droves.

He had publicly pledged to decapitate the American government. Twice now, he had come dangerously close to achieving his objective. Yet twice in twenty-four hours, the president had refused to mention his name or the name of his movement.

Who was the commander in chief trying to convince by such obvious denial? I wondered. Did he really believe that what had just happened was evidence of our "success" in the war against the caliphate rather than a damning indictment of our failures? The president was living in fantasyland, and it was getting Americans killed.

None of this would be happening, of course, if he had thrown the entire weight of the American intelligence community and military into hunting down and destroying the emir of ISIS. Yet rather than vowing to ramp up our attacks and destroy every last vestige of Abu Khalif and his genocidal forces, the president was repeatedly signaling his intent to end our involvement in Iraq and bring U.S. troops home from the region as rapidly as possible.

That was tantamount to surrender, and I was about to explode.

18

★ ★ ★

I went straight to the nurses' station, dressed only in a hospital gown and slippers.

I demanded my suit and my phone. The head nurse said that wasn't possible. I could get my things back when I was released, and only my attending physician could authorize that, and he wouldn't be available for another ninety minutes.

"This is still America, isn't it?" I asked her. "This is still the land of the free and the home of the brave?" Through gritted teeth I made it clear she had two minutes to turn over my personal effects. She dug in her heels.

I was about to go ballistic when Agent Harris stepped up behind me and calmly intervened.

"Ma'am, my two colleagues and I are leaving here in five minutes," he said in that firm, authoritative, no-nonsense tone they must teach new recruits down at the FBI training center in Quantico. "Now, we would be grateful if you would provide us our personal effects immediately."

It worked. Within moments, Matt, Harris, and I had everything we needed. Less than five minutes later we were in a cab heading straight to the J. Edgar Hoover Building.

Harris kept his cards close to the vest. He wouldn't tell us what he had in mind, but he didn't disabuse me of the notion he was taking us to look at some of the evidence the bureau had compiled so far on who might be responsible for these attacks so I could write a story for the *Times*. For the moment, though, he merely assured us that at the bureau we could get a change of clothes and a shower before we went any further.

The District of Columbia looked like a ghost town. In normal times, the five inches of snow alone would have led to the shutdown of all government buildings, schools, shops, and private businesses. But these were clearly not normal times.

The fires at the Capitol building had finally been put out, but all of Capitol Hill was now a hazmat disaster area. Specialists in chem-bio gear were swarming over the grounds and through the rubble of the Senate Chamber.

The cab driver had a local news station playing. We learned that every unsecured building in a twenty-block radius of the Capitol had been evacuated due to the threat of chemical weapons contamination. Meanwhile, the entire corridor between the White House and the Capitol had become a crime scene. It had been cordoned off from the public as the FBI, Secret Service, D.C. Metro police, and other law enforcement agencies gathered evidence. At the same time, a massive manhunt was under way for any and all suspects who had participated in the highly coordinated attacks.

Harris sat in the front and made several calls. Matt and I sat in back, with Harris's crutches across our laps. Matt immediately called Annie. He assured her—and our mom, who was on the extension—that we were alive and safe and had just been released from the hospital. He apologized that we hadn't been able to call earlier and explained what we'd been through.

Meanwhile, I speed-dialed Allen. After assuring him I was okay, I dictated an eyewitness account of what it had been like to be inside the House Chamber and on Pennsylvania Avenue during the attacks. It was all I could do not to let my personal outrage at the president come through, and for the most part I was successful. Allen was relieved to know I was all right, and he was grateful to get my first dispatch. He told me it would be posted on the *Times* homepage within the hour. I told him I was en route to FBI headquarters and would keep him posted on what I learned.

Moments later, we arrived at the Hoover Building. The main entrance was closed and heavily guarded, so the cabbie pulled up to the E Street entrance. I got out first and helped Harris with his crutches, then turned to Matt and suggested he head to my apartment in Arlington and get some rest.

"No, J. B. I want to stay with you," Matt insisted.

I shook my head. "I need to focus. And you need to rest. Go to my place. I'll link up with you as soon as I can."

"You sure?" he said.

"Absolutely," I said, then had an idea. "In fact, you should find a way to get up to Bar Harbor. You need to be with Annie and the kids. Don't worry about the cost. I'll cover it."

"You're serious?" he asked.

"Hey," I said. "It's the least I can do."

I hoped this might ease my conscience a little. My pursuit of the ISIS story had put my family in danger. I was single, making decent money, and had very few expenses. Matt, on the other hand, was a seminary professor. He wasn't exactly swimming in cash, and he had a wife and two young kids to support. I was sure he'd blown a good part of his meager savings to buy last-minute airline tickets to evacuate himself and his family out of Amman. Paying for him to get to Bar Harbor really was the least I could do.

"Let's go, Collins," Harris said, glancing at his watch. "We need to move."

I nodded and paid the cabbie the current fare plus enough to get my brother back across the Potomac to Arlington. I gave Matt my apartment key and my Visa card. He thanked me and made me promise I'd call home and tell Mom I was okay. Then the cab pulled away.

"Come on," Harris said. "There's something you need to see."

19

★ ★ ★

J. EDGAR HOOVER BUILDING, WASHINGTON, D.C.

We cleared security and boarded an elevator.

Harris positioned himself so I couldn't see what button he had pushed.

"Why are you doing this?" I asked.

"Doing what?"

"Taking risks. Feeding me information."

Harris said nothing. The elevator headed up.

"The two agents who took my statement," I said.

"What about them?"

"They wanted to know who'd leaked me the info about the mortar shells."

"What'd you tell them?"

"I think you know exactly what I told them," I said. "In fact, I think you *told* them to ask who fed me the information and to keep pressing me to see if I'd crack."

"And why would I do that?" he asked as we passed the second floor and kept heading up.

"To see if I could be trusted."

Harris said nothing as we cleared the third floor.

"Can you be?" he asked finally.

"You tell me," I said.

The elevator dinged. The doors opened. We had reached the fifth floor.

"Guess the answer is yes," I said, then stepped off.

I nodded to several uniformed agents holding automatic weapons, but they neither stopped nor searched me. Then I followed Harris to a suite of offices on the Pennsylvania Avenue side of the building. A secretary waved us forward. The security men posted nearby nodded but didn't say a word. The name on the door was *Lawrence S. Beck, Director*.

Beck was a legend in D.C. He had been a special agent for the bureau for almost twenty years before being appointed to serve as the U.S. attorney for the southern district of New York. Later he served for three years as U.S. assistant attorney general. During his career, Beck had successfully prosecuted some of the most notorious serial killers, embezzlers, mobsters, and terrorists in the country's history. At fifty-six, he was tough as nails, straight as an arrow, and as bald as I was after a fresh shave.

We'd actually met once in Baghdad at an embassy function in the Green Zone just after the liberation of Iraq in the summer of 2003. He was helping advise the Iraqis in how to set up their justice department. Tall and lanky, brimming with energy, he hadn't been real chatty. Instead, he'd chain-smoked through the evening, and given that he didn't really affect my beat directly, I'd not paid any more attention to him. Now I was standing in his office.

"Mr. Collins, have a seat," the director said.

I did as I was told. Harris sat beside me. Beck didn't sit at all. Rather, he paced and chewed—constantly—what I guessed was nicotine gum. I saw no ashtrays in the room. There was no smell of smoke. No stains on his fingers. Just the telltale signs of a man who wished I were offering him a light.

"Impressive work on tracking the ISIS story, Mr. Collins—the chemical weapons in Syria and all," he began. "Three separate intelligence agencies were pursuing that story. But you're the one who confirmed it."

"Lot of good it did," I said, in no mood to take credit given all the carnage that had ensued.

"Not your fault," he said, striding over to the enormous plate-glass windows overlooking Pennsylvania Avenue and the crime scene five stories below. "Those were political decisions, and—off the record—foolish ones. Nothing you could've done about that. You got the facts. You got them right. You put them out there for the world to see. There was nothing more you could do."

He was right. But so what? Where was he going with this? I was tempted to ask but held my tongue. Beck had summoned me. He had something to say to—or ask—me. He'd get to it in due time. There was no point seeming overeager.

"Did you catch the president's speech this morning?" he asked.

I glanced at Harris, then back at Beck.

"Of course," I said.

"Any initial reaction?"

It seemed a strange question for the director of the FBI to ask any reporter, especially a *New York Times* correspondent. His was an apolitical position. So was mine. At least, it was supposed to be. What *should* my reaction be? And why would he care?

I shrugged. Beck stopped pacing. He just stood behind his desk and waited for me to answer. But I said nothing.

"You had no reaction at all?" he asked.

"I'm not sure what you're asking, sir," I said cautiously.

"It didn't seem odd to you the president didn't accuse ISIS, didn't mention Abu Khalif, didn't suggest this was the emir's payback for Alqosh?" Beck pressed.

For a moment I stayed silent.

Beck didn't move. Didn't resume pacing. Didn't say a word.

"Okay," I said finally, seeing nothing to lose. "Off the record, yes—it did seem odd."

He waited for me to go further.

It wasn't just odd, of course. It was insane—an epic dereliction of duty. But why did Beck care what I thought? Again, I wasn't a columnist. I wasn't a pundit. I was a news reporter. My personal views were supposed to be irrelevant.

"Look, Director," I said at last, "if you've got something to tell me, I'm all ears. But I'm afraid I can't comment on the president's speech. Yes, I found it odd. But beyond that, I'm trying my best to stay objective."

Beck nodded. "Fair enough," he said. Then he opened a file on his desk and began sliding one eight-by-ten glossy color photo after another over to me. And one after another, I gathered them off the desk, reviewed them, and passed them to Harris to look at. The photos showed an abandoned facility, a relic of D.C.'s history.

"You're looking at what used to be the Alexander Crummell School," Beck said. "It's a twenty-thousand-square-foot building set on two and a half acres on Galludet Street."

"Just off of New York?" I asked.

Beck nodded.

"The Ivy City district," I said.

"That's right. You know it?"

"Sure." I had recognized the neighborhood immediately. "I had an apartment near there years ago when I first started with the *Times*."

"Then you might know the school was built in 1911 and shuttered in 1977," he continued.

I didn't. Nor did I care. I was waiting for the punch line.

Beck slid more photos across the desk. The first three weren't interesting in the slightest. They showed several angles of an unmarked tractor trailer bearing Alabama license plates, sitting in the snowy parking lot of the abandoned school. The fourth photo, however, sent a jolt of adrenaline through my system.

20

★ ★ ★

"You found the weapon," I said, stunned.

I stared at the photo, trying to take it all in. When I didn't immediately hand it to him, Harris leaned over and gasped.

"One of them," Beck confirmed. "What you're looking at, gentlemen, is a World War II–era U.S. Army M114-model howitzer. It's capable of firing 155-millimeter shells—each weighing about ninety-five pounds—up to a maximum range of about nine miles."

"How far is the school from the Capitol?" I asked.

"Just over two miles," the director noted. "And there's more." He handed us more photos. "Now you're looking at Our Lady of Perpetual Help Parochial School—or what's left of it. It was a Catholic elementary school for, I don't know, half a century or more. Three stories. Playground. Parking lot. Used to take in hundreds of kids, mostly African American, but it's been abandoned since 2007."

"Where is it?" I asked.

"1409 V Street Southeast."

"Anacostia," I said.

"Right," Beck agreed. "Just a block from the Frederick Douglass National Historic Site. Used to be a jewel. But the diocese ran out of money and shut her down."

"How far is it from the Capitol?" I asked.

"Two and a quarter miles," Beck said.

"Straight shot, no obstructions?" Harris asked.

"'Fraid so," Beck said, nodding, then showed us a photo taken from the roof of the school. The smoking wreckage of the Capitol Dome was clearly visible, and every muscle in my aching body tightened.

Next Beck showed us photos of another abandoned, unmarked 18-wheeler, also bearing Alabama tags, and another M114 howitzer.

"Unbelievable," I said, shaking my head. "Please tell me you've got suspects in custody."

"Not yet," Beck said, but then he corrected himself. "Not exactly."

"What do you mean?" I asked.

Rather than telling me, Beck simply passed more photos across the desk. These next shots had been taken at a construction compound just off of Douglass Road in Anacostia, not far from the Suitland Parkway. Another 18-wheeler. Another set of Alabama plates. But unlike before, these photos revealed stacks of intact, unfired 155-millimeter mortar shells—nineteen, by my count. Then came a photo of an African American security guard, graying, probably in his late fifties. He'd been murdered, double-tapped to the chest.

"Where's the howitzer?" I asked.

Beck handed me more eight-by-ten glossies. One showed the twisted, scorched remains of a World War II–era howitzer. Others showed bits and pieces of the howitzer spread all over the compound.

"What happened?" I asked, my thoughts racing.

"Apparently one of the mortar rounds exploded inside the barrel of the howitzer before it could be fired. Or perhaps it blew up as it was being fired. Our technical teams are still on site, doing their analyses."

"And whoever was manning this thing fled when the howitzer blew up too?"

Beck shook his head. "Worse."

The final seven photos were each more gruesome than the last. They revealed dead men in their mid- to late twenties. Each had dark skin and a beard. And they all had clearly been killed by exposure to sarin gas. I had seen it before—in Amman, in Mosul, and in Alqosh. I knew the signs. Their eyes were glassy and dilated. Their hands and fingers were twisted. Some were curled up in a fetal position. There was unmistakable evidence that each of them had lost control of their bodily functions in their final moments. They had urinated and defecated all over themselves. Several were covered in their own vomit. They had died just the way they had intended their victims to die, the way they had intended the president to die, the way they had intended my brother and me to die.

I couldn't look any longer. Shuddering, I stood, walked over to the windows, and looked out at the fresh snow falling on a city reeling from the latest wave of evil. The death toll—at 136—wasn't as high as the 9/11 attack on the Pentagon, which had claimed 184 lives. But the al Qaeda attacks had taken place almost two decades earlier. A generation of young people had been born and raised since those attacks. They'd only heard about them through textbooks, documentaries, and annual memorial services. These attacks by ISIS were as fresh as they were horrific, and since they had come on the heels of the disaster in Amman, every American knew two things: First, it could have been much worse. And second, it wasn't the end; much more was surely coming.

Abu Khalif had launched an unprecedented chemical weapons attack inside the heart of the American democracy. This was the first time weapons of mass destruction had ever been used against the American people inside the American homeland, and it had taken place in prime time, during a nationally televised State of the Union address, when an estimated 70 million Americans had been watching.

"Have you ID'd the seven yet?" I asked, fixated on the smoke still rising from the House Chamber but forcing myself to do my job.

"We have," Beck said. "Five are recent Syrian refugees. Each entered the U.S. in the past year as part of the president's program to welcome and absorb fifty thousand refugees fleeing ISIS. The sixth was an Iraqi national. He was captured by U.S. forces as a member of AQI and sent to Abu Ghraib. He got out the night Abu Khalif escaped."

"The night I was there, interviewing Khalif?" I clarified.

I saw Beck's reflection in the window as he nodded.

"And the seventh man?" I asked, turning to see Beck handing his entire file over to Harris.

This time Harris answered, reviewing the notes. "Jordanian. Twenty-six. Graduate of MIT. Studied chemical engineering. Son of a Jordanian member of Parliament."

"You're kidding me," I said.

"Wish I were."

"What else?" I asked, my thoughts reeling.

"They're all ISIS," the director said. "Every single one of them. None of them were carrying passports or other forms of ID. But we've recovered their phones. We've got their fingerprints. We're still crossing the t's and dotting the i's, but the evidence is over-whelming. They're all in our databases. They've all sworn allegiance to the caliphate and to Abu Khalif personally. Several of them posted videos of themselves doing so on YouTube. And if these seven are ISIS, we can be pretty sure the teams who ran the other two locations were ISIS as well."

"So the president was lying," I said. It wasn't a question. It was a statement of fact.

"I wouldn't say that," Beck countered.

"Of course you wouldn't," I argued. "You're a career lawyer, and you're the director of the FBI, personally chosen and appointed by the president. But facts are facts."

"Let's stick to what we know for now, Mr. Collins," Beck replied.

"Didn't the president just tell us it's 'too early to say who is responsible for these attacks'?"

Neither Beck nor Harris responded.

"Didn't he say, 'We must not make the mistake of jumping to conclusions that this was the work of a single organization'?" I pressed.

"Mr. Collins, the president is operating in the midst of a fast-moving crisis," Beck replied. "He didn't say it wasn't ISIS. He merely said it was too soon to point a finger. And he's right. Our investigation is still ongoing."

"Sir, with all due respect, Abu Khalif just tried to take out the entire American government," I said. "Then he and his men tried to slaughter me and Agent Harris in front of your own building, blocks from the White House. The president should be ordering the annihilation of ISIS strongholds in Syria. He should be unleashing the entire might of the American military toward finding and killing the head of ISIS. You know it. The entire country knows it. Don't start making excuses for him. Not now. Not after all we've been through."

"He's not making excuses," Harris responded. "He's telling you to keep your head in the game and stay focused on the mission at hand."

"Yeah? And what's the mission?" I asked, my face red, the back of my neck burning. I knew I was about to lose it.

Harris held up the file. "Putting everything he just told you on the front page."

21

★ ★ ★

ARLINGTON, VIRGINIA

"J. B., wake up."

I groaned, rolled over, pulled the blankets up over my head, and flipped my pillow to the cool side. But then I heard it again.

"Come on, wake up, J. B.—listen to me—it's important."

Was that Matt's voice? How could it be? It was way too early. I had to be dreaming. But then I heard it again.

"J. B., seriously—you need to get up."

That was definitely the voice of my big brother. I forced my groggy eyes open.

The room was dark and quiet but for the howling winter winds rattling my windows and the low hum of a space heater a few feet away. I glanced at the clock on the nightstand next to me. *You've got to be kidding me,* I thought. It was 4:36 in the morning. I'd been back in my apartment for less than three hours. There was no way I was getting up now.

"Go back to sleep," I mumbled, then shut my eyes again.

Suddenly all the lights came on and Matt kicked the side of the bed. I sat up, shielded my eyes with my arm, and tried to imagine why in the world Matt would want to provoke me into punching him in the face.

"Are you crazy?" I snapped. *"Turn it off."*

"Here," Matt said, tossing a fresh copy of the *Times* on my lap. "Check out the front-page headline, top of the fold."

Annoyed, I tried to rub the sleep out of my eyes and concentrate on the paper in my hands. **Evidence Strongly Suggests ISIS Responsible for Chemical Attack in D.C., Says FBI Director**, read the headline.

"It's all over cable news and it's blowing up Twitter right now," Matt said.

My exclusive interview with FBI Director Beck was the lead story, along with insider details of the bureau's ongoing investigation. Below the fold was my two-thousand-word firsthand account of the terror attacks. Allen had been ecstatic. These stories were going to drive the national news cycle. But they were no cause for getting up at zero-dark-thirty.

"Drink up," Matt said before I could snap at him again. He handed me a piping hot Starbucks mug.

"Not bad," I said, taking my first sip and savoring the perfect aroma. "Now what in the world is going on?"

"Didn't you get my note?" he asked.

"What note?"

"The one I left on your bathroom mirror last night."

"Why—what'd it say?"

"How could you not have seen it?"

"I don't know," I said. "I just didn't."

"What time did you get in?"

"I don't know—one fifteen, maybe one thirty."

"And?"

"And what?"

"Didn't you brush your teeth?"

"What are you, Mom?" I asked, my annoyance growing.

"I left you a note."

"Fine—but I missed it. What does it matter?"

He just looked at me like I should know what he was talking about. "What's today?" he finally asked.

I shrugged. "Thursday."

"Yeah, but what day?"

"Who cares?"

"I do."

"Just let me go back to sleep."

"What day is it, J. B.?"

"I don't know—the sixteenth."

"No, it's the seventeenth—it's right there on the front page."

"Okay, fine, it's the seventeenth. So what?"

"So it's February 17," Matt said.

I just stared at him.

"Three days after Valentine's Day?" he said. "Ring any bells?"

I sighed and took another sip of the coffee. It had been a long time since I'd thought or cared about Valentine's Day, and Matt knew it. I was divorced. I wasn't seeing anyone. The only woman I really cared about had nearly died in my arms on the other side of the world, and now I barely ever heard from her. Then it hit me. Matt and Annie had gotten married three days after Valentine's Day, three months before she graduated from college.

"Got it," I said finally. "Your anniversary's today. So are you flying home today?"

"I can't," he said. "The airports are all shut down, remember? Trains, too. But . . ." Rather than finish the sentence, he dangled the keys to my new Audi in front of me.

"You're not serious," I said.

"I am," he replied.

"You want to drive all the way to Maine?"

He nodded.

"Today?"

Another nod. "I plotted it all out on MapQuest. It'll take us eleven hours and forty-five minutes door to door, without stops."

"Us?"

"With fuel stops and bathroom breaks, I'm guessing we can be there in thirteen hours. If we get on the road by five, we can be there by six tonight. We'll surprise them. It'll be fun."

"And then what?" I asked, in no mood for a thirteen-hour road trip.

Matt smiled. "I take Annie out for a nice romantic dinner, and you . . ."

"What?"

"You and Mom can babysit," he said, like it was the greatest idea in the world.

"You've really lost your mind."

"It'll be great. You and Mom can catch up. She'll love it. The kids'll be so excited to see you. You can hang out for a few days, then drive back on Sunday."

This was a terrible idea. I hated it. All of it. I had a job. I had a story to pursue. I couldn't afford to be diverted. Not now. I'd been off my beat far too long already.

But I stopped myself. I really did owe Matt. What's more, I owed Annie and Katie and Josh. I owed my mom, as well. I was on the front page today with two big stories. The least I could do now was take Matt up to see his bride and his kids and spend a few days together as a family, something we hadn't done since . . . I couldn't remember when.

"Okay," I said at last.

Matt stared at me. "Really? You're serious? You're not just messing with me?"

"Nope—I'm serious," I said. "I'm in."

"Wow," he said, visibly dumbfounded.

"Just give me a few minutes to pack," I said.

"Already done," Matt replied.

"What do you mean?" I asked.

He nodded to my garment bag on the floor.

"You packed for me?" Now I was the one who was dumbfounded.

"Last night, while you were working," he said. "It's all in the note."

"The one on the bathroom mirror?"

Matt shrugged.

"Guess you thought of everything," I said.

"Not quite," he replied.

"What do you mean?" I asked.

"I never thought you'd really say yes."

22

★ ★ ★

Matt gathered our bags and took them down to the car.

I threw on jeans and a flannel shirt, brushed my teeth, read the note on the bathroom mirror, and shrugged. I was going on a road trip. The timing couldn't have been worse. But I knew I had to do it.

Matt offered to take the first shift driving, but I said no. With a good, strong cup of coffee and a double shot of adrenaline, I was wide-awake now. In my head I was already working on my next story, and I needed time to think, not talk. So Matt adjusted the passenger seat in the Audi until it was all the way back and drifted off to sleep. I'm sure he was thinking about celebrating his wedding anniversary with Annie. I had other things on my mind.

My lead article for the *Times* that morning would, I knew, make a big splash, and for good reason. It told the public for the first time about the three howitzers and the three locations in D.C. where they'd been positioned to fire mortars at the Capitol. It also broke the news about the murdered night watchman at the construction company in Anacostia, the identity of the seven dead Arab men, and the solid, conclusive evidence that each of them was a member of the Islamic State.

With Director Beck's permission, Agent Harris and I had visited the crumbling Alexander Crummell School, the boarded-up Catholic school, and the construction company. Allen MacDonald had sent along a *Times* photographer to take crime scene pictures. Then Harris and I had visited the city morgue. I'd seen the bodies of the seven ISIS terrorists for myself. I'd interviewed the D.C. medical examiner about the cause of death. I'd been allowed to look at her notes. The science was clear. All seven had died of complications triggered by sarin gas poisoning, and initial tests strongly indicated that the chemical fingerprint of the gas found in the remaining mortar shells matched the gas used during the attack in Amman.

It was good info, but I knew Allen would want more soon.

I figured once Matt got a few hours of rest, he could drive and I could write. By midafternoon, I could probably have a new draft that I could send, a draft that could significantly advance the story. But I was going to need Agent Harris's help.

Dawn rose and the sky brightened. Before long we had passed the city of Wilmington and were crossing the Delaware Memorial Bridge. I checked my rearview mirror again. I'd been doing so constantly since we'd pulled out of my parking garage. Nothing seemed out of the ordinary. But I couldn't shake the feeling that something wasn't right. I told myself the jitters in my hands and stomach were just frayed nerves from all that had happened to me in recent months.

But I had to admit that for the first time in my life I was scared. Abu Khalif had promised to kill me. And I believed him. He had just demonstrated to the entire nation that his reach extended deep inside the United States. Who could say he couldn't reach me?

I checked the mirror again. Still nothing suspicious, so as I got off I-295 and onto the New Jersey Turnpike, I put on a mobile phone headset and dialed Harris's number. It was early, but I was in no mood to wait.

"Collins, is that you?" Harris asked.

I could hear the fatigue in his voice. But I could also hear phones ringing and people talking in the background. He wasn't at home. He was already at work at the bureau. Maybe he'd never gone home.

"I need your help," I said.

"For what?"

"I need more info on some of the things we came across last night."

"Sorry—I can't," he replied. "You've gotten all you're going to get out of us."

"Harris, come on; your boss gave me this story on a silver platter," I said calmly. "He wants this stuff out there. I just need a little more."

"Can't do it, Collins," Harris said, speaking almost in a whisper. "You got your story, and it's breaking big inside the administration. You had details the president and NSC didn't even have yet. And they're furious. The AG has already called the director and read him the riot act. There's no more. That's all you're going to get."

"Wait," I said. "At least tell me how the ISIS guys got the how-itzers."

"I can't."

"Just give me a clue, a lead—something—and I can do the rest."

There was a long pause.

"Harris, you still there?" I asked.

"Write this down, Collins."

"What?"

"Three words—you ready?" he asked.

"Ready," I said, and Harris spoke the three words slowly, enun-ciating clearly.

"Lowell, Coon, Marion."

Then I heard a click, and the line went dead.

23

★ ★ ★

I speed-dialed Allen immediately.

He didn't pick up the direct line in his office, so I tried his mobile phone. He picked up on the second ring but said he wasn't in the newsroom yet. The snowstorm was still wreaking havoc on D.C. area traffic, and he was sitting in gridlock on the Beltway, still trying to get downtown. "Why, what've you got?" he asked.

"Do you have a pad and pen handy?"

"Of course."

"And are you stopped right now?"

"Yes, unfortunately."

"Good. Take this down—three words," I said. "Lowell. Coon. And Marion."

"Got it," he said. "What does it mean?"

"I have no idea," I conceded.

"Then why are you telling me?" Allen asked.

"I got them from a source—a good one—who says they're clues to finding out how ISIS got their hands on howitzers. Can you get someone to run a search and see if anything pops?"

"Sure," he said. "I'll text Mary Jane and get her working on it right away. What else have you got? We're already getting great feedback on your pieces from this morning."

For the next ten minutes, while Matt slept, I laid out for Allen the contours of my next story—the feverish federal manhunt for the remaining ISIS terrorists, the ones who hadn't accidentally blown up their howitzer and killed themselves with sarin gas. It was all material I'd gotten from Beck but hadn't fit in this morning's article.

I explained to Allen that according to the bureau, all three 18-wheelers that had been abandoned at the three crime scenes had been rented. Each was from a different rental company, but the rigs had all come from Alabama. The FBI was working with local and state investigators to determine exactly who had rented them and when.

Then I shifted to the howitzers themselves. "Apparently the terrorists needed tractor trailers to transport the howitzers because each one weighs about six tons," I said. "Beck told me all three were World War II–era, built in the early 1940s. All three saw action in Europe—two in France and one in Italy."

"How do they know?" Allen asked.

"They've got serial numbers on them," I said. "Somebody in the basement of the Pentagon was actually able to look up their records and figure out where they'd been used."

"So how does one go about acquiring a howitzer?" Allen asked.

"I wouldn't think there's much of a black market," I said.

"How about an Army surplus store?"

"For a seven-decade-old weapon that weighs six tons?"

"Right—so then how would a terrorist get his hands on one, much less three?"

We discussed all kinds of scenarios—private collections, auctions, Hollywood studios, museums. None of them struck us as particularly plausible, but Allen promised to get some people on it.

Then he abruptly changed the subject. "Listen, J. B., I need you to go back to Amman."

"What?"

"Someone needs to interview this Jordanian member of Parliament," he explained. "Who is he? Why was his son found dead in Anacostia with a group of ISIS jihadists? Did the father know his son was involved in terrorism? Have the Jordanians arrested the father? Who else is he linked with? You know the drill. And you know the king. You need to get on this angle right away."

"Allen, I—"

"I've got you on the next plane to Amman. It's all booked. Lufthansa flight 9051 out of Dulles. It leaves at 5:20 tomorrow afternoon, assuming the Homeland Security secretary lifts the travel ban. You'll route through Frankfurt and arrive in Amman by dinnertime Saturday. Mary Jane will e-mail you the details in a moment. And don't worry; I talked to the brass in New York. They know what you've been through and they're very grateful. They let me bump you up to first class. No need to say thank you. Just pack a bag and make sure you're at Dulles tomorrow by three."

"Allen, I can't do it," I said.

"This isn't a request, J. B. This is a huge story, and no one on my staff has better sources in the Middle East—and certainly not in Amman—than you."

"I get it, Allen, but . . ."

"But what?"

I took a deep breath.

"I'm not in D.C."

As I said it, I glanced down at the dashboard, saw the fuel gauge, and realized I was running low. I started looking for a service station where I could top off the tank and get some coffee and maybe a breakfast sandwich.

"What do you mean you're not in D.C.?" Allen asked. "Where are you?"

"My brother and I are driving up to Maine to see our family."

"Without telling me?"

"It was, you know, spur of the moment."

"What time did you leave?"

"Five this morning."

"So where are you now?"

"Not far from Philly, heading north on the New Jersey Turnpike."

"And when were you planning to tell me?"

"I'm telling you now."

"When will you be back?"

"Sunday, I guess. Maybe Monday."

Allen sighed. "Okay, listen," he said. "I'll make a deal with you. You need to go see your family. I get that. Really, I do. Take a day or two with them. Then fly out of Boston on Saturday evening. I'll have Mary Jane reissue the tickets. But you're going to Amman, J. B. I need you there."

I took a deep breath.

"What?" he asked, clearly sensing my resistance and somewhat uncharacteristically trying hard not to express his frustration.

"What if I take a leave of absence?" I said.

"You just had a leave of absence."

"Then how much vacation time do I have saved up?"

"No, J. B. You need to do this, and you're going to do it. I'm saying this for your sake, believe me. If you give up on reporting now, you're going to regret it for the rest of your life. I know you. And I'm telling you, my friend—you need to get back on the horse."

"How much vacation do I have coming to me, Allen?" I pressed.

"Forget it, J. B."

"It's got to be at least twenty weeks," I said. "I never take time off." Another sigh. "Twenty-six."

"Then I'm taking a vacation, effective immediately."

"J. B., please, you need to stay on this story," he insisted. "Hunt down these killers. Run them to ground. Force the administration's hand. Make them bring Abu Khalif to justice. And *then* take the rest of the year off if you'd like. Write a book. Go to the Caribbean. Sleep on a beach. Marry that Israeli girl you're so fond of. But not now, J. B.—not right now."

24

★ ★ ★

"What was that all about?"

My heated conversation had just woken Matt up. I glanced over at him as I finally found a service station and pulled off the main highway. "Nothing. You want some breakfast?"

"Sure, that sounds good," Matt replied as I pulled up to the gas tanks and asked the attendant to top us off with premium unleaded. I still couldn't believe New Jersey prohibited self-service gas fill-ups, but given the brutal weather, I certainly wasn't going to complain today.

"So what exactly can't you do, and why?" Matt asked.

"Forget about it," I said. "It's nothing."

"J. B., give me a break. It's obviously not *nothing*. You just talked about taking a leave of absence from the only job you've ever loved. Now what's going on?"

"I said forget it!" I snapped. "Now do you want some breakfast or not?"

It came out far more harshly than I'd intended. But rather than apologize, I just glared at Matt.

He'd seen this before, and far too often, I'm afraid. So he sighed, shook his head, and let it go. "Whatever," he said, getting out of the Audi. "Text me what you want. I'll be back in a few."

As I watched him head inside, I felt guilty and confused. I'd barely spoken to Matt for the better part of a decade. Now things were finally beginning to thaw between us. Why had I just lashed out at him? Why was I reverting to my old patterns? I wasn't sure. I didn't like it. But I didn't know how to change it, either. I knew I should apologize to him. At the same time, I didn't want to waste any time psychoanalyzing myself. I had work to do.

I picked up my phone and checked my e-mails. There were five new ones.

None were from Yael.

The first was from an old friend, Youssef Kuttab, senior advisor to Palestinian Authority president Salim Mansour. He was checking to make sure I was safe after the terror attacks in D.C. But he was also updating me on Mansour's recovery. In December, the Palestinian leader had been shot twice in the back by ISIS forces right in front of me during the attack on the royal palace in Amman.

At the time, the official story put out to press said President Mansour had been lightly wounded, but I knew the truth was far more serious. One bullet had missed the man's spine by less than a centimeter. The other had ripped through the left shoulder and caused a tremendous loss of blood. Only the fast actions of the impressive IDF medics on the chopper out of Jordan, multiple blood trans-fusions, and later three highly complicated operations in Ramallah at the hands of skilled Palestinian surgeons had saved Mansour's life. Trying to downplay the seriousness of the president's injuries, every few days the P.A. press team released a new photo of Mansour rest-ing in a hospital bed, smiling, laughing, chatting with his wife and kids, talking by phone with one world leader or another, reading briefing papers, and so forth. But not one of the photos had actually been taken during the days following the attempted assassination, I knew. They'd all been taken nine months earlier when Mansour had undergone a rather simple hernia operation. Yet the P.A. media team now put them out there—to great effect, I might add—and no one was the wiser.

During those dark days when Mansour's life hung in the balance—and could have literally gone either way—I had kept in close contact with Youssef Kuttab, who himself had only narrowly escaped being severely wounded or killed in the Amman attacks. I gave him my solemn word that nothing he told me would be published. I just wanted to know how the man was doing, as I had such tremendous respect for Mansour. The Palestinian president was one of the most humble, strong, and wise leaders I'd ever met. He was a true man of peace, and I genuinely and deeply feared the prospect of his death.

The president is doing much, much better, still off the record, Kuttab's e-mail began after inquiring about my safety. *The last few weeks have seen a nearly miraculous recovery. He's not just walking now; he's actually exercising. His appetite is returning. His color looks good. He still struggles with severe pain and, between us, even more severe depression. He smiles for the cameras, for the videos, for the media. But the man you saw in Amman—the man you remarked on who seemed so relaxed, even full of joy—that man, I'm afraid, is gone. Will he return? I don't know. We have seen other miracles, so I guess anything is possible. Inshallah.*

With every sentence, I found myself wincing. My heart grieved for Mansour. He had sacrificed so much to serve his people and try to hammer out a comprehensive peace accord with the Israelis, only to see the process literally explode in his face just before the final deal was signed. Now there was nearly zero interest in reviving the peace process among the Palestinian and Israeli populations, or among their leaders. Everyone knew ISIS was responsible for the terror attacks in Amman. But conspiracy theories had metastasized. Suspicion ran deep on both sides of the Green Line. Bloggers and activists on both sides blamed the other side for sabotaging the peace process, and emotions were running high.

At the end of Kuttab's note was an invitation to come and visit him and the president at my earliest convenience. I appreciated the gesture, and I liked the idea of sitting with these dear friends and sipping mint tea and seeing firsthand how they were doing. Perhaps if I headed over to Amman, I should go to Ramallah, too, and do an exclusive interview with Mansour—something to make Allen happy. Or at least get him off my back.

But then I glanced in my rearview mirror and suddenly my blood ran cold.

25

★ ★ ★

A black Mercedes pulled into the service station, covered in snow.

It eased into the line behind me, about six cars back. I was pretty sure I'd passed it several times before, but each time it had caught up with me. About twenty minutes earlier, I thought I'd seen it exit the turnpike. Now it was back.

The snow had turned to sleet. Visibility was getting worse. The Mercedes's windshield wipers were going full blast, and its front windshield was fogged up. I strained to see faces, but there were too many cars between us to get a good look. Then, in my side mirror, I saw the back passenger door of the Mercedes fling open, and despite the cold I broke out in a panicked sweat.

But out of the car came two figures I did not expect. They weren't Syrian or Iraqi men. They were two blonde little girls with pigtails and a puppy. They were wearing matching pink snowsuits, boots, mittens, and scarves, and they bounded out of the car without a care in the world. They didn't seem bothered by the cold and the sleet. Nor were they paying attention to the traffic around them.

In my rearview mirror, I stared in horror as the girls started racing across the parking lot toward the front door of the restaurant, oblivious to a Ford F-150 pickup bearing down on them. Their mother was now out of the car. She was screaming as the driver of the pickup laid on his horn and hit his brakes. Every driver in every car watched helplessly as the truck—which had been coming off the highway far too fast—fishtailed and skidded across the ice toward the girls, who stopped in their tracks, paralyzed in terror. I expected to see the truck smash into the girls and at the last moment turned away. I expected to hear the impact, but it never came. I expected to hear more screaming, but everything grew quiet.

Finally I forced myself to look again. To my amazement, the truck had come to a full stop just inches from the girls. The mother bolted to her daughters and grabbed them. The father was right behind her. Eventually I started breathing again. My heart started beating again.

But then I was startled by someone tapping on my window. I turned quickly only to find it was the service attendant, a young Hispanic kid no more than nineteen or twenty, motioning me to roll down my window. "Sixty-three bucks," he said.

Had I been in a different frame of mind, I might have asked this kid why the state of New Jersey didn't trust ordinary citizens to pump their own gas without blowing the place up, why the governor and the legislature were stuck in the twentieth century. Instead, I pulled out my wallet and handed him my Visa card. When it came back with a receipt, I pulled over to the rest area's entrance. Matt hadn't come out yet, so I returned to my e-mails.

I sent a quick note to Kuttab, assuring him that I was okay and telling him I would be honored to come see him and his boss soon. But for the moment, that's all I said. I knew I could work that into a trip to Jordan. But I genuinely had no desire to go to Amman. What I really wanted to do was go see Yael in Tel Aviv or Jerusalem. If I did that, a stop in Ramallah might still make sense. For now, however, a visit with the Palestinian president would have to wait.

The second e-mail was from Allen MacDonald's executive assistant. As promised, Mary Jane had sent me the details of the flights she'd booked for me from Bar Harbor to Boston, and then from Boston to Amman, via Istanbul, on Turkish Airlines. I didn't respond. I didn't know what to say. So I just moved on.

The third e-mail in the queue was from someone claiming to be a top aide to General Amr El-Badawy, commander of Egyptian special forces. I had met the general on a remote Jordanian air base in the final hours before the joint assaults on Dabiq and Alqosh. We hadn't spoken much then. I hadn't heard from him since. But now his aide was writing to tell me El-Badawy wanted to speak to me. The subject was too sensitive to discuss by e-mail, the message writer indicated, asking if I could please call the general—through him—at the private number he provided. I glanced at my watch. I couldn't call now, of course. Matt would be back at any moment. But I was curious, so I sent a note back that I would call at my soonest opportunity.

The fourth e-mail was a somewhat-cryptic message from a partner in the law firm claiming to represent the estate of Robert Khachigian. The firm apparently had "important business" to discuss with me concerning the final will and testament of the former senator and CIA director, who had been assassinated the previous November in D.C. This, too, was apparently a sensitive matter and required an in-person meeting in the firm's office in Portland, Maine. The partner indicated it was not something he could discuss by phone. I couldn't imagine what that was all about, nor did I care to guess.

Normally I'd be nowhere near Portland, but as fate would have it, I was about to be. Maine's largest city was a mere 175 miles south of my hometown of Bar Harbor, roughly a three-hour drive, depending on traffic. I decided I would find the time to make the trip. Khachigian, after all, had been a dear friend of our family and a personal mentor of mine. He had been shot and killed right in front of me while helping me track down one of the most important stories of my career: the capture of chemical weapons by ISIS forces in Syria. Whatever this lawyer had to say about my old friend, I would hear him out. I owed Khachigian and his memory and his family nothing less.

The newest e-mail was from Allen. He apologized for getting testy with me. He assured me that he understood what I was going through, and was ready to request a two-month sabbatical of sorts for me—not counted against my vacation time—so long as I would first go to Jordan and then take the next few weeks to follow this story about the manhunt for the ISIS jihadists that had just hit Washington. After that, he said, he would fully support me taking a "much-needed" break. I read it twice but didn't reply. My answer hadn't changed, and frankly I was peeved at him for pushing. I wasn't going to Amman, and that was final.

Again I glanced at my watch. Matt still wasn't back. I was about to put the phone down and turn the radio on. But suddenly—and somewhat oddly—I found myself thinking of our home in Maine. It occurred to me that I was actually looking forward to the visit. I craved a hot, home-cooked meal, prepared in that old kitchen, served on that old wooden table, in that old drafty house—the house I grew up in—with my mom and Matt. I couldn't wait to play with my niece and nephew, to laugh and giggle with them, maybe play hide-and-seek. Most of all, I wanted not to talk about ISIS or the manhunt or my work or anything related to Washington or the Middle East. Instead, I wanted to sleep in my childhood bed, and awake to a blanket of new-fallen snow and the smell of fresh coffee and bacon and sausages frying in the kitchen. I couldn't remember the last time I'd had anything like that, and the fact was I missed simple times and a quieter life.

I made a snap decision and sent a quick e-mail to my mom. I briefly described the anniversary surprise Matt was plotting, gave her our location and estimated time of arrival, and said I was looking forward to seeing her. Then I swore her to secrecy and hit Send.

Matt finally got back in the car with to-go cups of steaming black coffee for both of us and a couple of breakfast sandwiches. It dawned on me that I hadn't texted him like he'd asked, hadn't told him what I wanted. But rather than apologize, I said nothing. I just nodded my thanks, drank in the infusion of caffeine, and pulled back onto the turnpike.

26

★ ★ ★

We had no music playing.

The interior of the Audi was silent, save the *whoosh-whoosh* of the windshield wipers and the hum of the road beneath the treads. Matt, still annoyed or at least disappointed in me, had eaten in silence and then quickly drifted back to sleep.

I was thinking about nothing in particular, just doing my best to stay alert, when I glanced at a passing road sign. I thought we might be getting close to Newark, but the sign didn't say anything about Newark. It didn't mention Trenton or Shore Points or Manhattan either. It wasn't a mileage indicator. It simply noted that VFW Post 8003 in the town of Lawnside had adopted this stretch of the turnpike to keep it free of litter.

Lawnside. *Lawnside.* Something about the sign caught my attention. But why? Did I know anyone from there? I didn't think so. Had I ever been to Lawnside? Not that I could recall. So why had I noticed that sign? Why had it caught my attention? Why did I care? Was there any reason at all, or was I just growing exhausted? Maybe it was time to switch with Matt and let him drive. After all, we still had nine hours to go.

Suddenly I realized it wasn't the name of the town but the

organization on the sign that had tickled my subconscious. I grabbed my phone, hit Redial, and got Allen on the third ring. He was finally in the office.

"What about a VFW post?" I asked.

"What?"

"Or an American Legion post?"

"I'm not following you, J. B. What are you talking about?"

"We have them all over Maine," I said. "Some of these places have old Revolutionary War cannons out front. Others have World War II tanks and other vehicles. Maybe some have howitzers. Maybe that's where ISIS got them from."

"Hmm, okay, that's interesting," Allen said quickly, catching up with my otherwise-random train of thought. "My father-in-law landed on Omaha Beach on D-day, and he was very active in the VFW in Topeka."

"Did his post have a howitzer?"

"No, an old half-track," he said. "But you're right; maybe some do."

"Agent Harris mentioned three names—Lowell, Coon, Marion. What if they're towns with VFW posts and missing howitzers?"

"I knew a town called Lowell when I was growing up in Wisconsin," Allen said. "It was about seventy miles northwest of Milwaukee, along the Beaver Dam River. My grandpa used to fish not far from there. But it's small. I mean, really tiny. I bet there's not a thousand people in the whole town."

"Did they have a VFW post?" I asked.

"I don't know—maybe," he said. "A lot of those small towns do."

"Can you look it up?"

"Right now?"

"Absolutely. This is important."

"Fine," he said. "Hold on."

The sky was brightening, but I couldn't see the sun. A layer of thick winter clouds obscured the sky. The digital display on my dashboard said the temperature outside was a mere nine degrees above zero. The forecast called for more snow, but it wasn't coming down at the moment. The turnpike was pretty clear, considering, but the snowplows and salt trucks were out. More was coming, and they were ready. Was I? It occurred to me then that I didn't have snow tires on my car. Why would I? Washington rarely had this much snow, and when it did, it usually melted away within a few days. Now I was headed to Maine in a sports car I'd bought well below the Mason-Dixon Line.

A moment later, Allen was back on the line. "Get this," he said. "Lowell's population is a whopping 340."

"That's it?"

"Yeah—just eighty-nine families and a post office."

"And a VFW post?"

"Yes—Post 9392."

"And are they missing anything?"

"As a matter of fact they are," Allen said. "I just pulled up an AP story from January 2. That's, what, six weeks ago? Turns out your instincts were right on the money. According to the story, an M114 U.S. Army howitzer used in World War II was stolen from outside VFW Post 9392 sometime after midnight on New Year's Eve. A police officer is cited saying the evidence suggests this may have been some kind of high school prank. They found empty beer cans and cigarette butts at the scene, rocks thrown through windows, spray paint on the walls, that sort of thing."

"Pretty smart," I said, "making it look like some kids out to goof around on New Year's."

"Right. I bet the theft wasn't even reported to the Feds. Why would it have been? No one could have imagined a World War II–era howitzer was going to be used in a terrorist attack."

Other pieces quickly started falling into place. Searching the *Times'* database of news stories from all manner of publications all over the country, Allen pulled up several promising articles. One was about a howitzer stolen on January 9 from a VFW post in Coon Valley, Wisconsin, population 765. Another concerned a howitzer gone missing from a VFW post in Marion, Massachusetts, population 4,907. The articles were brief, little more than curiosities mentioned in the police blotter of obscure newspapers. In each case, the thefts were described by authorities as apparently the work of local youths. The details of the crimes were nearly identical—beer cans, cigarette butts, spray paint, and other forms of vandalism, all suggesting a high school prank of some kind. There was no indication that the police in any of the jurisdictions were aware of the other stolen howitzers. And there certainly was no mention of any notion that a larger plot was being set into motion.

Allen promised to work with his counterpart on the national desk to send *Times* reporters and photographers immediately to each location. For the moment, we were operating on a hunch. It was a good one, a plausible one—indeed, one Harris himself had set me onto—but before we went to press, we needed more hard information. We couldn't rely on old stories in local papers. We needed our own people to talk to the VFW folks in each town and interview the local cops. We also needed to confirm that the FBI had been talking to the local authorities and try to pick up any other useful tidbits that would help our readers better understand the ISIS plot.

After I hung up, I drove for another hour.

Then Matt's phone rang—the ringtone of a dad, some song from *Toy Story*. He woke up instantly and groggily fumbled to take the call. It was Annie. He motioned for me to be quiet, not wanting me to spoil the surprise of our visit. But no sooner had he said hello than I saw the anxiety in his eyes. He said only a few words before ending the call and reaching for the car radio.

"What is it?" I asked. "What's going on?"

"Annie says there's been a terrorist attack in New York."

27

★ ★ ★

Matt quickly found a news station out of Manhattan.

The attack had occurred in the subway system. But it wasn't a stabbing, a shooting, or a bomb. We tuned in just in time to hear a reporter broadcasting from outside of Penn Station say that this was another chemical weapons attack. Terrorists had somehow pumped sarin gas into the subway tunnels through the ventilation system.

"One transit official has confirmed to me that there have been simultaneous and closely coordinated attacks at nine different subway stations in Manhattan, Brooklyn, and the Bronx," the reporter said. "We have no casualty figures yet, but hundreds of ambulances are being called in and hazmat teams are being deployed."

As the minutes ticked by, the situation devolved from bad to worse. The news anchor said the Associated Press was now reporting that Washington D.C.'s Metro system had been hit as well. Soon there were reports of chemical weapons attacks in Philly, Boston, Chicago, Minneapolis, Dallas, and Atlanta.

The first detailed reports came from Atlanta. There, the city's transit systems hadn't been targeted. Instead, several large luxury hotels had been hit, including three Hiltons, a Marriott, and a Ritz-Carlton. The news station played a sound bite from the Atlanta fire chief, who said the terrorists had apparently employed some kind of aerosolized dispersion system to pump the gas through the hotels' ventilation systems. In so doing, they had effectively reached every room in the building and had killed nearly every guest and employee. Hundreds were reportedly dead in Atlanta alone, and several hundred more were wounded and battling for their lives.

Then came an update from Boston. The correspondent—reporting live from an emergency command center that had been set up at city hall—said that terrorists had found a way to pump sarin gas into the city's underground train system known to locals as "the T."

"I'm standing here with Police Chief Ed McDougal," the reporter said after setting the scene. "Chief, this is a fast-moving, fast-changing story. What can you tell us so far?"

"Thirty years on the force and I've never seen anything like it," the chief responded. "This is without question the worst terrorist attack in the history of the city. As of five minutes ago, we had over six thousand casualties. We're calling in ambulances from all over the state to come help us right now."

"Did you say *six thousand* dead?"

"No, no, I said *casualties*—six thousand *casualties*," the chief clarified. "I don't have an exact breakdown right now between dead and wounded."

"Can you give us your best guess, based on the information you're seeing?"

The chief refused to speculate, so the reporter asked, "And do you know at this point who is behind this attack?"

Again the chief refused to comment.

"But you suspect it's connected to the attacks in Washington, is that correct?" the reporter asked.

"That seems like a reasonable guess, but at the moment that's all it is—a guess. Give us some time. I've got my best officers and detectives on this. We're getting lots of help from federal and state authorities. We're going to figure this out and bring the people who did this to justice. You can take that to the bank."

"How many first responders have fallen to the gas?"

"I don't have any figures on that, but quite a few."

"And we're talking about sarin gas, like the kind that was used to hit the Capitol building on Tuesday night?"

"That seems to be the case, but again it's too soon to be definitive," the chief explained.

"You think it's ISIS?" the reporter pressed.

"I'm not going to speculate," the chief replied. "Like I said, we have no suspects at the moment. We're just trying to respond to the crisis. But the mayor and I are planning a press conference later in the day once we have more hard information."

On the radio, we could suddenly hear more sirens rapidly approaching. "Look, I've got to go—sorry," the chief said, and he was gone.

The reporter summarized what she'd heard for listeners just tuning in, then threw it back to the anchor in the main studio in Manhattan.

I reached over and turned the radio off.

"What are you doing?" Matt asked, incredulous. He'd never seen me turn off a breaking news story, probably because I never had.

"I don't know," I said. "I just—I can't listen anymore."

I realized I was gripping the steering wheel so hard my knuckles were white. I saw Matt glance at my hands and then look away. He didn't say anything, didn't press. We were both traumatized. We'd both seen things no one ever should. Now more people were dying, all over America. It just never seemed to end.

The phone rang. The caller ID said it was Allen. I knew what he wanted. This wasn't about going back to Jordan. This time he was calling to draft me into covering this fast-breaking story. He knew I was approaching Manhattan. He needed all hands on deck. But the last thing I wanted to do was head into the scene of another terrorist attack. My hands were shaking. My heart was racing. I just couldn't do it. I let the call go to voice mail and kept driving.

Matt and I continued in silence for more than an hour. We didn't talk to each other about the attacks or anything else. I think I was in shock. Too many thoughts were racing through my head, and I wasn't ready to share them. But eventually I couldn't help myself. I turned the radio on again.

The updates came fast and furious. In Chicago, several elementary and high schools had been hit. In Minneapolis, the Mall of America had been targeted. In Dallas and Philly, several luxury hotels were attacked. There were no hard numbers on casualties, but the numbers of dead and wounded were mounting rapidly.

For a long time, Matt and I said nothing. We just listened in complete shock. I kept thinking about the 1995 attack on the Tokyo subway. That had been sarin gas as well. Only twelve people had died, but more than 5,500 others were injured. That attack, though carefully planned, had not been nearly as effective as the terrorists had hoped.

Somehow I knew Abu Khalif had studied the planning and strategy of those attacks in Japan. Clearly, he'd found a way to make his attacks far more deadly. So what was coming next?

28

★ ★ ★

"I'm going to call Annie," Matt said, giving up on the element of surprise.

We were nearly through Connecticut, heading for Massachusetts. Matt tried several times, but no one answered. Finally he left a message, then called the house, and after that Mom's phone. Getting no one, he sent them a few texts, gave them an update on our progress, and noted that according to our GPS we should be in Bar Harbor by around seven and that he couldn't wait to give her and the kids a big hug.

Just then, my phone rang. Again the caller ID said it was Allen. Again I let it go to voice mail. But a few moments later, Matt's phone rang.

"It's your boss," he said. "Should I take it?"

The newest D.C. bureau chief was nothing if not persistent.

"No," I said and kept my eyes on the road.

"You going to tell me why?" he asked.

"Allen wants me to cover the attacks in Manhattan and then catch a flight to Jordan."

"To do what?"

"Interview the MP whose son was involved in the attacks in Washington."

"And?"

"And that's why he keeps calling. He says he's got no one else to interview this guy, and he's insisting I do it."

"And you don't want to?"

"You're kidding, right?"

"No, I'm not," Matt said. "That is your job, isn't it? And he is your boss, right?"

"Matt, you really want me to stop driving to Maine and cover sarin gas attacks in Manhattan? And then you really think I should go back to Jordan? You can't be serious."

"What if I am?"

"Are you?"

"J. B., when have you ever listened to my advice?"

"Well, I'm listening now."

"You're serious?"

Actually, I was. Perhaps it was my clumsy way of apologizing for being so distant for so many years or so rude earlier in the day. But Matt wasn't buying it, and I could hardly blame him.

"Listen—I'm in a jam," I said. "Allen's right; this is my story. But given all I've been through, I don't want anything to do with it."

"I understand that," Matt said. "It is Manhattan, after all—the *Times* certainly has more than enough reporters to throw at the story. But why not go to Jordan? That I don't get."

"Matt, tell me you're kidding."

"Why?"

"Because honestly, I can't imagine anything worse than going back to Amman right now."

"Don't the king and his forces have everything back under control at this point?"

"Yeah, pretty much."

"So it's probably not so dangerous anymore."

"Not like it was, no."

"Couldn't you see the king again while you're there and, you know, after interviewing the MP, do a story on how His Majesty and the royal family are doing two months after the crisis, what he sees for the future, how he views the fight with ISIS at this point?"

"Maybe."

"Don't you want to see him again?"

"Of course I do."

"I thought you were impressed with him."

"I am. I was before I met him, but even more so now."

"So what's the problem?"

"What do you mean?"

"I mean those all seem like pretty good reasons *to* go to Amman, even if you don't cover the attacks in Manhattan," Matt said.

I didn't respond. I just kept driving. After another few miles, Matt tried again.

"Answer me this, J. B. Is your job on the line if you keep defying Allen's orders?"

I shrugged. "Maybe."

"Didn't you tell me you and Omar and Abdel snuck into Syria when Allen ordered you not to?"

Reluctantly I nodded.

"And Abdel died on that trip, in Homs, and Omar died later in Istanbul?"

I said nothing, but it was all true.

"And you nearly got killed too."

"Your point is?" I asked, feeling more and more defensive.

"I just don't want you to lose your job; that's all," Matt said.

"Since when?" I shot back.

He looked surprised and a bit hurt. "Why would you say that?"

"Face it, Matt—you and Annie and Mom never approved of me being a war correspondent. You all think I've put my career ahead of everything else—my family, my marriage, my spiritual life, you name it. So maybe it'd be better if Allen canned me and it was over and done with, right?"

"J. B., you're a great reporter, but you're a real piece of work, you know that?" Matt said. "I've always read your stuff, and I've always been proud of what you do. And as long as you keep pursuing the truth, I'll always be proud of you. If you decide to give this thing up, that's your call. But don't get fired for blowing off your boss. Don't get canned for acting like a jerk."

I grew quiet and kept driving without looking at him.

"What's the matter?" Matt asked after a while.

I didn't respond.

"You don't like my advice?" he asked.

"No, as a matter of fact, I don't," I said.

"Okay, fine—I can take it—but why not?"

"I don't want to talk about it," I snapped.

"Of course you do," Matt said. "You just asked me for my advice for the first time in . . . well, forever. You may not like it, but you asked for it, and I'm telling you—you should do what your boss wants and go to Jordan. After that, should you step down from your job and do something else with your life? Maybe. *Maybe.* But for heaven's sake, don't get fired. Do what Allen wants you to do. Then go see Yael and take some time to figure out what you really want, what she wants, what the future might hold. *Then* make a decision about your job. But not right now. Not like this. Not when all hell is breaking loose and all your instincts are telling you Abu Khalif is the one responsible. Right now you need to stay focused, or you're really going to mess things up."

We drove in silence for several miles. Then Matt tried again. "J. B., come on; I've known you for too long. This isn't about some quick trip to Amman. Something else is wrong. Talk to me—what is it?"

29

⋆ ⋆ ⋆

Matt was right—something else was eating me.

I was just too embarrassed to admit it.

But who else was I going to talk about it with? This was my brother. I'd barely talked to him, or even seen him, since we were in college. I wasn't used to confiding in him. But I had no one else, and we still had a good six hours to go before we got to Bar Harbor.

"It's Yael," I said at last.

"What do you mean?" Matt asked.

I tightened my grip on the steering wheel, took a deep breath, and checked my mirrors again. "She hasn't written back."

"At all?"

"Well, hardly at all."

"I don't understand. I thought you two were getting close."

"So did I."

"Wasn't she the one who insisted you be allowed to go into Iraq with the Delta team even though one of the generals was against it?"

"Forget it," I said. "Let's talk about something else." I reached for the radio and turned it back on.

But Matt turned it off. "J. B., you obviously want to talk about this. So go ahead. We're off the record. I'm not going to tell anyone else—not even Annie or Mom. You have my word."

We drove in silence for several miles. Then I finally began talking again.

"She sent me an e-mail during Hanukkah."

"Okay."

"She thanked me for reaching out to her so many times," I said. "And she apologized for not writing back sooner."

"Well, that's good, right?"

"I guess."

"What else did she say?"

"She said she hoped I had a good Christmas."

"Okay, that's nice."

"Two sentences, really, you think that's nice?" I said. "I'd written her probably four or five pages' worth by that point."

"J. B., she was lucky to be alive. She'd already been in the hospital for a month. And she'd had three or four surgeries by then, maybe more. Isn't that what you told me?"

"I know, but—"

"But what? Cut her a break. Was that the last time you heard from her?"

"No, she sent me a text message a few weeks ago."

"All right, now we're getting somewhere. What was that one about?"

"She'd just been offered a new job."

"Doing what?"

"Working for Prime Minister Eitan as his deputy national security advisor."

"And she wanted you to be the first to know?"

"No, she wasn't sure if she should take it."

"Really? She was asking you for advice?"

"I guess."

"Why would she do that unless she valued your opinion?"

"I don't know."

"Certainly she has other people to ask, right?"

"I would hope so."

"But she asked you."

"Well, yeah."

"And what did you say?"

"What could I say? I told her to take it."

"That's it?"

"I told her I was proud of her, she deserved it, what a cool job, that kind of thing."

"Okay, so what's wrong with that?"

"Nothing."

"But there's something you're not telling me."

"Like what?" I asked.

"I don't know," Matt said calmly. "You tell me."

"I *am* telling you."

Matt shifted in his seat and tried another tack. "Did you really want her to take the job?"

"Why wouldn't I?" I asked. "She deserved to be promoted. She's amazing at what she does."

"I'm sure she is, but that's not what I asked."

I drove in silence for a while longer. "Look, I wasn't *against* her taking the job," I finally said. "I mean, who am I to be against her getting a big promotion?"

"Okay, I get it, but you would have *preferred* she not take the job, right?"

"I couldn't tell her that."

"Why not?"

"It wasn't my place."

"She was asking you."

"Yeah, but this was a huge honor. It was a really big deal for her. I didn't want to stand in her way. What kind of jerk do you think I am?"

"J. B.?" Matt said, clearly trying to choose his words carefully.

"Yeah."

"Let me ask you something."

"Okay," I said, bracing myself.

"Did it ever occur to you—I mean, seriously, did you ever consider the possibility that Yael wanted you to tell her *not* to take the job?"

"No, of course not," I said instantly. "That's ridiculous."

Matt was quiet.

"You don't understand," I protested. "She was perfect for this job. I mean, she'd have been crazy not to take it."

"Then why did she ask you?"

"I don't know," I said. "Just being polite, I guess."

I glanced over and saw Matt raising his eyebrows quizzically. He obviously wasn't buying my analysis.

"What are you saying, exactly?" I asked, seeing where he was heading but needing to hear it spelled out all the same.

"You said Yael was hardly in touch at all after her surgery, right?"

"Right."

"And when she did reply to your messages, it was just short responses?"

"Exactly."

"And then suddenly—out of the blue—she asks you this huge question, a really personal question about her future."

"So?"

"So you really still think she was just being polite?"

30

★ ★ ★

I grew quiet.

We were making decent time. The snow was coming down harder now, but the plows and salt trucks were out, and in the immediate aftermath of the attack in New York, traffic was light.

"You think she was testing me?" I asked finally.

"I don't know about *testing*," he said.

"But you think she wanted to see if I'd say no?"

"Maybe."

"You think she wanted to see if I'd tell her she *shouldn't* take the job?"

Matt didn't say a word. But when I glanced at him, he shrugged. "It's possible, isn't it?" he asked quietly.

Was it? I wondered. *Had she really wanted me to give her a reason to retire from the Mossad and . . . and what? What did she want? What did I want?*

"After you told her to take the job, did you hear back from her?" Matt asked.

"No."

"She never told you whether she took the job?"

I shook my head.

"Do you think she did?"

"I don't know—I mean, I assume so," I sputtered, suddenly realizing how ridiculous I must sound. I was an award-winning journalist for the world's most influential newspaper. Wasn't it my job to figure out the facts, not make assumptions or jump to conclusions?

"But you don't know for sure?" Matt asked.

"No," I said, embarrassed. "I guess I don't."

"So for all you know, she could have passed on the offer."

"Why would she?"

"You're saying the bottom line is you believe Yael Katzir is currently serving as the prime minister's deputy national security advisor?"

I hesitated. I really didn't know. When I didn't respond, Matt shifted gears.

"J. B.?" he asked.

"What?"

"Do you love this woman?"

I was startled by his directness. But he was right. That was the question.

"I don't know. Maybe."

"You're not sure?"

"I've touched that stove before; you know that," I said.

"And you're not exactly eager to get burned again."

"Of course not."

"Just because of Laura?" he asked.

Yes, Matt, "just" because my cruel, heartless ex-wife ripped out my heart and drove over it with the SUV I'd just bought her. I didn't say that, of course. I didn't need to. He could see my whole body stiffen.

"Okay, fine—you're not sure if you love her," he said. "That makes sense. You hardly know her. But you want to *get* to know her, to see if there's really something there. Right?"

"Yeah, I guess—yeah."

"So?"

"So what?"

"So isn't that a good reason for getting on a plane, going over to see the king—and while you're over there, seeing Yael—and letting the *New York Times* pay for the trip?"

★ ★ ★

Matt took the next shift.

The snow had stopped falling, and the road crews had been able to keep the streets clear, but our prospects of getting to Bar Harbor more or less on schedule were dimming. We still had almost five hours to go.

I climbed into the backseat, stretched out as best I could, put in my earbuds, and zoned out to Paul Simon's *Graceland* album. Scrolling through my e-mails, I found several from Allen and a blizzard of messages from other *Times* reporters comparing notes about the terror attacks. But for the first time I could ever remember, I had no interest in reading them. I didn't want to scan the headlines or track the story. I didn't want to reach out to any of my sources by e-mail, text, or phone. It wasn't that I didn't care. I did. Deeply. But I was spent. I simply didn't have the emotional, physical, or intellectual energy to engage in any of it. It was as if all my circuit breakers were going off. There was nothing I could do about any of it, and so I set down my phone and faded off to sleep. And kept sleeping for hours.

I don't remember the sound of the road or even the music in my ears. I don't remember Matt stopping again for gas or my phone ringing, which, according to the log, it did several times, as Allen continued trying in vain to get ahold of me. What I do remember was Matt suddenly shaking me and a sudden blast of winter air.

"J. B., wake up."

"Why? What's going on?" I said, trying to get my bearings and wondering why it was so dark.

"I need you to drive," he said. "I'm starting to weave all over the road."

The brutal cold of Maine quickly snapped me back to reality. "Where are we?" I asked as I forced myself out of the Audi, stretched my legs, and let Matt climb into the back.

"Just outside of Bangor," he said.

It had been a long time since I'd been home, I realized, and longer still since I'd driven all the way from D.C. The few times I had been up here in recent years I'd flown to Bangor and rented a car. Feeling decently rested, I agreed to take the next shift, then climbed into the driver's seat, shut the door, turned on the seat warmer, and tried to get comfortable. The LED display on the dashboard indicated the temperature outside was in the single digits. Inside it was only seventy. I turned up the heater a few notches to get it to seventy-five.

I pulled back onto I-395, heading southeast now, having skirted Penobscot Bay. I kept my speed around fifty, well under the state limit. It was snowing hard again. The roads were slick. The last thing I wanted to do was wipe out so close to home. We had less than ninety minutes to go.

I glanced in my rearview mirror. Traffic was light. No one seemed to be following us. But for some reason I couldn't shake the feeling that someone might be. I didn't say anything to Matt. I didn't want to worry him. His anniversary had already been ruined by a day of terror attacks ten times worse than 9/11. There was no point adding my paranoia to the mix.

The clock on the dashboard said 7:27 p.m. Matt had fallen fast asleep. With the rough weather, we were well behind schedule. Pulling out my phone, I noticed the battery was running low, so I connected it to the car charger. I didn't need the GPS. I knew my way from here. But I did want to give my mom a call and let her know we were coming. I tried twice but got voice mail both times. I tried Annie's cell phone too but got her voice mail as well. I left brief messages on our whereabouts and let them know that at the rate we were going, we would likely pull in sometime after eight thirty. Then I kept driving through the darkness and the blowing snow.

31

★ ★ ★

My phone rang.

I hoped it was my mom or Annie. But it was Allen MacDonald again. I ignored him. Then he called again, and a third time and a fourth, in rapid succession. He was determined to reach me. I was determined not to let him.

Then Matt's phone began ringing, and Matt woke up in a fog. "Good grief, doesn't your bureau chief ever give up?" he said from the backseat.

"I wish," I said.

"Maybe you should take it this time."

"Not a chance," I said. "I'm still mulling what you said. But I'll get back to him tomorrow, I promise."

Then Matt, too, got a second call from the *Times*' Washington bureau, and a third.

"Maybe something's going on," Matt said. "Seems pretty important."

"No, it's not important," I said. "Just annoying. Turn off your ringer and go back to sleep. We'll be there soon."

"You sure?"

"Absolutely," I said. "I'll wake you as soon as we're close."

"All right, thanks." Matt yawned again, then hunched over, pulled his coat up over his face, and went back to sleep.

Before long we passed the Hancock County Airport and then drove through the sleepy town of Trenton, population less than fifteen hundred. This was the last stop on the mainland. It swelled in the summer but was practically a ghost town this time of year. There was no reason to pull over. We had plenty of fuel, and we were anxious to get back to our family. So I continued driving, over Trenton Bridge and onto Mount Desert Island, hugging the shoreline and snaking along Highway 3 around the north side of Acadia National Park. We passed through Salisbury Cove and Hulls Cove until the highway turned into Eden Street, which led us directly into the town where Matt and I had both been born and raised.

I tried to recall the last time I'd been there and concluded it had to have been at least three years, though it might have been four. I'd never thought of myself as particularly nostalgic, but just seeing the sleepy coastal town with its ubiquitous churches, their steeples covered in a fresh blanket of snow, brought back a rush of warm memories. Hunting and fishing with my grandfather. Making blueberry pies with my grandmother. Cross-country skiing with Matt and hiking Cadillac Mountain with our friends. Christmas caroling in bone-chilling temperatures with the church youth group. My mom making us hot cocoa with marshmallows afterward. Sitting in front of a roaring fire in the parsonage while Pastor Mike regaled us with all kinds of crazy stories from his childhood. And his wife, Sarah, serving us bowls of her homemade chili. I hadn't thought about such things in years.

Now, as I turned right on Main Street, I could see the streetlamps glowing yellow in the frosty-blue air and the white lights illuminating a giant wire outline of a moose set atop one of the shops. Most establishments were shut down for the evening. At this hour, no one was shopping for gifts or getting their hair done or buying supplies from the hardware shop or taking letters to the post office. But all of the town's restaurants were open and doing a brisk business, perhaps packed with couples celebrating a belated Valentine's Day. Despite the attacks, people here were still trying to live normal lives. They were a resilient, rugged people. I envied them. And though I was loath to admit it even to myself, I missed them.

In the distance, a siren broke the Norman Rockwell–esque tranquility. Soon a fire truck raced up behind me. I slowed and pulled to the side of the street to let it pass. Moments later two more fire engines were tearing down Main Street as well. As I began to drive again, I was cut off by two police cars and an ambulance coming down the street, each with lights blazing and sirens blaring. Matt woke up and asked what in the world was going on. I had no idea, but clearly it was a big deal and would undoubtedly be the lead story in the next morning's edition of the *Mount Desert Islander*.

We passed the hospital on our left and on our right the snow-covered Little League fields where we'd played ball for so many springs and summers. Soon we reached the south side of town and took a left on Old Farm Road. It had been freshly plowed, which was good. Then we saw flashing blue lights ahead and a police squad car blocking our path. I rolled down the window to ask what the problem was and immediately smelled the smoke.

"Sorry, gentlemen, 'fraid I can't let you through," one of two uniformed officers said as he sipped a thermos of coffee.

I didn't recognize him, nor he me.

"House fire?" I asked.

"'Fraid so. And a nasty one—three alarms."

Matt and I peered through the snowy forest around us but couldn't see any fire trucks, much less the house in question.

"Whose house?" I asked.

"Dunno," he said. "I'm kinda new here. Moved here from Portland. Just two months on the job."

"So you got roadblock duty?"

"'Fraid so."

"What number, then?" I asked.

"Uh, I don't exactly . . . Eighty-five, maybe?"

My heart stopped. "Which street?"

"Sols Cliff," he said.

"That's *our* house," Matt shouted from the backseat, the fear in his voice palpable.

"Yours?" the young officer asked, skeptical.

"We grew up there," I said, my heart racing but trying to keep my voice calm. "Our mom's still there. Please, we need to get through."

"Let's see some ID," he said.

I had no time for this guy. I knew exactly what was happening. I knew why my calls to Mom and Annie hadn't connected. I knew why Allen had been calling me repeatedly for the past hour. I threw the Audi in reverse, then shifted gears again and hit the gas. We shot around the back of the squad car and raced up the road, taking a sharp left onto Sols Cliff Road. Suddenly I had to slam on the brakes. The road was full of emergency vehicles, and I could see our family's home—and the woods around it—going up in flames.

32

★ ★ ★

Matt bolted out of the car and ran toward the house.

Shutting down the engine, I threw open my door and raced after him. Matt was nearly tackled by a uniformed police officer trying to keep him from reaching the inferno. By the time I caught up to him, two more officers had blocked our path.

"My family!" Matt screamed. *"They're in there—my wife, my kids, my mom."*

"Who are you, sir?" one of the officers asked.

"Matt—Matt Collins," he stammered, his face ashen, his body shaking. "Please, I have to get to them."

"Do you have ID?" the officer said.

Matt stiffened. His eyes went wide. I'd never seen him like this. I actually thought for a moment he was about to throw a punch. So I stepped forward, put myself between Matt and the three of Bar Harbor's finest. I showed them my driver's license and my press pass. Then I explained again who we were and why we were here.

"Okay, boys, I've got this," said a voice from behind us.

I turned around, expecting to see the young officer whose roadblock we'd blown through. Instead, I found an older gentleman, probably in his sixties. He wasn't dressed in a police uniform but had on a black North Face snow jacket, a black ski cap, a red plaid flannel shirt, faded jeans, and old boots. He flashed his badge and identified himself as the chief of police. I didn't recognize him. But then again, I'd never had any run-ins with the local cops—not since leaving for college, anyway.

"You're J. B. Collins?" he asked.

"Yes, sir."

"And you're Matthew Collins?"

"*Where's our family, Chief?*" Matt shouted, blowing off the question and causing each of the officers around him to tense.

The chief waved them off and took a step forward. "I'm afraid I have very bad news for you two boys," he said over the roaring of the searing flames as ash and embers swirled around us like snowflakes.

"No," Matt said, shaking his head and backing away.

I grabbed my brother's arm to hold him steady. All the bravado in his voice had evaporated. His knees were beginning to buckle. I was afraid mine might too.

"Two are gone," the chief said. "Two are severely wounded."

My grip on Matt tightened, as did his on me. He was shaking his head but could no longer speak.

"What do you mean, gone, Chief?" I asked, my voice trembling. I resolved to stay strong for my brother's sake, knowing full well what was coming next.

"There's no easy way to put this, gentlemen—your mother is dead," the chief said without emotion, looking first at me, then at Matt. "And, Mr. Collins, I'm afraid your son is dead as well."

"No—no, I just—" Matt stammered, nearly inaudible, shaking his head, tears streaming down his face. "That can't—that's not—"

An explosion on the north side of the house suddenly sent all of us, including the first responders, scrambling for cover. I pulled Matt to safety behind one of the pumpers. A moment later, I heard one of the firemen say the heating-oil tank had just blown.

I stared in horror as the flames consumed what was left of the historic home. Our great-great-grandfather had built it in 1883 in a Greek Revival style. The half-acre waterfront plot alone was now worth a thousand times what he'd paid for it. The house had been enormous, with thirteen rooms, including six bedrooms, four and a half baths, and a grand living room with huge bay windows looking out over the Atlantic. Not a month went by without someone inquiring if it was for sale. But Mom would never sell. She had always said she was going to die in this house, and now she had.

"Annie? Katie?" Matt demanded. "They're still alive—the chief said so."

So he had. I grabbed Matt's jacket and we found the chief again and demanded to know what had happened to my sister-in-law and niece.

"They're alive," the chief confirmed. "But they're in critical condition."

"Where are they now?" I asked.

"We airlifted them to Maine Medical Center not ten minutes ago," he said.

"In Portland?"

"Yes."

"Come on, Matt, let's go," I said, turning back toward my car.

"Follow me, gentlemen," the chief insisted. "I'll give you an escort."

PART THREE

33

★ ★ ★

PORTLAND, MAINE

The next seventy-two hours were a blur.

Matt and I split most of our time between the ICU at Barbara Bush Children's Hospital, part of the Maine Medical Center, and the adult ICU in the hospital's other wing. The doctors urged us to remain hopeful, but both Annie's and Katie's situations could hardly have been more dire. Both were unconscious, badly burned, and suffering from severe smoke inhalation, and though I didn't dare say it to Matt, I had little hope for their recovery based on what we'd been told so far.

On Friday evening, Agent Harris came to see us at the hospital. Unbeknownst to us, he and a team of investigators from the bureau had arrived in Bar Harbor early Friday morning. They'd spent the day collecting evidence and interviewing witnesses.

"I'm going to tell you something few others know at this point," Harris told us as we stood outside the ICU, surrounded by uniformed local police and armed federal agents who had been personally tasked by President Taylor with providing round-the-clock security for our family. "You can't print this, J. B., any of it. I'm ·

letting you know this as a member of the family, as a courtesy, *not* because you're a reporter."

"I understand," I said, and Matt nodded as well.

"Look, this is hard to say, but I think you need to know," Harris said. "The deceased victims were double-tapped with a 9mm pistol."

"Double-tapped?" Matt asked.

"Shot twice in rapid succession," I explained, then turned back to Harris. "You're saying this was a professional hit."

Harris nodded. "The ME determined from his autopsy that your mom and Joshua died instantly from the gunshot wounds. Their bodies were severely burned in the fire, but they didn't feel a thing. There was no smoke in their lungs, indicating that they were killed before the fire was started."

The image of Matt's face at that moment—as pale and queasy as when we'd first arrived on the scene of the fire—would be forever seared into my memory. I put my arm around him and helped him sit down in the waiting area. He looked terrible. He was unshaven. He'd barely eaten. His eyes were bloodshot and moist, but thus far he was containing his emotions. Barely. Under the circumstances, he'd been remarkably strong, but I wasn't sure how much more he could take.

"And Annie? Katie?" he asked. "Were they shot too?"

"I'm afraid so," the agent explained. "Your wife was shot twice. Your daughter only once. Whoever did this apparently thought they were both dead. But when the firefighters found them, they weren't in the kitchen like the others. They were huddled in the basement, in a closet, bleeding and unconscious but away from the worst of the smoke."

Neither Matt nor I said anything, so Harris continued. "As best we can ascertain, when the shooters left, your wife must have checked the others, realized Katie was still breathing, and dragged her downstairs to where she hoped they'd be safe until help came. We found a cordless phone in her hand. Turns out she managed to call 911 before she passed out."

"She called 911? What did she say?" Matt asked.

"She told the dispatcher there were four terrorists in the house and that they'd been there for quite some time. She said they were all wearing black hoods, all speaking in Arabic, though the leader spoke some broken English. They were ransacking the place. And the leader kept demanding to know where you were, J. B. He kept shouting that you were supposed to have gotten there by seven. He thought you were hiding and that the family was lying to protect you or had warned you away somehow."

Now I had to sit down. I felt light-headed and shaky. The bitter truth was now crystal clear—my mother and Josh had been murdered because of me. Annie and Katie were fighting for their lives because of me.

Harris then told us that the arson investigators believed the fire had been set around seven thirty. Matt and I knew full well what that message was and who had sent it.

"Seven thirty, you're sure?" I asked.

"Give or take ten minutes," Harris said.

I was coming to the painful realization that if we'd gotten home when Matt and I had originally planned, we might have been able to break up the attack—or been killed with the others. The storm had slowed us down, and in doing so it might also have saved our lives. But that was little comfort.

"What else can you tell us, Agent Harris?" I asked. "Please tell me you have some suspects."

"Not yet, but we've got some leads," he replied.

"Like what?"

"The clerk at the Shell station on Main Street said two men in their thirties came in yesterday around dinnertime. They looked Middle Eastern. One used the restroom. The other bought bottles of water. He paid with cash. But we ran the video from the closed-circuit cameras and came up with a car and a license plate. We've got an APB out and my team is looking at footage from every camera in Bar Harbor. We'll find it—I promise you that."

Six hours later, they did, on some side street in Augusta. Little good it did, however. There were no security cameras in the area, so the FBI had no idea what these two were driving now, who they were, or where they were headed. As far as I was concerned, the trail had gone cold.

On Sunday morning, I sat with Annie and Katie, who were now in the same ICU. I insisted Matt take a break, go get a hot shower, and get some sleep or at least lie down for a while and rest. He'd been understandably reluctant to leave his wife and daughter, of course. But there had been no movement, no progress, no news, and the two of them didn't even know he was there. I promised to call him if either or both of them woke or if there were any developments at all. Finally he agreed.

By Sunday evening, Matt was back at the hospital and it was my turn to take a break. I sat on my bed in a Motel 6 on the outskirts of Portland, surrounded by containers of half-eaten Chinese food and empty bottles of Coke Zero and craving a real drink more intensely than any time in days. But there was no minibar, and with killers out there somewhere hunting for me—and a messy nor'easter bearing down on us—I wasn't about to head out to find a liquor store. I took a shower instead.

Just after nine, a text message came in from Allen. It said the president was about to give his third press conference in as many days, and the press pool was picking up rumors there might be an important update on the hunt for the terrorists. I thought of the two FBI agents parked in the room next door, assigned to watch my back, and the dozen federal agents and handful of local cops at the hospital, watching over Matt and his surviving family.

I didn't think ISIS was likely to come after me again—not now, not with a media feeding frenzy surrounding us.

But Harris refused to take any chances. And I was grateful.

34

★ ★ ★

As I waited for the president to speak, I was going stir-crazy.

For much of the last twelve hours, I'd been responding to a bliz-zard of e-mails concerning the memorial service, and once again my circuit breakers were blowing. For one thing, my mom's church was in the midst of extensive renovations due to a burst water pipe sev-eral weeks earlier, and the sanctuary was in no condition to host an event that was drawing national media attention. That necessitated finding another church facility, and I eventually chose St. Saviour's Episcopal Church, located close to the center of town. The building was beautiful and historic, and its sanctuary held 280 people, making it one of the largest on the island.

That, it turned out, had been the easy part. Now I was dealing with a torrent of questions from the director of the funeral home, the church secretary, the florist, the driver of the hearse, and dozens of my mom's friends and hundreds of other well-wishers.

Hour by hour, the condolences kept pouring in by e-mail and text message, not just from the local area but from all over the country. I couldn't keep up. I wasn't cut out to be a social secretary. But I knew I had to keep it all off of Matt's shoulders. He was proving himself stronger than I'd feared, but he didn't have the bandwidth for any of this right now.

I finally sent a text to Allen, apologizing for not being in touch sooner. He wrote back immediately, offering his own condolences and saying he'd already had Mary Jane cancel my flight to Amman. He told me I didn't need to come back to work anytime soon. He knew I couldn't write about what I was going through or be a source for other *Times* reporters covering it, even though this was big, front-page news. He was just happy to know I was still alive.

As I hit Send on a response to yet another e-mail, President Taylor entered the White House pressroom to a thousand camera flashes. I set my phone down, picked up the remote, and turned up the sound on the TV perched atop the dresser.

"Tonight I want to update you on the tragedy of the past few days," the president began. "As you know, terrorists have unleashed attacks in nine American cities and towns, beginning with our nation's capital and most recently in the small seacoast town of Bar Harbor, Maine. These cowardly attacks came without warning and without remorse. These are despicable, cold-blooded acts. They were unprovoked and unconscionable, and they will not be tolerated."

There it was again. *Without warning.* Was this really what the intelligence community was telling him? No attacks in American history had been more clearly telegraphed. Abu Khalif had done everything but fax a map and a timeline to the White House Situation Room. The president and his national security staff simply didn't want to believe it. They still had no idea what they were really up against, and we were all paying the price.

"As of this hour, some 4,647 American citizens and residents, and 62 foreign nationals—not counting the perpetrators—have been killed in terror attacks on the American homeland over the course of the past week," the president continued.

It was a chilling statistic. It represented 1,651 more deaths than the 2,996 people killed during the 9/11 attacks in 2001. I could only imagine Abu Khalif's twisted pleasure upon hearing the news that he had, in one day, killed half again as many Americans as his onetime mentor, Osama bin Laden.

The president then added that the sarin gas had wounded an additional 6,114 people, many of whom were in critical condition. He asked the nation to send "thoughts of peace and healing" to the families of the deceased and to those "suffering from the cowardly actions of these violent extremists."

Even with the nation under attack, he refused to utter the phrase *Radical Islam*, much less *apocalyptic Islam*.

Disgusted, I reached for the remote to mute the TV and get back to work. But then the president said that he had ordered U.S. bombers and fighter jets to attack ISIS positions inside Syria. That caught my attention. A map flashed up on the large monitor mounted over his left shoulder. The graphics indicated the position of the most recent air strikes, just inside the Syrian border with Iraq. The president claimed that in the last twenty-four hours, American forces had killed 612 fighters loyal to Abu Khalif, all of whom were hiding out in these border regions. Most of them, he said, had previously fought in Iraq but had been pushed back into Syria due to U.S. operations to liberate Mosul and other northern Iraqi towns and villages.

Did this represent a fundamental shift in U.S. strategy against ISIS, or a weekend diversion? I wondered. Now that Abu Khalif had struck inside the American homeland, was Taylor finally heeding my advice to take the gloves off and go after ISIS and its leader inside Syria, regardless of how much the Russians and Iranians and the U.N. secretary general protested?

For the moment, I could only hope. The president didn't say. Not exactly. Instead, he offered another tantalizing nugget. He explained that he was expanding authority for the CIA to use drone strikes against high-value ISIS targets inside Syria as well as in Yemen, Libya,

Afghanistan, and the Bekaa Valley in northeastern Lebanon. Then a face flashed up on the screen. I recognized it instantly: Tariq Baqouba.

"I can report to the American people that these expanded drone strikes are already having a devastating effect on the enemy," the president said. "Just hours ago, U.S. forces identified, targeted, and killed Tariq Baqouba—ISIL's number-three-ranked leader—in a drone strike near the Syrian-Iraqi border. In recent months, Baqouba was ISIL's operations chief, responsible for terrorist activity through-out the Middle East and North Africa. While we do not believe he was the mastermind of last week's attacks inside the United States, we have solid intelligence indicating he played a key role in execut-ing those attacks. Last fall, Tariq Baqouba led ISIL forces in a raid against a Syrian military base near Aleppo. It was this incident that allowed the group to capture precursors for chemical weapons—specifically for sarin gas—and thousands of artillery shells to deliver them. Tonight, a savage killer was brought to justice, and you have my word: there is more to come."

At this point, Taylor took a few questions.

No, the FBI still had not made arrests of anyone in connection to the attacks in Washington or in any of the six cities where chemical weapons had been unleashed against the American people.

No, the FBI had made no arrests in the attack on the Collins family in Maine.

Yes, the bureau had offered a $5 million reward for information leading to the arrests and convictions of suspects in all of these cases.

Yes, there had been a huge spike in calls to the FBI tip line.

No, he couldn't comment any further on ongoing investigations. Then it was over.

That was it? I thought. *That's all the detail you're going to give us?*

I shouted something profane and threw an ashtray at the wall. I didn't need vague answers to meaningless questions. I needed real results, and I needed them now.

35

★ ★ ★

Suddenly there was rapid knocking at the door.

The two agents assigned to protect me had come to check on me. They'd heard my yell and the crash of the ashtray and wanted to know if I was all right. I cracked the door open, apologized, and told them I was fine. They looked skeptical but eventually went back to their room.

When I heard them open and shut their door, I walked over to the windows. I pulled back the curtains, ever so slightly. It was snowing hard. The cars in the parking lot were covered with another several inches of fresh powder. What I wouldn't give to be free for a few days and head to Killington with some friends on a ski getaway.

My mobile phone rang. The number was Allen's.

I was about to ignore it but thought better of it. Maybe my brother was right. It wasn't exactly a wise career move to chronically blow off the boss. If I was going to leave the *Times*, then I should do so on my own terms, with a plan of what I was going to do next. To get myself fired for no good reason was just plain stupid.

"Hey, Allen," I said, my voice hoarse and laced with fatigue.

"Hey. I didn't actually expect to reach you. How are you?"

"I honestly don't know how to answer that," I admitted.

"I'm so sorry. I can't imagine what you're going through."

"No, look, I'm the one who's sorry—about Jordan, about not answering your calls, about being, well, you know."

"Forget it, J. B. You don't have to apologize. I understand. Believe me."

"Thanks," I said. "And thanks for your text, too, by the way. I appreciate it. So what's up?"

"Well, I just landed in Bangor, just rented a car. I should be in Bar Harbor in about ninety minutes."

"You're serious? You're going to Bar Harbor?"

"Of course," he said.

"Well, thanks, but—and please don't take this the wrong way—but why?"

"I spoke to your mom's pastor this afternoon," he explained. "He and his staff have gotten calls from every network and every national paper, the AP, Reuters, you name it. They're all coming up to cover the service. CNN wants to broadcast it live. It's becoming a major media event. Plus, with the VP flying up, the Secret Service is getting involved. The pastor's being deluged. He asked me for some advice. I said I'd be happy to come up and help, and he jumped at the offer."

"The vice president is coming?" I said, my stomach tightening.

"You didn't know?" he asked.

"No, but then again, why would Holbrooke tell me? I'm just running the thing."

"Well, according to my source at the White House, he's coming. Anyway, the pastor said he needed someone to manage the media at the memorial service—said it's going to be a madhouse. He didn't know anyone else who could do it, so I decided I would."

"That's very kind of you, I guess," I said.

"It is, actually, but that's not even the reason I called."

"What is?"

"I have news."

"What kind of news?"

"A front-page exclusive."

"By whom?"

"Bill Sanders."

"On what?"

"The hunt for Abu Khalif."

"What are you talking about?" I said. "Why is Sanders writing about Khalif?" Bill Sanders was the Cairo bureau chief for the *Times*. ISIS and Khalif were not his usual beat.

"Because you aren't," Allen said. "And because after you, he's the best Mideast correspondent we have. I asked him to work his sources and find out what's being done to track down the emir of ISIS and bring him to justice."

"And?"

"You'll see when you read the article. Make sure to pick up a copy of the *Times* bright and early tomorrow. Look, I gotta go. I'll call you in the morning."

With that, Allen MacDonald was gone. But there was no time to process all that he'd just said. For no sooner had Allen hung up than the phone rang again.

"Hello?" I said, not recognizing the number. I wondered if it might be the VP's office.

"Is this J. B. Collins?" asked the man on the other end of the line.

"Who's asking?" I said.

It was not a voice I recognized.

"My name is Steve Sullivan."

"Okay." The name was familiar, but I couldn't immediately place it.

"I'm the lawyer in Portland who's representing the Khachigian estate. I've written you a number of e-mails but haven't gotten any replies."

Now I remembered the name and the e-mails. I'd fully intended to write back, but I guess I never actually had. Sullivan's first e-mail had been rather cryptic. He'd indicated that he'd had important business to discuss with me concerning Khachigian's will. He'd said it was a sensitive matter that necessitated meeting in person. The rest of his e-mails were all variations on that theme. Since I had no idea what Khachigian's will could possibly have to do with me, it hadn't seemed that urgent given everything else going on.

I apologized and started to explain what had happened with my family.

"Yes, I know, and I'm very sorry for your loss, Mr. Collins," he said. "Truly, I am."

"That's very kind, Mr. Sullivan," I replied. "So you'll understand why I'm not in a position to meet at the moment."

"Actually, Mr. Collins, I must inform you that this is an urgent matter that cannot wait any longer," Sullivan countered.

Generally I applauded tenacity. But this was going too far. "Well, it will have to, Mr. Sullivan. I'm afraid I'm far too busy for this right now. But please, have a good night."

Before I could hang up, however, Sullivan quickly explained that he was in possession of a sealed envelope that I needed to see. "It's marked in Khachigian's own handwriting," he said. "The note reads, 'If I am killed in mysterious circumstances, please get this to James Bradley Collins immediately.'"

36

★ ★ ★

PORTLAND, MAINE

My return to Bar Harbor would have to wait.

I arrived at the offices of Sullivan & Sullivan, attorneys at law, at precisely 8 a.m., briefcase in hand. The firm didn't typically open until nine, but I didn't care. I'd told this guy if he really wanted to meet with me, that's when I'd be available. Not a moment later.

I'd been driven by two agents from the bureau, and the agent behind the wheel of our unmarked bureau sedan kept the engine running while his partner went inside to check things out. Five minutes later, he exited the three-story brick building and gave us an "all clear" signal. The driver parked and escorted me inside.

The decor was humble but tasteful. This wasn't a high-powered firm with a lot of Washington and Wall Street connections. Indeed, I suspected Robert Khachigian had been the Sullivans' highest profile client by far. The walls needed a fresh coat of paint. The chairs in the foyer were ready to be reupholstered. The magazines were out of date. The computer on the receptionist's desk looked like it had to be a good ten years old. The aroma of pipe smoke, carpet cleaner, and instant coffee wafted through the air.

Steve Sullivan greeted me with a firm handshake. He was younger than me, no more than thirty-five, I thought, despite the receding hairline that no doubt came from too many hours and too much stress. He wore a gray three-piece suit that looked like a throwback to a different generation, despite the brand-new and rather stylish dress shoes that squeaked when he walked. He asked if I wanted some coffee or a glass of water, both of which I declined, and then he ushered me down a hallway and into a moderately sized corner office overlooking Portland's main thoroughfare.

An elderly man, surely in his eighties, stood when I entered.

"Mr. Collins, please meet my grandfather and the founding partner of this firm, Link Sullivan," the younger man said.

"Link, did you say?" I asked as I reached out to shake the grandfather's hand.

"Lincoln, actually, but my friends call me Link," he said.

He was gray and balding and frail but had a warm smile and trustworthy eyes. As he offered me a seat, it occurred to me to wonder whether there was another Sullivan. Where was Lincoln's son, Steve's father? I glanced around and saw no pictures of the three men—separate or together—in any of the many frames on the large executive desk or on the walls. I was tempted to ask but decided the best thing was to get through whatever they wanted to talk about as quickly as possible and be on my way. There was too much else on my plate; getting to know the history of the Sullivan family wasn't exactly on the list.

The grandson sat in a weathered wooden chair across from his grandfather. I followed his lead and sat in a similar chair a few feet to his right. The FBI agents stepped back into the hallway and shut the door. The three of us were now alone.

"We understand you're pressed for time," the elder Sullivan began after verifying my identity by checking my driver's license. "We would not have insisted you come here unless it was of the utmost urgency."

"The sealed envelope," I said.

"Yes, the envelope. And one other matter," he said.

"What's that?" I said. "Your grandson didn't mention anything beyond the envelope."

"Mr. Collins, are you aware that my client left nearly his entire estate to you and your brother, Matthew?"

For a moment I just stared at him. "I beg your pardon?" I finally said.

"It's true."

"I don't understand. What about his family?" I asked.

Sullivan leaned back in his creaky leather executive chair. "As you know, Robert's wife, Mary, passed away three years ago from ovarian cancer. They had no children. Their parents are deceased. Robert's sister, Ellen, died a decade ago. And Ellen's children . . ." He looked at me expectantly.

I said nothing.

"I believe you knew Ellen's son, Chris."

"Yes," I said guardedly. "He was an Army Ranger. He was killed in Afghanistan in 2006."

"Exactly," the elder Sullivan said. "And you and Ellen's daughter were . . ."

He paused. I tensed. He was referring to Laura.

". . . married, I understand," the grandfather continued.

"And divorced," I hastened to add. I stood, walked over to the window, and stared out at the snow and the traffic and people hustling and bustling, to and fro.

"As the executor of Mr. Khachigian's estate, I can tell you that has no bearing on his final will and testament."

"But shouldn't she inherit everything?" I asked, turning now to face the two Sullivans. "I mean, Laura is his only living heir, right?"

"A man is entitled to leave his estate to anyone he so chooses," said the elder Sullivan. "In this case, my client chose to leave his estate to you and your brother."

"His *entire* estate?" I asked, incredulous.

"Well, no. Not quite. Laura will receive one quarter of the assets, once the house is sold and everything else is liquidated." Lincoln Sullivan pulled a copy of the will out of a folder and handed it over to me. "You and your brother will receive equal shares of the rest. We will need to have the house reappraised, of course. But it's quite valuable, as is his portfolio of stocks and bonds. All told, we believe you and Matthew will each receive about $15 million, give or take, before taxes."

I took the thick document in my hand. I tried to read it over but my thoughts were reeling and my vision was blurring. "And Laura?" I finally asked. "What will she receive?"

"About $10 million, give or take."

I didn't know what to say. "I had no idea."

"That the Khachigians were that wealthy, or that you and your brother were in the will?"

"Either—both," I said, rereading the first paragraph of the document before me for the third time and still not absorbing it. My eyes were filled with tears but I was fighting them back, embarrassed to show such emotion in front of two complete strangers. The grandson reached for a box of tissues on the desk and handed it to me. That embarrassed me even more, but I nodded my thanks, took a tissue, and wiped my eyes. "So this is what was in the envelope you mentioned? The will?" I asked, fighting to compose myself.

"No, the will was always in my possession, in my safe," said the grandfather. "That wasn't what was in the envelope. That's something entirely different."

"Meaning what?" I asked.

"I can't say," Sullivan said.

"Why not?"

"Because whatever he put in the envelope, he chose not to show me," Sullivan explained. "Frankly, I have no idea what's in there."

"But that's what you used to get me here."

"It was very important to my client."

"So may I see it?"

"You may," he said, reaching for his cane and rising—shakily—to his feet. "I'll be right back."

37

★ ★ ★

Lincoln Sullivan hobbled over to a door I hadn't previously noticed.

With Steve at his side, helping him keep his balance, he opened it to an adjacent conference room and disappeared from view.

Alone for the first time, I suddenly noticed that the office was dimly lit and quite chilly, as though someone had forgotten to turn the heat on, or perhaps the heater was broken. The whole situation seemed a little odd, and I wondered why in the world I had come. My mother had been murdered. So had my nephew. My brother was in a hospital across town, pleading with his God to save his critically wounded wife and daughter. I'd barely had time to accept what had just happened, much less grieve. Yet here I was in some dilapidated old law firm I'd never heard of, being told that Matt and I had just inherited thirty million dollars from a man to whom we had no blood relation. I hadn't come for money. I didn't even want it. I just wanted my family back, and now I regretted coming here at all.

I considered bolting but thought better of it. I'd come here for something far more valuable to me than money. There was something Khachigian wanted me to know, some bit of information he wanted me alone to see. Not Matt. Not even his attorneys, though he clearly trusted them a great deal. Could it be clues to the identity of whoever had leaked him the information about ISIS capturing chemical weapons in Syria? Or even clues to who might have ultimately killed him? Whatever it was, Khachigian had obviously left something deeply important to him, in my name, with the executor of his estate, and he'd done so shortly before his death. For that reason alone, I forced myself to stay and see this thing through.

As I waited for the Sullivans to return with the mysterious envelope, I checked my phone. There were dozens of new text messages and e-mails, but only two were critical. Allen's caught my eye first. He noted that Vice President Holbrooke had just confirmed that he was, in fact, going to attend the memorial service. Air Force Two would be wheels down at 7 a.m. the following morning, and the VP would arrive at the church by motorcade. Allen also said that he had found a place to set up a full-blown media filing center and was now trying to track down card tables, mult boxes, and a lot of extension cords. Lastly, he asked if I'd seen the front page of the *Times* yet. I had not. In fact, with everything else going on, I'd forgotten to look, so for now I moved on.

The other significant e-mail was from Agent Harris. He reported that his colleagues had lifted partial prints from the car abandoned on that side street in Augusta. They belonged to an Iraqi national who had served as a translator for U.S. forces in Fallujah in 2003 and 2004. Later, he'd been arrested as a mole. It turned out he'd been secretly working for Abu Musab al-Zarqawi, the leader of al Qaeda in Iraq, the forerunner of ISIS. He'd been tried and convicted and sent to the Abu Ghraib prison facility near Baghdad in 2005. But he'd escaped along with Abu Khalif the previous November. While Harris conceded the FBI couldn't yet prove in court that this guy was a member of ISIS or that he had been personally sent by Abu Khalif to kill my family, he said the evidence was moving steadily in that direction, and he wanted me to be in the loop.

I opened the attachment Harris had sent. There was a thumbnail picture of the guy from the FBI's most wanted list. In the photo, he was no older than thirty with dark, soulless eyes, closely cropped black hair, a dark complexion, and a thick scar across his neck. I burned the image into my memory. This guy had slaughtered my family. I had no doubt who had sent him or that he was coming for me next. He had a mission. It wasn't yet accomplished. And this wasn't the kind of guy who just gave up and went home.

When Lincoln Sullivan reentered the office, he was holding a small sealed envelope—the envelope I'd come for. He set it on the desk and slid it across to me without a word. Then he excused himself and departed again through the same door.

I sat there by myself for a long moment, listening to the ticking of my grandfather's pocket watch, staring at Khachigian's handwritten scrawl on the outside of the envelope, and wondering what I would find inside.

38

★ ★ ★

Two minutes later, I blew out of the Sullivan firm and headed straight for the car.

"Gorham Savings Bank," I said to the two agents hustling to catch up. "172 Commercial Street—*let's move.*"

On my lap sat the envelope from Khachigian. I held its entire contents in one hand. There wasn't much—just a brass key and a business card for the manager of the Gorham Bank branch on Commercial Street. That was it.

We pulled up precisely at nine o'clock, just as a security guard was unlocking the front door. I grabbed my briefcase and dashed out of the car and into the bank, only to find that the branch manager whose name was on the business card was out sick. Nevertheless, a young assistant manager offered to help me. She led me to a vault filled with safe-deposit boxes, and soon I had Khachigian's box in my hands. The assistant ushered me to a small room containing only an oak table and a swivel chair, then left me there so I could open the box and examine its contents in privacy.

I nervously fumbled with the key but finally opened the steel box and found myself astonished. Inside were stacks of crisp, new one-hundred-dollar bills, wrapped in rubber bands. In all, I counted nine thousand dollars, all in U.S. currency. Underneath the cash was a brand-new satellite phone. There were also three different passports—one Canadian, one Australian, and the third from South Africa. The passports had different pictures of me and different fake names for me. Beside these were three leather wallets. In each I found a half-dozen credit cards with the same names as the ones on the passports, along with driver's licenses, business cards, and various other materials corresponding to the fake names and appropriate countries of origin. There was also close to a thousand dollars in local currency in each of the billfolds.

Underneath all this were two more sealed white business envelopes. I opened the first one to find a handwritten letter, personally signed by Khachigian. I glanced back at the door to the windowless office to make sure it was fully closed, then sat down in the chair, facing the doorway in case someone suddenly entered, and began to read the letter.

Dearest James,

If you have this in your hands, then I am dead and you have met the Sullivans. Please know that you can trust them implicitly, as I have. Link was my father's banker and worked with your grandfather years ago as well. I doubt he told you that. He is far too discreet. Link's grandson, Steven, is as trustworthy as any young man you'll meet. Before returning to Portland, he used to work for the Treasury Department—specifically the Secret Service—for nearly a decade, handling dozens of bank fraud and other cases and putting countless crooks and international terrorists behind bars.

If I know you, you're probably wondering about Steve's father, Link's son. We'll get to that in a moment. You're also likely reeling from what the Sullivans just told you about my estate.

There is a reason for all this. Whoever has killed me did so to silence me, to keep me from telling the world urgently important facts about ISIS and its plans. So the torch now passes to you. Below I have listed three people whom you need to contact immediately. Go visit them in person. Show them this letter. I trust them. They're good people. Now you must win their trust. Learn what they know, and tell the world as quickly as possible.

Do not wait. Do not hesitate. I believe far greater attacks are coming against the American homeland. Perhaps your reporting can save many lives, including your own.

By now it has become painfully clear to me that Harrison Taylor has no idea what he's doing. He won't listen to wise counsel. He doesn't understand the nature and threat of the evil he faces. And I fear he—and the nation—will soon be blindsided as a result.

Over the many years of my career, I have known many presidents, good and bad. But I have never feared for the future of America as I do right now. We are not merely in a rough season, James. We are hurtling toward implosion. The president is selling out our allies and appeasing our enemies. He is gutting our military and dispiriting the brave men and women throughout the intelligence community and the military. Too many are giving up and moving on. And the more that leave high-level government service, the more danger America is in. People with such tremendous experience cannot easily be replaced.

Meanwhile, our enemies smell blood in the water. They see weakness, and they are probing, probing, probing, looking for vulnerabilities to exploit and waiting for the right time to strike. I fear they are planning something catastrophic.

Go stop them, James—before it's too late.

And one other thing. Whoever killed me is coming after you, James. Make no mistake. They're coming after Matt and his family and your mom as well. Your family is not safe in Bar Harbor. Not anymore. Persuade them to leave. Get off the grid—out of sight, out *of mind. It's that serious. They need to hide. You need to help them. This is why I've left you and Matt the lion's share of my estate. Matt must use the money to get his family to safety. But you must use your share to defeat ISIS. To that end, I have left you with cash, new identities, and access to your own jet.*

I know you want to go get these guys. Especially now. Good for you. That's what I've always loved about you. You're not afraid to go on offense, to seize the initiative. I can't promise you won't meet my same fate. I just hope you'll do a lot of damage to the caliphate before all is said and done.

Last thought: I'm not a preacher. I'm not a pastor. But as your friend, I need to urge you, James—please read your Bible, humble your heart, and give your life to Christ. I let too many years go by before I got serious about the things that matter most. I don't have many regrets about my life, but this is one. If it weren't for Matt patiently answering my questions and guiding me through the Scriptures and urging me to make a decision for or against Christ once and for all, I don't know where I'd be. I'm not a humble man by nature, James. It was excruciating for me to admit I needed a Savior. But I did. I do. And so do you. Go find him before it's too late.

I leave you with the verse that changed my life, the words of Jesus, from the Gospel of John. "Greater love has no one than this, that one lay down his life for his friends."

Godspeed, son—I hope to see you on the other side.

Your biggest fan,
Robert

For a moment, I just sat there, staring at the pages. There was so much to take in.

For starters, so much of it was too late. The catastrophic attacks had already come. So had the hit on my family. Why hadn't the Sullivans brought me all this sooner? Why hadn't they come down to Walter

Reed right after I'd gotten back from Iraq? On the other hand, why hadn't I responded sooner to their calls and e-mails? The weight of my failures was almost overwhelming. I set the letter down in the box, leaned back in the chair, and closed my eyes. Everywhere I went, people were getting killed, and I knew I bore a great degree of responsibility.

That said, I feared Khachigian had me all wrong. Clearly Khachigian wanted me—expected me—to personally go after Abu Khalif and these ISIS devils. Given all that he'd done for me—in the past and certainly now—how could I refuse? Yet I wasn't sure I had the energy or desire to go back on offense. What's more, how could I leave Matt, Annie, and Katie now, after all that had happened? They were all the family I had left.

Then there was the mention of his faith. Of all the conversations we'd had over the years, I couldn't recall any about his religious beliefs. I knew Matt had had a profound influence on him, but Khachigian himself had never discussed his faith with me. He was a secretive man by nature. It's what had made him an effective keeper of the nation's secrets. But that only made his urgent appeal that I follow his spiritual journey and wrestle through the claims of Christ for myself all the more surprising. He was urging me to study the Gospels and make a decision, once and for all, for or against, before it was too late. Was I going to listen to him . . . or ignore him?

I sat silently for several minutes, then suddenly opened my eyes and picked up the letter again. I reread it, more slowly this time, word for word, sentence by sentence. Then, on instinct, I flipped the page over, and there on the back I found three names: Paul Pritchard, Walid Hussam, and Mohammed bin Zayed. Beside each name was a mobile phone number. None of the names rang a bell. I didn't recall Khachigian having ever mentioned them before. But these were his sources for the chemical weapons story. Of this I had no doubt.

Which left me with two questions: Who were they, and would they talk to me?

39

★ ★ ★

We raced the 175 miles back to Bar Harbor.

The bureau was transferring me from the Motel 6 in Portland to someplace in my hometown, where I could make the final preparations for the funeral. As I sat in the backseat of the bureau's sedan and watched the snow-covered trees and hills and barns of rural Maine blur by, my thoughts raced as fast as the car. I felt conflicted about heading back to Bar Harbor. My brother needed me with him at the hospital in Portland. But someone had to finish planning the service. He couldn't. I owed him. The memorial service was set to begin in less than twenty-four hours.

On a good day, the drive took less than three hours. But with so much snow falling overnight, I knew we'd be lucky to get there in four.

With my briefcase resting on my lap, I pulled out my grandfather's watch. It was 9:47. I made a quick call to Matt to check on him. He said he was just about to go into the ICU and would have to call me back. He would be making the trip to Bar Harbor in a couple of hours with another team of FBI agents.

Next I called Allen but got voice mail. I didn't leave a message. Then I called Harris, hoping for an update.

"How are you holding up, Collins?" he asked, answering on the first ring.

"Surviving," I said.

"How did the meetings with the Sullivans go?"

"Fine."

"Anything interesting?"

"Just some loose ends they were trying to clear up."

"So what was in the safe-deposit box?" Harris asked.

"Personal stuff."

"Nothing relevant to my investigation?" Harris pressed.

"No," I said. "Just some private things, family things."

"Don't lie to me, Collins. You know it's a crime to lie to a federal agent, right?"

"So I've heard."

I hadn't crossed that line, not exactly, but I had come pretty close. The letter *was* personal. It contained Khachigian's thoughts, emotions, and desires for me and Matt and our family. It included his personal assessment of the president and the administration. It didn't contain evidence relevant to a murder investigation—not precisely, anyway. I certainly wasn't going to tell Harris that I now had new passports, driver's licenses, and credit cards. Khachigian had given me those for the very real possibility that I would need to slip away unnoticed, undetected by the ever-watchful eye of the American government. Telling Harris would obviously and completely undermine that intended escape hatch.

As for the three names, at the moment I had no idea who they were. Clearly they were old friends of, and trusted sources for, Khachigian. But beyond that I knew nothing about them, and as far as I was concerned, I was under no obligation to disclose them to the FBI. I wasn't under investigation. I hadn't been served a subpoena. I didn't have to tell Harris anything I didn't want to, and for the moment, I didn't want to tell him this.

Harris had no new information for me, so I ended the call and thought more about the three names. I was dying to know who they were. At the moment I had no time to do a background search on them, much less contact them, but I needed to connect with them soon. I needed to know what they knew and follow whatever clues they could give me. Yet I hesitated even to do a basic Google search for these names on my own mobile phone. Partly I was concerned that Harris might be monitoring my calls and online activity—mostly to protect me, of course, but perhaps also to keep an eye on me. Was that paranoia? Maybe. But for the moment, I decided extra caution was prudent.

I was even more concerned that ISIS might somehow be monitoring Matt's and my phones. How else had the terrorists known we were supposed to be at my mother's home by seven o'clock that Thursday night? If they'd been physically trailing us, I was pretty sure I would have spotted them somewhere during our fifteen-plus-hour drive from Arlington. The more I thought about it, the more likely it seemed that they must have intercepted the e-mail I'd sent to my mom from the service station on the Jersey Turnpike, giving her a heads-up that we were coming home and estimating our time of arrival. Matt had also sent a text to Annie telling her we'd be there by seven. They must have intercepted that one too.

On the other hand, what about the voice messages I'd left later, updating both Mom and Annie on our progress and telling them that due to snow and traffic we likely wouldn't reach Bar Harbor until closer to eight thirty? If the terrorists were truly tracking our calls and text messages, wouldn't they have intercepted those messages as well? Then again, I'd made those calls at 7:27 p.m. Based on what Harris had told me, maybe it had already been too late. Maybe by then Abu Khalif's men had already struck.

Just then, I remembered there was still another envelope from Khachigian I had not yet opened. Fortunately, the agents in the front seat were engrossed in a conversation of their own. I wasn't paying much attention, but from the fragments I'd caught so far, they were discussing the arrival of the vice president and how they were being instructed to interface with the Secret Service. That seemed as good an opportunity as any to investigate further without the FBI looking over my shoulder, so I opened my briefcase and pulled out the other sealed envelope. Opening it carefully, so as not to attract their attention, I was stunned to find paperwork detailing my new fractional ownership of a private Learjet.

I quickly scanned the documents in my hands and learned that Khachigian had prepaid for 100,000 flight miles, including fuel costs, pilot time, landing fees, taxes, and other assorted fees. Included in the envelope was a membership card. It did not have my name on it. It didn't have anyone's name on it. It just had a membership number and a PIN code. Reading through the instructions, I learned that all I needed to do was call the 800 number on the back of the card—or the international toll-free number from anywhere outside the U.S.—and punch in my number and PIN. At that point, I would be immediately connected to a flight coordinator who would simply ask where I wanted to depart from, at what time, what my destination was, and how many passengers would be accompanying me. The entire process was anonymous. They didn't care who I was. They just needed the number, the PIN, and six hours of advance notice before departure.

That could come in handy, I thought as I finished reading. Then I put the card in my wallet, the paperwork back in the envelope, and the envelope back in my briefcase.

40

★ ★ ★

An hour later, we were tearing up I-295, heading north.

I used my iPhone to check the financial markets. They were up and running again as of that morning, after having been shut down for several days by the Feds. But already they were tanking. The Dow was down more than six hundred points. The NASDAQ was down more than 5 percent. It shouldn't have been surprising, given how bad the Nikkei, Hang Seng, and other international markets had been in recent days. But seeing everything so deep in the red—and knowing the satisfaction that must be giving Abu Khalif—sent a chill down my spine.

I knew I should be responding to the avalanche of e-mails and phone calls that were pouring in regarding the service, but all I wanted to do just then was play hooky. I'd had no time to think, no time to grieve. I wasn't sleeping well and had no one to talk to. Matt was in even more pain. Allen had his hands full with all the media inquiries. And I certainly wasn't going to pour out my emotions to these agents from the FBI.

Thinking of Allen reminded me of the article he wanted me to read. I pulled up the *Times* app on my phone and looked for the front-page piece by my colleague Bill Sanders. The headline immediately caught my attention: **Egypt Emerges as Unexpected Ally in Hunt for Abu Khalif**. It was datelined Cairo.

As I scanned the story, it became immediately apparent that congressional leaders on both sides of the aisle were furious that the Taylor administration was doing so little to bring the ISIS leader to justice. Yes, the president had ordered new bombing runs and drone strikes. But according to Sanders's reporting, this was not a fundamental change of U.S. strategy. Rather, unnamed congressional leaders—and the unnamed head of a foreign intelligence service— said these attacks were "short-term fixes" aimed at "satiating America's bloodlust for revenge." The air strikes might last for a few weeks, said an anonymous member of the Senate Armed Services Committee, but they would be curtailed again once all the anger at ISIS had calmed down a bit.

"President Taylor has no appetite for a serious and prolonged war against the Islamic State inside Syria," said the unnamed senator. "It doesn't fit his strategy of containing the caliphate rather than crushing it."

Now, Sanders wrote, attention was shifting to Arab intelligence services for help in taking out ISIS leaders and operatives, and Egypt was emerging as chief among equals.

There were several more quotes by Republican senators speaking on background, chastising the White House and State Department for "not being serious" about winning the "great war of our time" and for "seeking sensational headlines, not serious solutions."

This struck me as shoddy journalism. Why was Sanders giving cover to GOP lawmakers, letting them take unnamed potshots at the president? If the Republicans had something of import to say, Sanders should have required them to say it on the record.

Far more interesting was a scathing—and very much on-the-record—statement by the ranking minority member of the U.S. Senate Select Committee on Intelligence, excoriating the administration for not taking specific and decisive action against Abu Khalif in the aftermath of the widespread ISIS attacks inside the U.S.

"Run this [expletive deleted] to ground and blow him to kingdom come," said Jane Oliphant, the senior senator from Rhode Island and former chairwoman of the Democratic National Committee. "What the [expletive deleted] is the White House waiting for? Are we really going to outsource this to the Israelis, the Jordanians, and the Egyptians? All three are great friends and capable allies. But we're the [expletive deleted] United States of America, for crying out loud. It's time for the president to show these [expletive deleted] what Uncle Sam is truly capable of."

Sanders dutifully quoted the president's national security advisor insisting that "every possible measure is being taken" to track down the emir of ISIS and counseling patience for "those in the peanut gallery who perhaps have read a few too many spy thrillers and think hunting terrorists is easy and quick."

However, Sanders also cited an unnamed CIA official who admitted that the fear of ISIS moles in senior positions in government agencies was "nearly paralyzing" the U.S. intelligence community. "No one knows who to trust," he said. "So no one is sharing information and things are getting missed."

"Enter the Egyptians," Sanders wrote. "Working quietly but in remarkably close cooperation with the Israeli Mossad and the Jordanian General Intelligence Directorate, senior officials in Cairo have made the hunt for Abu Khalif a top priority. In the past thirty days, Egyptian police and security forces have arrested twenty-three ISIS operatives. In the process they have scooped up an enormous amount of intelligence about ISIS methods, and more raids and arrests are expected in coming days."

As I kept reading, I forgave Sanders for letting a few Republican senators snipe at their political adversary on background. The rest of his reporting was as riveting as it was detailed. He described intense interrogation sessions of ISIS terrorists by Egyptian agents, the seizure of cell phones and laptops, the cracking of passcodes and encryption software, and even a list of confirmed locations where Abu Khalif had been sighted over the past two months. On that list were the Iraqi cities of Mosul and Dohuk and the Syrian cities of Raqqa, Aleppo, Deir ez-Zor, and al-Mayadin. Given that I myself had theorized that Khalif might be in Raqqa, the ISIS capital in Syria, the story rang true. But Sanders had pieces of the puzzle I did not.

He cited a senior Egyptian intelligence official saying he had actually been privy to grainy photos of Abu Khalif getting into the back of an ambulance in Raqqa, reportedly headed for Deir ez-Zor. However, the official noted, none of the witnesses indicated that Khalif was injured.

"The ISIS leader appears to be using Red Crescent ambulances as his personal taxicabs to obscure his movements," said the Cairo-based official, speaking on the condition of anonymity.

The article didn't quote any sources saying the Egyptians, Jordanians, or Israelis were close to actually finding the ISIS leader. But in the infuriating absence of American leadership, the three countries had apparently banded together on a mission each regarded as vital to its own national security.

Clearly the hunt for Abu Khalif was on. But according to Sanders, the White House wasn't exactly taking the lead.

41

★ ★ ★

We arrived at the Harborside Hotel, and I checked in.

The agents secured my room, then left me to myself and occupied the rooms on either side of mine, though not before cleaning out the minibar, at my request.

"Two years, six months, and three days," I told them as they removed all the alcohol from my room. "One step at a time. One day at a time."

I said it. I meant it. But there was no question I intensely wanted to drink and drink heavily. The pain of the last few days was sinking in more and more, and I desperately wanted an escape. The brutal truth was that I was an alcoholic. It had nearly destroyed me in the past. It was a constant temptation, and though I was determined to manage it, I genuinely feared I was going to crack.

My phone buzzed. It was a text message from my friend Carl Hughes, the longtime deputy director of intelligence at the CIA. In December, after the arrest of then-Director Jack Vaughn on charges of espionage, the president had named Carl the agency's acting director. I immediately dialed the number he gave, eager to hear his voice.

I'd known Carl, now fifty-two, for nearly twenty-five years. We'd first met at American University, where I was an undergrad majoring in political science and he was a grad student studying international affairs. We'd become friends and kept in reasonably close touch over the years as he'd gone off to work at Langley while I'd gone to Columbia for an MA in journalism before taking a job with the *New York Daily News* covering local crime stories prior to landing a position as a foreign correspondent for the Associated Press. We'd both done well for ourselves. Eventually I'd moved over to the *Times* and emerged as the paper's chief national security correspondent. Carl had proven himself one of the most impressive analysts who had ever risen through the ranks of America's intelligence community. Now he had finally been named to the top spot.

His secretary answered. I gave my name and said I was returning Carl's message and wanted to thank him for his condolences. She immediately transferred me to his executive assistant, a man with a military background who, among other responsibilities, was tasked with making sure not just anyone got through to the acting director. Again I explained who I was and why I was calling. I stressed that I was calling as an old friend, not as a journalist. Finally Hughes came on the line.

"J. B., I'm so sorry not to have called sooner," he began. "I just . . ."

His voice trailed off, and as it did, the weight of all that had happened hit me again, and hard.

"Don't worry about it, Carl," I said. "You've got a very full plate."

Nevertheless, he apologized profusely for not being able to come up for the funeral. I told him that was fine, but he insisted on explaining. He'd initially arranged to join the vice president on Air Force Two the following morning and surprise me, but the president had suddenly decided to send him to Moscow on agency business. He was leaving in a few hours.

He asked me how I was doing. He asked how Matt was holding up and what the doctors were saying about Annie and Katie. I told him what I knew, which still wasn't much, then took a deep breath and shifted gears.

"Carl," I began. "I have to ask—"

But he immediately cut me off. "Don't, J. B."

"What?" I said, taken aback. "You don't even know what I was going to say."

"Of course I do—we've known each other too long. You want to ask whether the president is serious about hunting down Abu Khalif. But you can't."

"Why not?"

"Just don't go there."

"Because you can't tell me anything?"

"No, of course I can't," he said. I expected him to say he needed to take another call and let me go. But to my surprise, he continued, perhaps taking pity on me. "Look, I can't say it on the record, of course, and you can never repeat this, but your instincts were spot-on. All the warnings were there. Every light on the dashboard was blinking red. We didn't know certain pieces, but we knew enough. We knew something was coming. We knew it for weeks. We knew ISIS had people here. It was inevitable with all the refugees the president's been welcoming into the country with open arms. We didn't know which ones, of course. There were too many to vet—more than fifty thousand—it was an impossible situation. But I personally briefed the president and the NSC on five separate occasions. I urged him to shut down the airports and seaports. I pleaded with him to delay the State of the Union. He wouldn't hear of it. Any of it. And then the NSA intercepted two calls and a text message. I personally called Larry Beck at the FBI. That's how they found the cell in Birmingham. We were hot on their trail, J. B. Another twenty-four hours, and we would have had them—some of them, anyway."

I was floored—not just that the head of the CIA was telling me so much, even as a friend, but much more by the damning nature of what he was saying. If the president had known all this before any of it had gone down, then he had stood there in the Oval Office and lied to my face. He had stood there in the House Chamber and lied to a joint session of Congress and the country. The state of the union was not strong. ISIS was not on the run. Abu Khalif had not been contained. Rather, he and his minions were coming to kill Americans, and the commander in chief wasn't doing all he could to stop them.

I'd gotten my answer. No, the president wasn't serious about hunting down Abu Khalif. Someone else was going to have to do it. Maybe the Egyptians were up to the task. Or the Israelis. Or perhaps the Jordanians.

But Harrison Taylor could not be trusted to do the job. That much was clear.

42

★ ★ ★

I worked straight through the afternoon.

No lunch. No breaks. I was burning pure rage and fighting a lust for hard liquor. My only hope was to stay busy.

By sundown, I'd finalized the service order, edited and signed off on the program and made sure it got to the printer on time, and talked to the florist multiple times, answering myriad questions while trying not to go insane. All the while, I did my best to make sure everything was coordinated with the pastor, the local police chief, the head of the advance team for the Secret Service, and the vice president's chief of staff. And there were still twenty-six e-mails remaining that had to do with the service, not to mention another thirty-nine from colleagues in D.C. and sources around the world offering their condolences or giving me leads I ought to be following up on.

Rubbing my eyes, I plugged my phone into a wall charger and stood for a moment to stretch. Then I stepped into the bathroom. I splashed warm water on my face and dried myself off with a towel and tried to decide what to do next. Order some room service? Turn my phone off and watch a movie on pay-per-view? Go down to the gym and work out? None of the options sounded attractive. I had no appetite. No interest in the latest garbage from Hollywood.

No desire to be babysat by my FBI handlers while I spent an hour on the treadmill. What I ought to be doing—what I wanted to be doing, I decided—was tracking down everything I could find on Paul Pritchard, Walid Hussam, and Mohammed bin Zayed and finding a way to contact them. The clock was ticking. The information was valuable, Khachigian had made clear, but it might also be perishable. *Use it or lose it.* I had to move quickly.

I still didn't want to use my own phone for anything sensitive, in case anyone—the FBI or ISIS—might be watching. Instead, I grabbed the satellite phone Khachigian had left me in the safe-deposit box. Powering it up, I quickly got a signal, pulled up Google, and ran a search on the three names mentioned in the spymaster's letter to me.

The first was Paul Pritchard. I didn't immediately find a LinkedIn bio for him, but I did find a 2012 profile on him in the *Washington Post* that would have to suffice for now. Pritchard, it said, was a former intelligence officer in the U.S. Army who had served in both Iraq and Kuwait in the first Gulf War before joining the CIA. From there, he'd been recruited into the Clandestine Service, working his way up to the rank of station chief in Damascus. But this was odd. The *Post* article said that Pritchard was ultimately fired from the agency by Khachigian for reasons that weren't immediately clear. Then, in 2013, the *Wall Street Journal* reported that he had been killed in a car bomb in Khartoum. Was that possible? Was he really dead? Then why was he on Khachigian's list?

I found several mentions of Walid Hussam, who, according to Al Arabiya, was a former chief of Egyptian intelligence back during the days when Hosni Mubarak was president. Once again I was confused. At first glance, it seemed like Hussam had been out of the spy game for a long time. He'd written a book on the Arab Spring that hadn't sold many copies, though I found a few unflattering reviews. He'd briefly taught at the American University in Cairo. Then he'd dropped off the radar screen. I couldn't find a single news story about him, or even mentioning him, from the past half decade. Why, then, would Khachigian send me to him?

The third name on Khachigian's "must-see" list was Mohammed bin Zayed. The name was vaguely familiar to me. I knew he was a member of the royal family in the United Arab Emirates, but I couldn't remember anything else about him. The Google search, however, struck pay dirt. I found a wealth of stories about him, all indicating he had served for almost two decades as the UAE's ambassador to Iraq before being severely injured in a bomb blast in Baghdad almost three and a half years earlier. That, apparently, had retired him, which was likely why I hadn't ever done any business with him. More recently, however, he had been named the UAE's chief of intelligence.

So, I thought, at least one of the people on Khachigian's list was still active in the intelligence business. The others seemed to be out of the game or, in Paul Pritchard's case, maybe even no longer alive. Was it possible the old spy chief's information was out of date?

Just then I heard footsteps in the hallway and a soft voice outside my door. *"You sure that's the room?"*

I quickly powered down Khachigian's satphone and put it back in the briefcase and tucked the case under the bed. Then I turned and faced the door, my heart pounding fast and hard. I waited for a movement and noticed flickering shadows under the door to the hallway. Someone was pacing. I couldn't tell exactly if it was one or two, but whoever they were, they were deciding what to do next.

Rising to my feet, I moved quickly across the carpet and pressed myself against the wall to the left of the door, straining to hear more of their conversation. I expected them to burst into my room at any moment, and I had no idea what I would do when they did. Everything got quiet. The pacing stopped. So did the talking. Whatever was happening, it was happening now.

I decided not to wait. Grabbing the handle with my left hand, I gave it a hard turn and flung the door open, determined to face the threat head-on.

I was prepared for the worst. Instead, standing in front of me—startled and alone—was Agent Art Harris, holding a cell phone against his ear.

"Never mind," he said to whoever was on the other end. "It's the right room. I'll call you back."

I started breathing again.

"Hey," Harris said calmly. "Expecting someone else?"

"Wasn't expecting you, that's for sure," I said.

He stood there for a moment, waiting for me to say something.

"Would you like to come in?" I asked finally.

Expressionless, Harris entered, and I shut the door behind him.

"Please tell me it's not that easy for someone to approach my room," I said.

"No, don't worry," Harris replied. "There are agents stationed in the lobby, at every exit in the hotel, and at both ends of your hallway. And video cameras feeding into a makeshift operations center on the first floor. Believe me, we've got you covered. I just forgot your exact room number, that's all."

"So why are you here?" I asked.

"We have a problem," he said.

"What's that?"

"We've arrested a suspect."

"That's a good thing, isn't it?" I said.

"Yes and no."

"Meaning what?"

"Meaning, yes, we've captured an ISIS operative. Wonderful. The problem is that from the information we've pulled off this guy's phone, we now believe there are at least two more ISIS sleeper cells operating in New England."

"And you're worried they're going to hit the memorial service tomorrow?"

"No. Between the Secret Service, the bureau, and the local authorities, we're confident the service will go safely and without a hitch."

"Then what?"

"We're worried about what could happen after the VP goes back to D.C. and the circus leaves town," Harris said. "We believe these two cells may have orders to kill you and the rest of your family."

It was as if Harris had just sucker punched me. "You're saying they're coming to finish us off?"

Harris didn't say anything just yet, but I could see it in his eyes.

"I see," I said, forcing myself to take deep breaths. "So what exactly do you recommend?"

"You're not going to like it."

"I already don't like it."

"I wish there was another way, but honestly, I don't see one."

"What is it?"

"We need to move you into WITSEC," Harris said.

"Into *what*?"

"The federal Witness Security Program."

43

★ ★ ★

"You've got to be kidding me," I snapped.

I had barely eaten. I had barely slept. I was completely over-whelmed by everything I had to do to get ready for the next day. And now this?

"That's your plan?" I asked. "You and a bunch of geniuses in Washington want the four of us to put on fake mustaches and move to Utah or New Mexico or Alaska or wherever, and change our names and raise ostriches and be completely cut off from our friends, our relatives, and everything connected to our previous lives? Are you nuts?"

"Well, I'm not sure about the ostriches and fake mustaches, but if you'll just take a moment and listen—"

"No," I said, suddenly feeling claustrophobic. "That's not some-thing I have time to listen to."

"J. B., you need to sit down and listen to me very carefully," Harris said calmly but with authority. "You and your family are being systematically hunted down by ISIS. Why? Because you know Abu Khalif. Because you've seen him. Because you've talked to him. Because you've watched him—personally watched him—kill people. And because he personally told you his plans to attack Americans inside the homeland. No other American citizen that we know of has met him. No other American could actually identify him in a lineup, could identify his voice. That's why he wants you dead. He needed you at the beginning to get his message out. And now that he's done with you—now that you're no longer of value to him—he's going to kill you. You're a threat to him. When we capture Abu Khalif—and we will; make no mistake about it—he's going to stand trial. He's going to give an account for all the blood he has spilled, all the lives he has destroyed. And then you're going to testify against him. If my colleagues and I do our job right, he will pay for his crimes against humanity. He will be executed by lethal injection. But that's going to take time, and at this moment, you and your family are in grave danger. And that's why I'm saying—"

"Forget it," I said, cutting him off. "You're wasting your time."

But Harris would not be dissuaded. "That's why I'm saying we need you as a federal witness. If you agree to this—"

"I said forget it. I'm a reporter, not an informant for the FBI."

Harris wouldn't let himself get derailed. He just kept on talking. "If you agree to testify, the federal government is empowered to protect you and your family. We can't force you. But if you agree, we can relocate you. We can give you all new identities. We can make sure Abu Khalif and his men never find you or your family. But only if you sign this." He pulled a document out of his breast pocket and handed it to me.

"What's this?" I asked.

"It's a memorandum of understanding," he said. "It explains exactly what will happen, how it'll all work, and what your responsibilities will be."

"Keep it," I said. "I don't want it."

"What about Matt?"

"He doesn't want it either."

"And Annie and Katie—what about them?" he countered. "You're saying they don't want federal protection after all they've been through? You're saying they don't want a chance to heal from their wounds and go on with their lives free from fear that one day Abu Khalif and his men will come and finish what they've started? Are you really going to blow this off and put their lives—all of your lives—in jeopardy again?"

I didn't want to hear any of it.

"Come on, Collins. You owe it to them—and to yourself—to at least read this over, talk to Matt, think it through, and then decide. But you're going to need to move quickly. We don't have much time."

My mind was reeling. I couldn't believe what I was being told. On the face of it, it all sounded ridiculous, like something out of the movies. But as much as I didn't want to admit it, Harris had a point.

"So how would it work—big picture?" I asked.

"First, you and Matt would need to read and sign this agreement. Second, we'd put you all on an air ambulance—preferably tomorrow afternoon, after the memorial service. I've been instructed to personally take you to the location we've chosen for you."

"Which is where?"

"You'll know when we get there."

"Don't we get to choose?"

"It's better if you don't."

"Why?"

"Less chance you'll pick someplace you've already talked about with family and friends, someplace people might know—or guess—where to look."

"Fine," I said, even less happy with that scenario. "What then?"

"You'd have a medical team taking care of Annie and Katie twenty-four hours a day, seven days a week, until they recover. You'd have private tutoring for Katie when she starts to recover, until she's well enough to go to a local school. You and Matt would each receive a stipend of about $60,000 a year for the first few years, until you find jobs and get on your feet. And of course, you'd all have new identities. You'd be completely off the grid—no linkage with your past life whatsoever."

"No contact with family?"

"No."

"Friends?"

Harris shook his head.

"Colleagues from work?"

"I'm afraid not," Harris said. "If you agree to this, it means you agree to all the stipulations—first and foremost that you can have absolutely no contact with anyone from your past. I realize that's hard to contemplate, but believe me, it's for your own safety."

"And if we do this, you think it'll work?" I asked. "You can really keep us all safe?"

"We can," Harris insisted. "Since we started the program in 1971, we've protected nearly twenty thousand people."

"And how many have you lost?"

"Of the people who followed the rules?" he asked.

"Yeah," I said.

"None."

44

* ★ *

Matt arrived at the hotel just after ten.

I'd already spoken to him briefly by phone to give him a summary of what Harris was proposing. Neither of us was permitted to use our own cell phones. So Harris had insisted I use his phone and that Matt use the phone of one of the FBI agents guarding him.

The bureau's technical division was still trying to determine how the terrorists had known we had been planning to be home by seven o'clock that fateful night. Until they could rule out the notion that ISIS had somehow tapped either or both of our numbers, Harris said we needed to be extra careful.

Matt greeted me in the lobby of the Harborside with a bear hug and wouldn't let go.

"You look horrible," I whispered, trying to break the ice.

"Thanks," he whispered back, finally releasing me.

"You eat anything today?" I asked.

He looked at me for a moment, then shook his head.

"I didn't think so," I said, motioning him to follow me down the hallway to the hotel's main restaurant. Since the bureau—in cooperation with the U.S. Secret Service—had commandeered the entire hotel, there were no other diners. I asked Harris if he could get someone to whip up a couple of omelets, some sausage and bacon, and a fresh pot of coffee. He radioed for one of his guys to make it happen. Then he and his colleagues took a few tables by the door.

Matt and I sat at a table in the back. As Matt removed his coat, scarf, and gloves, I asked about Annie and Katie. There was still nothing to report. Nothing good. But nothing bad either. I asked if Matt had been getting any sleep. Not much, he said. He'd tried, he insisted. But sleep simply would not come. He'd experienced too much horror, and now the FBI was telling us we had to give up our very identities and all contact with family and friends.

"So what do you think?" I began, bracing myself because I already knew the answer.

"What do I think? *What do I think?* I think Harris is insane," Matt replied. "Who does he think we are? Cowards? He thinks we're just going to give up our lives? Absolutely not. No way."

"That's what I told him," I said calmly.

"What we need is for the president to go after Abu Khalif and take him out—period," Matt continued. "Khalif should be on the run, not us."

"You're right," I agreed.

"Then why are we even having this conversation?"

"Because the president isn't going to do it," I said. "The country might be buying this latest bombing attack—and the new drone strikes—but it won't last. He's not serious. You know it. I know it. Abu Khalif knows it. And though he won't say it, Harris knows it too. That's why he wants to get us out of harm's way now, while there's still time."

"But it's crazy, J. B.—completely nuts."

"I know."

"I'm not going to do it—*I'm not*," Matt insisted. "Are you?"

Just then one of the agents brought over a pot of coffee, two mugs, some fresh cream, and some sugar. I kept quiet.

The moment the agent had gone back to the kitchen, Matt pressed me for an answer. "Is that what you want to do, J. B.? Hide for the rest of your life? Is that how we were raised?"

"It's not just about us, though," I said in a hushed tone, leaning toward him. "It's about Mom and Josh. More important, it's about Annie and Katie. If we stay out in the open, they're going to hunt us down and kill us. That's it. That's the deal."

"Can't these guys protect us?"

"Yes, if we go into the program."

"And if we don't?"

"Then pretty soon we're on our own."

Matt said nothing. He poured us each a cup of coffee, put a packet of sugar in his, and started stirring with a fork, as the agent had forgotten to bring us any spoons. But he didn't take a sip, and neither did I.

"Look—if it was just me, I'd probably take my chances," I said quietly. "And maybe if it were just the two of us, we'd do the same. But if we could wind the clock back and give Mom and Annie and the kids the chance to slip away and live safely in Montana or Arizona or wherever, just the six of us, don't you think they'd have taken that in a millisecond?"

Matt remained quiet, and in the silence I suddenly realized I was talking myself into a decision I couldn't have imagined making just a few hours before.

"Matt, this is my fault. I know that, and I'm sick about it. But I can't undo what's happened. This is it. This is our reality now. And you and I can't simply think about what we want. We need to do what's best for Annie and Katie, and as much as we're resisting it, I think we both know what that is."

45

★ ★ ★

The agent brought us the omelets and the side dishes.

We nodded our thanks and waited again for him to leave us.

"There's something else I have to tell you," I said.

My older brother just looked at me. He was already on information overload. What I was about to tell him wasn't going to help.

After making sure there was no one approaching us, I told him about my visit to Sullivan & Sullivan, about the will and the $30 million—give or take—we had just inherited. I didn't tell him about the fake passports or my new fractional ownership of a Learjet. Those weren't details he needed to know right now, or maybe ever. The first part was enough.

"Even as we speak, the Sullivans are setting up two untraceable bank accounts in the Cayman Islands, one for you and one for me," I said. "At the same time, they're liquidating all of Khachigian's assets. The house will take time to be sold, obviously. But the rest will be in our accounts in the next twenty-four hours."

He looked pale, close to being in shock. "What about Laura?" he asked.

I nodded. "I asked that too. She'll get a big share as well."

"And taxes?"

"I've already instructed the Sullivans to set aside whatever they think we'll need to pay into a separate account and to pay our tax bills as soon as possible."

"And their share as executors?"

"All taken care of."

"J. B.—I can't believe this," Matt said. "I don't even know what to say."

I shrugged. "I know. I had the same reaction. I've just had an extra day to process it."

"And you told all this to Harris?"

"Of course not."

"Why not?"

"He doesn't need to know. It's none of his business."

"But if we end up going into the Witness Protection Program— which still sounds ridiculous to me, by the way—isn't he going to find out eventually?"

"I don't know. Maybe. We can worry about that later. For now, all we have to worry about is keeping you and Katie and Annie safe. And that means we have to come up with an answer for Harris."

"But you're not—"

"Keep your voice down, Matt."

Harris and his colleagues turned toward us. I smiled and nodded.

"Fine," Matt said, more quietly this time. "But you're not *seriously* considering this, are you?"

"Yes, I am, actually. But that's not the point, Matt. It's not about what I do. It's about keeping you all safe. If I don't go into the program, none of you can. I'm the witness. I'm the one they need to protect."

I could see in my brother's eyes he couldn't tell whether to laugh in my face or get up and punch Harris in his.

"You wouldn't be able to write for the *Times* anymore."

"No."

"You couldn't write your memoirs."

"No."

"Couldn't write op-eds."

"Not if I want to have a long and happy life," I said softly, knowing how hard it was for him to hear it. "Eat your omelet."

"It's cold."

"Whose fault is that?"

Matt stared at the eggs, then at me. Finally he sprinkled on some salt and pepper and wolfed down the entire meal in just a few minutes. I took a few bites of my own meal but couldn't summon any appetite.

"So how does this play out?" Matt asked when he had finished and had washed it all down with another cup of coffee.

"What do you mean?"

"I mean they have to get rid of us, right? So how do they do that?"

I took that as a good sign. Despite his resistance, he was asking questions, which meant he was finally considering the idea, which meant he might actually get to yes.

"Once we're safe in wherever they're going to resettle us, the news will come out that we've all been killed in a car bombing just outside of Portland."

"Kinda grim."

"Yeah."

"When would that happen?"

"Next few days."

"And then?"

"There'll be another memorial service, I guess. I imagine there will be a lot of press. Big story, right? Another terrorist attack and all? And then that's it."

"Everyone we know will think we're dead."

"Yeah."

"And that's all right with you?" he asked again.

I pushed my plate away angrily. "No, it's not all right with me. But, Matt, how many ways can I say it? The guy the FBI caught? He had your private mobile phone number. He had mine. He had floor plans of Mom's house. He had dozens of photos of your family, notes on their daily routines, friends, acquaintances, church attendance, favorite restaurants, you name it. And he had a trunk full of automatic weapons and plastic explosives. The guy was a professional. And there are three more just like him in his cell—three more the FBI haven't caught yet. Harris says the guy was also in contact with two other cells in the region. He isn't just being dramatic. This is real."

"Can't they catch these guys and be done with it?"

"Maybe, maybe not," I said. "Harris says they've got more than three hundred agents hunting them down. So yeah, he's confident they'll catch them. He's just not confident that will be the end of it."

"'Cause he's never going away," Matt said, half under his breath, looking out the windows again at the twinkling lights across the water.

There was no hint of a question, just a statement of a bitter reality. And he was right. I couldn't tell him what Carl Hughes had told me. But it wasn't even necessary.

"No," I said quietly. "Abu Khalif is never going away."

46

★ ★ ★

BAR HARBOR, MAINE

It was the dead of night, and I lay in my bed, tossing and turning.

Unable to sleep, I just stared up at the ceiling fan as the moonlight streaming in through the windows cast long, dark shadows across the stucco surface. The fan itself was off, of course. After all, the temperature outside was well below zero and sinking. A new storm was approaching. I could hear the howling winter winds gusting across the North Atlantic, rattling the windows.

My hands mindlessly toyed with my grandfather's pocket watch, which now read 3:18, but my thoughts were a thousand miles away—well over five thousand miles away, actually, in Israel. Against my better judgment, I'd sent Yael a text. Told her I missed her. Asked what she was up to. Told her I wished she would write and hoped she was well. In Jerusalem, it was now after 10 a.m. on a workday. She was, no doubt, immersed in meetings, perhaps with the prime minister, perhaps with the full security cabinet. I didn't really expect to hear from her. But if I was about to "die" in an FBI-staged car bombing, I guess I just wanted to say good-bye. Inside, I raged against the notion that I would never be able to see her again, never be allowed to talk to her again. Not that we'd interacted much in the last few months anyway. But *never*? If not for the need to make sure Matt and his family were finally and truly safe, the thought would be inconceivable.

The latest news from the hospital was not encouraging. Annie's vital signs were stable. But earlier that night, Matt had received a call from the ICU that Katie's breathing had suddenly stopped. They'd caught it instantly, thank God. They'd gotten her breathing again within seconds, and she was now on a respirator. At this point there was nothing we could do but pray. And try to sleep.

If only I were following my own advice.

I got up and got a glass of water. However frigid it was outside, I was soaked with sweat. Was I coming down with something? Did I have a fever, or was I just consumed with anxiety? I had no idea. But one look at my bloodshot eyes in the bathroom mirror was enough to make me wonder if I needed to check into the hospital for a few days myself.

Matt was clearly going through the five stages of grief. At the moment, he seemed to be shifting from denial to anger. I, on the other hand, was calm and functioning better than Matt. But that was simply because I was still fully immersed in a state of denial—and not just because of the murders of my family members, but because of the murders of so many people I loved.

All around me, the death toll kept mounting, and I just kept moving. Somewhere deep in the recesses of my mind, a faint and distant voice was telling me I had to stop. I couldn't keep up this pace. I couldn't keep living off adrenaline. I had to face the reality that my world was crashing down all around me, or I was going to crash too. Everything I'd known, everything I'd trusted, everything I'd ever taken for granted, was rapidly coming to an end. My career. My connections with everyone I'd ever worked with or befriended. Even my name, my very identity. I knew it, but I certainly hadn't accepted it. How could I?

Clicking off the bathroom light, I walked back through the

bedroom to the windows overlooking the water and pulled aside the drapes. I stared out into the oncoming storm. Thick, heavy clouds rolled in off the sea, obscuring the full moon and shrouding my room with darkness.

I still had no idea what I was going to tell Harris in the morning. Matt and I had spent more time arguing about it before going to bed. He'd kept trying to convince me how ridiculous the FBI agent's plan was. And everything he'd said had made perfect sense.

There was only one argument I could make in response: We were all going to die unless we accepted Harris's offer. It was a compelling argument because it was true. But that didn't make it any easier to accept.

I flipped on the television and roamed through a hundred and fifty channels, but there was nothing I wanted to watch. I scrolled through my iTunes account, but there was nothing I wanted to listen to. I checked my messages again, but Yael hadn't responded. Why would she? She had a life of meaning and purpose. I was about to give mine up.

★　★　★

I suddenly woke up to someone pounding at my door.

Groggy and disoriented, I forced myself out of bed and stumbled to see who in the world was making such a racket so early. It was Matt, and the look on his face told me I was in serious trouble.

"J. B., what are you doing?"

"Sleeping," I said. "Why aren't you?"

"We're waiting for you."

"For what?" I asked.

"It's 9:15."

"And?"

"You were supposed to meet us in the lobby ten minutes ago—it's time to go."

47

★ ★ ★

Fifteen minutes later, Matt and I were in the lobby.

I told Harris we'd have an answer for him after the memorial service. Then I told him Matt and I were going to drive ourselves to the church, not be driven by him and the agents he'd assigned to us. He didn't like it. But I refused to budge. I told him he could follow behind us, but my brother and I needed to be alone before the service, and that was final. We weren't under arrest. We weren't employees of the federal government. We hadn't yet agreed to enter the Witness Protection Program. The FBI had no legal basis to prevent us from doing what we thought was best, and at the moment, this was it.

We immediately exited the hotel, not waiting for Harris's response. I headed straight for the driver's side of the black Lincoln Navigator assigned to us. Matt headed straight for the passenger's side.

"Out," I told the agent behind the wheel.

He just stared at me with a blank expression.

"Please," I added.

A moment later, he pressed on the wire running to his ear. He radioed back, asking if he'd heard right. Apparently he had. Mystified at such an unprecedented turn of events, he got out. I got in, and Matt climbed in beside me. The agent moved to get in the back, but

I hit the gas and shot out onto the street without him. I turned left on West Street, then took a right on Main, as the agents scrambled into their vehicles to catch up.

"Good work," Matt said as he quickly fastened his seat belt and held on to the handle over the door. "Now you've got the FBI mad at us. Brilliant."

It was snowing again. Another inch and a half of fresh powder had fallen overnight. The forecast was calling for another few inches throughout the day, and the temperature was a mere twelve degrees. I notched up the heater and flipped the headlights on. "We need to talk," I said.

"About your driving or your manners?" he asked.

"About Harris's offer," I said.

"I thought last night you said we had no choice, that we'd die if we didn't accept."

"I did say that. But I was up most of the night thinking about it from every angle, you know, to see if there was any other way."

"Is there?"

"I haven't come up with anything yet."

"Then we have to say yes, right?"

"Maybe not," I said.

"But what about Annie? What about Katie?" he asked. "You kept saying we had to put them first."

"We do—absolutely," I said as we approached the first of several police checkpoints in a town that today looked like an armed camp.

"And?"

"And I don't know," I admitted as I slowed to a halt. "As far as I can tell, we have until the service is over to come up with an alternative, or we're going to have to say yes. And I don't want to say yes. I really don't."

We both handed over our photo IDs to the heavily armed officer, then showed him the pins we were wearing, one from the FBI, the other from the Secret Service, indicating that we had all-access clearance for the event at the church and the reception to follow back at the Harborside. The officer checked them carefully, then nodded and told us to pop our rear cargo door.

"I got the first good night's sleep I've had in days last night," Matt said as we idled. "You know why? Because I stopped fighting this thing and decided to believe you."

"That we'd be safer by saying yes?"

"Yeah."

"That this is the best chance—and maybe the only one—to protect Annie and Katie?"

"Exactly."

The officer radioed ahead our names and the license plate number. Meanwhile, a K-9 unit sniffed for explosives as another officer used a mirror attached to a long metal pole to check the underside of the car for explosives. Finally we were waved through, just as Harris and his men pulled up behind us in two more Navigators.

I took a right onto Mount Desert Street and passed the church parking lot that Allen was using as a media staging center. It was lined with rows of satellite trucks and cars bearing the logos of dozens of media outlets. Then we turned into the parking lot beside St. Saviour's Episcopal Church. There were local police and Secret Service agents everywhere. But beyond their vehicles with all their flashing red-and-blue lights, the lot was mostly empty, and there were no reporters or cameras in view. This clearly was not the parking area for the general public. Not today.

An officer wearing a bright-orange safety vest pointed us to our spot. I parked and turned off the car but didn't get out.

"Matt, do you remember what I told you in Amman?" I asked.

"You mean that Abu Khalif had threatened to kill you and all of us if you didn't report exactly what he wanted you to report?" Matt asked.

"Right."

"Of course I remember. How could I forget?"

"Well, before we go in there, I just need to say this face-to-face."

"What?"

"I'm sorry."

"For what?"

"I never should have written those stories. It wasn't just my life at stake. It was all of yours. I had no right to put you all in harm's way."

"No, don't say that, J. B.—you had to do those stories. I know that."

"No, I didn't."

"Yeah, you did—the world had to know."

"But I got Mom killed. I got Josh killed. And for what?"

"This isn't your fault, J. B.," Matt shot back with a vehemence I didn't expect. "You did your job, and I'm proud of you. This isn't your fault. It's Abu Khalif's and his alone."

"But I—"

"Stop it. Seriously—just stop. You've done a lot of stupid things in your life, a lot of stuff I would never have done. But telling the world who ISIS really is—who Abu Khalif really is—wasn't one of them. Yeah, it cost us—more than we ever imagined. But it also saved a lot of lives. And the truth is, I know where Josh and Mom are. They're in heaven, right now, with Christ. They're safe. They're free. And someday Katie and Annie and I are going to be there with them. No more pain. No more sorrow. No more tears. God will wipe them all away. The only thing that really scares me—terrifies me, actually—is the thought that you won't be there with us."

48

★ ★ ★

As we got out of the Navigator, Harris and his men pulled into the lot.

A moment later, we could hear the sirens and the motorcycles, and soon the motorcade roared up, stopping just a few yards away from us. Secret Service agents in long winter coats and black Ray-Bans fanned out to set up their perimeter. I watched as the head of the detail surveyed the scene and received a status check from each of his agents. Then he opened the door of the armor-plated and snow-covered black Chevy Suburban. Immediately Vice President Martin Holbrooke stepped out and came directly over to Matt and me.

"Mr. Vice President, thank you for coming," I said, taking off my gloves and shaking his hand.

"Gentlemen, it's an honor to be here," Holbrooke replied. "I'm so sorry for your loss. On behalf of the president and me, I hope you'll accept our sincerest condolences."

"Thank you, sir, that's very kind," I said. "I don't believe you've ever met my brother, Matt."

"No, can't say I have had the pleasure—good to meet you, son," the VP said, turning to shake Matt's hand. "I can't pretend to understand the pain you're both going through. But I want you to know how much the president and I—and the nation—respect you both and how committed we are to bringing those responsible to justice."

I stiffened—not visibly, I hoped. I wasn't looking for a fight. Not here. Not now. I just wanted to make it through the day and help Matt do the same. But to hear the second most powerful man in the world lie to my face—on the grounds of a church, no less—was almost more than I could bear. Neither Holbrooke nor the president was serious about tracking down and terminating the emir of the Islamic State.

Why not just admit it? I thought. *Why not just walk into the press center down the street, gather a bunch of reporters around, look into the cameras, and say to the American people, "Look, the president and I feel really bad about all the terrorism that Abu Khalif and ISIS have unleashed over the past days, months, and years. We didn't see the attack on the peace summit in Amman coming. We didn't pay attention to the warnings about the coming attacks on the Capitol or the rest of the country, much less on this little fishing village on the coast of Maine. Sure, we feel bad for the Collins family—and for all who have suffered at the hands of Radical Islam. And sure, we're comfortable lying and telling you we're winning, that we'll never rest until we make Abu Khalif pay. But the truth is we've got better things to do than be obsessed with Abu Khalif. Dealing with the Middle East isn't why we ran for office, and frankly we're getting tired of thinking and talking about it constantly. There are much bigger priorities to deal with here at home than wasting so much time and money on events half a world away. So we're cutting our Sunni Arab allies loose. We've offered the Jordanians barely any financial assistance to rebuild their capital. We're not providing the Egyptians enough helicopters or drones or night-vision goggles or other state-of-the-art equipment to hunt down ISIS leaders. Neither of us attended the funeral of the Israeli prime minister. We're slashing the American defense budget. We're demoralizing our armed forces and intelligence community. We're forcing a whole lot of good, experienced, irreplaceable men and women out of the military at a time we need them most. And we really couldn't care less. This is what we're doing. And there's nothing you can do to stop us."*

As far as I was concerned, *that* was the truth—and it made my blood boil.

But I held my tongue.

It wasn't as much of a struggle for Matt. It's not that he didn't have strong views, but he was a genuinely nice person. He didn't hold a grudge. He simply didn't see the value in it. And for all his disagreements on policy, he really was grateful the vice president of the United States had traveled from Washington to attend a memorial service for his family members. So as we stood there in the parking lot, the snow swirling about our faces, he thanked Holbrooke with a sincerity that both impressed and eluded me.

At the encouragement of the Secret Service, we began walking up the freshly shoveled sidewalk and across a courtyard, Matt and Holbrooke taking the lead, me a few steps behind.

As we entered a side door, we were greeted by Pastor Jeremiah Brooks, my mom's pastor, and the rector who officiated here at St. Saviour's, a kindly silver-haired woman. She handed each of us a program, and then the bells started ringing. It was precisely ten o'clock. Everyone but us was in their seats. The service was set to begin.

49

★ ★ ★

Pastor Brooks led Matt and me out into the sanctuary, to the pew in the first row.

The vice president and his security detail followed right behind us.

The first people we saw were Annie's parents and two younger sisters, all of whom had arrived in town just a short time earlier after visiting the hospital in Portland. They were sitting in the second row, dressed in black, right behind our assigned seats, and they were a picture of grief. The youngest, still in her teens, was sobbing. Matt handed her a handkerchief I suspected he'd planned to use himself. Annie's mother was barely keeping it together. Her mascara was already smeared and the service hadn't even started. Annie's father, a onetime Anglican priest and now an Indiana farmer with a tanned, leathery face and thick, calloused hands, was doing his best to be the stoic comforter for his family, but he looked like he'd been run over by a truck. He gave Matt an awkward hug. This was not a man comfortable with any displays of affection, least of all in public.

When we were all seated, the rector stepped to the front. She welcomed everyone and then introduced Pastor Brooks.

Brooks, a lanky man in his sixties, looked somber as he stepped to the pulpit, opened his Bible, and organized his notes. "Thank you all for coming," he began, taking his reading glasses off to look out over the crowd of nearly three hundred people. "We are gathered this morning to honor, remember, and celebrate the lives of Margaret Claire Collins and Joshua James Collins."

The two caskets—one long, one short, each adorned with flowers—stood on metal supports at the front of the sanctuary. That put them about two yards away from us, and I found myself staring at the caskets as the pastor continued his opening remarks. Brooks explained that he had been my mother's pastor for more than thirty years. He thanked Matt and me for asking him to officiate, and thanked the St. Saviour's rector and staff for their hospitality. Finally he thanked the vice president for "honoring us with your presence." Then he began his message.

I had no intention of listening. If I was going to come up with an alternative to the plan proposed by Agent Harris, now was the time to do it. Still, I was sitting in the front row, directly beside the vice president. I couldn't exactly flip the program over and begin sketching out my plan. I had to at least look interested, and for me that posed a distinct challenge. Because I wasn't.

To make matters worse, Brooks kept looking at Matt and me. Not the whole time, of course. He was addressing the entire congregation, but his gaze kept returning to us again and again, and it made me uncomfortable. After today, I couldn't imagine I'd ever see this man again. I didn't need him preaching to me. And yet he did.

"In the New Testament, the apostle Paul teaches us that 'to be absent from the body' is 'to be present with the Lord,'" Brooks explained. "If you knew Maggie and Josh at all, you know that both of them had placed their simple trust in the shed blood of Jesus Christ on Calvary and that they are with him now and forever."

His accent suggested southern New Hampshire roots, possibly even Boston, not Maine. It was vaguely reminiscent of how my grandfather used to talk.

"Both Maggie and Josh knew they were deeply loved by God. They truly believed the Word of God as recorded in the Bible: 'I have loved you with an everlasting love; therefore I have drawn you with lovingkindness.' They truly believed what the Lord said through the prophet Jeremiah: 'I know the plans I have for you, plans for good and not for evil, plans to give you a future and a hope.' What's more, they both believed that Jesus was, in fact, the Messiah, the Savior, who fulfilled the messianic prophecies, who died on the cross, and who rose from the dead on the third day. I had the privilege of kneeling down and praying with Maggie the day she received Christ as her Savior and Lord by faith, the day she was forgiven of her sins and born again by the Holy Spirit. And almost three decades later, I had the great joy and honor of praying with Josh as he, too, decided to give his life to Christ. I know what they prayed, and I know how their lives changed as a result. That is why I can say with absolute certainty that they both knew the blessed hope of the gospel message."

Again Brooks looked at Matt and me. I looked away.

"Now, there are many things I loved and admired about Maggie Collins. But perhaps at the top of the list was that she was a faithful member of our choir. She was there every Sunday morning, rain or shine, and she sang with all her heart. She sang not for me or the congregation but to her Savior. You could hear it in her beautiful voice. You could see it in her lovely, sparkling eyes. She didn't just believe she was going to heaven when she died—she *knew* it. She believed Christ's promise, 'I am the resurrection and the life; he who believes in Me will live even if he dies.' She believed his words to the repentant thief on the cross that 'today you will be with Me in Paradise.' Without a shadow of any doubt at all, she absolutely *knew* that when she breathed her last breath here on earth, she would take her first breath in heaven in the very presence of her God and Redeemer forever and ever—and frankly, she couldn't wait."

Memories of my mom singing in the choir came flooding back.

And she didn't just sing in church. I suddenly found myself remembering her singing or humming old hymns of the faith all the time—while she was cooking, while she was cleaning, while she was driving to the supermarket. The woman simply wouldn't stop. It used to drive me crazy. But what I wouldn't give now to hear her hum "It Is Well with My Soul" one more time.

"And little Josh—oh, what a heart for Jesus," the pastor continued. "He would come up to Bar Harbor in the summers to visit his grandmother, and he would participate in our vacation Bible school, and he was such a joy. Two summers ago Josh memorized sixty-two Bible verses in six weeks. *Sixty-two!* His favorite was not exactly one you'd expect for a young boy. It was John 15:13—the words of our Savior: 'Greater love has no one than this, that one lay down his life for his friends.' Now, I have to say, I've been pastoring a long, long time, and I've met a whole lot of kids, but I never met anyone quite like Josh."

The more the pastor spoke, the deeper my remorse became. I thought about how little I really knew Matt's kids and how much I had missed in their lives. I'd never known Josh had memorized so much Scripture. Nor that he'd had a favorite verse. Nor what it was. And then it struck me that this was the very verse Khachigian had quoted in his letter to me.

"Last Thursday night, what looked like a tragedy to us was not a tragedy for Maggie and Josh," the pastor continued. "The spirits of these beloved family members and friends were taken from us. But they are not lost. Oh no. Maggie and Josh are gone, but they are not dead. They are more alive today than they have ever been. These two saints are alive and well in the throne room of heaven. Right at this moment, Maggie and Josh are worshiping at the feet of the King of kings and the Lord of lords, our great God and Redeemer, Jesus Christ. Their race is finished. Their mission here on this earth is complete. They are home, safe and sound, awaiting us to join them, if we, too, are in Christ. But, my friends, your only hope of seeing them again is to give your soul to the God they entrusted their souls to, and to do it before you breathe your last here on earth."

As I stared at those coffins, the finality of it all hit me hard. For the past several days, I'd been living on adrenaline, duty, and denial. But sitting there in that church, looking at those wooden boxes, the brutal, unfair, cruel reality finally came crashing down on me. Mom and Josh were gone. Forever. They were never coming back. And all the family events I'd missed, skipped, ignored—they were gone too, never to be recaptured.

"My friends, one day, whether we want to or not, whether we're ready or not, you and I will stand before the judgment seat of Christ," the pastor continued, his voice unexpectedly calm, his manner surprisingly gentle, not like the hellfire-and-brimstone preachers of my cynical imagination. "We're all going to pay the piper. If you're still an unforgiven sinner when you die, the Bible says you'll be the one who pays for your own sins. That is, you'll go to hell, forever, with no way of escape. But the Bible also says that if we repent and receive Christ, then he pays for our sins—in fact, he already did, when he died on the cross in Jerusalem two thousand years ago.

"So today you have a choice to make: say yes to Christ, receive him as your Savior—as Maggie and Josh did—and God promises in his Word to forgive you. He'll adopt you as his child. And when you stand before him one day, you'll stand there as one forgiven, not one condemned, and he will welcome you into his open arms—just as he so eagerly and lovingly welcomed Maggie and Josh on Thursday night. Or say no, and roll the dice. It's your choice. But I beseech you as a man of the cloth: don't gamble with your eternal future."

I shifted uncomfortably in the pew. As much as I wanted to resent the pastor and all he was saying, I couldn't. He was speaking to me, and he was connecting. I was trying not to listen, but I simply couldn't help it.

When the pastor finished, we sang a hymn, and then it was my turn to speak. I had a pit in my stomach as I stared out at the congregation through tear-filled eyes, feeling racked with guilt so overwhelming I could barely breathe. In pursuit of my dream of being an award-winning foreign correspondent like my grandfather, I had essentially abandoned my family. I hadn't been there when they'd needed me. I hadn't been there for the big moments in their lives. And now, because of me, two of them were dead, and two others were lying in an intensive care unit, fighting for their lives.

The truth is, I don't remember what I said for the next few minutes. I hope I thanked the pastor for his beautiful words. I hope I said some nice things about Mom and about Josh. I honestly cannot recall a single word that came out of my mouth. It couldn't have been too bad. I do remember people coming up to me after the service, in the receiving line, thanking me for honoring my family so beautifully.

But I'll never forget what the vice president said after me because it so infuriated me. Holbrooke dutifully expressed his and the president's condolences to Matt and me and to our family and assembled friends. Somebody had fed him a few details about my mom and Josh—even some tidbits about Annie and Katie—that he sprinkled throughout his prepared remarks as though he'd known them personally, as though he'd been an old friend. That didn't bother me. Nor did it bother me—too much, anyway—that he was using the administration's boilerplate language about "the scourge of violent extremism," and about the "cowardly attacks of those who claim to speak in the name of Islam but have no idea what this great religion of peace is truly all about." What did bother me—what absolutely enraged me—was something he said almost in passing toward the close of his remarks.

"As we lay to rest these two heroes—not victims, but true American heroes—let there be no doubt: We are winning the war against ISIL. We have liberated Mosul. We have liberated northern Iraq. We are killing their leaders. We have them on the run. What we have seen this past week is tragic, but rest assured, these are among the last violent spasms of a cruel but vanquished movement."

The last violent spasms? A cruel but vanquished movement?

What planet was he living on? Nearly twice as many Americans had just died at the hands of the Islamic State as had on 9/11. Nearly as many Americans had perished in one week at the hands of Abu Khalif as in ten years of fighting in Afghanistan and Iraq. ISIS was hardly "vanquished." It might have lost its grip on northern Iraq, but it was solidifying its grip elsewhere. It was expanding its caliphate into Yemen, Somalia, and Libya. It was recruiting tens of thousands of new foreign fighters and raising millions of dollars for its jihad against the West. Yet this administration couldn't or wouldn't see it. They simply refused to throw their full might into crushing this evil force once and for all.

At that moment, something in me snapped. I was suddenly consumed by a toxic and rapidly intensifying feeling of humiliation, compounded by guilt and fused with rage. By the time the service was over, I was seething. Something had to be done. Abu Khalif was engaged in nothing less than genocide. He had to be stopped. Who was going to do it? The president? The vice president? Not a chance. They were abject failures, and nothing about that was going to change. The world couldn't wait for a new administration and a new plan. Neither could I. Neither could what was left of my family. That much was clear, and that certain knowledge left me with no other choice and not a shred of doubt.

I knew what I had to do, and I now had a plan.

PART
FOUR

50

★ ★ ★

TEL AVIV, ISRAEL

A brutal winter thunderstorm was bearing down on Israel's largest
coastal city.

I sat in the Royal Executive Lounge on the fourteenth floor of
the Carlton Hotel, a few blocks north of the U.S. Embassy, nursing
a Perrier as I watched the driving Mediterranean rains pelt the windows. Outside, palm trees bent in the forty-mile-per-hour winds.
Streaks of jagged lightning illuminated the dark sky, and crashes of
thunder rocked the building.

My pocket watch said it was five o'clock. I'd come to the same
place, sat in the same leather chair, looked out the same window for
the fourth day in a row. My contact had yet to show up. Maybe this
was a complete waste of time. But I didn't see any other way. So I sat,
and I waited, and I tried to be patient. Not exactly my strong suit.

What bothered me most was that I'd nearly blown up my newly
mended relationship with my brother to get here. Matt was furious
with me. And I certainly understood why he felt betrayed.

Initially he'd liked my plan, but that's only because I hadn't told
him all of it.

The part I told him about when we were alone in the rector's

213

office after the memorial service had been straightforward enough. We would accept Harris's proposal to put us into the Witness Security Program, but with one caveat: the FBI couldn't kill us off.

We would agree to disappear from our daily lives for several months, perhaps even a year or more, until Abu Khalif was arrested and my testimony was needed or until Khalif was dead and my family and I were no longer in danger. I'd take an indefinite leave of absence from the *Times*. Matt would take an indefinite leave of absence from Gordon-Conwell Theological Seminary. With the bureau's help, we would slip away unnoticed, undetected, and undetectable. Harris would provide us with new identities, complete with driver's licenses and passports and credit cards and mobile phones. We'd have fake names. We'd live by the aliases Harris provided. We would live, in other words, like anyone else in the Witness Security Program, with one difference. We would not be "dead." There would be no car bomb. There would be no funeral. The world wouldn't think we were dead. They would just think we'd gone away to recover from the attacks and get the physical and psychological and spiritual help we so obviously needed. When we were better, we would come back.

My plan provided my brother full anonymity and protection and first-rate medical care for his wife and daughter. But it also provided Matt the ability to reenter his life at some point. It was almost elegant in its simplicity. It was the best of both worlds, and Matt loved it.

Harris? Not so much.

For the bureau, it was the worst of both worlds. We would be costing the American taxpayers just as much as if we were entering the formal program and playing by all the rules, except that we wouldn't be entering the formal program and we wouldn't be playing by the rules. We'd get all the benefits, but the bureau would still face many of the risks. Abu Khalif would know we were still alive. He'd do his best to track us down and take us out. If we made a single mistake—and we probably would, Harris insisted, given that we weren't intelligence professionals—then I might not even be alive long enough to testify.

So my plan called for a compromise. We would split the costs of our "disappearance" fifty-fifty with the bureau. Yes, the U.S. government would be going to considerable expense. But Matt and I now had sufficient financial resources to defray some of these costs. I didn't think we should have to pay for all of it. After all, I would eventually be providing an enormously valuable service to the government by way of my testimony. But we would agree to cover half the costs to defray the added exposure for the FBI.

Harris had blown a gasket when we presented him with our counteroffer. He told us in a dozen different ways that he could never sign off on such a foolish and pathetic plan. But Matt and I held our ground. We made it clear we appreciated the bureau's concern for our well-being, and we were willing to hide for a time, but we weren't going to hide forever.

It was near midnight on that Tuesday by the time Harris finally met us back at the Harborside. He told us the request had gone all the way up the chain of command. Neither the director of the FBI nor the attorney general liked the idea, Harris said, but in the end they had agreed to it, provided Matt and I sign waivers indemnifying the U.S. government from any criminal or civil liabilities in what they called "the not unlikely possibility" that one or all of us were murdered by ISIS.

We had, of course, signed the waivers. In triplicate. On video. With a half-dozen federal agents there to sign affidavits as witnesses.

The next thing we knew, we were being rushed by helicopter to the Portland International Jetport in the dead of night. There, we boarded an unmarked Gulfstream IV business jet that had been retrofitted to serve as an air ambulance. Annie and Katie were already on board. They were lying on stretchers, hooked up to IVs, respirators, heart monitors, and who knows what else, attended to by a doctor and a nurse, both of whom worked for the FBI.

As we gained altitude, Matt had sighed, then leaned over and thanked me. We were safe from ISIS, and we were together as a family. Given the alternatives, that wasn't bad, he said. Then he leaned his seat back, pulled a blanket over himself, closed his eyes, and drifted off to sleep, a calm and peaceful man.

I knew it wouldn't last. I'd have to tell him the rest of my plan. But not just then. He needed his sleep, as I'd needed mine.

51

★ ★ ★

"Sir, can I get you anything from the bar?"

The twentysomething waitress who had just interrupted my daydream had kind eyes and a pleasant, gentle manner. She meant no harm. She was just doing her job. But she had no idea what she was asking.

Yes, I want a Scotch on the rocks with a twist.

Yes, bring me the whole bottle.

Yes, please deliver a case to my room.

There were only a handful of people in the lounge, and none of them knew me. I'd been here four days, and my contact hadn't even called me back. Or sent an e-mail. Or a text. Yael hadn't responded to any of my messages either. She knew I was here. She knew I wanted to see her. She was just blowing me off. *So why not have a drink?* I asked myself. I deserved one.

"Maybe just a cappuccino," I said, forcing myself to smile.

Another boom of thunder, and the hotel trembled once more.

I checked my pocket watch again. It was closing in on six. I'd been here almost nine hours. For the fourth day in a row.

How much longer was I going to wait? What was I even doing here? Khachigian had, after all, drawn me a road map. He'd given me names, sources he trusted. Yet instead of tracking down the contacts he had given me, I was wasting time in this hotel lounge.

I got up to stretch and walked around the lounge for a bit. There was nothing to see. There was no one I wanted to talk to. A happy couple on a date, drinking champagne, laughing it up. A handful of executives discussing a telecom deal. Two gray-haired ladies, clearly tourists. One was reading Agatha Christie's *Murder on the Orient Express*; the other was leafing through a copy of the *National Enquirer*.

Really? I thought. *You've come all the way to the Holy Land and you're wasting your time with tabloid trash?* Then again, what was she supposed to be doing? She hardly wanted to be outside just then. Nobody did. The storm bearing down on Israel's coastline was unbelievable.

I sat down and opened the Bible app on my phone. With nothing else to do the past four days, I'd finished reading the Gospel of John, not because I had really wanted to but because I'd promised Matt I would. In fact, when I'd finished John, I'd read through the other three Gospels, too, and then much of the rest of the New Testament. It was actually kind of interesting to read it here in Israel, where so much of it had taken place. I'd found myself particularly intrigued by Luke's account. Luke was a Gentile. A physician. An educated man and a good writer. He hadn't been an eyewitness like the apostles, apparently, but he'd set out to write an "orderly account" of the life of Christ. Like a journalist. A foreign correspondent. And a good one. His report provided a compelling narrative. Rich in details. Direct quotes. Colorful anecdotes. I'd never read anything quite like it.

The waitress came back with my coffee. I paid her, then tried to stare out at the storm. But the sun had set. Darkness had fallen. All I could see was my reflection in the window, and I winced in regret. I took a sip of my coffee, closed my eyes, and suddenly the clock turned back and I could feel the Gulfstream touching down.

I remembered Matt being startled awake. I remembered him

trying to reestablish exactly where he was. I remembered his sudden sense of anticipation as he rubbed his eyes and checked his wrist-watch, then leaned over to me and whispered, "Ten bucks we're in Wichita."

"Kansas?" I'd said, rubbing my eyes as well. I hadn't slept at all.

"Yeah."

"Why Kansas?"

"I don't know. We were flying for about four hours, give or take. If we were heading west, I'm thinking that puts us around Wichita."

"Why not Oklahoma City?"

Matt had shrugged. "You'd rather live there?"

"Hardly. But I'm sure we're not in Kansas."

"How do you know?"

"It's not nearly cold enough."

In my mind's eye I pictured Agent Harris opening the door near the cockpit. The cabin had been flooded with brilliant sunshine and a warm, sultry breeze. We hadn't flown west. We'd flown south.

"Your new home, gentlemen," Harris had said, standing beside the open door. "Welcome to St. Thomas."

As we exited the plane and headed toward a white Ford Explorer that was waiting for us, Harris explained, "Your wife and daughter will be taken to a specialized medical clinic on the other side of the island. You can visit them this afternoon, but first I need to show you the house, get you settled in, and explain a few things. Then I've got a noon flight back to D.C."

"Why did you bring us *here*?" I asked, more coldly than I'd meant, as we wound our way up narrow roads, covered in dense foliage, driving on the left side of the street as if we were in Great Britain.

"Ever been here before?" Harris asked. "Either of you?"

I didn't bother to answer.

"That's why you brought us here?" Matt asked. "Because we've never been?"

"Think about it," Harris replied. "You don't know anyone here. No one knows you. Not a lot of people read the *New York Times* down here. You can't imagine yourself visiting, much less living here. It's not you. I get it. I can see it in your faces, your body language. You're mountain people. Lake people. You like to ice fish and hunt. You don't hate deep snow and bitter winters. In fact, you love both. You'd be skiing at Killington right now if I'd let you. Which is why this is perfect. No one would think to look for you here. Wichita? Maybe. Oklahoma City? Perhaps. But the Caribbean? Never."

We'd come to a fork in the road. To the right was a sign to Magens Bay, but we took the road heading left, snaking up the mountain, heading north toward a place called Tropaco Point.

"You're actually still on American soil, gentlemen," Harris continued. "These are the U.S. Virgin Islands. You don't need a passport to fly from here to the mainland or back. You can operate in U.S. currency. And there are plenty of pasty-white tourists and businessmen—just like you two—who visit here, live here, retire here. So you're not exactly going to stand out."

I had to admit, Harris was right. Neither Matt nor I had ever had any interest in coming down here. But as we pulled into the driveway of a three-story house painted in a pale yellow with blue shutters, I could see Matt was warming to it.

And why not? The temperature was a perfect eighty-one degrees. The view from each of our three balconies was absolutely spectacular. The clouds were white and puffy. The bay, directly below us, was the most gorgeous shade of azure I'd ever seen, rimmed by white sandy beaches and dotted by sailboats gliding along in the lovely tropical breezes.

We'd never even imagined living in a place so gorgeous.

Inside, things got even better.

The tour started in the basement, where Harris showed us the secure room—or "panic room"—which by Middle Eastern standards was a full-blown bomb shelter. Hidden behind a sliding bookshelf, the room had a cement floor and two-foot-thick reinforced concrete walls. The ceiling was also concrete-lined with steel plates to prevent attackers from drilling into it from the first floor. The door was made of thick steel and Kevlar, and the entire structure was blast resistant and hermetically sealed to prevent smoke, tear gas, or other toxins from entering.

The room had sets of bunk beds that could sleep six, a separate toilet and shower facility, a small kitchenette, and a supply of water and canned and freeze-dried food that could last for up to thirty days. There was also a communications console that would allow us to monitor video cameras positioned all over the house and connect with local authorities, including the St. Thomas FBI field office, just in case. Harris walked us through the system of high-tech batteries that could provide all the power we needed if somehow we were cut off from the local grid.

The rest of the massive six-bedroom house—complete with a fully equipped medical suite—was no less impressive. The place was furnished and had all the linens, towels, dishes, silverware, and other necessities we might need. There was a large entertainment center in the basement and TVs in every bedroom, all hooked up to a satellite dish on the roof. And in the back, there was a two-car garage, where we found a bronze Toyota RAV4 and a forest-green Jeep Grand Cherokee.

The bureau, it seemed, had thought of everything.

"Have you ever seen anything so beautiful?" Matt asked later that evening after Harris left and we were finally seated together, looking out over Magens Bay.

"Can't say I have," I said, glad Matt was happy.

And then I told him the next stage of my plan.

52

★ ★ ★

TEL AVIV, ISRAEL

I paid my bill at the front desk and headed out the front door of the Carlton.

It was windy and wet and gray, but sometime in the night the rains had stopped. The bellman whistled for a cab and it pulled up momentarily. It was just before seven in the morning. There had been no time for breakfast or even a good cup of coffee, but I wasn't staying in this country a minute longer. I'd wasted almost four and a half days, and I was done.

"The airport," I said, and we were off.

I still felt bad about the way I'd left things with Matt. When I told him I wasn't staying on St. Thomas, he'd been furious. "Are you crazy?" he'd said. "You just got here."

"I know, but I never planned to stay. I wanted you and Annie and Katie to be safe, to enter the FBI program, albeit with modifications, and now here you are. You've got this great house—better than either of us could have imagined. You've got first-rate medical care for your family. You've got new passports, new IDs, everything you need. So you'll be fine. But I can't stay."

"You can't go," Matt had replied. "I know I did everything I could to persuade you to do what Allen asked and go write those stories about the MP's son and the king and his family and all. But everything's changed. We negotiated with Harris. We made a deal. It was approved by the attorney general of the United States. You can't just renege on it now."

"Look, Matt," I'd said, "what you and I agreed to was that the only way this *ever* ends—the *only* way we ever get our lives back—is if Abu Khalif is taken out once and for all. Now you and I both know the president's not going to do that. But the Egyptians might. The Jordanians might. The Israelis might. Maybe a few others. Khachigian gave me information that might help take Khalif down. I need to go make sure this thing gets done right. Then we can all go home."

"Help? You?" Matt had asked. "J. B., have you completely lost your mind? What, you suddenly think your initials stand for James Bond? Jason Bourne? Jack Bauer? What are we talking about here? You're not an assassin. You're not trained for any of that. You're going to get yourself killed. And then you're going to get us all killed."

But in the end, I had left anyway. I had no other choice. I'd come to Israel first, hoping to link up with folks at the Mossad who might be able to make use of the information I had. But that hadn't happened. I was on my own.

It was going to take a while for my taxi driver to work his way through the morning rush-hour commute to Ben Gurion International Airport, but at least the plane would wait. I was no longer flying commercial, after all. There was a Learjet waiting for me on the tarmac, fueled up and ready to go, a jet I partially owned. By lunchtime I'd be in Istanbul. By dinner I'd be in Dubai, having hopefully secured a meeting with Mohammed bin Zayed, the UAE's intelligence chief.

I had no intention of reaching out to bin Zayed directly until I arrived. He had no idea who I was, and I didn't want to give him much time to find out. But if everything went according to plan, I'd be sipping coffee with him soon and discussing the hunt for Abu Khalif.

I pulled out my iPhone—a new one I'd picked up en route to Tel Aviv—and checked the headlines. This was a phone even Agent Harris didn't know about and thus one he couldn't trace.

My eye was drawn immediately to the lead story in the *Washington Post*, our fiercest competitor, though never our equal. It was an exclusive, lengthy, and stupefying interview with President Taylor, conducted in the Oval Office. In it, the leader of the free world had just gone on the record as saying some of the most incendiary comments of his presidency.

"Yes, this is a difficult moment," Taylor had told the editorial board of the *Post*. "We have been hit by extremists who fundamentally reject modernity, who reject our values and our way of life. And I grieve for the families who have suffered losses. But we must maintain a sense of perspective. We are waging a war against these extremists, and we are winning. We are taking back the lands they've ravaged. We are killing their leaders. We are cutting off their money supply. And they are reeling. So they are lashing out, and these recent attacks, as terrible as they are, are simply death spasms of a movement whose day is over. Let me be clear: my job, and that of the American military and our allies, will not be over until these extremists are shut down once and for all. But they are trying to lure us into a much-larger conflict. They want us to come back to a full-scale war in the Middle East. And that's not going to happen. America's days of fighting endless wars in the Middle East—for the oil companies, for Israel, for democracy, for freeloader despots, or for whatever other reasons the neocons and the warmongers and the foreign policy establishment in this town are itching for—those days are over. They are over. And we are never going back."

This was a new low. In a single paragraph, the president had once again demonstrated his absolute unwillingness to properly defend the American people and our national security interests in the world's most dangerous and volatile region. That was nothing new. But now he had unleashed what amounted to an unprecedented anti-Semitic slur, and from the Oval Office no less, by accusing our Jewish allies in Israel and the "neoconservatives" in Washington—referring primarily to conservative Jewish foreign policy experts, many of whom were Republicans but some of whom were Democrats—of dragging America into war time and time again.

Not Osama bin Laden and al Qaeda and the 9/11 hijackers.

Not the Mullah Omar and the Taliban.

Not Saddam Hussein, the Butcher of Baghdad.

Not Abu Musab al-Zarqawi and the forces of al Qaeda in Iraq.

Not Abu Khalif and the forces of the Islamic State.

No, in the president's worldview, apparently it was the Jews—in Israel and the United States—along with the oil companies and also our "freeloading" Sunni Arab allies (presumably Jordan, Egypt, the Saudis, and the Gulf emirates)—who were responsible for every war the U.S. had ever fought in the region.

The implications of the president's remarks were far-reaching, but for the moment I couldn't go there. I was still trying to understand the mind-set of an American leader—a Democrat backed by more than 70 percent of the American Jewish community—turning so harshly against people who had so wholeheartedly supported him.

There was no time to think about any of it much further, however, for suddenly the taxi lurched onto some Tel Aviv side street and then down a series of ramps into the bowels of a dark parking garage, and before I knew it, we had screeched to a halt.

My door was opened by one of several large, swarthy men, all wearing black leather jackets and jeans. "Excuse me, Mr. McClaire," he said. "Would you please follow us?"

For a moment I thought they had the wrong guy.

"Mr. McClaire, please—your contact is a busy man, and he has a schedule to keep."

Finally I recognized the alias. I had used it, along with one of the fake passports Khachigian had left me, when I'd flown to Israel several days earlier.

I stepped out of the taxi, hoping these men were connected to my source and that they weren't going to double-tap me and stuff my body in the trunk of one of the dozens of cars and minivans parked all around me. Either way, there was no point resisting. I wasn't armed. I wasn't trained in self-defense. No one even knew I was here. Why not just get on with it?

I followed my escorts through the garage, through a filthy exit door, into a putrid stairwell, and up several flights of concrete steps. The more steps we climbed, however, the less concerned I was about getting shot in the back of the head execution-style and the more certain I was that my fishing expedition had been successful after all.

We soon exited on the ground floor. The air was chilly but fresh— almost sweet—as my handlers walked me across the street. Yesterday's storm had subsided. We were in the heart of the ancient town of Jaffa, just south of Tel Aviv, and once we entered a park overlooking empty beaches and crashing surf, they told me to sit down on a wooden bench. One of them lit a cigarette. The other pretended to tie his shoes.

"Mr. McClaire," said a kindly, older voice just over my right shoulder. "What an unexpected pleasure. Welcome to Israel."

I turned and found Ari Shalit, the head of Israeli Mossad, coming around the far side of the bench, bundled up in a long navy-blue winter coat, a plaid Scottish cap, a scarf, and leather gloves.

"Ari," I said, standing to greet him and shake his hand, as surprised as I was relieved. "It's so good to see you. Thanks for making some time."

"Of course—you didn't really think I'd let you fly off to the Gulf without saying hello, did you?"

I held my tongue. That was exactly what I'd thought, but I was glad to be wrong.

"So," he said, "how's life in the Caribbean?"

I was so stunned I didn't know how to respond. My mouth opened, but no words would form.

"Don't look so surprised," he said. "It's my job to know such things, is it not?"

It took me a moment to recover. "Is it really that easy?" I finally asked.

"If you know what to look for, yes."

"Does Abu Khalif know what to look for?"

"No, not yet," said Shalit. "Besides, he has his hands full right now. For the time being, your brother and his family are safe."

I stared out at the whitecaps on the roiling Mediterranean, unsure whether to be relieved or worried.

"There is one thing I don't understand, and I must ask you," Shalit said. "Why did Agent Harris let you come? I mean, your being here is quite a risk for someone in the Witness Protection Program."

"He didn't let me," I said.

"I don't understand."

"I didn't tell him."

For once, it was Ari Shalit who didn't know what to say.

"Although," I continued, "if you know I'm here, the CIA probably knows. And if the CIA knows, the FBI must know. And if they know, Harris knows. Am I right?"

"I doubt it."

"Why?"

"Because you did everything right," Shalit said. "Flew to New York—not commercial but by private plane. Then changed planes. Flew to London. Bought a new iPhone. Changed planes again. Flew to Madrid. Changed again. Came here. All different tail numbers. Different names, different passports, different credit cards. You were careful. I've been impressed. It was like you'd been a spy all your life. I doubt the guys at Langley saw any red flags."

"But you figured it out."

"Yes, but we were expecting you to come," Shalit said, staring out at the sea. "They were expecting you to stay."

53

★ ★ ★

"You were expecting me to come here?" I asked, once again surprised.

"Of course."

"Why?"

"We were right to do so, weren't we?"

"Yeah, but if you knew I was coming, why did you just let me sit alone at the Carlton for four days, doing nothing, without even responding, without even telling me you'd gotten my message?"

Shalit shook his head. "You weren't alone."

"What's that supposed to mean?" I asked.

"Everyone in that executive lounge was Mossad," he explained. "We were watching you. Testing you. Waiting to see if you'd start drinking again. To see if anyone was following you. See how you'd react to disappointment. And to see if you had a plan after us."

"And what did you learn?" I asked.

"You booked a flight to Dubai. So you did have a plan. And you hadn't been drinking. And you had been quite patient, after all. And no one was following you. So here you are."

"Then you know why I came?" I asked.

"I think so," Shalit replied. "But I want to hear it from you."

"Fair enough," I said, then paused for a bit, watching the waves crash against the rocky Jaffa shoreline. "I want in."

"In?" he asked. "What exactly does that mean?"

"You're hunting for Abu Khalif," I said in a hushed tone, even though at this early hour, and season and temperature, no one but the bodyguards was around. "He murdered your prime minister. You want to make him pay. But you're getting almost no help from Washington. Or the Europeans. And ISIS is still on the move. They're still slaughtering innocent people, still on offense, still planning bigger and more deadly attacks. You know they're coming here, to Tel Aviv, to Jerusalem, to Haifa and Tiberias. You know they don't just want to kill Americans. They also want to murder Jews—Israelis in particular—and as many as they can. So you need help, and you need it fast. That's why I've come."

At this, Shalit turned and looked directly at me. "You came to *help* us?" he said, appearing genuinely perplexed.

"Yes."

"To help us find and kill Abu Khalif?"

"Exactly."

"This is why you've risked your life, and your brother's and your sister-in-law's and your niece's lives, to crisscross around the world, to come all the way over here, to meet with me, to tell me you want to join the Mossad and help us assassinate Abu Khalif?"

"Why else?"

Shalit sat there for a long while, searching my eyes, trying to read me. It was rare to see him caught off guard. The fifty-seven-year-old spook had built his career on knowing everything about everyone, on knowing all secrets, large and small. This was what had made him one of the most interesting operatives I'd ever met in the Middle East. The fact that we'd been friends for almost two decades had made him an invaluable source. But right now I wasn't looking for a story. I was looking for a job.

"I am not easily surprised, *Mr. McClaire*," he said, emphasizing my new alias. "But I must confess, today I am. I thought you were here for something else—something else entirely."

"Like what?" I asked.

He smiled. "Honestly? I thought you were here for Yael."

"Yael Katzir?" I asked.

"Who else?"

"Well, who says I'm not?" I asked.

"You haven't brought her up."

"What are you, her father?"

He laughed. "No, no, of course not."

"Then with all due respect, why would you care?"

"I'm her boss," he said.

"I thought she was working for the prime minister."

"You thought wrong," he said simply. "She turned that job down. You didn't know?"

"No," I said. "Can't say I did. Why didn't she take it?"

"Why didn't she tell you herself?" he replied.

"I have no idea," I said.

He shrugged. "Then it's not my place to say. For that, you'll have to talk to her directly. But for this other topic, I can honestly say I did not see this coming."

"Clearly."

He turned back to the sea. "You're not a spy," he said after a long silence.

"True."

"You haven't got the training."

"Obviously."

"And you already have a job."

"*Had,*" I corrected him.

"You quit?"

"Not exactly."

"Fired?"

"Let's just say I'm on an extended leave of absence."

"Paid?"

"No."

"Then how can you afford not to work?"

"Again, Ari, with all due respect . . ."

"You think that's none of my business?"

I shrugged.

"Think again. If you want to work for me, Mr. McClaire, *everything* is my business."

There was no guarantee he was going to let me in if I told him, but I was guaranteed to be shut out if I refused to say anything. So I explained as concisely as I could what Robert Khachigian had done for my brother and me.

"J. B.," he sighed, finally abandoning the pretense of my alias. "If this were anyone else, I wouldn't even be giving you the time of day. You have no training. You have no security clearances. You're not Israeli. You're not Jewish. The list of reasons I should be putting you back on your private jet to the Caribbean is a mile long."

"But . . . ?"

"You tell me."

"What do you mean?"

"Make the case," he said. "Sell it to me."

"It's simple," I said. "I'm the only Westerner on the planet who has ever met Abu Khalif. I'm the only Westerner to have ever spoken with him at length. I know what he looks like. I know what he sounds like. I've met his closest advisors and spoken to them. I've read everything ever written about him. I know how he thinks. I know what he wants. I speak Arabic. And he thinks I'm in hiding. That's my competitive advantage. I'm in his blind spot—he doesn't see me coming."

"Maybe not," Shalit said. "But I've got a pretty sharp team. They've studied him too. They're trained. They're experienced. They've been doing this a long time. How are you going to find him if they can't?"

"They can, and they will, but they need my help—and so do you," I said. "Before Bob Khachigian died, he wrote me a letter. He made it clear that his final wish was for me to track down Abu Khalif. And he gave me several leads."

"What kind of leads?"

"Names," I said. "Three of them, to be exact."

"What names?"

"Not so fast," I said. "First you agree to put me on your team."

"But why come to us? Why not go to the CIA?"

"I can't."

"Why not?"

"Because the acting director's hands are tied."

"By whom?"

"By a man blaming your country for all the wars in the region."

"No comment," Shalit said.

I nodded.

"To be fair, your president says he wants to take down all the ISIS leaders. He's authorizing drone strikes, bombings. And ISIS leaders are dying—two more just yesterday."

"The president wants headlines," I snapped. "I want Abu Khalif's head."

Shalit said nothing.

"We've known each other for a long time, Ari. You trust me, and I trust you. That's why I'm here."

Again Shalit looked out at the Mediterranean. "Do you really understand the risks you're taking, my friend?"

"I'm willing to die for my country," I said as though I meant it, though I wasn't entirely sure I did. The truth was, death flat-out terrified me. I had no idea what the afterlife really held or how to determine my eternal fate. Maybe my mom and Josh were right.

Maybe Pastor Brooks was. Maybe not. But that was all a different subject for a different time.

"Perhaps you are willing to die for your country, J. B., but are you willing to die for mine?" Shalit asked.

"Honestly? No. But this isn't about me dying for anyone's country; it's about making Abu Khalif die for all he's done."

"So you're here for vengeance?"

"No," I said. "Not really."

"Justice, then."

"In part," I said.

"What else?" Shalit asked. "Why do this? Why take such risks?"

"I want my life back, Ari," I said. "But even more, I want Matt and Annie and Katie to have their lives back. I want them to live free and safe and without a care in this world. I owe them that. Actually, I owe them much more. But I have nothing else to give them than this. Now what do you say? Are you going to let me help you guys hunt down Abu Khalif or not?"

54

★ ★ ★

The Mossad chief abruptly stood.

"It's time," he said, adjusting his scarf and collar to protect himself from the wind.

"Time for what?" I asked, standing as well.

"Let's go for a little ride," he said, pointing to a black sedan that had just pulled up, followed by two black Chevy Suburbans.

"Where?"

"You'll find out soon enough."

"What about my luggage, my briefcase, my laptop?" I asked, picturing them in the trunk of the taxicab in the nearby parking garage.

"Don't worry," he said. "All your belongings are safe. But I will need your new mobile phone."

When I asked why, he explained he was going to take the battery out of it so no one could track our movements.

"We're going someplace no one can know about," he added. "Now come. We don't want to be late."

Our driver worked his way out of Tel Aviv's morning gridlock and got us on Highway 2, heading north along the coast toward Haifa. Just before we reached Herzliya—the elite seaside community filled with enormous overpriced homes owned by high-tech Israeli CEOs and former government ministers now serving on their boards—he took a right on Highway 5, then turned north on Highway 6.

Eventually we arrived at the Ramat David Air Base in the Jezreel Valley. This was the country's main air base in the north and home to some of Israel's most advanced fighter jets, including the new F-35i stealth fighters.

I pulled out my pocket watch. It was a little before ten. Our driver turned off the main road, pulled to the first guard station, and came to a halt. Young soldiers holding machine guns watched us carefully as we all handed over our photo IDs—even the acting director of the Mossad.

A few minutes later, we were cleared to proceed. The gates opened, and our driver eased us forward.

We took a quick right and wound around the inner perimeter of the base. In the distance I could see rows of F-15s and F-16s being cleaned and refueled, and I could hear several taking off and landing. Then we reached the far side of the base and stopped in front of a nondescript, unmarked concrete building with a few cars parked out front and a sentry standing post.

Two of Shalit's bodyguards got out, surveyed the area, nodded to each other that the coast was clear, and then opened Ari's door and mine. The base was remarkable in how unremarkable it looked. All the buildings were badly in need of fresh paint and basic repairs. The pavement on the roads and tarmacs was cracked, and weeds were growing everywhere. The barracks for the rank-and-file soldiers looked like they hadn't been spruced up since the Independence War, and even the accommodations for the pilots and other officers were largely unimproved. The reason was obvious enough. The Israelis had no money to spend on improving their bases. They were funneling every shekel into the planes themselves, their weapons, their avionics, and the training of the men and women who flew and serviced them. Little else mattered, so little else got funded.

Inside the nondescript building we were greeted by a major who led us through a series of electronically locked doors, down a long hallway, and onto an elevator.

"Okay, Mr. McClaire," Shalit said as the doors closed and we descended, "you asked for it. You got it. You're in."

"Thank you, Ari," I said, suddenly feeling the weight of such an honor and enormous responsibility.

"Don't thank me now," he said. "You have no idea what you just signed up for, my friend."

The elevator door opened, and Shalit led me into a rather spacious but windowless office. "Have a seat," he said. "The major here will help you fill out some paperwork. I'll be back to get you when you're done."

Shalit wasn't kidding about the paperwork. The waivers and non-disclosure forms and all kinds of other legalese took me almost an hour to read through carefully. The short version was that I was not an employee of the State of Israel. I was not an employee of the Mossad. I was not an independent contractor for Israel or the Mossad or any other government or private institution in Israel. I was not being paid or compensated in any way by the State of Israel, the Mossad, or any Israeli entity. I was not receiving from Israel any medical insurance or any life insurance or any of two dozen other listed benefits. What's more, I agreed to completely indemnify the State of Israel, its citizens, and its agents from all future claims of liability related to my volunteer services. I would not disclose the names, ranks, or other personal or professional details of any Israeli citizen or resident I met during the course of my volunteer work. I would treat all paperwork and electronic documents as the property of the State of Israel, handle it all as highly confidential and sensitive, and not share, give, pass, transfer, transmit, or in any other way communicate their existence or their substance, even in a redacted or summary fashion, to any unauthorized foreign national, including my own lawyers, family members, or friends, without express written permission—which I would never receive. *Ever.* And on and on it went.

Counterintuitively, perhaps, the more I read, the calmer I became. Shalit knew what I was asking. He knew my weaknesses and liabilities. He knew the risks I was taking as well as the risks he and his government were taking. Yet he was bringing me in anyway. It wasn't out of charity. Shalit had to sincerely believe I brought something critical to the table and possessed something he urgently needed. It wasn't just the three names. It was my unique set of experiences and insights. I really did know Abu Khalif in a way no other Westerner did.

When I finished reading the final page, I went back and signed each document one by one. When I was done, the major led me along a darkened basement corridor to a lounge, where we met Shalit.

"All set?" he asked.

I nodded.

"You're sure?" he pressed.

"I'm sure."

"Good."

Shalit led me through a labyrinth of corridors and past a series of workstations where analysts quietly labored on computers displaying satellite images of various remote towns and villages. Then we arrived at a large conference room. A guard holding an Uzi stood outside the door. At Shalit's command, he stepped aside. Shalit then entered a password into a keypad and opened the door.

The moment we entered, everyone stood to attention.

Even Yael Katzir.

55

★ ★ ★

RAMAT DAVID AIR BASE, ISRAEL

"At ease," Shalit said, taking a seat at the head of the large oak table.

The group of five—four men and Yael—just stared at me. One guy's mouth literally dropped open. Yael's hand shot to her mouth, perhaps to prevent a similar reaction. I scanned each face and forced myself to look at her last. I saw shock in her eyes along with a flash of anger. The shock I could understand. She knew I was here in Israel because I'd told her in numerous e-mails and text messages over the last few days, though clearly Shalit hadn't told her he was bringing me to Ramat David. But the hostility? Where was that coming from?

"I said, at ease," Shalit repeated.

The team members took their seats. Most of them were dressed casually—jeans, sweaters, and a few plaid wool shirts over white cotton T-shirts—suggesting that none of them were military. Not currently, anyway, though they certainly all had been and probably still held fairly senior ranks in the reserves. They were older than most of the others I'd seen on the base, ranging in age from late forties to early sixties, making Yael—still in her early thirties—the youngest person in the room.

I tried to pick out the team leader. A guy on the far side of the table struck me as the most likely suspect. He was the oldest of the group, aside from Shalit. He was also the only one wearing a crisp, white oxford shirt and had a pair of reading glasses dangling from a chain around his neck. His small, intense eyes stayed locked on me even as the others shifted their attention to the head of the table.

Shalit motioned for me to take an empty chair to his left. The table was cluttered with open notebook computers, thick three-ring binders, and half-filled ashtrays. The walls were covered with maps, satellite imagery, and eight-by-ten black-and-white photos of various ISIS commanders, all high-value targets. A much-larger photo of Abu Khalif—a screen capture from the video of him speaking to the American people from Alqosh—was hanging front and center.

I noticed, too, photos of Jamal Ramzy and Tariq Baqouba, each with a big red X drawn over their faces. Ramzy had been the commander of ISIS rebel forces in Syria until Yael and I had gunned him down in the king's palace in Amman. Baqouba, his replacement, had been taken out by an American drone strike just days earlier.

As I sat down, I looked back at Yael. Her eyes were riveted on me. I couldn't read what she was thinking. Her expression was inscrutable. But one thing was clear: until sixty seconds ago, the last thing she had expected was for me to walk through that door.

"I'd like you all to meet Mr. Mike McClaire," the Mossad chief began.

The room was deathly quiet. *Was this a joke?* they were wondering. They didn't say it, but I could see it in their eyes.

"Officially, Mr. McClaire is an ISIS specialist on loan to us from NATO—from the Canadian government, to be precise," Shalit said. "That's our cover story. Of course, like everything else that happens in this room, on this floor, in this building, and on this base, Mr. McClaire's presence here is classified. You won't discuss his presence or reveal his identity to anyone outside this room. Not to your best friend on this base. Not to the janitor in the mess hall. Not to the minister of defense. Not to the prime minister himself. And certainly to no one on the outside. Any violation will be prosecuted to the fullest extent of the law. Are we clear?"

Everyone nodded.

"To anyone who asks about him, he's just 'the new guy.' If anyone has questions—they shouldn't; they know better, but if they do—you tell them to come to me. Understood?"

More nods.

"Good. Now, we all know who this really is," Shalit continued. "And you are all well aware that aside from the president of the United States, there is no one Abu Khalif wants to kill more than Mr. Collins here. His life and the lives of his family are in grave danger. Thus, I need you to treat him as one of the team and protect him like family. Am I clear?"

Reluctantly I scanned the room and made eye contact with each one as they all nodded again. Even Yael.

Still, Shalit could read the room better than I could, and he addressed their understandable cynicism head-on. "Okay, now why have I brought a civilian—an American, a goy, and a journalist, no less—to our illustrious little base camp here on Ramat David? One reason and one reason only: James Bradley Collins is the only person in this room who has ever actually met Abu Khalif. He's the only one of us who has ever spoken to him, ever looked into his eyes. He's also the only one of us who has had family members murdered by Khalif's men. He found him before. He's going to do it again with our help. And together we're going to take him out once and for all. Any questions?"

There were none. Or rather, there were a thousand, but no one was stupid enough to ask them.

"Fine," Shalit said. "Now let's get to work. Miss Katzir, would you introduce your team to Mr. Collins?"

Her team?

Shalit hadn't mentioned that.

56

★ ★ ★

"Of course, sir," Yael replied.

She took off her reading glasses and set them on the notebook in front of her. Then she went around the table and gave me the first name and brief background of each of her colleagues. I assumed the names were false and didn't even try to remember them. The backgrounds, though, were fascinating.

First, on my immediate left, wearing the oxford shirt, was a dark-skinned and somewhat brooding Sephardic Jew of Yemeni origin with closely cropped graying hair and two fingers missing from his right hand. He'd lost them when wrestling a hand grenade away from a Black September member in Beirut, Yael said, and he was lucky to be alive. Now in his early sixties, I guessed, the man was a thirty-two-year veteran of the Shin Bet, Israel's domestic intelligence service, roughly equivalent to the American FBI. He was, Yael noted, the most experienced tracker of high-value targets in the Shin Bet and had been highly decorated.

Sitting beside him was a Russian immigrant who, to me at least, bore a striking resemblance to Leon Trotsky, one of the leaders of the Russian Revolution and the founder of the Red Army. Thin and wiry—almost gaunt—he had a salt-and-pepper mustache and matching goatee even uglier than mine. But unlike me, he had a wild, unkempt shock of graying hair and wore round, black-rimmed spectacles. Yael explained that years before, the man's father had been the KGB's station chief in Baghdad, Cairo, and later in Damascus before being posted in Vienna, where he walked into the Israeli embassy one fall Friday and defected. Remarkably, nobody in the Kremlin had ever so much as suspected that the family was Jewish. Today, she concluded, this "son of the KGB" was now the Mossad's most senior analyst of Islamic terror movements.

Across the table sat a short, stocky redhead in his mid- to late fifties who Yael said was a major general in the Israeli military and one of the top analysts from Unit 8200, Israel's signal intelligence–gathering operation, roughly equivalent to the NSA. His father had been a top Mossad agent serving in Arab lands, and his mother was an English teacher who, despite her husband's job, was a peacenik through and through. Little did she know what her only son had grown up to do. Even today, his mother thought he was an executive with HOT, the Israeli cable TV company. Instead, he'd become one of the best Arabic speakers on her team, Yael said, not to mention the best chef she'd ever met in Israel. "His ginger couscous is to die for," she concluded.

I'd just learned I had made another mistake. Not only had I wrongly ID'd the guy in the oxford as the team leader, it now turned out that we actually did have an active military man—a senior officer, no less—in our midst, despite the fact that at the moment he wasn't wearing a uniform. Zero for two, I thought. How exactly was I supposed to add value to this team?

Next to the redhead sat a rather tall, well-built man in his late forties, perhaps early fifties, with thinning, sandy-blond hair and a face that struck me as Swedish or Danish or perhaps Norwegian. Yael explained he was a highly decorated—but now officially retired—former commander of the Sayeret Matkal, the IDF's most elite commando unit. No Israeli had personally captured or killed more high-value targets than he had, Yael said, and his ability to drive the intel-gathering process in order to produce hard, clear, actionable, accurate information that led to the actual takedown of HVTs was unparalleled in the Israeli military. And by the way, she added, he's from Holland.

Well, I thought, I'd been close. Still, it had been a foul ball, at best. At this point my batting average was .000. At least no one else in the room knew it.

So here they were—the team Yael had assembled to hunt down Abu Khalif—Israel's best and brightest. Fingers, Trotsky, Gingy, and Dutch.

All but Dutch were native Arabic speakers. They'd learned the language growing up, not in the army or university. They all had significant time operating in the Arab world as spies or commandos. And they had real-world military experience, including decades of experience searching for high-value targets.

As Yael added some details and explained their mandate, I had my first chance in two full months to look at her. She was breathtaking in a chocolate-brown sweater, black bomber jacket, faded blue jeans, and brown leather boots, and it was all I could do to stay focused and listen carefully and retain all the details she was saying. Even with the scars on her face and neck, visible despite the fact she was growing out her hair to cover them up, she was beautiful. Even with her left arm in a cast. Even though she had clearly lost weight. Even with the obvious lack of consistent sleep, the sadness in her eyes, and the dark rings underneath them. I found her stunning. I couldn't help it. I was falling for this girl, no matter how little she reciprocated.

"Thank you," Shalit said when Yael was finished. "Now, as all of you except Mr. Collins know, I've just gotten back from London, Paris, Berlin, and Rome. I met with each of their intel chiefs. I reviewed all they have on ISIS. And the bottom line is I'm coming back empty-handed. Their files are virtually blank. None of them have any real assets in Syria to speak of. None of them have penetrated any ISIS cells. They have no idea where Abu Khalif is, and frankly they don't seem to care all that much."

"Then what are they doing all day?" Fingers asked.

"Hoping against hope they can identify and thwart the next terror attack in their own countries," Shalit replied. "They're purely in defensive mode and have little interest in going on offense. The head of MI6 told me ISIS has weaponized the Syrian refugees coming into the U.K. He and his team are tracking twenty-two different ISIS cells right now. The Brits are identifying a new one every few days. He said he and his team are drowning in refugees. His people can't possibly vet them fast enough. They're trying to watch to see who links up with these terror cells. They're trying to keep them from buying weapons. But they're completely overwhelmed. Yet the prime minister keeps letting more and more refugees into the country despite all the polls that show the public's concern rising. And in every other capital, I heard essentially the same story."

"So once again, we're on our own," said Dutch.

It wasn't a question. It was a cynical, almost bitter statement of fact, and Shalit made no attempt to tell him he was wrong.

57

★ ★ ★

"Okay, now tell our guest where we are at the moment," Shalit ordered.

"Honestly?" Yael replied. "Nowhere."

"Why?" I asked.

"Where do I start?" Yael replied, her body tense and her eyes cold. "Lots of reasons, but at the top of my list at the moment would be the Americans."

"Meaning President Taylor isn't taking the hunt for Abu Khalif seriously, isn't willing to sign an executive order to take him out, and isn't willing to authorize an invasion of Syria to find him?" I asked, sure we agreed on that much, at least.

But Yael threw a curveball. "No, meaning the White House is obsessed with drone strikes," she replied. "They keep finding ISIS leaders and killing them, one after another after another."

Now I was confused. "Isn't that a good thing?"

"No, Mr. Collins, it's not a good thing—not if the objective is finding the head of ISIS," she said. "Last week my team tracked down Tariq Baqouba, the number-three guy, head of all military ops for the caliphate. We hunted him down. We knew exactly where he was. Then, as good allies, we dutifully briefed the Americans, told them his precise location, and asked for their assistance in capturing him. Next thing we know, Baqouba is killed in a drone strike and President Taylor is boasting about it on TV. There's just one problem. You don't kill a man like Tariq Baqouba. You snag him and shake him until he tells you everything. Killing him gives you a headline for a day. Capturing him gives you a gold mine of intelligence that can keep you going for weeks, sometimes months. And this wasn't the only instance. Yet no matter how hard we protest, the president won't listen to us. He's become Mr. Drone Strike, and I'm telling you, that's never going to get us to Abu Khalif."

"Whoa, whoa, Katzir, let's pull this thing back," Shalit said. "We're not here to bash the chief executive of our most important ally. Let's focus on what we know and don't know. A month ago, you all thought Khalif was in Mosul. Walk Mr. Collins through what you've learned since then."

"Fine," she said, glaring at me, clearly unhappy with the request but even more unhappy, it seemed, with my very presence. "Well, we know for certain that Khalif was in Mosul last November, because you interviewed him there, right? And we know for certain that he spent at least some time in Alqosh because after President Taylor was captured in Jordan, the video ISIS released showed both the president and Khalif together there. Unfortunately, Khalif somehow slipped away in the hours before coalition forces took Alqosh and rescued the president. So the first question is, where did Khalif go after Alqosh?"

"Do you believe he went back to Mosul?" I asked.

"We do," Yael confirmed. "Mosul was the perfect place to hide. It used to be a city of about two and a half million people, one of Iraq's largest. When ISIS took over in the summer of '14, a good deal of the population fled. Still, there were hundreds of thousands of Iraqis living in Mosul last December. Khalif had allies there. He had a network of safe houses there. He had money, weapons, communications equipment, everything he needed to hunker down and ride out the storm."

"But Khalif obviously heard the rumblings that U.S. forces were coming to retake Mosul," I said.

"Correct," Yael agreed. "For some bizarre reason that eludes everyone around this table, including yours truly, the White House and Pentagon were telegraphing the impending military operation for the better part of a year. President Taylor—big surprise—had been dithering, refusing to sign off on the operation for this reason or that. But the ISIS attack on the summit in Amman and the president's capture were the last straw. The moment Taylor was safely back in the White House, he finally authorized the formation of a Sunni Arab alliance—Kurds, Egyptians, Saudis, and the emirates, plus whatever King Abdullah could spare from Jordan—to come help the U.S. liberate Mosul and all of northern Iraq. The Arab leaders all said yes. They all sent men and matériel. But when the coalition stormed through Mosul, Khalif was nowhere to be found. He'd slipped the noose again."

"To where?" I asked.

"Well, that's the billion-dollar question, isn't it?"

Yael looked at Trotsky.

The Russian immediately took the baton. "We all would have said Raqqa," he began, referring to the Syrian city east of Aleppo with roughly a quarter of a million people, making it the sixth-largest city in a country that was imploding by the hour.

"But . . . ?"

"But we've found no trace of him. No sightings. No signals. Just rumors."

"Still, it makes sense that he'd be there."

"Maybe yes, maybe no," Trotsky said. "On the plus side, Raqqa has certainly been the capital of the caliphate for the past several years. We're picking up lots of SIGINT out of there. The Americans keep finding and killing top ISIS commanders there in one drone strike after another. It's practically become the drone strike capital of the world, there are so many high-value targets coming in and out. On the minus side, why would Khalif hunker down in a place so carefully watched? It's not his style. And for all his talk of martyrdom, we don't see him volunteering to lay down his own life for his team or his cause."

"Then why do all the other HVTs keep going there?" I asked.

"Good question," Trotsky said.

"And one we don't have the answer to," Yael added.

"Why not?"

"Because we've got no assets on the ground," said Gingy, the guy from Israel's Unit 8200. "We've got no spies, no moles, no human assets inside Raqqa to explain what's going on. We're trying to monitor calls and e-mails and movements of thousands of jihadists all across Syria, Lebanon, Iraq, Gaza, Iran, you name it. But our systems are overwhelmed. We don't have the manpower to sift through everything we have."

"What about the NSA?" I asked. "Aren't they vacuuming up everything? Can't they help?"

Yael took that one. "I'm sure they are, but they're not exactly sharing what they have with us. And frankly, over the last two months, retaking Mosul and northern Iraq has been the top priority in Fort Meade and Langley and certainly at the White House."

"Not finding Abu Khalif," I said.

"No," Yael said.

"Could that mean Khalif might actually be in Raqqa, but you just haven't isolated him yet?"

"No, he's not there."

"How can you be so sure?"

"It doesn't fit his profile."

"What do you mean?"

"The man just launched a devastating series of attacks on Washington and seven other American cities and towns," she noted. "The American administration's position notwithstanding, these were *not* the last gasps of a dying movement. This was a brilliantly designed and almost flawlessly executed series of terrorist operations with precision timing and deadly effect. You can't put a plan like that together in a city that is being watched 24-7 by the Americans, the Russians, the Iranians, us, and the bulk of the Sunni Arab world, not to mention one that's being bombed every few days. Everyone knows Raqqa is the ISIS capital, which means Khalif isn't there. He may not be far away, but he's not in Raqqa."

"Then where?" I asked again.

"We have no idea."

My first reaction was raw anger. This was the best this elite Mossad team could come up with? *He's not in Mosul. He's not in Raqqa. Beyond that, we're clueless.* Every armchair analyst in the world writing a blog in his underwear could come up with that. With a two-month head start, spy satellites, drones, thousands of spies and analysts on their payroll, and billions of dollars a year in U.S. military aid, how in the world could one of the premier intelligence forces in the world not be closer to catching the man who had killed their prime minister?

I wanted to scream at someone—all of them.

I'd left my brother and his family for this?

I knew I had to calm down, take a deep breath. Of course they didn't know. Not yet. That's why I'd come. That's why I wanted to help.

But these weren't kids. These were highly trained, highly experienced combat intelligence veterans. They'd hunted down a whole lot of bad guys in their day. They'd also been the team that had turned the eyes of the Mossad—and thus the Americans and the Jordanians—to Alqosh in the first place. These were good people—sharp, clever, outside-the-box thinkers. So why weren't they further down the road?

The answer—once I'd cooled down enough to accept it—was entirely obvious.

Their prime minister and nearly his entire protective detail had been killed in Amman two months before, and the entire Israeli security establishment was suffering vertigo. Two weeks after the attack, the head of the Mossad had died of pancreatic cancer, further destabilizing the Israeli intelligence culture. Then came the joint U.S.–Sunni military push into Mosul and across northern Iraq. On top of all this, the new leader of this new unit was a woman who'd nearly been killed in Alqosh. How long was it since she'd been released from the hospital? How long since she'd turned down the new prime minister's offer and been approved to take this post? Having come on board, hadn't she needed to be brought up to speed on everything she'd missed while in the hospital and in rehab—mountains of field reports, cable traffic, satellite imagery, telephone intercepts, e-mail intercepts, and text message intercepts, not to mention countless meetings, verbal briefings by each of her new team members, and intense pressure from on high to deliver results?

All of it took time.

And then, of course, the White House—as risk averse as any I'd ever seen—was taking out every valuable source with a Hellfire missile before the Israelis could snag 'em and bag 'em.

No wonder the team was running behind.

I needed to calm down and cut them some slack—starting with Yael.

58

★ ★ ★

There was a knock on the conference room door.

Shalit glanced at a security monitor, then pushed a button, electronically unlocking the door. A colonel burst in with breaking news—Abu Khalif had just released a new video, and it was about to be shown on Al Jazeera.

Yael quickly turned on a bank of monitors behind her. On the largest flat-screen, mounted on the center of the wall, she put a live feed from the Arab news network based in Doha, Qatar. On four smaller screens, hanging by steel mounts from the ceiling, she brought up Israel's Channel 2, Al Arabiya, CNN, and Sky News. Then she grabbed her chair and moved it to my end of the conference room, setting it down to Shalit's right. This gave her a clear view of each of the screens. It also put her about five feet away from me.

Yael turned up the sound on the center screen, and every eye in the room turned to Al Jazeera—except for mine, which I admit lingered perhaps a moment too long on this woman who had all but captured my heart yet was still treating me like a stranger.

The new video was not yet running. Instead, the network was showing a still photo of Abu Khalif wearing his signature kaffiyeh and flowing white robes while their commentators were discussing what he might say.

Shalit was riveted on the screen, undoubtedly listening for any tidbits of hard news the anchors might have. But Yael glanced at me quickly, awkwardly, and then looked away. I was dying to talk to her alone, to really know what she was thinking, to know why she was being so hostile. What had I done wrong?

But then I heard the voice of the man who had murdered my family.

"My name is Abu Khalif," he began, looking straight into the camera. "I greet you in the name of Allah, the most beneficent, the most merciful, the only ruling judge on the Day of Recompense, the day of coming judgment. Truly all praise belongs to Allah. We praise him, and we eagerly await the day that he sends Imam al-Mahdi, the promised one, the rightly guided one, who will expand the caliphate over the entire globe and send the infidels into the hellfires forever."

The emir now went off on an interminably long and nearly incomprehensible rant about some ancient battle that occurred in the seventh century. I tried to focus, but my mind soon wandered back to the day I'd met Abu Khalif in Abu Ghraib, Iraq's most notorious prison. I'd been hunting for an exclusive, and to my regret, I'd gotten it. Even now, I could still see myself stepping into that barren interrogation room. I could see the face of the man in handcuffs, wearing the orange prison jumpsuit. He had struck me as part religious fanatic, part terrorist mastermind—a serial killing lunatic and by far the most dangerous and disturbing man I'd ever met.

Back then, Khalif had sported a wild, unkempt black-and-gray beard. Now the beard was neatly trimmed. But those eyes had not changed. They were full of murder. They still haunted me, and I could literally feel the hair on the back of my neck stand erect.

I forced myself to look away from his eyes, and only then did it strike me that this video wasn't a wide shot like in Alqosh. This was a tight close-up on Khalif's face. There was a bookshelf behind him, but it was empty. Apparently he had learned from his past mistakes. The last video had shown Khalif standing in the courtyard of a crumbling mausoleum, and Matt had immediately recognized the location. Then he'd quickly contacted me to let me know Khalif was in the town of Alqosh, on the plains of Nineveh, in the heart of northern Iraq, standing in the ruins of the tomb of Nahum, the ancient Hebrew prophet who had foretold the coming judgment of the wicked Assyrian capital. This time, there was nothing for foreign intelligence analysts to focus on, no clues as to what kind of building he was using or what city or even country he was in.

Suddenly the emir's message shifted gears, and I tuned back in.

"Let all of humanity know the words of the holy Qur'an, that 'he who deceives shall be faced with his deceit on the Day of Resurrection, when every human being shall be repaid in full for whatever he has done, and none shall be wronged.' When Imam al-Mahdi comes, when the final judgment comes, every infidel will see the error of his ways. Every infidel will experience the flames of justice. But even now, the infidels have begun to pay for their crimes—in Amman and throughout the kingdom of Jordan; in Washington, D.C.; in Philadelphia and Boston and Chicago and Minneapolis and Dallas and Atlanta; and even in the remotest village in Maine. As of this recording, more than 6,300 criminal American souls have perished at the hands of the jihadists of the caliphate in just the last few weeks. We can praise Allah for his faithfulness."

The number jumped out at me. The president had told the nation that the number of deaths was 4,647. Taylor had also said another six thousand Americans had been wounded in the ISIS attacks. Maybe more had succumbed to their injuries. Then again, I wasn't exactly about to depend on facts and figures provided by Abu Khalif.

"I tell you today, let all who abide in the caliphate know—let the entire world know—this is only the beginning," the emir continued.

"Soon—very soon—the faithful warriors of jihad, along with all Muslims everywhere, will celebrate the festival of *Isra* and *Mi'raj*. This will be a celebration like no other. Together we will celebrate not just the journeys of the Prophet, peace be upon him. No—together we will celebrate the fall of the apostates, the slaughter of the infidels, the fulfillment of the prophecies, and the coming of the end of the age. O Muslims everywhere, glad tidings to you! Raise your heads high, for soon—very soon—you will see what the faithful have longed to see for so many ages. Keep your eyes fixed on *Isra* and *Mi'raj*. Remember what the Prophet, peace be upon him, saw on that blessed journey. Remember the night visions. Remember what was revealed in the heavens. It is coming, O Muslims. It is coming, and it cannot be stopped."

What was coming? I wondered. *What was ISIS planning next?*

"All praise and thanks are due to Allah," Khalif concluded. "Therefore, rush, O Muslims, rush to do your duty; rush to join our jihad. Time is short. The end is nigh. What will you say on the Day of Judgment? What will the scales of justice reveal? As our brother from Jordan—Abu Musab al-Zarqawi—first told you: the spark of the consuming fire was lit in Iraq. It spread to Syria. Now it has spread to Jordan. And it has spread to America, but more is coming—so much more. This spark has become a raging, uncontrollable fire. And this fire will intensify until it burns all the crusader armies in Dabiq. Let there be no doubt, O Muslims—Rome is falling. The Caliphate is arising. The hope of all the ages is truly coming to pass."

59

★ ★ ★

"Thoughts?" Shalit demanded when the video had ended.

Yael muted the TV, and for a moment there was quiet as everyone processed what they had just seen and heard.

"Clearly another attack is coming," Trotsky said. "Khalif says a celebration is coming because more infidels are going to be killed."

"I'm afraid he's right," Yael said, getting up and walking over to a large whiteboard hanging on the wall in between the maps and photos of ISIS leaders. "Khalif boasted that 6,300 Americans have already died at the hands of the jihadists, but he said, 'This is only the beginning.'"

"Plus he said, 'More is coming—so much more,'" Gingy noted.

"Right," Fingers said. "And he said the attacks are becoming a 'raging, uncontrollable fire.'"

"So we're agreed that he's not just bragging about the attacks in the U.S. but signaling more attacks to come?" Shalit asked the team.

Everyone nodded.

Shalit turned to Yael. "Now it's a question of location. Is ISIS going after the Americans again or heading to Europe—or coming here?"

Yael said she was going to reserve judgment until she'd had the chance to review the transcript and go over precisely what was said, word for word. But her instinct was that Khalif meant both—more attacks in the States as well as more around the world, specifically in the West.

"Why do you say that?" Shalit pressed, not indicating she was necessarily wrong but trying to better understand her thinking.

"Khalif wasn't clear, and he wasn't clear for a reason," Yael replied. "He's not trying to give away his game plan. He's trying to dominate the global news cycle. He wants to be larger than life, larger than bin Laden. He wants to be seen as the most important and most powerful Muslim in the world. He sees himself as the leader of the caliphate—not just the Islamic State but the global Islamic empire. He truly believes he is going to take over the entire world. He's trying to inspire more Muslims to join the caliphate, become jihadists, and bring their expertise and their resources to the team. Where he hits next is important, but I don't believe that was his central point."

"You think this was a recruitment video?" Shalit asked.

"Not primarily," she clarified. "Though I'm sure it will function as one. Given all the success ISIS has had in recent days, I expect he's going to have ten thousand new recruits by the end of the week. But I don't think that was his main objective."

"Go on."

"I think Khalif put this video out not to tell his followers *where* he was going to strike next," she said. "He put it out to tell them *when*."

"Soon," I said.

"Very soon," Dutch clarified.

"Yes, yes, but it was more than that," Yael prompted. "He was clear. He was precise. Did anyone catch it?"

The room was silent, and then Trotsky spoke up. "He mentioned the festival to celebrate *Isra* and *Mi'raj*."

"Exactly," Yael said. "But why? What's important about this festival?"

She was circling the room now, trying to get the group energized, thinking, participating. Her entire demeanor had shifted. Her body language was no longer cold, no longer reserved. She was engaged, even passionate. Her eyes had lit up. It was clear she respected the men in this room enormously and loved leading this team.

"The festival marks Muhammad's journey to the Al-Aksa Mosque and his supposed visit to heaven," Trotsky said.

"Right," she said. "This is a big deal in the Muslim world—the Night Vision and the Ascension. Where does it come from?"

"The Qur'an and some of the hadiths," Fingers said.

"Good, good—which sura?" she pressed.

Gingy took that one. "Seventeen. But why does it matter?"

"Because we're hunting a man who has a doctorate in Islamic jurisprudence," she insisted. "He memorized the Qur'an before he was nine. This is a man who eats, thinks, and breathes the Qur'an and the hadiths. I'm not saying he's interpreting it correctly. But he knows his stuff. Everything he says comes from his religious beliefs, and we're not going to find him unless we can understand him. We need to outfox him, people. We need to get ahead of him, anticipate where he's going next."

I glanced over at Shalit. He was sitting back in his chair and I detected a slight smile on his face. He, too, was enjoying Yael's energy, her passion, her commitment to this mission. If Shalit had ever had any doubts about his choice to head up this team, I suspected they were long gone.

Still, I wasn't clear where she was going with this. But before I could ask her, she turned to me.

"Now, Mr. Collins, since you supposedly have so much to offer us," she said, her demeanor rapidly cooling, "perhaps you would like to enlighten us on the story of the Night Vision and the Ascension and why Abu Khalif might be referencing it?"

Her voice held an edge once again. She was standing at the other end of the room, under the video monitors. I looked into her eyes. They were hard and unforgiving. She loved this team, but she wasn't welcoming me onto it. She wasn't accepting Shalit's decision to bring me in without consulting her, without giving her the courtesy of a heads-up before springing me on her. Indeed, she was challenging my very qualifications for being in this room at all.

I looked at her, then at the others in the room. They were waiting for me to answer. I could feel the tension mounting, and I was under no illusion that Shalit was going to step in and bail me out.

This was my test, and I had about ten seconds to pass it.

60

★ ★ ★

I didn't claim to have a PhD in Islamic theology, and Yael knew it.

I certainly didn't know much about the brand of Islamic eschatology driving the leaders of ISIS, though I'd been scrambling to learn everything I could over the last few months. I'd studied the Qur'an and the hadiths as an undergraduate majoring in political science. And I'd studied them more closely on my assignments in Iraq and Afghanistan. I'd discussed them at length with various Arab government officials, scholars, and even terrorists I had interviewed in the field over the past decade.

But this wasn't about my education or my job or my qualifications or lack thereof. Something else had angered Yael, and I still had no idea what. For the moment, I needed to stay calm and pass her test.

"Well, Miss Katzir, let's see," I began. "As a young man in his thirties, Muhammad used to climb up into the caves of Mount Hira, not far from Mecca, to pray and to meditate. As I recall, he began having dreams and visions in the year AD 610, which would have made him about forty years old. At first he couldn't decide if it was Allah or Satan speaking to him. I think it turned out to be his first wife, Khadijah, who convinced her husband he was hearing the voice of Allah. She ended up becoming his initial convert. She encouraged him to keep going to the cave and listening to the voice. And soon Muhammad came to believe that Allah was commanding him to proclaim a new message to the pagans on the Arabian peninsula."

I paused for a moment to gather my thoughts, then looked back at Yael. "It was about ten years later—around the year 620—that he experienced what became known as the Night Vision and the Ascension. Muslims believe the angel Gabriel appeared to Muhammad in Arabia and gave him a mystical winged horse, or maybe a donkey, named Buraq. If I remember, one hadith says that Buraq bucked when Muhammad tried to mount him, but Gabriel put his hand on the winged creature and rebuked him. Anyway, this creature ostensibly flew through the night sky and took Muhammad to 'the farthest mosque,' otherwise known as 'the mosque in the corner.' Today it's called Al-Aksa Mosque."

"In Jerusalem?" Yael challenged, showing no evidence she was impressed by my answer thus far.

"Well, nobody actually knows for sure where 'the mosque in the corner' was located," I replied.

"What are you talking about?" Yael snapped, suddenly pacing again. "Every Muslim on the planet claims Jerusalem is their third-holiest city, right after Mecca and Medina."

"They do," I agreed. "But the Qur'an never actually mentions Jerusalem. Not by name. Not even once. And of course, there was no mosque on the Temple Mount in AD 620. When the mosque was later built there, it was named Al-Aksa to comport with sura seventeen. So how could Muhammad have flown to a mosque that didn't exist? But that's a different discussion."

"Go on," she said, circling the table. "What about the Ascension?"

"Well, again, according to the Qur'an and the hadiths, once he arrived at the mosque in the corner, Muhammad prayed and earnestly sought the counsel of Allah," I explained, straining to remember everything I'd ever read or been taught on the subject. I tried hard not to ad lib or embellish, knowing I couldn't afford even one false step. "As I recall, it was at this time that Allah supposedly reassured Muhammad that he was on the right path, that he was doing the right thing, that despite all the opposition he was encountering, he was in fact submitting to the divine will. Then Muhammad was told to climb up a ladder—the *Mi'raj*—right up into the seven levels of heaven, where he met and spoke with the prophets of old—prophets like Abraham and Moses and even Jesus. These revered holy men, according to the ancient Islamic texts, assured Muhammad that he was one of them, that he was a true prophet just like they were, and that he was truly hearing the voice of God."

Every eye turned back to Yael. It was as if we were playing singles at Wimbledon. *Serve. Smash. Return. Smash.* But I wasn't done yet.

"What I find particularly interesting is that this all came during—or perhaps right after—what Muslims call the Year of Sorrow. That was the fateful year that Muhammad's beloved uncle died. Then his first wife, Khadijah, died as well. This was the wife he truly loved, the wife he'd apparently been faithful to. In fact, he didn't marry another woman until Khadijah passed away. So these dreams and visions were occurring during a time when Muhammad was grieving—and facing many other challenges as well. Most Jews and Christians, unsurprisingly, were rejecting his insistence that he was their rightful religious leader and that Islam was the divine successor to Judaism and Christianity. Some people were saying he was a heretic, that he was listening to the voice of Satan, not God. So this was a time of great distress and confusion. Muhammad was in deep mourning. He was desperately seeking a sign from Allah, and in the Night Vision and the Ascension, he suddenly believed that he had received what he had asked for."

Yael just glared at me, and that's when Shalit stepped in. "Perhaps it's fair to say Mr. Collins knows the story of the Night Vision and the Ascension after all," said the Mossad chief.

"Maybe so, but I'm still waiting for him to answer my questions," Yael shot back.

"Which were what exactly?" Shalit asked. "Remind me."

"She's asking why," I said before she could respond. "Why would Khalif reference the festival marking these events? What exactly is he trying to say? Is he hatching a plot connected somehow to the Al-Aksa Mosque or the Dome of the Rock? Is he going to attack Jerusalem?"

Yael stood motionless.

"And?" Shalit prompted. "Do you have an answer, Mr. Collins?"

"My answer is Yael's answer," I said, wanting her to know I'd been listening.

"Meaning what?" Shalit asked.

"Meaning I can't say whether Khalif is planning to strike Jerusalem and the Temple Mount," I said. "But Yael said it herself. The reason Khalif released this video isn't to tell Muslims *where* he's going to strike next. It's to tell Muslims *when* he's going to strike, during the festival marking the Night Vision and the Ascension."

"Precisely," she said. "And when is that?"

Everyone looked at me. I struggled to recall the date. I so wanted to pass this test. But in the end I simply could not remember. "I'm sorry," I said. "I don't know."

"Do you?" Shalit asked, turning back to Yael.

"Of course," she said.

"Then when?" he asked.

"This year the festival occurs on April 3."

My stomach suddenly tightened.

That was only thirty-three days away.

61

★ ★ ★

Yael's analysis sparked a firestorm.

For much of the next hour, the group dissected every sentence—every word—of Khalif's statement. For now the group was split. Fingers and Dutch agreed with Yael that Khalif was marking April 3 as the date of the next attacks. Trotsky and Gingy weren't convinced. Shalit didn't take a side. Nobody asked me for any further analysis.

In the end Shalit told the group he wanted them to test their theories against every other piece of intel they had on Khalif and ISIS. He said he was supposed to brief Prime Minister Eitan in person at four o'clock that afternoon. Thus he needed the best they had no later than three, when he would be boarding a chopper to the Kirya—the IDF's headquarters—in Tel Aviv.

Soon everyone had been dismissed, leaving the conference room and racing back to their workstations. It was closing in on noon. They had less than three hours, and the stakes were high.

"So what do you think?" Shalit asked me as he pushed away from the table.

I hadn't left the conference room. I had no workstation, no place to go.

"I think you've put together an impressive team," I said.

He nodded. "With an impressive leader, no?"

"Very," I said.

"Not so happy with you."

"Apparently not."

"Don't forget she's got a very personal stake in the success of this mission," Shalit added. "That's why she's good. That's why I have no doubt she'll succeed."

"That's why you recruited her away from the prime minister's office."

"That's why she said yes."

"And that's why you let me join your team—because I've got a personal stake in this too?" I asked.

"Of course," Shalit replied. "You've just met the best of the best, J. B. These guys are in a class of their own. But you two are the key. You and Yael will work harder and longer, drive deeper, look more thoroughly, and think about this mission every moment of every day, because it's not a job for you. You're not here because you're experts. Neither of you. You're here—both of you—because you want Abu Khalif found and taken out even more than I do."

He leaned forward. "Now tell me: does it concern you that the team is divided?"

"You mean that they almost came to blows over the significance of April 3?"

"Exactly."

"Welcome to Israel," I said. "Five Israelis. Six opinions. Right?"

"For better or for worse," Shalit said, nearly smiling, though not quite.

"For better," I said. I was actually glad to see how divided the team was. It required each side to dig hard, fast, and deep into all the intelligence they had at their disposal to see if there was anything that would bolster their case. That was good. Skepticism in the face of even the most impressive intelligence analysis was not only justified but essential.

Groupthink, by contrast, was dangerous, especially when it came to national security. Too often it led to blind spots, caused people to be unaware of their own misguided assumptions and biases. Too many in Washington had been blindsided by the catastrophic attacks by the Islamic State. Some of the best and the brightest intelligence, security, and political officials in the world had tragically missed the signs of what was coming.

Shalit motioned for me to come and sit beside him. When I did, he said very quietly, "James, it's time. Tell me what you have."

I nodded. He was right; it was time. I walked him through the three names Khachigian had left me, the research I'd done on them, and all the information on each that I'd been able to track down.

Shalit listened carefully but looked disappointed. When I was finished, he sighed. "I'd expected more."

"More names?"

"More quality. More depth. These men are fine. I know two of them—Pritchard and Hussam. They were competent operatives in their day. But Pritchard was fired and now he's dead, and Hussam was jailed, and these are the names you bring me?"

"I'm not giving you these names," I clarified. "Bob Khachigian is. I don't know any of the three. I have no idea what they can tell me. But if Bob says these guys can help me, I believe him."

Shalit sighed again. "I certainly agree with your assessment of Bob. He was a great spy. He was a great analyst and one of the finest men to lead the CIA, certainly the finest I ever knew. I'm skeptical about these names, but clearly he must have known something I don't."

"So?" I asked.

"So let's get moving," he replied. "We trusted him in life. Why not trust him in death? I'm putting you and Yael on a plane to Cairo this afternoon. You're going to start with Walid Hussam and find out where this trail leads."

62

★ ★ ★

Walid Hussam was not the first name on Khachigian's list.

But Shalit had insisted on sending us to see Hussam first. Initially I'd pushed back, arguing Yael and I should go first to Dubai and meet Mohammed bin Zayed, the UAE's intelligence chief and the only name on the list who was still an active intelligence agent. That had been my original plan, and I thought we should stick to it.

But Shalit had overruled me. "Cairo first, then Dubai," he'd said, explaining that he had better contacts in the Egyptian capital.

Upon hearing this new development, Yael was not happy, to say the least. I could clearly hear her even through the closed conference room door as she told Shalit she had better things to do than go off on a wild-goose chase, spending what could be upwards of four or five days crisscrossing the Arab world with me. But in the end Shalit outranked and overruled her, just as he had me. She might not like it—she didn't, in fact—but Yael was stuck with me now.

Just after 3 p.m., with the initial written assessment of Khalif's videotaped address complete, Yael and I said good-bye to the team, headed upstairs to the flight deck, and approached the Sikorsky S-76 executive helicopter piloted by two Israeli air force colonels who would fly us to the airport where my private jet was waiting.

I stepped forward and offered to help Yael, who looked a little uncomfortable with the cast on her left arm, into the chopper. She ignored me and did just fine on her own, taking the leather seat immediately behind the pilots. *So much for chivalry,* I thought as I scrambled into the back and slid across the leather bench to the left window seat. Two security guys climbed in next and sat beside me. Then one of the ground crew shut the door behind us and tapped the fuselage twice. The moment we were all buckled in, we lifted off and headed south.

As the chopper banked to the right—southwest—I snuck a glance at Yael. She looked exhausted, and while the wounds to her face and neck were healing nicely, short of extensive plastic surgery, they were going to leave some serious scars. It didn't matter. She was still the most beautiful woman I'd ever met, even though she hadn't said a word to me since storming out of her meeting with Shalit.

I gazed out the window at the Jezreel Valley below and thought of Matt. I tried to picture what he was doing just then. It was only eight in the morning on St. Thomas. He was probably having breakfast and reading his Bible out on the veranda overlooking Magens Bay. He was probably praying for me, and even though I still didn't believe what he believed, I was grateful.

I grabbed my briefcase from the floor and retrieved the briefing paper I'd prepared at Shalit's request, summarizing my research on Walid Hussam. If I was going to meet this guy, Ari had told me, I might as well know as much as possible about him.

Hussam had been born in 1954 in the Egyptian port city of Alexandria. He was only thirteen in 1967, too young to fight in the war against Israel. But in 1973, when Egypt launched a surprise attack against "the criminal Zionists" on Yom Kippur, the holiest day of the Jewish year, Hussam was on the front lines as a nineteen-year-old deputy commander. When his superior officer was mortally wounded in a ferocious firefight with IDF forces near the Gaza Strip,

Hussam had to take over. His bravery in combat caught the attention of those up the chain of command.

In time, Hussam became the aide-de-camp for Omar Suleiman, the notorious head of the Egyptian General Intelligence Service. After Suleiman fired two of his deputies and another was later mysteriously murdered on a visit to Tripoli, the spy chief named Hussam his new deputy in late 2009. But soon the Arab Spring erupted in Tunisia and rapidly spread to the streets of Egypt. Egyptian president Hosni Mubarak promoted Suleiman to vice president on January 29, 2011. That same day, Mubarak promoted Hussam to become head of EGIS.

But by then all hell was breaking loose. Millions of Egyptians had taken to the streets, burning cars, burning police stations, calling for Mubarak to step down, calling for the entire Egyptian government to be arrested and tried on charges of treason. To Hussam's astonishment, even the White House was openly calling for Mubarak to step down. Once that happened, it didn't require being an intelligence professional to read the handwriting on the wall. Mubarak was going down.

On June 30, 2012, the once unthinkable occurred. The Muslim Brotherhood was swept into power, and that very day, Hussam found himself arrested, thrown into prison with thousands of other Mubarak loyalists, tortured, and left to rot and die without a trial.

What no one had foreseen that day, not even Hussam, was how rapidly the Egyptian people would then turn against the Brotherhood and their leaders. Less than a year later, a stunning 20 million Egyptians—roughly a quarter of the population—signed a petition calling for the Brotherhood to relinquish power. Many turned out on the streets, demanding the same. They didn't want Sharia law imposed on them. With Egypt teetering on the brink of full-blown civil war, the army finally stepped in, launching a coup in late June of 2013. It was bloody but successful. Within weeks, the military was in full control of the capital and the country. Most of the Brother-hood leadership was dead or in prison, and suddenly Hussam and thousands of his colleagues found themselves released from prison.

Now sixty-four, Hussam was out of the intelligence game. He hadn't reentered government but had started teaching at various uni-versities. He wrote a book on the Arab Spring, though it sold poorly. He joined a few corporate boards, probably making a few bucks, and spent far more time with his children and grandchildren than he ever had.

How he was going to help us find Abu Khalif, I had no clue. But like Shalit, I was operating on the basis of my confidence in Robert Khachigian. He hadn't steered me wrong yet. Except perhaps with Laura.

Just then our chopper touched down. When the door opened, it was immediately apparent we were not at Ben Gurion International Airport but rather at an airfield in Herzliya, the upscale community up the coast from Tel Aviv. I saw my Learjet being fueled up and readied for departure. How it had gotten here, I had no idea. Who had authorized the flight, I had no idea. Why I hadn't been told a thing about it, I also had no idea. But frankly, at the moment, I didn't care. I was in the world of the Israeli Mossad. They operated differently than the *New York Times*. I knew I'd better get used to it, and fast.

63

★ ★ ★

Yael and I hurriedly boarded, took our seats, buckled up, and roared down the runway.

The whole process from start to finish took less than fifteen minutes, and it was a good thing we'd moved so quickly. It was 4:37. It was already getting dark. A storm was rolling in, and winter rains were pelting the plane.

As we reached cruising altitude, I was tempted to lean my chair back and get some rest, which I desperately needed. So did Yael. Instead, Yael opened her laptop and buried herself in her work.

I stared out the window, trying desperately to think of something to say. "Yael, do you remember General El-Badawy?" I asked.

I knew full well she remembered the commander of Egyptian special forces, whom we had first met in the war room with King Abdullah as he and his fellow Sunni military commanders made their final plans to assault Dabiq and Alqosh.

Yael kept typing furiously, albeit only with her right hand.

"Well, the other day I got an e-mail from someone saying he was an Egyptian colonel who worked for El-Badawy. Said the general wanted to speak with me. The subject was too sensitive to discuss by e-mail."

Again, nothing.

"I was thinking we should probably call him when we get to Cairo," I continued. "Maybe you're right. Maybe Hussam is a dead end. But El-Badawy is a key player. What do you think?"

Zero.

I didn't know whether to laugh or scream, but this silent treatment was getting ridiculous. I glanced around the cabin. The cockpit door was closed and surely locked. The pilots couldn't see or hear us. There were no other passengers on the flight, and unlike on the helicopter, we could actually hear ourselves think. We could have a conversation if we wanted to, and I wanted to. This was the first time I'd been alone with Yael Katzir since the underground bunker with the king and his generals in northeastern Jordan, before we headed out to Alqosh, and there were things that had to be said.

"Yael," I began, "we need to talk."

"Not now," she replied, hunting and pecking on the keyboard with her right hand since her left was still healing.

"It's not even an hour-long flight."

"I said, not now."

"Look, you're not happy with me being here, with Shalit putting me on this team. That much is clear. But you owe me the courtesy of telling me why."

At this, she looked up. "The courtesy?" There was astonishment in her voice. "The courtesy? Seriously? Where do you get off, *Mr. McClaire*?"

"What are you talking about?" I said. "I thought we were friends."

"I thought so too."

"Then what happened?"

She just shook her head. "You've got a lot of nerve, Collins, you know that?"

"I've obviously done something to offend you. But I have no idea what. So just tell me."

"No, J. B., this isn't the time or the place. People's lives are at stake. So just give me some space and let me do my job."

No matter what I said, it was clear I wasn't going to break into the ice palace. I regretted it, but there was nothing I could do about it. Except perhaps one thing—keep talking. If she didn't want to tell me what was bothering her, fine. But I hadn't come halfway around the world to get shut down. We both had a job to do. She didn't like it, but that was tough. At this point, I didn't care. Shalit had brought me onto this team. He'd forced her to work with me, over her numerous—and vociferous—objections. So we'd better get started. I pulled out my grandfather's pocket watch. We'd be on the ground in twenty-two minutes.

"Did your team find any intercepts referencing *Isra* and *Mi'raj*?" I asked.

"No," she said, still typing.

"Did they find anything in Israeli databases indicating any terrorist detainees have referenced *Isra* and *Mi'raj* in recent months?"

She mumbled something.

"What's that?" I asked. "I'm sorry; I didn't catch that."

"*No*, they didn't," she replied.

"What about the U.S. or Interpol databases?"

"Nothing."

"What about historic connections between *Isra* and *Mi'raj* dates and acts of war or terrorism?" I pressed.

"What about them?"

"Did your team find any?"

"Not yet."

"But they've picked up chatter about coming strikes in the U.S.," I said.

That stopped Yael cold. She quit typing and looked at me.

"What do you mean?"

"The papal visit," I said. "The pope is coming to the States soon for Palm Sunday in Chicago, Easter in Los Angeles, then back to New York to address the U.N. Your guys are picking up chatter from ISIS operatives. You think Abu Khalif is plotting to take out the pope?"

Yael looked astonished. "Who told you that?"

"I'm on your team," I said. "I think you were supposed to."

"How did you find out?"

"I didn't," I said. "It was a guess. A pretty good one, as it turns out. Remind me to play poker with you someday."

She cocked her head to one side, then nodded and leaned back in her seat. "Touché," she said at last. "You saw the Reuters story out of Vatican City that the pope had just accepted an invitation to return to the States. You saw the dates. You saw all the flurry of activity, and you guessed."

"Khalif doesn't even have to hit the pope—not directly," I said. "There are 69 million Catholics in the U.S. They're 22 percent of the population. Bomb a few dozen churches around the country—all soft targets with little or no security—and you'll create enough panic."

She looked at me long and hard, then closed her laptop. "Unfortunately, you're dead-on. Ari already briefed the PM, and the PM is going to call the president. Given everything that's unfolded in recent weeks in the States, I suspect the Vatican will call the trip off. But there's more."

"Like what?"

"We're picking up all kinds of chatter that ISIS is plotting major attacks against theme parks across the U.S.—Disney World, Disneyland, SeaWorld, Universal Studios, Kings Dominion, Six Flags, you name it."

"Spring break," I said.

"Exactly. Schools let students off for a week at a time, right?"

I nodded.

"But different schools in different states take different weeks?"

"Right."

"So all together it's about a five- to six-week period—and it's coming up fast," she said. "And while you're thinking about that, think about this: Three hundred million guests visit American theme parks, water parks, and amusement parks each year. These businesses are responsible for over $220 billion in overall economic impact and something like six hundred thousand jobs. If Khalif successfully targets that industry, he's going to do real and lasting damage to the American economy."

"When does the spring break season begin?" I asked. It had been at least two decades since I'd gone down to Miami or Daytona or Panama Beach.

"This year it starts on Saturday, March 12," she said.

That was only eleven days away.

PART
FIVE

64

★ ★ ★

"I thought we were going to Cairo," I said.

"We are," Yael replied.

"Then why are we flying southeast? Cairo is southwest."

"Because we're making a stop on the way."

Yael explained that the Sinai Peninsula had become infested with jihadists of all stripes. ISIS was there. As was al Qaeda, Islamic Jihad, members of Hamas, and factions of the Muslim Brotherhood, among others. And some of them, she said, had shoulder-mounted surface-to-air missiles.

"But I thought the Egyptians were rooting out the jihadists," I said.

"They are. And President Mahfouz is making progress. The Mossad even provides targeting assistance and other aid sometimes. Still, it's not safe for a business jet coming out of Israel to fly across the peninsula. There's too high a risk we'd be shot down, and I for one don't want to wander in the desert for forty years."

"Okay, so why aren't we arcing out over the Mediterranean?" I asked.

"We're heading to Aqaba first," she said, referring to Jordan's resort city at the northern tip of the Red Sea.

"Why?"

"We'll land. We'll refile our flight plan. We'll change our transponder number and even our tail number. *Then* we'll head to Egypt."

"I don't understand. Israel has a peace treaty with Egypt."

"True. And we have a close working relationship with Cairo on the security side. But it's not normal for business flights to emanate out of Tel Aviv and head straight to Cairo. Not at this time of year. Not in this weather. We don't want to draw attention."

"So, what? We're going to play an Arab couple flying to Cairo for a few days?"

"Canadian, actually," she said. "You're Michael McClaire. I'm your wife, Janet. We're from Edmonton—on holiday."

"No wonder you're not happy," I laughed.

"This wasn't my idea, believe me," she snapped.

"Oh, I believe you. This has Ari's name written all over it."

"Shut up, and just let me do my job."

"Fine," I said. "When do we land in Cairo?"

"We're not landing in Cairo."

"Isn't that where Hussam is?"

"Yes, but we're flying to Asyut."

"Why?"

"Again, security precautions. We should land around seven."

"And then?"

"We'll drive to Cairo."

"You and I are renting a car together?"

"Of course not," she said. "We'll have a driver."

"Well, won't this be interesting."

★　★　★

We landed a few minutes ahead of schedule.

By my watch, it was now 6:48 p.m. As we disembarked, we were met by two Mossad agents. Our driver and bodyguard was a tall and lean young man who never smiled and introduced himself as Mohammed, though I was certain that wasn't his real name. He struck me to be about Yael's age—early thirties. The Mossad's station chief in Cairo was a somewhat-older and somewhat–less fit guy who looked to be in his early forties, about my age. He introduced himself by the name Abdel.

I would never have suspected these men were Jewish or Israeli or worked for the Mossad. Both looked like the native-born Egyptians they were, and both spoke fluent, flawless, native Egyptian Arabic. Whoever had recruited them had done a remarkable job, and I had no doubt we were in good hands.

"What time do you think we should get to Cairo?" Yael asked as our large black Mercedes crossed a bridge over the Nile and flew along the Asyut Desert Highway.

"Just before eleven," the station chief said.

"So when do you think Michael here should reach out to Hussam and ask for a meeting?"

"I'd do it now," Abdel replied, turning to me. "Say you're having dinner with a source in Alexandria but you need to see him immediately, at Khachigian's insistence. Say you could meet him anywhere in Cairo at, I don't know, eleven thirty tonight. Say it's very important and very time sensitive."

"Why lie about being in Alexandria?" I asked. "The man is a former spymaster. Won't he be able to find out where we're coming from?"

"You'd better hope not. Because if he gets so much as a whiff that you're with the Mossad, you'll have big problems."

"I thought you all were close."

"Not that close, my friend," Abdel replied. "Not right now."

"But your prime minister went to Amman to sign a comprehensive peace deal with the Palestinians, with President Mahfouz's full approval," I protested. "When Amman was attacked, Mahfouz sent the head of Egyptian special forces to Jordan to be part of the coalition to rescue President Taylor. I was there. We both were. We met him. We spoke with him. Everyone was working so closely together."

I looked at Yael to back up my assessment, but she wouldn't—or couldn't. "That was then," she said. "Now everything's changed. After the slaughter in Dabiq, there was a tremendous backlash against Mahfouz and the government. People were angry that Egyptian forces had died fighting in Syria, of all places. Then Mahfouz made a mistake. When Yuval Eitan was sworn in as the new Israeli prime minister, Mahfouz immediately called to congratulate him, and it leaked."

"And what?" I asked. "I don't see the problem."

"It was too quick," Yael said. "Emotions were too raw. The street was red-hot, and Mahfouz looked like he was being too friendly with 'the Zionists.' It was like lighting a match and tossing it into a sun-scorched forest. The country erupted. Demonstrations in front of the Israeli embassy. People burning tires, cars, Israeli flags. It got ugly fast. I think it rattled Mahfouz and his team. They recalled their ambassador and made us pull ours out too. Mahfouz stopped taking the prime minister's calls. The defense ministers stopped talking. The spy chiefs stopped talking. It's been like that for almost two months."

"So despite the fact the Egyptians are scooping up dozens of ISIS fighters, you don't know what they know?" I asked.

"Just what we read in the *New York Times*, I'm afraid," Yael replied.

So here we are, I thought.

I looked back at Abdel. He nodded and glanced at my phone.

I made the call.

65

★ ★ ★

Unfortunately I got Walid Hussam's voice mail.

I left a message, then sent a text and an e-mail as well.

By the time we approached the outskirts of Cairo, I still hadn't heard back.

Yael told me to call Hussam again. Again I got voice mail. I was getting worried. Yael told the station chief to call his men who were trailing Hussam and find out what was going on.

Two minutes later we got the report. The former spy chief and his family had been at a party but were just now leaving the restaurant and getting into cabs. "They should be home soon," Abdel reported. "What do you want to do?"

"We proceed as planned," Yael said. "Take us to the hotel. There's not going to be a meeting tonight. We just have to hope we can arrange something tomorrow morning."

A few minutes later, we pulled up to the entrance of the Mena House, the oldest and most beautiful privately owned resort in all of Cairo. Sitting in the shadow of the Great Pyramid of Giza, it looked more like the grand palace of one of Egypt's ancient pharaohs than a modern luxury hotel.

Yael pulled a wedding ring out of her pocketbook and put it on

her left hand. Then, to my surprise, she gave one to me. It fit perfectly. Shalit had thought of everything.

"I do," I deadpanned.

She didn't find me funny in the slightest.

Playing my part as doting husband, nevertheless, I opened my
door and got out of the Mercedes. The rain had stopped, but the
pavement was wet and the air was cold and the brisk winds made
it feel colder still. I stepped around the back of the car, opened the
door for my bride, and offered her my hand. This time she took it,
smiling at me for the first time all day, and even kissed me gently on
the cheek.

I knew she was only acting, but I liked the role, and I liked the
scene.

We walked into the lobby with Yael leaning on my arm. We passed
through the airport-like metal detector, and Yael put her pocketbook
through the X-ray machine—standard operating procedure at hotels
in the Middle East these days.

I went to the reception desk and checked us in as a couple and made
sure to pay with one of the credit cards under the name McClaire.
Abdel, playing the role of the dutiful valet, brought in our bags and
helped us up to our room. He unlocked the door and motioned for
us to wait. Then he drew a silencer-fitted pistol I had no idea how
he got past security and entered the room without us. We watched
as he checked the closets, the bathroom, under the bed, behind the
curtains, and outside on the veranda. When he was certain no one was
waiting for us, he wheeled in our luggage and handed Yael the pistol.

"Sweet dreams," he said without expression. "I'll be in the room
across the hall. Mohammed will be in the room to your right. Let us
know if you need anything."

Then he walked out the door and shut it behind him, and Yael
and I were alone.

We looked around and found ourselves standing in an enormous suite overlooking the palm trees and the heated pool and the dazzling four-thousand-year-old pyramids rising high and proud and surreal into the night sky. I glanced at Yael, then at the king-size bed with its soft Egyptian cotton sheets and small chocolates wrapped in gold foil sitting atop the pillows.

"I'll take the floor," I said.

Some things were not in the script.

⋆   ⋆   ⋆

Suddenly I heard my phone buzz.

I'd fallen almost instantly into an uneasy sleep. Now, bleary-eyed and disoriented, I fumbled around in the darkness for my glasses and my phone. It was 11:53, and there was a text message from Hussam. He said he'd been at a family gathering and had just seen my e-mail. He apologized for not getting back to me sooner. Khachigian had been an old and dear friend, he said. He'd be happy to meet me. Was I available now?

I texted back saying of course and asking where to meet him.

A few moments later, Hussam sent back his address. I recognized it immediately. It was a high-rise building right on the Nile, close to the American embassy, close to the Hilton where I'd stayed a few months earlier to write the story that had started it all, the one revealing that the Islamic State possessed chemical weapons.

I found Yael asleep on the bed, still in her jeans and brown sweater. I woke her up, explained the situation, and then called the guys on their mobile phones. Ten minutes later, we were rolling.

⋆   ⋆   ⋆

"So, Mr. Collins, what brings you to Cairo on such urgent business?"

The introductions and small talk were over. So were the condolences for the deaths in my family and so many other Americans in recent weeks. So were the condolences I gave him on the loss of fifty-three Egyptian commandos who had participated in the daring—and disastrous—raid in Dabiq. We had covered it all, but it was time to get down to business.

Hussam poured us both cups of freshly brewed mint tea as we sat looking out over the twinkling lights of Egypt's largest city from his thirtieth-floor penthouse suite. It was now past one in the morning. Much of the capital was asleep. But I had clearly piqued Hussam's curiosity.

I was alone, of course, and operating under my real name. That's how I'd known Khachigian, and that's how I'd initially reached out to Hussam. Yael had stressed again how important it was that I not be connected in any way, shape, or form to the Mossad. My alias, Michael McClaire, was to be used only when I needed to present a passport. Under no other circumstances should I mention that name.

Since Yael and her team needed to be able to hear everything I said and everything that was being said to me, I was wearing a wire that was beaming an encrypted version of our conversation down to a communications van parked a block from the apartment. That signal, in turn, was being transmitted directly and in real time to the Mossad safe house in Cairo, which was sending it back to the bull pen at Ramat David. There it was being digitally recorded and would be carefully analyzed by Gingy, Trotsky, Fingers, and Dutch.

I took a sip of the piping hot tea. It was too sweet for my liking, but it was laced with the caffeine I desperately needed, so I quickly took two more sips. Then I set the glass cup down and leaned forward in my chair. "Mr. Hussam, I came because I need a favor."

"Of course, Mr. Collins. Whatever can I do for you?"

"We had a mutual friend," I said, referring to Robert Khachigian.

"We did."

"And before our friend was murdered, you tipped him off to the fact that ISIS had chemical weapons in their possession."

"Go on," he said, not confirming my instincts but certainly not denying them.

"That's why he was murdered," I continued. "Because ISIS decided he was a real and immediate threat."

Silence.

"You both instinctively understood what could happen if Abu Khalif were to gain control of weapons of mass murder."

Hussam sat stone-faced.

"And now your worst fears have been realized," I continued.

At this he nodded.

"This is not the end," I said.

"No," he replied. "I'm afraid not."

"He will kill many more unless he is stopped."

"That is why you've come?" he asked.

"Yes, Mr. Hussam," I said. "I need you to help me find him."

66

★ ★ ★

CAIRO, EGYPT

"Why me?" Hussam asked. "I've been out of the game a long time."

I shook my head. "Not that long. And clearly you're still wired in. That's how you knew ISIS had seized that base near Aleppo with the sarin gas precursors. That's how you saw the satellite and drone photos and heard the audio intercepts. That's how you became convinced of the gravity of the situation—because you'd seen the evidence. You gave it to Robert. Robert gave it to me. I put it on the front page of the *New York Times*. Suddenly the whole world knew, while you stayed under the radar the whole time."

Hussam did not respond immediately.

"Mr. Hussam, please understand—I don't blame you for his death. Not in the slightest. You absolutely did the right thing. Robert knew the risks, and he was more than willing to take them. Because he trusted you implicitly and because he loved his country and had devoted his life to keeping her safe."

Hussam rose and walked over to the sliding-glass door to the balcony.

"You just made one mistake," I continued. I saw his head turn ever so slightly. He was listening—carefully. "You calculated that once the story was out there, the president of the United States would take action, that he would order military strikes on ISIS forces in Syria and Iraq, that America would destroy a mortal enemy of the Sunni Arabs once and for all. Except it didn't happen. ISIS crossed the red line, but the American president refused to take action."

"No," Hussam said quietly, still staring out at the Nile. "You're right. I honestly never seriously considered the possibility he wouldn't act. I'm not sure I considered it at all."

I stood and walked over to him. "The world has taken a very dark turn, Mr. Hussam," I said softly. "The America you thought you knew—the friend of Egypt, the ally of peaceful Arabs, the superpower who confronts evil with courage and overwhelming might—I'm afraid that America is gone."

"You're saying it's just us now?" he asked.

I nodded but said nothing.

We stood there in his living room, silently looking out over a city of some eight million souls, a once great and mighty regional power—the world's only superpower for a long stretch in ancient times—now humbled and teeming and increasingly endangered. Then I said, "It was you, wasn't it? You're the one who e-mailed me and asked me to contact General El-Badawy."

He didn't respond.

"So call him," I said.

Hussam thought for a moment. Then, to my surprise, he walked to his kitchen, picked up a phone, and started dialing. "General, it's me. Yes. . . . I did. . . . I think so. When? . . . Fine—bye." He turned to me and sighed. "Okay. You have a driver?"

"He's waiting downstairs."

"Then let's go. It isn't far."

Encouraged, I asked to use the restroom while Hussam put on a sweater and a coat. He pointed me down the hallway. Locking the door behind me, I quickly sent a text to Yael and the team to confirm that we were heading to see General Amr El-Badawy, commander of Egypt's special forces. I thought it was likely El-Badawy had given Hussam the critical intel on ISIS that Khachigian had passed to me. If Cairo's intel on ISIS operations in Syria had been that good several months ago, they might very well be able to help us track down Abu Khalif now.

Then I asked Yael to forgive me for what I was about to do next.

Unbuttoning my shirt, I quickly ripped off the microphone that had been taped to my chest and the transmitter that had been secured to the small of my back. I tossed both into the toilet and flushed. I had no idea what that had just cost the Israeli government, nor did I care. I wasn't going to be caught wearing a Mossad wire when I entered the Defense Ministry—period.

I washed my hands, took a deep breath, stepped out of the bathroom, and turned off the light.

"Ready?" Hussam said, waiting for me in the vestibule.

"I am," I said, and we were off.

By the time we walked out the front door of the high-rise into the brisk night air, Mohammed was alone with the Mercedes, standing at attention and holding the rear door open. There was no sign of Yael or Abdel or the communications van, and for this I breathed a sigh of relief.

Hussam gave Mohammed the address and we began cruising down nearly empty city streets. Ten minutes later, however, we did not pull up to the Defense Ministry. Rather, we stopped at a small café in a suburb called Heliopolis, just blocks from the presidential palace. The café was closed. The lights were off and there was no movement inside. It was, after all, 2:17 in the morning. Yet Hussam insisted that this was the place.

Mohammed stopped the car and let us both out. Then Hussam guided me down a dimly lit alley, past two Dumpsters overflowing with putrid garbage, to a back door, where he knocked twice.

I could only imagine what Yael and the team were thinking. They had no way to see where I was, what I was doing, or whom I was about to meet. Nor did they have any way to listen in to my conversation, as per the explicit plan. But when the door opened, I knew I'd done the right thing. Three large bodyguards greeted us and pulled us inside. I was immediately given a pat-down that was, in a word, thorough. The wire would have been found instantly, and the meeting would have been blown. But in the absence of the wire, I was cleared and led down a hallway, with Hussam, to a small private dining room where the fifty-six-year-old general was waiting.

El-Badawy greeted me warmly and told his men to step outside and interrupt us only to bring in some coffee. When they left and closed the door, he bade Hussam and me to sit down.

"Thank you for coming, Mr. Collins," he began.

"Forgive me for not coming sooner," I replied.

"I am so sorry for your loss."

"And I am for yours."

He nodded and tapped his right hand to his chest. "It is not easy to lose those you love."

"No, sir," I said. "It is not. Still, I wish I could have come sooner."

"Not at all," he said. "Obviously when I heard of what had happened to your family, I knew I could not expect you to come."

"So you gave the story to Bill Sanders," I said. "You told him about how closely Egypt is cooperating with Washington in the hunt for Abu Khalif."

"Perhaps," he said.

"You made the right call. Bill is an excellent journalist. The story made a big splash."

"Maybe," El-Badawy said, "but it's not true."

"Pardon?"

"You heard me. The story is fundamentally untrue."

"You're not helping the Americans?" I asked, suddenly puzzled.

"We want to," he said. "We're trying to. But the fact is . . ."

He stopped midsentence as someone knocked on the door. Coffee was brought in. Thick, strong Turkish coffee. With a plate of baklava. And a bowl of crisp red apples, bananas, and fresh pears. This wasn't going to be a quick meeting. We were going to be here for some time. When the agents were finished serving, they stepped back out of the room and again shut the door.

"Mr. Collins, are we off the record?" El-Badawy asked.

"I'm not here for a story."

"Then what are you here for?"

"I want your help."

"With what?"

"Finding the man who killed my family."

"The man who killed my men."

"The very same."

"And when you find him?"

"That's my business."

"Not if I'm helping you."

"Then let me be clear, General," I said. "Abu Khalif is not going to Guantánamo. Not if I can help it. If you help me find him, he's going to die."

67

★ ★ ★

"So you're not here on behalf of the *Times*?" the general asked.

"No," I said.

"Then you're working for Langley?"

"No, this is personal."

"But you and Carl Hughes are old friends, and he now runs the agency, right? By all measures, he's itching to take the gloves off and go after Khalif—whatever it takes, however long it takes, wherever the trail leads. And I'm supposed to believe he didn't send you?"

"He didn't."

"Does he know you're here?"

"I hope not."

"Then who are you working for?"

"I told you: this is personal."

"Don't insult me, Mr. Collins. You want my help? Then answer my questions. Somebody sent you. Somebody's helping you. Who?"

I'd known the question was coming. It was obvious. Inevitable. Still, I wasn't fully prepared to give a plausible if not entirely accurate answer. Frankly I didn't know what to say. So I froze. I wasn't trained for this. All I knew was I had to keep the Mossad out of it. "I'm not at liberty to say."

It was all I could think of, and even to me it sounded lame.

"Suffice it to say," I quickly added, "that if we find Khalif, I have people who can take him out."

"People?" the general asked, his eyebrows raised.

"Yeah."

"What kind of people?"

I didn't reply.

"Editors from New York?" he pressed. "Reporters in tweed jackets?"

I kept silent.

"Hunters from Maine?"

I sipped the coffee and almost instantly felt the jolt of caffeine.

"The boys from Blackwater?" he probed. "Mossad? The Jordanians? You sure aren't working for the Saudis."

"General—" I began, but he cut me off.

"I know," he said. "You're not at liberty to say."

"No."

"Mr. Collins, do you remember what I said in the bunker, in Jordan, about Khalif's endgame?"

I remembered all right. "You said Khalif wants Mecca. He wants Medina. He wants Cairo. He still wants Amman. And that's just for starters."

"And do you remember what your guy, General Ramirez, said to me?"

"He said something like, 'I don't have time to get sidetracked.' The president of the United States was being held by ISIS. We only had sixteen or seventeen hours to find him and rescue him before he was executed on YouTube."

"Correct. So it's understandable that Ramirez wasn't interested in the long-term goals of Abu Khalif at that moment. But I am. Khalif is indeed coming after Mecca. He is coming after Medina. But he's also coming after Cairo. He wants to do what the Brotherhood failed to do. He wants to make the world's largest Sunni city—and largest Arab country—part of his caliphate. I can never allow that to happen. But your government doesn't seem to get it. You've had 9/11. You've had the attacks in Amman. You've just had all these attacks inside the American homeland. And still your president thinks ISIS is less of an existential threat than climate change. How can he dare say such a thing?"

"That's why I'm here, General. That's why I need your help."

"And that's why I can't give it. Not if you aren't going to tell me who the information is for."

I was desperate. This meeting was sliding off the tracks. "General, you need to trust me," I said. "You gave me critically important information on ISIS, and I put it on the front page of the paper of record. You asked me—admittedly, indirectly—to do something that advanced your interests, and I did it."

"Because it advanced yours, too."

"And now I'm back. I didn't come on my own. You invited me. And even if you hadn't, Bob Khachigian sent me. Because he trusted me. And I'm telling you: you can too. Give me what I need, and I'll make sure Abu Khalif pays for his crimes. I promise you that."

"Look, Mr. Collins, with all due respect, I invited you here as a reporter. You're not a spook, not an assassin. Don't get me wrong. I see what Khalif has done to your family. I know you're out for vengeance, and I don't blame you."

"Not vengeance," I said. "Justice."

"Call it what you want, but if you're not here on behalf of the Central Intelligence Agency, then you can't possibly assure me that if I help you track down Khalif, you'll be able to bring him to justice. That's impossible. You'd never get close to him—not you or the mercenaries you've hired."

"I haven't hired any mercenaries."

"Then they've hired you—or the Mossad recruited you, or the GID did," he speculated, referring to Jordan's General Intelligence Directorate.

"Don't be ridiculous, General," I retorted. "You know I'm not Jewish. How could I have been recruited by the Mossad?"

It was a deceptive question, but it was true in a way. After all, I hadn't been recruited by the Mossad. I'd volunteered.

"So you're working for King Abdullah," he concluded.

I shook my head. "I've met King Abdullah. I admire him enormously. I think he's doing a remarkable job under horrific conditions. And I think if the cards had been dealt a little differently, he'd be leading the charge to get Khalif. But his hands are full just now rebuilding his country."

"Which is why he's outsourcing the job to you."

"You're fishing, General, and you're wrong. I don't begrudge you asking. You have to ask. But I can't tell. But that doesn't mean we can't work together to find Khalif and bring him to justice. I'm not just asking for your help. I'm offering to help you. I know this man. I've met him. I've studied him. And I truly think we can help each other."

"I'm sorry, Mr. Collins."

The general took a final sip of coffee, then stood. It was over. I'd blown it. My only hope now was to tell El-Badawy about my connections to Mossad. It was my only shot. It could backfire. But wasn't it worth trying?

"Wait," Hussam suddenly said in Arabic, standing as well. "Listen to me. Collins found Jamal Ramzy. He found Abu Khalif once. He found the president. Maybe he really can find Khalif again."

"He's just a reporter," the general shot back.

"Maybe so, but his instincts are spot-on. You know it. That's why you invited him here."

"Be serious. He didn't use his own instincts—he had help."

The general moved toward the door, but Hussam physically blocked his path. *And what do you think he's asking for now?* he asked, directly in the general's face. "Look, Amr, this guy is good, and we need him. What's the worst thing that could happen? We work with him. We hunt for Khalif together. If he finds him, maybe you and your men get to go kill him. Imagine what that would do for the country, for Egypt's standing in the world. Remember, Wahid personally tasked us with getting this done. We can't just blow it off. We need to try. I'm not saying it's going to work. But it's clear the White House isn't going to help us. The Kremlin isn't going to help us. This is it. This is our last play."

They were arguing in heated, rapid-fire Arabic. I wasn't catching all of it, but what I did get was chilling. Both men believed that what had happened in Amman and in Washington was going to happen in Cairo—Abu Khalif and his forces were coming to kill Egyptians, in large numbers, unless someone stopped him.

What's more, it was quickly becoming clear that the directive to find me and bring me into the mix had come straight from the top. Hussam wasn't out of the game after all. And he wasn't simply an old friend and confidant of the commander of the Egyptian special forces. Formally or informally, Hussam was working for Wahid Mahfouz, the president of Egypt.

And I was their last option.

68

★ ★ ★

The next thing I knew, I was being hustled out the back door of the café.

We spilled out into a deserted alley, under the hazy glow of a streetlamp. Two black SUVs awaited us, doors open, armed guards at the ready. It was raining again—a biting, sleety, gusty mist. I turned up the collar of my coat as Hussam and I hurried into the second vehicle. The general and his men piled into the first. A moment later, we were peeling down empty streets. The windows were tinted. I couldn't see much. I certainly couldn't see the black Mercedes or the communications van anywhere, and as much as that worried me, it had to be driving Yael crazy.

"Text your driver," Hussam said, apparently noticing me looking in both directions and craning my neck to see out the back. "Tell him to stay put."

"Where are we going?"

"I can't say."

"So what should I tell him?" I asked.

"Tell him you'll stay in touch—you just have a quick detour. When we're done, this driver will drop us both back at the café."

I did as he suggested, increasingly sure where we were headed. A moment later came the reply.

U safe?

That had to be Yael, not Mohammed.

Yes, I wrote back. **All good.**

Lost contact.

I know. I'm sorry.

Boss very upset.

Yes, I wrote. **Gotta go.**

I put away the phone and noticed Hussam eyeing me, but he didn't say anything more.

Just then we pulled off the main street and passed through a heavily guarded security checkpoint. Soldiers in full combat gear atop armored personnel carriers gripped .50-caliber machine guns while other soldiers in ceremonial garb stood erect and saluted. Seconds later, without any words being spoken, the steel barriers ahead of us were lowering into the pavement and a massive steel gate was electronically opening.

"Welcome to Al-Ittihadiya Palace, Mr. Collins," Hussam said.

I had never been to the presidential residence in Cairo, but I'd heard of it. In the early 1900s, this immense building was the largest and most luxurious hotel in all of Africa. At the peak of its private glory, kings and queens, presidents and prime ministers, movie stars and business tycoons from all over the world stayed here. Today it was the Egyptian White House.

We followed the general's SUV around to the back of the monumental structure. I glimpsed the gorgeous dome, beautifully illuminated by a large flood lamp. As we pulled up to a rear entrance and were led into the foyer, the thought occurred to me that this had never actually been the palace of a Middle Eastern potentate. More likely, it was what some European architect had imagined such a palace should look like.

Inside, I was again carefully searched, and I again found myself grateful I had ditched the wire, no matter how angry Shalit was.

The interior of the palace was even grander and more exquisite than the exterior. An aide met the general, Hussam, and me at the security center and walked us down marble corridors, each wall covered with ancient artwork, swords, and various archaeological artifacts. Then we took a right into another labyrinth of corridors adorned with framed photographs of President Wahid Mahfouz being sworn into office, Mahfouz speaking to the masses, Mahfouz meeting with the king of Saudi Arabia, Mahfouz meeting with the emirs of Dubai and Abu Dhabi, Mahfouz meeting with the presidents of Russia, China, and India, and on and on it went. What I didn't see—though maybe I just missed it—was Mahfouz with President Taylor.

We reached another security checkpoint. When we were cleared, we were ushered into an enormous office, at least two stories high and a hundred feet long. The walls were wood paneled and lined with grand bookshelves, and above us hung not one but two enormous crystal chandeliers. I had barely looked around when a half-dozen bodyguards entered the room. The general and Hussam immediately stiffened, and there—entering from a hidden door behind one of the bookshelves—was President Wahid Mahfouz.

"Mr. Collins, thank you for coming to Egypt," he said, shaking my hand vigorously and with a warmth I had not expected from a man so routinely attacked in the media as a ruthless authoritarian. "It's a pleasure to finally meet you. I've read most of your work, especially over the past year. I am a great admirer."

"Thank you, Mr. President—that is very kind," I said. "I just wish more of it was good news rather than bad."

"So do we all, Mr. Collins," he replied. "So do we all."

69

★ ★ ★

I knew Mahfouz had an agenda.

It was obvious from the way Hussam and El-Badawy had been vetting me. They'd been determining whether I merited this meeting. Clearly Hussam thought I did. The general wasn't so sure. So undoubtedly it had been the president's call, and he'd decided yes. It was a risk, to be sure. We were about to discuss very sensitive matters, matters the Egyptians most certainly did not want splashed across the front page of the *New York Times*.

Complicating matters further, the editors of the *Times* had not exactly been kind to Mahfouz and his administration. An editorial the previous summer had charged that "human rights abuses under Egyptian president Wahid Mahfouz have reached new highs" and that "thousands of Egyptians have been arrested and imprisoned without due process, without fair trials, and some have been tortured and killed." Another recent editorial urged the White House to "increase pressure on the Mahfouz government," possibly even suspending the $1.3 billion in aid the U.S. annually gave to Egypt.

I was not on my paper's editorial board, of course. Nor did my views always reflect theirs. I wasn't paid to opine. I was paid to report. In print, I had always kept my opinions to myself and striven to be as fair and neutral as humanly possible. But would Mahfouz know that? Wasn't his view of me likely to be tainted by the opinions of my employer? Personally, I *was* concerned about allegations of human rights abuses in Egypt, of course. But I wanted this man to know I was grateful that he and the Egyptian military had, in fact, seized control of their country back from the Muslim Brotherhood. I was glad he'd worked so hard to restore order in the streets and to get the economy moving again, sluggish though it still was. I was glad he was building closer security ties with the Jordanians, the Israelis, the Saudis, and the emirates. And I was glad he was taking ISIS—and all of the Islamic extremists—as seriously as he was.

A few years earlier, Mahfouz had delivered an address at Al-Azhar University, the Harvard of Sunni Islam, located in the heart of Cairo. The speech was absolutely riveting, unlike anything I'd heard from any other Muslim leader. He'd stood before the intellectual and spiritual hierarchy of the Sunni world and demanded that they make serious, radical, sweeping reforms. He had called for a religious revolution.

"It is inconceivable to me that the world should see Islam as a religion of violent jihad, extremism, murder, mayhem, beheadings, and wanton cruelty," he'd bellowed before the stunned gathering of clerics, scholars, and students. "This is not Islam! Yet the extremists are making the world believe this is who we are. On Judgment Day, you will have to answer for what you did and did not teach. You imams are responsible to teach peace. Show the world that our religion is made for peace, not for war. The burden is on you!"

I couldn't say firsthand whether the human rights abuses the *Times* and many others were writing about were as bad as portrayed or whether they were being exaggerated by media. Was Mahfouz using harsh and heavy-handed tactics to restore calm in a country nearly undone by the Brotherhood? I didn't know, but I wasn't about to bring such matters up. They were important, to be sure. But they were not my immediate concern. Right now I had to stay focused.

But before I could say anything at all, the president cut me off.

"Mr. Collins, I've asked you to come because I want your help," Mahfouz began.

I kept quiet and listened carefully.

"When I was elected by the people of this great country, I thought nothing could endanger Egypt and the Islamic world more than the Muslim Brotherhood and the extremist rhetoric they were preaching and exporting all over the region and the world. But since taking office, I have come to believe that what Abu Khalif is doing and saying is far, far worse."

70

★ ★ ★

I nodded for the president to continue.

"This notion that mankind can somehow speed up the coming of the Muslim messiah—the Mahdi—and hasten the establishment of Allah's kingdom on earth—this is foolish, dangerous talk," Mahfouz said. "Yet this seed has taken root in many Muslim men, and not a few women, and it is bearing poisonous fruit. This apocalyptic thinking would be toxic enough on its own, of course, but the way Khalif teaches it, the way he and his men practice it, is pure evil. Khalif has convinced himself that committing outright genocide is the surest and most effective way to speed up the coming of the caliphate. This notion should be dismissed by all Muslims as sheer lunacy. Yet it has metamorphosed into a lethal virus. The number of ISIS-related Egyptian deaths in the past few days alone is evidence of that. Khalif's sick ideology is spreading—rapidly—across the region, across the planet, and we must stop it before it's too late."

"I agree," I said.

"And ISIS is not the only threat," he continued. "The Iranians—at least the Ayatollah and his inner circle—they, too, want to bring about the End of Days. Yes, they want to resurrect the glory of the Persian Empire. But what they really want is to hasten the establishment of the caliphate and the appearance of the Mahdi. They come at it all from a different angle, of course. Their theology and eschatology is not precisely the same as ISIS, though it might look the same to you, to the West. But that is not the point. The point is they are just as dangerous. They have a whole country, a whole nuclear industry, and a missile-building complex. And now—thanks to your country—they have international legitimacy and another $100 billion to make mischief with. I know you've come to talk about ISIS. I know your focus is Khalif. But you must understand how I look at the world. The ayatollahs threaten Egypt and our way of life. They've said as much. They're not hiding it. One of the Supreme Leader's top advisors just said the other day, 'We have captured three Arab capitals. We're working on a fourth. And we have another in our sights.' What do you think those three capitals are, Mr. Collins?"

"Beirut, Damascus, and Baghdad."

"Precisely. And do you know the fourth capital Tehran is trying so hard to capture?"

"Sana'a," I said, referring to the largest city in Yemen, "but I'm guessing you fear Cairo is next."

"Cairo and Amman—they want us both," Mahfouz said. "But ultimately we are not their primary objective. Whom do you think they want most of all?"

"Jerusalem," I said.

The Egyptian leader shook his head. "No. Remember, Israel is only the Little Satan to them. You—Washington, America—you are the Great Satan, and they're coming after you. ISIS and Khalif have already struck. The ayatollahs want to be next."

"So what are you doing to stop them?" I asked. "And how can we work together?"

"Egypt is facing the most serious internal and external threats in our modern history, but there are limits on how much we can do. We have our hands full with the jihadists in the Sinai. We are fighting them, and we are gaining ground. But the situation there is far worse than most people realize. Your president isn't giving us enough arms and ammunition. I have asked repeatedly. He has repeatedly said no. What's more, your own newspaper's editorial writers are urging him to cut off American aid to us."

So he did read the *Times* editorial page.

"But back to Khalif," Mahfouz said. "We aren't just killing ISIS jihadists on the battlefield. We're capturing them. We're inducing them to talk to us, to tell us what they know. Don't ask me how. Just know that we are developing solid, actionable intelligence on Khalif and his forces in real time."

Now we were getting down to it. I could feel my heart pounding. This was really happening. I was exhausted. I was grieving the deaths of my mother and nephew. I was battling clinical depression and craving a drink so badly it was physically painful. But I was also in Cairo. Inside the presidential palace. Shalit and Yael had told me exactly what to ask for if I got to this moment. "Find the couriers," they had said. "Ask about the Baqouba brothers."

Tariq Baqouba, recently killed by an American drone strike, had been the third highest ranking man in the ISIS hierarchy. His brothers, Faisal and Ahmed, were both trusted deputies. Yael suspected one of them—probably Faisal—was a courier, possibly *the* courier for the ISIS leader himself. If we could find Faisal and Ahmed, she had argued, we would find Khalif.

"Do you have anything on either or both of the Baqouba brothers?" I asked. I needed something concrete. Something I can use. A phone number. A location. And I was about to hit pay dirt.

"Of course," Mahfouz said. "I'll give you everything we have, on one condition."

My stomach tightened. "And what's that, Mr. President?"

"You need to tell me whom you're working with, or I'm afraid there's nothing more I can say."

71

★ ★ ★

I could hardly blame him.

Who was I that he should give me state secrets when I wouldn't even tell him whom I was working for or what exactly I was going to do with the information? This was highly classified intelligence that some Egyptian agent might very well have paid the ultimate price to secure. Still, I needed to know.

"Mr. President, I completely understand your position," I began, trying to build trust while finding a way through this minefield. "But I'd be grateful if you would keep in mind a few things—"

Mahfouz cut me off. He wasn't curt. I can't say he was impolite. But he made it clear this wasn't a negotiation. "We aren't in the souk, Mr. Collins," he said calmly. "Even if we were, you want to buy something, but you have no currency and no credit. You want to make a purchase you can't pay for."

"I realize that, sir, but—"

Mahfouz held up his hand. "Tell me something, Mr. Collins. How did you arrive in my country?"

The question jarred me as it seemed to come out of nowhere. "Why do you ask, Mr. President?"

"I find it curious that we have no record of a James Bradley Collins landing at Cairo International Airport, or any airport in Egypt, in the last two months."

I felt as if the wind had been knocked out of me. Suddenly I wished Yael and Shalit were listening to this and feeding me answers. I wasn't trained for this. I was tempted to blurt out the truth right then and there, to tell Mahfouz that I'd gone to the Mossad, that Ari Shalit wanted to work with him—in the shadows if necessary—to bring down Khalif before it was too late. I was sure it would be well received. But the stakes were too high to violate the confidence of my only allies and patrons at the moment.

"You obviously slipped into my country with false papers," Mahfouz said. "Which, I'm sure I don't have to tell you, is illegal. You have committed a crime. Perhaps I should just lock you up and then wait to see who—if anyone—would come to bail you out. You're walking a dangerous line, Mr. Collins. So let me remind you. This is not a game."

"I understand," I said, my mouth bone-dry.

"Good."

"If you'll give me some time, Mr. President," I said, desperately trying to recover, "I'll confer with my colleagues and see if they will agree to let me share their identity with you."

The president stood, and the rest of us followed suit.

"I will give you till noon," Mahfouz said. "Walid is your contact. Let him know what your friends decide."

★　★　★

Dawn was rising as Hussam and I headed back to the café in silence.

Morning rush hour started early in Cairo. It wasn't in full swing yet by any means, but with the rain, which was coming down harder now, and the growing traffic, the drive took us longer than it might normally have. The silence was awkward, and I was glad when we turned onto Baghdad Street, for I knew we were now just a block from our destination.

I pulled out my phone and texted Yael and Mohammed that we would be there momentarily. A large delivery truck partially blocked our path. Annoyed, our driver laid on the horn, but two men were wheeling large crates of something into an open garage. They weren't going to be getting out of our way anytime soon. We eased around the truck and finally reached the café.

As we pulled to a stop, the retired spy chief broke the ice, telling me he wouldn't need a ride back home. The president wanted him to return to the palace. I assumed they were about to have a debriefing. I could only imagine what they were going to say. As one of the bodyguards opened the door for me, I thanked Hussam for his time. "If it were up to me, I would have already told you whom I'm working with. It makes sense. But . . ."

"You have your orders," he said graciously. "We all do. You must be a loyal soldier. There is nothing more important than loyalty, James. Nothing."

"Life was simpler when it was just me and the Gray Lady."

"Maybe so. Just do what you have to do—and let me know by noon."

"No hard feelings?" I asked.

"Of course not," he said. "None at all."

The next moment, I spotted the Mercedes. It was parked a block down from the café. Mohammed stood in a doorway, smoking a cigarette and waiting for me. I started to get out. But Hussam grabbed my shoulder.

"What is it?" I asked, turning back to him. "What's wrong?"

"You asked about the Baqouba brothers," he whispered.

"What about them?"

"They're the key," he said. "Whatever you decide to do with us, that's fine—but I want you to know you're on the right trail. That's all I can say for now. I hope that's enough."

I looked in his eyes. He seemed sincere, like a father giving a son a gift. I sensed I could trust him. "Thank you," I said. "Stay safe."

"Inshallah," he replied. "You, too."

I turned toward the Mercedes and motioned for Mohammed to start the car. He quickly dropped his cigarette, stamped it out with his shoe, jumped in the car, and started the engine. I looked up and down Baghdad Street but didn't see the communications van. I had no idea where Yael was. I hoped she was close. I didn't want to debrief her by phone, but the forty-five-minute drive back to the hotel was too long to wait. There were decisions to be made, and they wouldn't be made by her. I doubted even Shalit had the authority to make this call. I guessed the prime minister himself would have to be informed.

As I approached, Mohammed got out and moved around the hood to open the rear passenger door for me. Thunder rumbled in the distance. It was as cold here as it was back in Israel.

But as I crossed the street, I suddenly saw a flash of light to my left. My first thought was lightning. But it was too low, too isolated. And then came the massive concussion. The SUV I'd just stepped out of—the one Hussam was still in—exploded. It flipped through the air and came back to earth with a deafening crash. The resulting shock wave sent me soaring. I smashed into the side of the Mercedes. Then I heard the distinctive whoosh of a second rocket-propelled grenade and once again felt the earsplitting explosion and the searing, scalding fireball.

I couldn't move, couldn't think, couldn't breathe. I couldn't hear or see. Thick, black, acrid smoke filled the sky, filled my eyes, and the last thing I heard was the rat-a-tat-tat of machine-gun fire.

And then everything went black.

72

★ ★ ★

When I came to, I was lying on the wet pavement, covered in glass.

My clothing was soaked and torn. My eyes stung. My ears were ringing. I had no idea how long I'd been out. As I pulled myself to my knees and then to my feet, I saw that all the windows in the Mercedes had been blown out. Then I saw Mohammed sprawled out on the sidewalk, his body ripped to shreds, a pool of crimson surrounding him. I stumbled over to him and checked his pulse. He was gone.

I looked around and stared at the carnage before me. The roaring, flaming wreckage of the SUV. The charred bodies of Hussam, his driver, and the bodyguard. The gaping, jagged holes where the windows of the café had been. They'd all been blown to bits, and the building was on fire. It was then that I realized I couldn't have been unconscious very long. There were no police cars on the scene, no fire trucks or ambulances. But they'd be here any moment.

Looking to my right down Baghdad Street, I noticed the delivery van was gone, and a chill abruptly ran down my spine. Did Abu Khalif somehow know I was here? Had he sent jihadists to kill me before I found him? How was that possible? How could he have known? Was one of the Israelis a mole? Someone in Mahfouz's office?

That didn't seem likely, but there were still only a handful of people who even knew I was here. That meant there were only a handful of possible suspects, and four of them were dead.

I felt my phone vibrating in my pocket. I took the call, but whoever it was, I couldn't hear what they were saying. A moment later a text message came in. It was from Yael.

Get out of there now! she insisted. **Meet at the safe zone—go!**

My head was pounding. My right knee was bleeding. I felt foggy and disoriented. I knew we'd discussed a rendezvous point, a safe zone, just in case something went wrong. But right now it was all a blur. I couldn't remember the name. I couldn't remember the address. But I had no time to think about that. I had to get moving. Yet I couldn't leave Mohammed there. I couldn't leave the body of a fallen Mossad officer on a Cairo side street.

I opened the back door of the Mercedes. Then I picked up the six-foot-one, two-hundred-pound Israeli and wrestled him into the backseat, even as a crowd was beginning to form. As I shut the door, I noticed that his pistol—equipped with a silencer—had fallen out of his holster. It was sitting in the gutter, in a puddle, and just the sight of it—along with the blood on the sidewalk, and the blood that was now all over me and all over the car—triggered a shot of adrenaline through my entire system.

I grabbed the pistol and raced for the driver's side. I could hear again—not perfectly, but it was slowly coming back. Sirens were approaching from multiple directions. Behind the wheel, I gunned the engine and took off, leaving the growing crowd of onlookers and knowing they were all witnesses.

As I barreled down Baghdad Street heading for El-Orouba Street, a major thoroughfare, I knew people had seen me. They'd seen my face. They'd seen the car, shot up with machine-gun fire. They'd seen me put a body in the backseat. And someone had surely taken down the license plate number. Someone always did.

I raced up the ramp, onto the highway and into thickening traffic. I tromped on the accelerator, weaving from lane to lane when I could, but knowing all the while I was running the risk of attracting the attention of the police. I couldn't afford to be stopped. Not the way this car looked. Not with who I had in the backseat. Not with the information I had to get to Yael.

The phone rang. I didn't want to answer it as I raced westward onto Salah Salem Street, heading for the Nile. But it was Yael and she could tell me where I was supposed to be going. So I put the phone on speaker and dropped it into the cup holder by the gearshift, knowing I would need both hands on the wheel from this point forward.

"You've got a tail," she yelled before I could even say hello.

"What are you talking about?"

"You're on Salah Salem, heading west, right?"

"Right."

"Someone's following you—a silver Audi—it's eight, nine cars back and it's coming up fast."

"How do you know?"

"'Cause Abdel and I are six or seven cars behind him."

"Cops?" I asked.

"No," she said.

"Secret police?"

"I doubt it, not with that car."

"Then who is it?"

"I have no idea, but you need to lose them."

"I can't," I said. "You need to get them off me—now."

I glanced in my rearview mirror and then in my side mirror. Yael was right. Whoever was in the Audi, they were coming up way too fast. I shifted into a higher gear, broke left and roared around a dump truck, then cut back to the right. In the process two other cars braked hard to miss hitting me, which temporarily blocked the

Audi's view of me as well as its approach. But I doubted it was going to be enough.

Edging to my right, I checked my side mirror again. I could see the Audi. It was only five cars back but boxed in between a Ford Expedition and a large moving van. This was my chance. I pulled onto the shoulder and then hit the gas. Fifteen seconds later, I reached an off-ramp and took it.

"No, no, don't get off!" Yael screamed over the speakerphone. *"What are you doing?"*

"I had to," I yelled back. *"They're gaining on me."*

"And we're gaining on them!" she countered. *"Now you'll be on smaller streets. More traffic. More lights. Get back on the highway."*

I braked and downshifted as I roared down the ramp and came to a dead stop. Yael was right. The traffic was brutal in both directions. Everything was gridlocked. Fear threatened to overwhelm me.

"I don't know what to do," I said. "I'm stuck."

"Don't worry," Abdel said into the phone. "I don't think they saw you."

"You sure?"

"Either way, they're trapped in the left lane. No wait—"

"What?" I yelled.

He swore loudly.

"What?"

"They just shot at the Ford. The Ford's braking. They're smashing into the Ford, pushing around him. They saw you. They're heading for the off-ramp."

I was still not moving. Traffic was at a standstill. And then I saw the Audi barreling down the ramp, coming straight for me. Inside were two men, both wearing black hoods. And they would be on top of me any second.

I should have panicked, but instead I had an idea. I grabbed for Mohammed's silenced pistol on the seat beside me. I would shoot these two just before they reached me, and that would be the end of it. But the pistol wasn't there. Frantically I searched everywhere, then realized it had slid off the passenger seat and onto the floor. I could see it, but with my seat belt on, I couldn't reach it.

73

★ ★ ★

I was out of time.

The Audi smashed into the back of the Mercedes at full speed. This should have driven me into the Volkswagen van that had been idling directly ahead of me, but at that moment traffic started moving again. The VW turned right and got clear just in time. I went straight ahead, but instead of folding up like an accordion from impacts on both sides—crushing me in the process—my Mercedes went ricocheting through the intersection.

I clipped the back of one car and the front of a pickup. But the velocity from being hit so hard from behind still sent me hurtling completely through the intersection and up the on-ramp on the other side. How the driver's side air bags weren't triggered, I had no idea, but I hit the gas and the Mercedes poured back onto Salah Salem Street, leaving the Audi trapped by the new chaos its driver had just created.

I could hear Yael and Abdel cheering over the speakerphone, but they were abruptly drowned out by the sound of automatic gunfire. At the same time, I could hear the Audi smashing its way through the intersection, and when I glanced in my rearview mirror, I saw the Audi surging back onto the thoroughfare behind me and one of the terrorists aiming an AK-47 at me.

For the moment, I was a good ten to twelve cars ahead of them, but they were fighting hard to close the gap. I pushed the accelerator down and zigzagged through the morning rush-hour traffic at forty, fifty, sixty miles per hour. Often I was on one shoulder or the other. But the guys in the Audi weren't just keeping up—they were gaining. I roared past the National Military Museum on my right and an enormous mosque on my left. Still the Audi kept coming, and now Yael and Abdel were nowhere to be seen, stuck in the mess the Audi had left behind.

Traffic was getting worse. My speed was dropping from fifty to forty to thirty miles per hour and then all I could see ahead of me was a sea of red brake lights. When I looked again, the Audi was only six cars back and coming on strong. Fearing I would soon be trapped, I again broke right at an off-ramp and began weaving through various side streets at ever-increasing speeds.

The Audi never missed a beat. My pursuers were tracking my every move as I increasingly feared for my life. These guys clearly knew who I was. They weren't going after Hussam. They'd been coming after me. When they saw me sprawled out on the street by the café, they must have initially thought they'd done their job. They couldn't have known I'd only been knocked unconscious. But someone had told them after I'd gotten up and driven away. Someone in that crowd. And now they were closing in for the kill.

"Where are you? We can't see you," Yael said over the speakerphone.

I had absolutely no idea. Office buildings and restaurants and parks and street signs were blowing by too fast for me to process, much less report them. I was trying not to get sideswiped by the traffic around me, and that was increasingly becoming a fool's errand.

Up ahead the street I was on was ending. Railroad tracks lay dead ahead. But there was no crossing. Not here. Just a cement wall on the other side of the tracks. I hit the brakes and pulled hard to the right, spilling into oncoming traffic and going the wrong way up a one-way street. I laid on the horn and flashed my lights as I wove my way forward.

Cars, trucks, and motorcycles were swerving to get out of my way and then, all of a sudden, the road completely cleared. I figured there must be red lights ahead. In another sixty or ninety seconds they would turn green, and then cars and trucks and motorcycles would be hurtling straight for me once again.

A freight train was now speeding past on my left. I was picking up speed on this clear straightaway—forty, fifty, sixty miles per hour—so I was slightly gaining on the train. But the Audi was gaining on me. They were a mere three car lengths behind me. Then two. And soon they were right on my tail and about to smash into me.

Then I heard something beeping. I glanced down at the dashboard and saw the gas gauge on empty. Just my luck. I'd made it through half of Cairo with ISIS butchers on my tail, and it was all going to come to an end because I ran out of gas. It had to be a leak, I knew. There was no way the Mossad guys had forgotten to top off the diesel before rolling out on this mission. Which meant I'd been leaking fuel since coming under machine-gun fire at the café.

A single spark, and the whole car could erupt.

I heard the train's horn blow twice. It was a sharp, piercing sound—the sound of danger, the sound of warning. And that's when I saw the railroad crossing ahead. Now I knew why the traffic was stopped. It wasn't for a traffic light. They were stopped for an oncoming train.

Less than a quarter mile ahead of me the road veered slightly left and crossed the tracks at an angle, and I could see the gates were down. I could see the lights flashing, and I knew I had a choice to make. Floor it and try to outrun this thing. Or slam on the brakes and get hit from behind by the Audi, a collision that could easily ignite what leaking fuel was left and blow me to kingdom come. And that's if I was lucky. More likely, if I could even come to a full stop before the crossing and not get boosted onto the tracks by the Audi, the ISIS guys following me would capture me and take me back to Abu Khalif. That would be a fate far worse than death, I knew, so the choice was clear.

As the train horn blew two more times, I pushed the accelerator to the floor. I was doing nearly seventy miles per hour as I pulled ahead of the locomotive—half a car length, then a full car length. Better still, I was pulling away from the Audi. Not much. Not enough. They were still far too close. But rather than right on my bumper they were about a car length back, and then two.

I looked ahead at the crossing. It was coming up fast. Again came the blast of the train's horn—and not just once or twice. This time the engineers laid on the horn and wouldn't stop. I glanced in my side mirror. I could see their faces. Looks of sheer terror. They could see what I was trying to do. They were sure I was suicidal. But there was nothing they could do to stop me, and there was certainly nothing they could do to stop their engine and the hundred fully loaded freight cars they were pulling.

A split second later, the moment of truth arrived.

At the speed I was going, the rubber-coated crossing and the slight rise over the tracks sent the Mercedes airborne. In my periphery I could see and feel and hear and even smell the rush of the oncoming locomotive. But I cleared it. It was close. Far too close. But somehow I cleared and slammed down on the pavement on the other side, metal crunching, sparks flying, and then I hit the brakes and closed my eyes. The car—shuddering, smoking, skidding, weaving—finally slammed into the side of an idling but empty city bus.

The air bags exploded. But the Mercedes didn't.

Not yet, anyway.

The interior of the car instantly filled with smoke. Coughing, choking, gasping for air, I groped about blindly for the firearm and my phone. I somehow found both and kicked open the driver's-side door and crawled out of the wreckage. Gripping the silencer-equipped pistol in hand, I turned back to confront my pursuers.

But then I saw the Audi—or what was left of it. Flaming chunks of German engineering were raining down from the sky. The Audi was gone. The men inside it had been vaporized. What's more, the train hadn't derailed. It had survived, and for the moment, so had I.

74

★ ★ ★

A crowd was gathering.

That was a problem. The police were already on their way. I could hear the sirens approaching. There were witnesses. They would be interviewed. The Mossad agent's body would be found in the backseat of the Mercedes. And I might be found too.

I pushed my way through the crowd, limping and in pain, yelling in Arabic for people to get out of my way but careful to keep my head down and avoid eye contact. Without stopping, I made sure the pistol's safety was on and then shoved the gun into my belt and pulled my shirt over it. Then I made my way to a subway station. I hustled down the stairs as quickly as I could, mopping sweat from my brow and trying desperately to suck in fresh air and get hold of my spiking heart rate.

I knew countless people had just seen me go into the subway station and would therefore point the police in my direction, so I hobbled my way to the other end of the station and took an escalator back up to ground level. The moving stairs ended inside an office building, out of the direct sight of anyone who was gathering around the crash. Immediately I bolted out the building's back doors, crossed a busy street clogged with rush-hour traffic, and passed through the lobbies and back doors of three more office buildings and then a shopping plaza. At that point I flagged down a taxi, jumped inside, thrust a handful of cash into the driver's hand, and told him to get me to the campus of Cairo University. Speaking in Arabic, I promised the man a very generous tip if he could get me there quickly, and he readily complied.

Soon we were weaving through traffic and crossing the Abbas Bridge, heading west. I texted Yael, telling her I was alive and where I was headed. Seconds later, she texted back with the address of a supermarket on the north side of the campus. I relayed the information to the driver and asked how long it would take to get there. He said ten to fifteen minutes, depending on traffic, and I shot that information back to Yael.

I'm on my way, she said. **I'll be there in no more than half an hour.** Then she gave me exact instructions about what to do when I arrived. **Pay the driver in cash. Go directly into the supermarket café, but don't order. Don't sit down. Head straight for the men's room. Step into a stall. Lock the door. Turn off the ringer on your phone. Wait there. And whatever you do, don't attract any more attention.**

Everything took longer than promised. The taxi driver's estimate was way off. So was Yael's. But I did as I was told, and eventually Abdel met me in the men's room. I gave him the gun, and he gave me a clean, dry set of clothes and a new pair of leather shoes. I washed my hands and face and changed quickly as he stuffed what I had been wearing into a duffel bag and rushed me through a back door into an alley, where Yael was waiting in the van.

Moments later, with Abdel at the wheel, we were working our way through traffic. Abdel was careful to maintain the speed limit, careful not to attract attention, and before I knew it, we were on the Ring Road heading north.

As we drove, I told Abdel and Yael everything that had happened in excruciating detail. She had me on speakerphone with a secure line directly back to her team at the Ramat David air base and Shalit at Mossad headquarters. They were firing questions at me left and right. *Had I seen the men who had fired the RPG that killed Hussam? How good a look had I gotten at the Audi that had followed me? Did I know what color it was? What specific model? What was the license plate number? Could I remember any other details about the attack?*

Unfortunately the answer to everything was no. I hadn't seen anything. I couldn't remember anything. I had nothing specific, much less actionable, to report. And then I began firing questions back at them. *How in the world could ISIS have tracked me to Cairo? How could they have known I was with Hussam? How could they have known my exact location? Even on the off chance that ISIS had picked up some whiff of intelligence that I was in Cairo, how could they have possibly known I would be at that café at that moment?*

I was angry, and I was scared. The attack made no sense whatsoever. I could count on one hand the number of people who had known precisely where I'd be that morning and when. No one on this call had known. Not even I had known.

"Maybe there's a mole inside the Egyptian palace?" one of the analysts mused.

The very notion sent a chill down my spine, especially as I explained to them everything I had just discussed with Hussam and the general and President Mahfouz. Shalit wanted to know what exactly Hussam and Mahfouz had said about the Baqouba brothers and whether I believed the Egyptians had specific intelligence on their whereabouts. He wanted to know if I had admitted, confessed, hinted at, or intimated in any possible way that I was working with the Mossad. He wanted to know why I'd destroyed my wire and flushed it down Hussam's toilet. And on and on it went.

I answered every question numerous times, but Shalit and the others kept asking in different ways, from different angles, both trying to force me to remember every single little detail but also trying to break my story. It was clear that some of them—Dutch and Fingers in particular—didn't believe me. "Why would you discard the wire unless you were planning to give them information you didn't want us to know?" Fingers demanded.

At that I went ballistic. "What exactly do you think would have happened when the general's men searched me? How would I have explained a wire? El-Badawy is the head of the Egyptian special forces, for crying out loud. If he caught me trying to secretly record our conversation, he would have had me thrown into a cell!"

Yael finally intervened and cut off the call. As we exited the Ring Road onto the highway bound for the Egyptian city of Ismailia, she turned to me and repeated the question Shalit had asked me. "Did you believe Mahfouz when he said he had solid intel on the Baqouba brothers?"

"Absolutely," I said.

"Why?"

"I don't know," I replied. "I can't give you anything definitive. Call it intuition. Call it a gut instinct. All I can say is, I've been doing this for a long time—interviewing subjects, assessing their honesty, assessing their motives and reliability—and I'm telling you, this is legit."

"So you think they know something important."

"I do."

"Because they're scooping up bad guys in the Sinai?"

"Among other places."

"Human intel?"

"You mean as opposed to a telephone intercept or an e-mail?" I asked.

"Or a hard drive or pocket litter or anything else," Yael replied.

"You want to know if they have an actual source with firsthand knowledge of where one or both of the Baqouba brothers are?"

"Right."

"That I can't say," I confessed. "I don't know what they have, and I don't know how they got it. But it's something. It's big. It's real. But I have no doubt it's perishable."

"Meaning if we don't get it today, it might not be true tomorrow?"

"Exactly."

Yael was quiet for several minutes. Then Abdel piped up as he drove. "You think Mahfouz is serious about helping bag these guys?" he asked.

"Yeah, I do," I said.

"He really wants to take down Abu Khalif?"

"Not directly," I said. "He said his hands are full with the jihadists inside Egypt and in the Sinai. But he's got something he wants to give to somebody. He just feels he has to be careful who that somebody is. He wants to work with the Americans, but they're not playing ball, and he doesn't trust them anymore. Why else would he meet with me? I wasn't asking for a meeting with him or the general. I only wanted to talk to Hussam because Khachigian told me to. Even you guys weren't sure if Hussam was an active player."

"Turns out he was," Yael said.

"I'll say—the man was working directly for President Mahfouz. It was Mahfouz who learned ISIS had chemical weapons. It was Mahfouz who wanted to get that intel to President Taylor. It was Mahfouz who wanted the world to know what Abu Khalif was planning. So he gave the intel to Hussam. Hussam gave it to Khachigian. And Khachigian leaked it to me."

"That was months ago," Yael said. "Doesn't mean they've got the goods now."

"Maybe not," I said. "But look at the article my colleague Bill Sanders wrote. The Egyptians told him they had photographs of Khalif getting into Red Crescent ambulances going in and out of Raqqa. Did you guys have that?"

"No," Yael conceded.

"Do you believe it?" I asked.

Yael shrugged.

"Well, do you?" I pressed.

"Probably."

"Then Mahfouz and his team are doing their job. They've got the sources. They want to help. They're willing to play ball. But not unless I tell them who I'm working for. Which is why I need to tell them."

"Absolutely not," Yael said. "That's never going to happen."

"We don't have any choice," I countered. "I need to call them back and make sure they don't suspect me for Hussam's death. And I need to tell them I'm working with you guys and why we all need to work together. I can't wait until noon. If ISIS really was responsible for that attack, then they could very well know what I'm fishing for, and that means the Baqouba brothers know or will soon. Whatever hard intel Mahfouz has on them is going to be useless unless we move fast."

75

★ ★ ★

Abdel dropped us off at the Ismailia airport just before 11 a.m. local time.

The business jet lifted off minutes later, bound for Dubai. As soon as we were in the air, I demanded Yael get Ari Shalit back on the phone. At first, she told me this was impossible, but when I threatened to call Carl Hughes at the CIA and get ahold of Shalit through him, she finally relented and put me on a secure phone to Mossad headquarters.

For much of the first hour of our three-hour flight to the commercial capital of the United Arab Emirates, Shalit and I battled over the efficacy of informing the Egyptian government of my connection to the Mossad. I was adamant that every minute going by was wasted time that could blow the only real lead we had to the killer of the Israeli prime minister, not to mention thousands of Americans. Shalit, however, countered just as forcefully that the future of the entire Israeli-Egyptian peace treaty lay in the balance.

"Listen, James," he said, "if Mahfouz thought for a split second that Mossad was running operations inside Egypt, the entire treaty could come unglued. Yes, it's that sensitive. And don't forget: your involvement has already led—directly or indirectly—to the death of Walid Hussam. Israel has enough crises to worry about without opening up an entire new front with the Egyptians."

I could not dissuade him, and when I raised my voice, Shalit hung up on me. Had I been a politician, I might have turned to Yael and spun the whole thing as a stalemate. But I wasn't a politician. I had no energy or desire to call this anything other than what it was—a complete and utter defeat. I'd made my case, and I'd lost, and now I was done. I'd put my life on the line to try to make a difference, to find leads that could help the Mossad crack this case and find Abu Khalif. And now we had a lead. With a single phone call from Ari Shalit to General El-Badawy, we had the potential to blow this thing wide-open. Yet Shalit refused to listen. He had his reasons, of course, but they weren't nearly good enough for me.

I slumped into a seat in the back of the plane and stared out the window at the vast expanse of the Saudi desert below us. I could see no cities, no towns, no villages—not even bedouin outposts. There were no trees, no rivers, no vegetation, no signs of life in any direction as far as the eye could see. I saw no roads, no cars, no people, no power lines. No evidence of human existence at all. It was like I was staring down at the surface of the moon. Uninhabited. Uninhabitable. Barren. Empty. And unforgiving.

In that moment, I felt more alone and helpless than at any other time in my life. I was doing everything I could to bring Abu Khalif to justice, to safeguard my family, to give us a chance at a life of freedom and security. But I was failing. I'd almost died—again. I'd seen far too many others die before my eyes—again. And for what? What good had any of it done? What, if anything, had I accomplished?

I thought about that as I looked down at the desert from thirty-nine thousand feet. I thought about that as we streaked through the atmosphere at five hundred miles an hour. And nothing at all came to mind. A half hour went by. Then an hour. And then two.

We were approaching the Gulf. We were told that in a few minutes we would need to fasten our seat belts and prepare for our descent. Absentmindedly I did both, but I just kept staring at the desert floor, and try as I might, I couldn't see any good that had come from this mess. Nor could I see a way forward. I was out of plays. Out of options. Yael had shut down on me and I didn't know why and she wouldn't say. Shalit wasn't listening to me and I did know why, but I wasn't wrong, yet I couldn't budge him. I owed the president of Egypt an answer I wasn't allowed to give. So what was the point of it all? I had no idea.

I was suddenly overwhelmed by the intense desire to get back to Matt and Annie and Katie. I missed them so badly it was physically painful. I'd wasted so much of my life covering other people's lives that I'd blown much of my own. My marriage. My relationship with my mom. My relationship with Matt and his family. I knew I couldn't go back and change the past. But maybe I could start fresh. Maybe, at the very least, I could go home, or to whatever passed for home at the moment, and make amends. Or try, anyway. At that moment, I resolved to book my flight back to St. Thomas the moment we landed in Dubai, and only then did I finally begin to breathe again.

I turned away from the window and found myself glancing at Yael. She was sitting toward the front of the plane, hunched over her laptop. I was dying to know what had gone wrong between us. Whatever spark I'd felt in Istanbul and then in Amman and even on that base in eastern Jordan just before we'd headed into Iraq was long gone. I wanted to fix it. I wanted to make it right. I wanted to go back to the way it was before, when even the mere prospect of a few moments with this fascinating, beautiful, mysterious woman was tantalizing and electric.

This was the moment. I had to know. And I had to know now— before we landed, before I boarded a flight back to the Caribbean, before I walked out of her life forever, never to see her again.

76

★ ★ ★

I was about to unbuckle my seat belt and go talk with her when we hit some serious turbulence.

The plane began to shake violently, lurching from side to side. The pilot came on and insisted we remain in our seats with our seat belts fastened and not attempt to move about the cabin. Yael's laptop suddenly slid off the tray in front of her and went crashing to the floor. I could see her trying to decide whether she should grab it or not, but as the jet shook even more intensely, she decided against it. She glanced back to make sure I was all right. I nodded that I was fine, but it wasn't true. Not even close.

I was feeling nauseated. I was beginning to perspire. I reached up and opened the vent above me to get more air, and then I closed my eyes and leaned back and tried to steady my nerves and my stomach. I was not prone to air- or sea- or carsickness, but I remembered that on the few occasions I had experienced motion sickness as a kid, my mother had always told me to focus on something else, something specific, something good. Now, as I closed my eyes, it was my mother's face that came to mind—not hazy and gauzy and distant but as crisp and vivid as if she were really with me. It wasn't a mystical experience. She wasn't speaking to me. I wasn't hearing her from the grave. It was just a memory, and after a split second the image faded, replaced by a feeling of intense regret. I missed my mom. I wanted to see her. I wanted to talk to her. I wanted her to tell me everything was going to be okay.

From the time I'd left for college at the age of eighteen, I'd always been a man in a hurry. Always on the go. Always making excuses why I couldn't come home, couldn't see her, couldn't even call home enough and say hi. And the sadness I felt was excruciating.

And then I began to cry. Sob is more like it. I felt embarrassed and ashamed but I couldn't help it, though I did everything to stay quiet and not draw Yael's notice. Still, I was completely overcome with emotion—with loss, with regret, with fear—and from the inner depths of my soul I wept. It wasn't only for my mother. I think it was for all the people I'd lost in recent months. I hadn't really grieved for any of them. Not properly. But at that moment all that I had kept buried came rushing to the surface.

Wave after wave swept over me, the tears accompanied by images. My father storming out our front door when I was twelve—the last time I ever saw him. Me walking past my mother's room when I was seventeen and seeing her on her knees, praying through tears. My friend and photographer Abdel Hamid stepping on a land mine in Homs. Omar Fayez starting the rental car in Istanbul and it blowing to smithereens. Matt in Amman, driving me to the airport, pleading with me not to go to Iraq.

All these and many others flashed like a strobe light through my mind and heart. There didn't seem to be a rhyme or reason, no theme or common thread that bound them all together.

The last image in the rapid-fire series was my mom's pastor, speaking at her memorial service back in Bar Harbor. In my mind I again heard one of the last things he'd said.

"Maggie and Josh are gone, but they are not dead. They are more alive today than they have ever been. . . . But your only hope of seeing them

again is to give your soul to the God they entrusted their souls to, and to do it before you breathe your last."

Those words thundered in my heart. They shook me to my core. And in that moment, I knew they were true. I can't explain how. I just knew that everything I'd heard the pastor say that morning was true. Everything Matt had been trying to explain to me for years was true. All of it. Jesus' life. His death. His burial. His resurrection. The way to heaven. The way of salvation. My sins. My need for a Savior. It all made sense. All at once, everything I'd been reading in the Gospels and the rest of the New Testament began to click into place. For the first time in my life, I could see it. And I wanted it. I wanted *him*. I wanted to be saved. To be adopted into God's family. To know beyond the shadow of a doubt that I would spend eternity with him and with my family.

So through my tears—silently but earnestly—I begged God to forgive me, to change me, to fix me, to rescue me and adopt me.

And something happened. I didn't see a vision. I didn't hear angels singing. I didn't see fireworks or have some out-of-body experience. But I felt clean in a way I'd never felt before. I had peace I couldn't begin to explain.

I was different. One moment I was lost and dead and grieving and alone. And the next moment I wasn't. In the blink of an eye. In the space of a prayer. I was different.

I was free.

77

★ ★ ★

DUBAI, UNITED ARAB EMIRATES

We touched down at Dubai International Airport at precisely 4 p.m.

It was sunny and breezy and eighty degrees, and as we taxied, I composed myself and tried to process all that had just happened to me. I wanted to call Matt. I wanted to tell him what I'd done. I wanted him to pray for me, and I had so many questions. But first I wanted to talk to Yael. Not about my newfound faith. Not yet. I just didn't want there to be any bad blood between us. Whatever I'd done wrong, I wanted to apologize to her and do what I could to make it right. She clearly didn't have any feelings for me. That hurt more than I cared to acknowledge, especially to her, but I wasn't going to make a thing of it. I just wanted to book my flight back to St. Thomas and say my good-byes on good terms.

Ignoring the still-lit seat belt sign, I moved up to the seat next to hers. She had just recovered her laptop and was putting it into her carry-on bag, but before I could start the conversation, her satellite phone rang. She answered it, then handed it to me, a surprised look on her face.

"Don't tell me that's Ari calling to reconsider," I said.

"Not exactly," she said.

"Calling to fire me, then?" I asked. "No need. I'm done."

She shook her head. "Quiet—it's not Ari."

"Then who?" I asked.

"It's the prime minister," she whispered.

A moment later I found myself on the line with the new Israeli premier, Yuval Eitan.

"Mr. Collins," the prime minister began, "I understand we have a problem."

"I guess we do, sir," I replied. "But I'm sorry you had to be bothered with this."

"Well, I'm not sure how it works in Washington, but around here the head of the Mossad tends to get the PM involved when, you know, the fate of a treaty with a major Sunni Arab neighbor is on the line."

"That would make sense," I said, not knowing what else to say.

"Ari tells me you two really got into it this morning."

"I'm afraid so, sir."

"Gave him quite an earful."

"Yes, sir. I was pressing him to put you on a call with President Mahfouz as quickly as possible."

"About?"

"Look, sir," I said. "I'm only doing this for one reason. I don't want money. I don't want attention. I don't even want vengeance. I want justice. I want to see the man who murdered my family stopped before he can hurt anyone else. I want this monster who's committing genocide stopped once and for all. That's why I dropped everything and came to you guys. I thought I could help. I thought I had something unique to contribute. Ari agreed. And he put me in the field. And I came back to him with a lead. A big lead. A serious one. But it requires your team coming clean with President Mahfouz, and apparently you're the only one who can authorize that. But Ari is dead set against you doing anything of the kind, and that's pretty much where things derailed."

"So now what?"

"That's up to you, sir," I said. "I'm going home."

"Unless I do what?"

"Pardon?"

"You heard me," the prime minister said. "Just say it plainly. What is it you want?"

I paused for a moment, caught off guard by the question. "Didn't Ari tell you?" I finally asked.

"I want to hear it directly from you," Eitan said.

I thought about that. It was a fair request. Surprising, but fair.

"Very well, Mr. Prime Minister," I said. "You need to call Mahfouz directly—and immediately. You need to tell him how and why I'm connected to you. You need to be clear, and you need to be precise. I came to you. You didn't recruit me. I don't work for you. I don't answer to you. But I want the same thing you want, the same thing he wants, and you're calling to offer to work together with him and his people to take down Abu Khalif before he does any more damage. You understand he's got information that could lead to the capture of the Baqouba brothers. And you understand he's offered to provide that information so long as he knows how it's going to be used. Then assure him there are no measures you're not willing to employ to see this job through to the end."

"That's it?" he asked.

"That's it," I said.

"That's a pretty high-risk proposition, Mr. Collins, given Cairo's stiff-arm toward us since the Amman attacks," Eitan said.

"No, sir," I countered. "With all due respect, the high-risk scenario is letting this moment pass. President Mahfouz was clear with me. You are not Egypt's problem. Israel doesn't threaten Egypt's way of life. Abu Khalif does. The ayatollahs do. He believes the next Arab capital that ISIS and Iran are coming after is Cairo. That's what Mahfouz told me. He told the same thing to Washington. He's been trying to reach out to the White House. He's even used the *New York Times* in recent days to send the message right to the top. But the White House isn't listening. President Taylor's convinced he's done all he needs to do. He doesn't want to take any more risks. He certainly isn't going into Syria to find Abu Khalif and take him down. He doesn't think the reward justifies the risks."

"And you think this creates a unique moment for us?" Eitan asked.

"I do, sir," I said. "Do what President Taylor won't. Make the first move. Reach out to Mahfouz. Show him you respect him. Show him you want to be his partner. Offer to work together on a major operation that will make both your countries safer. And do it right now—before the window closes."

There was silence on the other end of the line.

I was tempted to keep talking, to push him, to try to seal the deal through the force of my reasoning, but something held me back. So I kept quiet. I just waited. And waited. And finally the prime minister spoke.

"All right, Mr. Collins, I'll make the call on one condition," he said.

"What's that, sir?" I asked.

"That you stay in the game and see it through to the end."

78

★ ★ ★

"So what do you think?" I asked Yael when I'd briefed her on the call.

"Why ask me?" she said as we finished taxiing and came to a complete stop.

"I value your opinion."

"You certainly seem to have no trouble *giving* your opinion," she said, getting up the moment the seat belt light was turned off and pulling her suitcase out from under her seat.

I just looked at her. "The job with the PM's office?"

"What about it?" she asked curtly.

"You asked me what to do," I replied. "I told you I thought you should take it. What's wrong with that?"

"Nothing. Get your things. We need to go."

"Yael, come on, what in the world is going on here?"

"This isn't the time, J. B."

"You brought it up."

"My mistake."

At that moment the cockpit door opened. The pilots introduced themselves, and I was surprised to learn that our plane had been piloted by the station chief and deputy station chief of the Mossad's Dubai office. They had orders to help us get through security and to our hotel and then link up with the head of UAE intelligence. To do that, we needed to change clothes, change IDs, and follow their lead.

Ten minutes later, the four of us exited the plane to blue skies and white wispy clouds. I was now dressed in a five-thousand-dollar Zegna suit, a gold Rolex, beautiful Italian handcrafted leather shoes, and sunglasses I suspected cost more than my first car. The cover they'd given me was that I was an Arab—a Sunni—and a highly successful CEO of a British hotel chain. I was coming to the Gulf to visit friends. The whole thing seemed implausible on the face of it and I nearly laughed in their faces when they first explained it to me. But the station chief—going by the pseudonym Ali—insisted we needed a reason I was flying into the UAE on a Learjet, and this was it. Once we made it through passport control and customs, he said, we could change our image and our cover for the rest of our stay. But for now I was an Arab businessman and Yael was my wife.

To her they gave a black silk *abaya*, the traditional floor-length dress worn by devout women in the Gulf, and a black *niqab*, a veil that covered her head and face completely except for a small slit she could see through. This was the only option, they insisted. Yael's facial scars, and the fact that her arm was in a cast, would raise too many questions unless we went this route. Yael had no problem with it. I did. But it was clear we didn't have a choice. So down the stairs and onto the tarmac we went.

The pilots handled all our paperwork with the local officials. My job was to keep checking my watch, look annoyed, and pay no attention to my wife, who was always several steps behind me.

Ali was right. It worked like a charm.

The moment we were cleared into the country, we were met by a silver Rolls-Royce and a black Toyota Land Cruiser. Out of the SUV jumped several aides who took care of our luggage and our personal effects. The driver of our Rolls opened the back door for me and Yael while the pilots got into the chase car. The whole process took less than fifteen minutes, and soon we were off to the Burj Al Arab Jumeirah, the most beautiful hotel I'd ever seen, much less stayed in, anywhere in the world.

Located on an artificial island in the Persian Gulf, the hotel—the third tallest in the world—was designed to look like the sail of a ship. Our rooms were on the twenty-fifth double-story floor, looking out over the city of Dubai. But we had no time to savor the place or explore the amenities. The moment I'd gotten off the phone with the prime minister, I'd sent an e-mail to the private account of His Royal Highness, Prince Mohammed bin Zayed, the chief of intelligence for the United Arab Emirates and the third name on Khachigian's list. As I'd done with Walid Hussam, I briefly explained my connection to the former CIA director and described the letter he'd left me upon his death.

By the time we checked in to the Burj Al Arab, I'd already received a message back to meet His Highness for a nine o'clock dinner at Al Muntaha, a restaurant located on the twenty-seventh floor of the hotel. That gave us a little over four hours to prepare, and we did our best to use the time wisely.

The first thing I did was send a text to Paul Pritchard's phone number. Pritchard, a former CIA operative, was the top name on Khachigian's list. He was also supposedly dead, as far as anyone knew. But I didn't buy it. Khachigian wasn't sending me to a corpse but to a trusted confidant. The man was alive. The only question was whether he'd respond to my message at all, much less come out of hiding and actually meet with me.

Yael handed me her laptop and instructed me to read a forty-three-page encrypted dossier she'd just received on the Islamic State. It had been developed by her team back at Ramat David, specifically authored by Trotsky, and updated overnight. The first section contained info on attacks perpetrated by ISIS over the past three days:

- Three car bombings in Baghdad—129 dead, 53 wounded
- An attack on a petrochemical plant in Egypt—more than 600 dead, more than 1,000 wounded, and some 10,000 people evacuated
- A suicide bombing at a Coptic church in Alexandria, Egypt—46 dead, 78 wounded
- A suicide bombing in a Catholic school in Luxor, Egypt—21 dead, 35 wounded
- Two suicide bombings in two Coptic churches in Cairo—64 dead, 212 wounded
- Two truck bombs at two different hospitals in Yemen—113 dead, 301 wounded
- And now, of course, the RPG attack near the presidential palace in Heliopolis—6 dead (including the two men driving the Audi)

What struck me immediately was that the pace of the attacks was accelerating. The second section of the dossier included a chart noting the number of ISIS attacks month by month for the last year. In the previous February, there had "only" been sixty ISIS attacks outside of Syria and Iraq, killing a total of 416 people and wounding 704. Yet as this February had come to a close, the chart noted there had been more than two hundred ISIS attacks—including those in the United States—for a total of more than nine thousand people dead and more than fifteen thousand wounded. Clearly the tempo was increasing, and so was the urgency of stopping these monsters.

The good news came in the third section of the report. This provided a summary of ISIS fighters killed and captured in the month of February, country by country.

- Iraq—3,102 jihadists dead, 26 captured (reflecting the ongoing allied operations to liberate northern Iraq)

- Syria—119 jihadists dead, 0 captured (reflecting limited allied bombing runs along the Syrian border with Iraq, and the lack of allied ground operations in the Syrian theater)
- Yemen—403 jihadists dead, 33 captured (reflecting the Saudi offensive there)
- Egypt—104 jihadists dead, 23 captured (primarily reflecting the Egyptian campaign against ISIS in the Sinai Peninsula, as well as raids against ISIS sleeper cells in several major Egyptian cities)
- Libya—63 jihadists dead, 2 captured
- Jordan—25 jihadists dead, 0 captured

The Jordanian figures appeared shockingly low until I sifted through the data more carefully and saw that in December and January, the Jordanian security forces had killed more than five thousand ISIS fighters and captured well over three hundred. By the beginning of February, the battle to retake Jordan was essentially over. So the low number reflected the stunning and rapid success of the king's campaign to secure his country, not his failure.

The remainder of the report provided summaries of the latest intel gleaned from interviews with ISIS detainees, material pulled off their phones and computers, and a review of their "pocket litter"—material taken from the jihadists upon their capture, ranging from airline boarding passes and used bus tickets to meal and purchase receipts to handwritten notes to or from their colleagues. The material was a treasure trove, but the amount of information—some valuable, some irrelevant—was overwhelming. Forty-three pages from just the past three days, and this was only a summary. Back on the Ramat David air base were hard drives full of thousands of hours of interrogation tapes, tens of thousands of transcript pages, audio recordings of intercepted phone calls, intercepted e-mails, intercepted text messages, reports by human agents and sources, satellite photos, drone footage, and on and on it went. All of it had to be carefully processed and collated and tagged and reviewed and analyzed and then stored in a way it could be readily found and searched and cross-referenced with other material. And more was coming in by the hour.

There was just one glaring problem. As potentially helpful as all of it was, none of it gave us a single actionable clue to where the Baqouba brothers or Abu Khalif were hiding.

79

★ ★ ★

The view from the twenty-seventh floor was exquisite.

I arrived at the restaurant a few minutes early but did not need to wait. The maître d' immediately led me to a private room in the back. Seated outside were two plainclothes security men. They patted me down and checked my ID, then radioed to more agents inside the room who opened the door and let me in.

The room was all glass from floor to ceiling, except for the wall I'd just entered through, and the twinkling lights of Dubai were dazzling to behold.

Wearing crisp white linen robes and a white headdress bound by a thick black cord, Prince Mohammed bin Zayed quickly rose from the table and greeted me warmly. But he was not the only person in the room. A tall, fit man stood right beside him. I wondered if he was a bodyguard—until he introduced himself.

"Paul Pritchard," he said, extending his hand.

To say I was startled would have been an understatement. Not only was Paul Pritchard alive, but he and the prince had come to this meeting together. They were friends. Probably allies. Very likely business partners. This was going to be quite an evening.

As I sat down, I adjusted my glasses. They were not my usual pair.

Before I'd headed to dinner, Yael had asked—again—that I wear a wire. I'd refused. But Yael had insisted that the situation was far too sensitive for her team to simply depend on my memory. She said they needed to hear, record, transcribe, and analyze the entire conversation, beginning to end. I pushed back just as hard that the risk of being detected was far too high. Prince bin Zayed was no amateur. This guy was the top spy in the Gulf region. He was going to have bodyguards. They were going to search me. They were, therefore, going to find the wire, and we'd be shut down before we even got started. What was the point?

In the end, however, the local station chief had proposed a compromise. Out of his briefcase he had produced a pair of eyeglasses that looked exactly like mine. Embedded into the frames was a highly sensitive microphone with a small transmitter that could broadcast the audio via an encrypted signal up to a half mile away. The lenses themselves, it turned out, weren't exactly my prescription, he'd conceded, but when I put them on, they were pretty close. I was impressed with his creativity and forethought, and in the end I agreed to wear them, ending the showdown.

Though younger than Paul Pritchard by a good decade, Prince Mohammed bin Zayed nevertheless dominated the room not simply by virtue of his office but by the sheer force of his personality. He did not strike me as arrogant, but he definitely had a commanding way about him. When he asked you to sit, you sat. When he asked you questions, you answered. When he gave you an answer, you believed him. He just had an air of authority without swagger or showiness that I actually found reassuring.

Like me, the prince was in his early forties. Unlike me, he was a billionaire several times over. He was a member of a royal family that was sitting on an ocean of oil. Even when prices fell, he was still wealthier than I could even imagine, a high-ranking member of the Forbes 400 list though he'd never worked a day in the private sector.

That said, I detected nothing in his manner that seemed consumed with material things. Admittedly, we were sitting in the most expensive restaurant at one of the most expensive hotels on the planet, but he didn't strike me as pompous or distant. Rather, he had a firm handshake and sharp, quick eyes that flashed with an intelligence that both impressed and somewhat intimidated me. When a young waiter approached, the prince ordered a Coke Zero with lots of ice, not a fancy bottle of wine, champagne, or liquor. When it was time for dinner, he ordered a simple garden salad. Pritchard, on the other hand, ordered the king crab and ratatouille ravioli accompanied by the 200 gram Wagyu fillet, cooked medium and served with a glass of the house cabernet sauvignon. I split the difference, ordering a salad and a bowl of lobster bisque.

For his part, despite the lavish dinner order, Pritchard wasn't playing the role of a flashy, jet-setting businessman. He wasn't wearing Zegna or Armani or some other designer suit. Instead, he wore a crisp new light-blue dress shirt under a navy-blue blazer, cotton Dockers, and loafers without socks. Graying at the temples and clean-shaven, he was lean and looked like he could handle himself with a weapon or in hand-to-hand combat. I had questions for him. So many questions. But for now those would have to wait.

The prince offered his condolences on the deaths of my mother and nephew. Then he asked about Khachigian—details about his death, how we'd known each other, and how I thought ISIS had discovered his efforts to expose their acquisition of Syrian chemical weapons. I answered all his questions as best I could while Pritchard listened. It was a professional yet relaxed conversation and I was grateful for their interest.

At the same time, I knew the prince was testing everything I said to see if I was being truthful and candid, and I suddenly felt self-conscious about having used an alias to enter his country. Surely as the head of UAE intelligence, he knew, but if it bothered him, he didn't let on.

Our meals came, but only Pritchard seemed interested in the food. The prince and I mostly just kept talking. He barely touched his salad. I barely touched my soup. In time, I apparently passed his test.

When the waiter finally removed our plates and served us coffee, we moved from the dining table to several leather chairs looking out over the water. When I commented on how lovely the Persian Gulf looked from such a vantage point, and especially at night, His Royal Highness gently reminded me that this was "not the Persian Gulf, but the Arabian Gulf, thank you very much."

I quickly apologized for my faux pas.

When it came time to get down to business, I started things off with a direct question of my own. "So do you guys know?"

"Where Abu Khalif is?" the prince replied.

"What else?"

"No," he said. "Not for certain."

I took a sip of coffee. "But you must have some idea, right? I mean, obviously we can rule out Mosul. The allies have gone through the city street by street, house by house. And we can pretty much rule out Raqqa. It's been scrutinized up and down for the past two months, and it's not that big to begin with."

"He's been there, though, in Raqqa," the prince said. "We've had multiple sightings, just like the Egyptians. But no, we don't think he's there now."

"Then where?" I pressed.

Bin Zayed did not reply. Instead, he turned to Pritchard, who floored me.

"At this point, we think he's with his wives and kids," the former Damascus station chief said. "Find them, find him."

"Whoa, whoa, what in the world are you talking about?" I asked. *"Abu Khalif is married?"*

"I just found out a few days ago myself," the prince said, clearly amused by my reaction.

"I had no idea," I said.

"Join the crowd," Pritchard replied. "Turns out he's got four wives and seven children."

"How do you know?" I asked. "How did you find out?"

"For the past several years, my firm has been working closely with the prince on making sure the UAE is safe from terrorism—from ISIS, Iran, and other chief threats," Pritchard explained. "Last week we picked up the scent of an ISIS cell operating in Abu Dhabi. We shared it with the prince, and as you can imagine, that got the leadership pretty spooked."

I could imagine. Abu Dhabi, a city of about a million and a half people, was the capital of the United Arab Emirates and thus far one of the safest cities in the region, nearly untouched by the kind of terrorism that seemed to be plaguing everywhere else.

The prince picked up the narrative. "As soon as Paul gave me the details, I ordered our special forces into action. It got pretty messy—a nine-hour gun battle. All five jihadists were killed, but we lost two officers in the process."

"I'm sorry."

"So am I. These were very fine men—smart, experienced. A difficult loss. But the site itself was a gold mine. The cell consisted of four Saudis and one Syrian. They all lived in a small apartment just blocks from the Sheikh Zayed mosque. The Saudis, it turned out, were the muscle—bodyguards for the Syrian."

"And who was the Syrian?"

Pritchard took that one. "An aide to Abu Khalif, and pretty high up the food chain. We recovered his laptop, and once we cracked the hard drive, we discovered the guy reported to one of the Baqouba brothers—Faisal—but essentially he was a courier for Khalif. Specifically, it turned out, he was an emissary between Khalif and his wives. In other words, well vetted. Highly trusted. On the hard drive we found some of Khalif's correspondence with his wives over the last several years. We found digital photos of the wives' and kids' passports. We also found digital photos of the kids, names, dates of birth, all kinds of stuff. A real bonanza. At first we didn't even know what we'd found. Like I said, we didn't know he was married either. But the more we kept looking, the clearer it all became."

For the next hour, bin Zayed and Pritchard walked me through what they themselves were just learning, starting with the names of the four wives—Aisha, Fatima, Alia, and Hanan—and backgrounds on each.

"Here's something interesting," Pritchard said. "We've got medical records indicating that Aisha is barren. She was treated for several years but apparently never was able to bear children for Khalif. And yet Khalif never divorced her."

"That *is* interesting," I said. "They're in love."

"That was my take," he replied, "which is one of the reasons I think she's with him. The Saudis insist she's not in the kingdom. Travel records say she flew to Islamabad four months ago, and from Pakistan to central Asia. But then the trail goes cold."

"Four months, you say?"

"Yes."

"That would have been about the time Khalif's men were planning to break him out of Abu Ghraib," I said.

"Exactly," the prince said. "My guess is they were moving her to safety, and specifically to a place he could see her after his escape and maybe even live with her."

"What about his other wives?" I asked.

Pritchard told me Fatima, who at twenty-seven was nearly a decade younger than Khalif's first wife, had a boy and two girls. Alia, only twenty-two, was the mother of two more Khalif boys and one girl. "We think Alia is the wife Khalif loves most," he said.

"Not his first wife, Aisha?" I asked.

"No."

"How can you be certain?"

"Most of the correspondence we've intercepted is to her," Pritchard said. "The language is flowery, passionate, laced with poetry, while letters and notes to the other wives are more newsy, more practical, less romantic."

The last of the four wives was Hanan, a Palestinian and a distant cousin to Khalif. Hanan had married the ISIS emir three years earlier when she was only fourteen. Now she was seventeen and the mother of a baby boy.

Bin Zayed then told me that Hanan's parents had just been found that morning—living on the outskirts of Dubai—and had been arrested and interrogated by the prince's men. They insisted they had no idea where their daughter was. They said they had not been to the wedding and swore they had never given their blessing to Khalif to marry their daughter. In fact, both the father and the mother—interrogated separately—went to great pains to renounce Khalif and ISIS.

"Do you believe them?" I asked.

"I'm not sure yet," the prince conceded. "We've just gotten started with them. Give me another few days."

"What did you find in the house?"

"Nothing that links the parents directly to Khalif or the Baqouba brothers, or even to ISIS," the prince replied. "But we're still looking."

"Okay," I said. "So this is a big breakthrough. Abu Khalif has four wives and at least seven children that we know of, right?"

"Right," Pritchard responded. "Four boys and three girls, ranging in age from two to twelve. And based on the correspondence we've captured, he seems to be very fond of the children. Remembers their birthdays. Sends them presents through the courier. Sends them cash. And keeps saying he misses them and wants them near him."

"So like you said, if we can find them, maybe we find him," I said.

"Exactly."

It made sense, but my head was still reeling.

"How come no one had this before?" I asked. "Marriage? Kids? How do you keep these things secret from the world's greatest intelligence services?"

"Good question," Pritchard said. "Painful—but fair. To be blunt, the first answer is simple: I don't know. We missed it. Everybody missed it. That's on us. On me. But the second answer is, the guy lives in the shadows, right? I mean, until your profile of Jamal Ramzy and then Khalif himself, we hardly knew anything about these guys. There had always been bigger fish to catch before them—bin Laden, Zawahiri, KSM, Zarqawi, the list went on and on. So Khalif and Ramzy came up through the ranks. We knew some basics, but until you put a spotlight on them—and they let you—they had stayed off the radar. That's how they survived. That's how they climbed to the top of the greasy pole. They didn't want their names in the papers—they didn't want to draw the attention of foreign intelligence agencies—because they knew that those who did had a very short life span."

"But somehow the Iraqis captured Khalif," I said. "They knew he was a threat. They obviously went after him. They caught him. They put him in Abu Ghraib."

"I talked to the Iraqis specifically about this after your story was published," the prince said. "They say they caught Abu Khalif in a raid aimed at scooping up other bad guys. Khalif just happened to be in the room at the time. They weren't targeting him. In fact, at first they didn't know who they had or how big a deal he was. Obviously that changed over time, but the Iraqis insist they didn't even have a file on Abu Khalif when they caught him. It was sheer dumb luck, and since he refused to talk—except to you—they never got anything out of him when they interrogated him. They didn't really know who he was, or anything about his associates, much less his family members. They certainly didn't know he was married or that he had kids."

I sat back and thought for a moment. This *was* a big deal. It gave us eleven new trails to follow. Only one of them had to take us to Khalif. But it was a race against time, for new attacks were being planned and they could be unleashed at any moment.

80

★ ★ ★

It was almost midnight when I got back to my hotel room.

But it was clear that sleep wasn't anywhere on the horizon. Yael and the local Mossad team were hard at work on their laptops, sitting around the dining room table in the executive suite with stacks of dirty dinner dishes and used glasses and coffee cups all around them. I was eager to discuss the conversation I'd just had. The new intel on Khalif's wives and children was astonishing to me. I also wanted Yael's take on the aggressive effort Prince bin Zayed and his men were making to hunt down Khalif himself. I knew she'd been listening in on the conversation. But that wasn't all. I also needed to process everything I'd learned about Paul Pritchard.

First of all, not only was Paul Pritchard still alive and well, he was still unofficially working for the CIA. Yes, he'd been publicly "fired" by Khachigian, but that, he'd told me, was only so that he could be sent on assignments that could not be traced back to the U.S. government. For nearly a year, Pritchard had maintained his own identity, using his supposed firing as motivation for wanting revenge against the agency. He'd managed to convince several jihadist leaders in Syria and Iraq that he was a turncoat and an ally of theirs. When the usefulness of that technique had run its course, Pritchard got himself officially knocked off in an elaborately staged car bombing in Sudan. Then he'd gotten plastic surgery, changed his name, moved to the United Arab Emirates, set up a small private security firm, and begun working as an intelligence advisor to Prince bin Zayed. Only a handful of people on the entire planet knew his real identity. Robert Khachigian was one of them. And now so was I.

Particularly interesting to me was the fact that Paul Pritchard's real name was actually William Sullivan. To my astonishment, he was the son of Lincoln Sullivan and the father of Steve Sullivan, my new attorneys back in Maine. It turned out that Khachigian had known the family forever and had personally recruited William into the agency some twenty-five years earlier.

This finally explained something I hadn't understood about Khachigian's letter to me, the one I'd been given that fateful morning back in Portland. There was an odd line early in the letter that read, *If I know you, you're wondering about Steve's father . . . We'll get to that in a moment.* I had indeed been wondering about Steve's father. And yet Khachigian had never come back to that point, never finished the thought, never explained himself. Rather, on the back of the letter there were three names I was supposed to track down, with contact information for each. Now it made sense.

I was eager to talk about all this with Yael and the team. There was just one problem. Yael and her team had neither the time nor the interest for such a debriefing. They had news of their own.

"The PM made the call," Yael told me when the hotel room door was shut and locked behind me.

"When?" I asked, taking a seat at the table across from her.

"He and Mahfouz finally connected about an hour ago. Ari just called to brief us."

"And?"

"We're in business," she said, leaning back in her chair. "Mahfouz really appreciated the PM's call. The two agreed to swap intel on the hunt for Abu Khalif, provided there be absolutely no leaks. It all has to be hush-hush."

"Wow, that's great," I said.

"There's more. The attack near the palace wasn't ISIS, and it wasn't directed at you."

"What?"

"Mahfouz says his people just arrested a Muslim Brotherhood cell—four men and two women—earlier today. They were found with weapons that matched exactly those used in the attack. Their vehicle matches one seen on several surveillance cameras. And one of the suspects has confessed. He said they were targeting Walid Hussam for his role in arresting Brotherhood leaders when he served as the head of Egyptian intelligence. It had nothing to do with you. The palace is absolutely certain of it."

I closed my eyes and said a silent prayer of thanks. It was my first prayer since getting off the plane, and I suddenly was overwhelmed by a desire to call Matt.

But Yael had more.

"Mahfouz didn't waste any time before sharing intelligence with us," she said. She explained that the Egyptians had an informant in Doha, the capital of the Gulf state of Qatar, 225 miles due west of where we were seated. The informant was the sister of three ISIS jihadists, one of whom was a bank manager in Doha. "But that's just a cover for his ISIS role," she insisted. "Turns out he's a key player in the ISIS courier system." She claimed that three times in the last eight months, video and audio recordings created by Abu Khalif, including the most recent, had been passed along to Al Jazeera through the bank manager.

"Why don't they just grab the bank manager?" I asked. "Interrogate him, put pressure on him, make him talk? We're running out of time."

"Because he doesn't know anything," she said. "Egyptian intelligence is waiting for another courier to make contact. It might be Faisal. Whoever it is, they could lead us to Khalif."

This was good news. Big news. A real lead.

Yael sent a flash message to Shalit via secure text outlining the basics of my conversation with bin Zayed and Pritchard. She promised a full report by daybreak. Then she recommended that he brief Prime Minister Eitan and that the PM brief President Mahfouz. The fact that Khalif had wives and children—and that they had been positively ID'd—was huge. We needed to get the Mossad's best people working on this. But we needed the Egyptians' help too. They might be able to tap sources we didn't have. What's more, it would be an act of good faith for the PM to share sensitive information back to Mahfouz just hours after receiving it himself.

"We need to get the Jordanians in on this as well," I said.

"You're probably right," Yael said, yawning and rubbing her eyes.

"I'm definitely right, and I don't think we can wait anymore," I said. "The prime minister should call the king first thing in the morning, right after he talks to Mahfouz."

Just after 5 a.m., the guys went back to their rooms, and Yael and I were suddenly alone. I went into the bathroom, brushed my teeth, and changed into gym shorts and a T-shirt. When I came out, I grabbed a spare blanket and pillow from the closet and lay down on the huge couch, leaving the king-size bed to her. She nodded and disappeared into the bathroom for a few minutes. When she returned, she said good night and crawled into bed.

I forced myself to close my eyes, then pulled the blanket over my head and said a prayer as she turned off the light.

She fell asleep almost instantly. I, on the other hand, had no such luck.

81

★ ★ ★

BAHRAIN AIRSPACE

J. B. Collins's life is in danger—we need to talk.

That was the urgent message we'd just received from Jordanian intelligence, and that was the totality of the message. We had no other details. We didn't know the specific nature of the threat or how the Jordanians knew it existed.

Yael and I had, however, been summoned to a private meeting with King Abdullah II at the royal palace in the port city of Aqaba. So suddenly we were back on the Learjet, racing from Dubai to the Hashemite Kingdom. Total flying time for the nearly 1,300-mile trip: just under three hours. A quick glance at my grandfather's pocket watch suggested that would put us on the tarmac by midnight.

To my surprise, despite the gravity of the threat, the truth was I wasn't particularly worried for myself. Not anymore. For the first time in my life, I was absolutely certain where I was going when I died, and while I didn't want to go prematurely, I felt ready for heaven. I wanted to see my mom. I wanted to see Josh. I wanted to see my grandfather and Khachigian and his wife, Mary, and so many other believers who had gone on before me. But far more, I wanted to meet my Lord and Savior face-to-face. I was new to the team, and

I had wasted so much of my life running from the truth. But I was done running. I was ready to go home, whenever that moment came.

What truly worried me now, however, was the thought that more harm might come to Matt, Annie, or Katie because of me. I couldn't bear the thought that Abu Khalif and ISIS might still be hunting them.

To her credit, Yael did her best to calm my mounting fears. She reminded me that my family was in hiding, under the protection of the U.S. government. She pointed out that the message from Amman indicated that I was in danger, not my family. Her words didn't do much to assuage my anxiety. But for the first time since we'd reconnected, she was acting like my friend and not my adversary.

After a while she switched tactics. She was, after all, a professional spy. She'd been trained in the art of misdirection. So rather than trying to convince me that my family wasn't in danger, she instead tried to keep me focused on the primary task at hand.

"What's your take on this new intel?" she asked. "Is it possible Abu Khalif is really in Turkey?"

Five days earlier, such a question would have seemed nonsensical. But no longer.

Following my meeting with Prince bin Zayed and Pritchard, the Israeli security cabinet had met in emergency session to discuss the progress Yael's team was making and the need for the Israeli government to make direct contact with the leaders of not only Egypt and Jordan but now the United Arab Emirates, as well. The vote was unanimous—direct contact was authorized. By seven that morning, Ari Shalit had called and given me explicit permission to formally introduce Yael and her Mossad team to the prince and to Pritchard. I was to explain why and how I was working with the Mossad to bring Abu Khalif to justice and request permission for Shalit to call the prince directly and discuss how the two countries could work toward this common objective.

Once so authorized, I'd called the prince immediately, requested another face-to-face meeting, and been invited to meet with him in his palatial office.

To my surprise, the prince wasn't caught off guard in the slightest. In fact, he told me he'd been quite certain I was in some way connected to the Mossad and had simply wondered when I would come clean. He wasn't offended or upset, and he agreed to take Shalit's call at once. Ten minutes later, the two spy chiefs were on a secure line, briefing each other on developments and comparing notes on their latest theories. When the call was over and the prince explained those theories to Yael and me, we could hardly believe our ears.

As the prince explained to Shalit, his agency's hunt for Khalif's wives and children was pointing not toward Syria or Iraq but toward the Republic of Turkey. Three of Khalif's wives, they had determined, had taken flights through Dubai, Abu Dhabi, and Doha in late November and early December. One had traveled to Beirut. Another had flown to Cairo. The third had gone to Cyprus. But none of them had stayed there. All of them—and several of the children—had eventually wound up flying to Istanbul.

These flights—the last ones Khalif's family members had taken on commercial airlines—raised all kinds of new questions. Were they still in Istanbul? Had they all been given false documents and flown on to Europe or some other destination? Or had they been picked up by ISIS operatives and driven someplace, perhaps deeper into the interior of Turkey?

For his part, Shalit briefed the prince on the latest from Egyptian intelligence. They'd struck pay dirt in their surveillance operation of the bank manager in Doha. By studying the usage of the manager's mobile phone, home phone, and office phone—along with e-mail traffic from several accounts he was using simultaneously—a curious picture was emerging.

The guy's tradecraft was stellar. Nothing pointed directly to a specific location for the Baqouba brothers or any other couriers. But the patterns were intriguing. Over the last year, there hadn't been a single call or e-mail originating from a single city or town in Syria. Zero. Zip. Nada. There had been many calls and e-mails to and from the Gulf states, North Africa, and Europe, as one would expect of a banker. But there were also thirty-seven messages from Turkey—twenty-one from in or around the Istanbul metropolitan area, the nation's commercial capital, and the rest from in or around Ankara, the nation's political capital. And a good 80 percent of these messages had come in the last three months.

Of course, a Gulf banker receiving messages from Turkey wouldn't normally be cause for interest, much less concern. The Republic of Turkey was a country of nearly 80 million people, at least 96 percent of whom were Muslims, and the country had a gross domestic product of more than $1.5 trillion. Naturally Turkish citizens were doing business in Doha, arguably the epicenter of Islamic business activity in the region. However, what made these thirty-seven messages unique, the Egyptian intelligence analysts noted, was that they weren't returned. The bank manager—whom we now knew for certain was an ISIS operative—had received thirty-seven phone calls and e-mails from people in Turkey over the past eight months, most of them in the last ninety days, yet he had not replied to a single one of them.

This raised even more questions. Were these unreturned messages from Turkey instructions or directives of some kind? Was it possible Khalif and the Baqouba brothers weren't in Syria after all? Was it possible they were actually in Turkey? Turkey was a NATO ally. Turkey was ostensibly part of the regional Sunni alliance against ISIS. Turkey was supposedly bombing ISIS camps in northern Syria. Why, then, might Khalif and the Baqouba brothers be in Turkey?

As I listened to the prince's report on his conversation with Shalit, it dawned on me how enormously complicated our investigation had just become. If Khalif were somehow in Turkey, of all places, who was going to go get him? What country would dare send fighter jets equipped with laser-guided missiles to take him out? I couldn't think of one. What country was going to send in drones equipped with Hellfire missiles to end Khalif's reign of terror? Again, I didn't see it happening. Who was going to send in a team of special forces commandos, or a team of assassins, to bring Khalif to justice? Not the Egyptians. Not the emirates. Certainly not the Americans. Maybe not even the Israelis or the Jordanians, though they had suffered the most from Abu Khalif's actions.

Simply put, the notion of launching an attack deep inside a NATO ally was virtually unthinkable. An attack against one NATO country could trigger Article 5 of the alliance, requiring a collective response by all NATO countries against the aggressor.

For me, that fact alone dramatically increased the likelihood that Khalif had specifically *chosen* to hide in Turkey. That's what I told Yael en route to Jordan while we both tried not to think about the new unspecified but apparently authentic threat on my life.

And to my surprise, she agreed.

82

★ ★ ★

AQABA, JORDAN

We landed in Aqaba just after midnight in the middle of a brutal winter thunderstorm.

Gone was the gorgeous, balmy weather of the Gulf we'd had no time to enjoy. Now, as the sky flashed and rumbled and driving rain made visibility limited at best, we were met by officers of the Royal Court, carrying large umbrellas, who hustled us into a small motorcade consisting of three silver Toyota Land Cruisers and six heavily armed bodyguards and drivers.

Minutes later we were exiting the airport grounds and driving at high speed along deserted roads under the cover of darkness and fog. Eventually, though, we slowed down and turned a corner onto a narrow, secluded driveway, lined by long rows of palm trees on either side, bending in unison in the gale-force winds. Ahead of us were massive steel gates under a stone archway. Jordanian soldiers in full battle gear stood at attention beside two armored personnel carriers with .50-caliber machine guns aimed directly at us.

We did not come to a full stop, however. We did not show IDs or even have a conversation. The driver of the first Land Cruiser saluted the guards as we approached and slowed down, and the gates immediately opened before us. On either side of us I could see high, thick walls and several well-lit guard towers and the silhouettes of sentries and sharpshooters. But soon we were picking up speed again, snaking our way along the winding driveway until we came to another set of steel gates and more armed soldiers. Again we slowed but did not stop. Again the driver saluted, and again the gates opened for us, and before I knew it, we had arrived at the palace.

The motorcade pulled up under an awning that gave us a bit of protection from the elements, though not nearly enough, and our doors were immediately opened by protocol officers who greeted us and whisked us into the vestibule. They showed us each to separate restrooms and gave us fresh towels and a few moments to dry off and gather ourselves.

As I shut and locked the door behind me, I closed my eyes for a moment. We'd been working eighteen to twenty hours a day for much of the last week. Even when there'd been time to lie down, I hadn't been sleeping well. There were too many interruptions—calls and e-mails and emergency discussions about new information constantly flowing to us—and even when there was a momentary break in the intensity, I constantly felt the weight of what we were trying to do.

When I finally opened my eyes and stared into the mirror, I winced at what I saw. My skin was pale. My eyes were red. Having not shaved my head since leaving Bar Harbor, I was no longer bald. Rather, my hair was growing quickly, though to my chagrin it was far more gray than the last time I'd let it grow out, maybe five or six years before. I hadn't shaved my face either since the funeral, and I no longer had a goatee but a rapidly thickening full beard, also far more gray than I'd expected or wanted. I was starting to look old and tired. I was starting to look my age—older, actually—and I wasn't a fan.

Tossing the towel into the sink, I opened the door and flicked off the light. A few moments later, Yael joined me, and the chief of protocol took us to the king's private study.

The room was empty. We were told the king was on a call but would be here momentarily. A steward brought in a large silver tray bearing a teapot and three teacups, each hand-painted with the royal coat of arms. The steward poured us each a cup of mint tea and then backed out of the room.

A moment later the king arrived with his several bodyguards, though they did not enter the study. Rather, the king entered alone and immediately closed the door behind him. He looked tired but greeted us warmly. "Welcome back to Jordan," His Majesty said with a broad smile and a firm handshake. "It's a joy to see you both again," he said in his flawless English with that trace of a British accent picked up from years of military schools and British special forces service in his youth. "Still, I do wish it were under more favorable circumstances."

"Thank you for having us to your home, Your Majesty," I said. "It is truly an honor to see you again—alive and well and victorious over such a cruel and heartless enemy."

"The fight is not yet over, I'm afraid," the king replied as he beckoned us all to take our seats.

He expressed his profound regrets for the attacks against my family and the loss of my mother and nephew, and as he spoke, it was quickly apparent he had tracked the news coverage and knew many of the details of what I had been through. He asked me how I was holding up, and then just as generously he asked Yael about her health and the status of her recovery. Even in the midst of a crisis, the monarch had a personal touch. It was one of the many qualities that impressed me.

We answered his questions and likewise shared our condolences for the tremendous loss of life he and his kingdom had experienced, especially for the deaths of Kamal Jeddah, the chief of Jordanian intelligence, and Ali Sa'id, the chief of security for the Royal Court, both of whom had died in the ISIS attacks during the peace summit in Amman, as well as our friend and comrade-in-arms Colonel Yusef Sharif, the king's senior advisor and personal spokesman, who had joined us on the mission to rescue President Taylor and had died in the firefight at the compound in Alqosh. Yael also asked how the queen and the children were doing. We hadn't seen the king since all these events had transpired, and we were both eager for an update on his family, the government, and all the reconstruction efforts that were under way.

It became immediately evident, however, that these were not the topics he wanted to discuss at present, as important as they were to him. He said his family was well and safe, and seemed to intimate—though he didn't say outright—that they were not currently in the country. But he turned quickly to the reason he had summoned us in the first place.

"J. B., I'm sorry to have to say this to you, but I'm afraid you're in grave danger," he said, looking straight into my eyes and ignoring his tea.

"Okay," I replied, trying to stay calm. "What exactly does that mean?"

"Over the last few weeks, we've been picking up a lot of chatter among ISIS operatives we're surveilling," he said, leaning forward in his chair. "They're furious that they weren't able to kill the president during the attack on the State of the Union. They're even more enraged that they didn't kill more members of Congress during the sarin gas attacks on the Capitol. They believe you're an easier target. They also believe you have a high enough profile—a high enough value—that they can score a major propaganda coup in the U.S. and perhaps globally if they can capture and behead you. From what we've been able to gather, they think you went into hiding after the funeral, and they've been pleading with Khalif to issue a fatwa authorizing them to find you and kill you posthaste."

83

★ ★ ★

"With all due respect, Your Majesty, this isn't really news," I said.

I explained that the FBI had expressed their concerns to me back in Bar Harbor, noting that they were particularly anxious about sleeper cells operating in New England.

"I know," the king said. "I've spoken directly to President Taylor and CIA Director Hughes—an old friend of yours, I understand. I also spoke to Director Beck at the FBI. Beck told me he personally gave Agent Harris the assignment to keep you and your brother and his family safe."

"Yes, he did, and that's very kind of you, Your Majesty, to discuss my safety with each of them," I said. "I'm touched—really—and I can tell you that Agent Harris has, in fact, gone to great lengths to make sure Matt, Annie, and Katie are secure and we're very grateful."

"Yet here you are, J. B. You're not in protective custody. You're not under the watchful care of Agent Harris and his team. You're jetting about the Middle East, hunting for the very man who is hunting you."

"I'm not worried," I said.

"You should be," the king retorted. "Really, J. B., this could not be more serious."

"Is there proof Abu Khalif has agreed to his men's wishes?" I asked. "Has he issued the fatwa?"

"He did," the king said. "Tonight, while you were flying here from Dubai."

At this, I set my cup down on the coffee table, sat back on the couch, and took a deep breath. This king had earned a special place in my heart. He was an Arab. He was a Muslim. He was a direct descendant of the founder of Islam. We didn't share the same background or ethnicity or theological views. But this was a good man. A man of peace. A man of tolerance and respect for Christians and Jews and those of a wide range of other backgrounds and beliefs. This was a man who had welcomed millions of refugees into his country, not because he had extra resources lying around to provide for their food, clothing, housing, medical care, and education, but because he felt it was the right thing to do—despite the potential risks. Because they were fleeing from Assad and the al-Nusra Front and from ISIS and from genocide.

In the face of extraordinary threats, this king had not surrendered or cowered in fear. To the contrary, he had courageously gone to war against the forces of evil and extremism. He was engaged in a winner-take-all civil war inside Islam, a war that pitted the forces of reform and modernity against the radicals and those pursuing the apocalypse.

His Majesty had aged considerably in the last few months. His hair was grayer. He had new lines etched in his face. Yet he was still in remarkably good shape for a monarch in his midfifties. I had to ascribe that to his lifelong discipline of being a soldier and even head of Jordanian special forces and to the singular commitment he had to protecting his people and his kingdom. But events were clearly taking their toll on him. He looked as tired as Yael and I did. Maybe more so.

"Look, J. B.," the king said since I had not replied, "the chatter about you was worrisome before the funeral in Maine. But it has spiked enormously since then. Now Khalif has issued this fatwa calling for your head with extreme urgency. Once it is announced publicly, probably in the next few hours—no more than a few days— your life is . . . Well, it's hard to explain just how serious this is. It won't just be active ISIS operatives who will be authorized to find and kill you. It will be any radicalized Muslim, anywhere in the world. That's why I asked you to come here. I wanted to tell you in person what we've learned and to impress upon you just how dire I view this. It's not safe for you to be out in the field. It's not safe to be here in the region like this. Not anymore. You were in Egypt—and were nearly killed there. You were just in Dubai. You're here now. The number of people who have seen you, who are talking to you, who are interacting with you—that number is growing by the day, by the hour. That's a problem, because it significantly raises the possibility that your presence in this region will be exposed and that the people who want to kill you will find you."

"So you want me to stop," I said.

"I want you to live."

"By stopping."

"By going home."

"Your Majesty, I don't have a home."

"Then going back to wherever Agent Harris put you, wherever he thinks you'll be safe."

"Or what?" I asked.

"Honestly, J. B.—if you remain here, I doubt you'll make it a month, if that. You're playing a very dangerous game, my friend, against very dangerous adversaries. You've beaten the odds so far, but now they're targeting you. It's time for you to stop. It's time for you to go back to your family and leave this game to us. We've been trained to play and win. And let's be honest, you have not."

84

★ ★ ★

RAMAT DAVID AIR BASE, ISRAEL

"J. B., can I talk to you outside?" Yael asked.

We were back at the command center at the Ramat David Air Base and had been here for four days. So far the question of whether I was going to voluntarily choose to go home, as the king had suggested, or be sent home by Yael or even Ari Shalit, had gone unaddressed. But I feared the time had come.

In the past four days, the team and I had been following every lead imaginable related to the new information about Khalif's wives and children. But there still was absolutely no concrete evidence that could direct us to a specific, definable location. The only thing we knew for certain was that chatter was growing of another coming mass casualty event, inside the United States, against civilian targets, and soon.

On that front, Unit 8200 was working miracles. They had terrifying Skype call intercepts of terrorists talking about "devastating" and "catastrophic" and "imminent" operations inside the American homeland. The attacks would come "soon" and "without warning," the jihadists insisted. Yet there were no details, nothing definitive and actionable. And tensions were rising.

The intel and the accompanying analysis had been given to the prime minister, who passed it along to President Taylor and his national security team. The White House wasn't showing any new interest in hunting down Abu Khalif, but the Israelis were determined to be good allies, passing along what they had, and not just to the American intelligence community but to Jordanian, Egyptian, and the Gulf state intelligence agencies as well.

The team was spent. We were eating and sleeping in the bunker. People's nerves were raw. Tempers were short. Arguments were flaring. I hadn't been aboveground since we flew back from Jordan, and I'm not sure the rest of the team had seen the light of day since Yael and I had departed for Egypt.

Now, responding to Yael's request, I followed her into the corridor. Suddenly we were alone.

"Let's go for a walk," she said.

The rain had stopped, and the grounds were surprisingly dry. Spring seemed to have sprung across Israel's northern tier when we weren't looking. The clouds had parted. The temperature was in the low seventies. A lovely breeze was coming in from the sea. Grass was starting to grow. Flowers were starting to bloom. Trees were beginning to bud. It felt amazingly good to be out of the bunker, breathing fresh, clean air.

"So what can I do for you, boss?" I asked, happy to be stretching my legs and walking with my friend, even if I had no illusions the conversation was going to be anything but professional. "And make it snappy, if you don't mind. I've been chewing on a new theory I want to run past you."

She took a deep breath, then stopped and turned to me. "I'm afraid there's no easy way to say this. But I have to. It's my job."

"Why? What is it?" I asked.

"J. B. . . . Ari and I think it's time for you to go back to the States."

"What?"

"Don't get me wrong. You've been an enormous help, especially these last four days. But Ari and I have been discussing what King Abdullah said, and the bottom line is the king is right. The risks to you and your family by you staying here in the region are way too high. Ari and I have been reviewing the intel over the last few days. The king was spot-on. The ISIS guys are gunning for you, and Khalif really has issued a fatwa calling for Muslims everywhere to find you and your family and kill you on sight. A spokesman for ISIS just released it on the Internet about fifteen minutes ago. By tomorrow, every radical Muslim on the planet will be looking for you."

I didn't say anything. I was hurt. Angry. But I knew there wasn't anything I could say to change her mind, much less Shalit's.

We started walking again, tracing the perimeter of the base along the interior fence. A jeep patrol rode by. We nodded to the security team and kept going. The final rays of the sun were slipping below the Carmel Mountains. Dusk was falling. The lights of the base were flickering to life.

"You're not going to say anything?" she asked.

"What should I say?"

"I don't know. I thought you'd at least make an argument to stay."

"Would it help?"

"No."

"So what's the point?"

We kept walking.

"It's probably best you call the Learjet company tonight," she said after a while. "Let them know you'll be ready to fly back tomorrow to wherever you came from. I don't want to know, so please don't tell me."

I said nothing.

"We can chopper you out of here after ten tomorrow. You can say good-bye to the team. I think you can schedule a departure for noon or so out of Ben Gurion or Herzliya, whichever you'd prefer."

Another five minutes passed, and I realized what a sprawling base this really was. We'd barely covered half of the perimeter, if that, but it was growing dark and even a bit chilly.

"Listen," she said, "it's getting late and I'm getting hungry. Can I drive us someplace and buy you a farewell dinner?"

I just looked at her. She wasn't kidding. After all we'd been through together, this was really the end. I was going "home" to hide, without winning the heart of this girl, and Abu Khalif was still out there killing.

"Sure," I said.

What else could I say?

85

★ ★ ★

It was a Friday night in Israel.

The Sabbath had just arrived. That meant no Jewish-owned restaurants would be open. So we climbed into her bright-red Jeep Grand Cherokee and drove to a little Arab restaurant in Nazareth.

"You really do hate me, don't you?" I said as we parked and I realized where we were.

"What is that supposed to mean?" she asked, looking a bit hurt.

"The leader of ISIS just put out a fatwa on my head, and you're taking me to an Arab hot spot for dinner?"

She smiled and lowered her voice. "Don't let on that you know, but every diner in this place tonight is a Mossad agent. We'll be very safe."

"Seriously?" I said, looking out the window at the bistro and already enticed by the aromas wafting from the kitchen.

Yael shrugged.

"They're here to keep me safe?" I asked, impressed.

"Well, technically they're here to keep me safe, but they're good guys—they'll take a bullet for you, too. At least for one more night."

We went in and were immediately shown to a table for two near the back by the kitchen.

The server was young and inexperienced and a bit harried and overwhelmed. But she brought us some water and finally came back to take our order. We didn't get fancy. We didn't have much of an appetite, so Yael simply ordered some plates of hummus and tehina and falafel and a couple of small salads and skipped the grilled lamb and chicken.

"So listen," she said after several minutes of awkward small talk. "I've been trying to find a good time to tell you this."

Every muscle in my body tightened. Now what?

"Yes?" I asked as calmly as I could.

"Well, the thing is, I . . ."

She couldn't get the words out. She asked a passing server for more water and more pita. She shifted in her seat. Clearly she was stalling. I couldn't decide if I wanted her to spit it out or change the subject. It turned out not to matter, because before she could continue, our meal came.

We waited until the waitress had served us everything and departed. Then Yael tried again.

"So, look, J. B. . . ."

"Just say it, Yael," I said quietly. "Whatever it is, I can take it. Just say it, please."

"Okay. What I'm trying to say is . . . I'm . . . well, anyway . . . I'm sort of . . ."

"Sort of what, Yael?"

"Well, I'm sort of . . . engaged."

The word just hung there in the air. I heard it. I just couldn't believe it. "Engaged?" I said, trying to force my brain to process the meaning of this perfectly simple English word.

"Yeah," she said, not meeting my eyes but staring at her food.

"To be married?" I asked like an idiot.

"Yeah."

"You're really engaged."

She finally looked up at me. "Yeah."

"To whom?"

"You don't know him."

I stared at her. "I don't understand."

"I know; it seems weird to me, too."

"Two months ago you weren't even dating anyone. In fact, I seem to recall you kissing me rather passionately in Istanbul."

"Yeah, I know."

"And I remember asking you out at the peace summit in Amman. And I seem to remember you saying—what did you say?—oh, that's right, you said yes."

"That's all true."

"So were you engaged then?"

"Of course not. Look, J. B., I'm sorry. I mean, I know this must seem kinda sudden—"

"Kinda?"

"Okay, very sudden, but I've actually known him a long time."

"How?"

"We dated in high school, before I went to the army, before I met Uri."

"Uri was your husband."

"Right."

"The one who was killed by Hezbollah."

She sighed and nodded. "What happened was that Moshe—his name is Moshe—anyway, he's a doctor. Specializes in physical rehab for trauma victims. I didn't know that. We broke up my senior year, and I lost track of him after high school. But it turns out he became a medic in the army and then he went to medical school, and the next thing I know, I'm lying there in the hospital after Alqosh and Moshe walks through the door."

"He was your doctor?"

"Yeah."

"And you thought, what a small world."

"Well . . . I guess, yeah."

"And you got chatting, and one thing led to another."

"When I was released, we went out a few times, nothing serious. I was still thinking about you."

"Oh, gee, thanks."

"But then I got offered the job in the PM's office, and I wrote to you, asking whether I should take it. I thought you would . . . I don't know. But you just wrote back saying I should take it and made a stupid joke about getting a raise, like you couldn't care less what I did. I was a little hurt, okay? And maybe a little angry."

"A little?"

"Okay, a lot. And I started thinking about my life, and what I really wanted, and it was a life here, in Israel, in my world. Then Moshe started getting more serious, and yes, one thing led to another. He asked me, and I said yes."

I stared at the untouched food before us, trying to process her words and silently berating myself for not coming clean about my feelings. For not bombarding her with flowers and letters and gifts. For not jumping on the first flight to Israel after being released from Walter Reed and tracking her down and telling her how much I liked her. I never imagined the window would close so fast. Now *I* was hurt and angry. But I forced myself to stay calm. There was nothing I could do to change any of this. She was engaged. In the movies, people try to break up engagements, but I couldn't do it. I wasn't going to fight for a girl to love me. Not after all I'd been through with Laura. If it didn't happen naturally, it wasn't meant to be. I wouldn't force it. I couldn't.

Finally I looked up. "I guess congratulations are in order. Mazel tov."

"Thanks," she said, her eyes moist and red.

Then we were silent again. I looked around the packed restaurant. Everyone was talking and laughing. It was so joyous and raucous and loud and festive, it almost made me forget for a moment that this was all fake. These weren't random residents of Nazareth. They were all Mossad agents. They were pretending to be unrelated to us. But we were—or more precisely Yael was—the entire reason they were in this place tonight.

"So," Yael said after a while, breaking the awkward silence. "You wanted to tell me something too, right?"

The last thing I wanted to do at this point was talk about my new theory of how to find Abu Khalif. I just wanted to pay the bill, excuse myself, and get out of there. I didn't want to be with her for another moment. I couldn't breathe. Not sitting here like this. I needed to be alone. I needed to think, to pray, to call my brother and see how he and Annie and Katie were doing. Talk about a fish out of water. I was a long way from home. I had no idea where home was. But it certainly wasn't here.

I loved this girl, I realized. If there had been any doubts in my mind, they were all gone the moment she told me she loved someone else. Now it felt as if someone had hit me in the chest with a two-by-four.

"Okay, fine, yes, there is something I'd like your take on," I said, forcing myself to go forward with the conversation, completely against my wishes, only because I knew it was the right thing to do for Matt and his family.

"Sure, what is it?" she asked.

There was no point waiting. I might as well get it out and get it over with. The sooner I did, the sooner we could head back to the base and the sooner I could go to my small apartment and be alone. "Khalif earned his doctorate in Islamic studies in Medina, right? That's when he fell in love. That's when he got married for the first time and all that, right?"

"Right."

"Well, for the past few days we've been looking at his wives and where they once lived, thinking maybe if we could find them, that's where he probably is."

"And?"

"And that's bothering me—I think that's the wrong premise."

"What's the right one?" she asked.

"We shouldn't be looking for the wives any more than we should be looking for the couriers," I said.

"Then whom should we be looking for?"

"The mentor."

"The what?"

"Khalif's mentor—the professor that had the most impact on him in Medina, the one who converted him from Palestinian nationalism to apocalyptic Islam."

"And who's that?"

"His first wife's father—Dr. Abdul Aziz Al-Siddiq."

She wasn't following, so I explained that for the past several days, I hadn't been looking at any of the intel regarding Khalif's wives. Instead, I'd been studying Aisha's father, Dr. Al-Siddiq. Aisha, it turned out, was the man's youngest daughter. Now seventy-one years old, Al-Siddiq was arguably one of the most prominent scholars—and advocates—of apocalyptic Islam in the entire Sunni Muslim world. He'd written nine books on the topic, I told Yael, including a textbook on eschatology that was required reading in most of the world's Sunni colleges, universities, and seminaries.

What intrigued me was that Al-Siddiq had overseen Abu Khalif while the future ISIS leader was researching and writing his doctoral thesis in Medina. The thesis, a five-hundred-page treatise on why the Mahdi would come back to earth to establish the caliphate sometime in the period between 2007 and 2027 if Muslims were faithful to prepare the way—starting with genocide against Christians and Jews and "apostate" Shia Muslims—was as convoluted and downright bizarre as anything I'd ever read.

"You actually read it?" Yael asked.

"Every page—what do you think I've been up to the last few days?"

"Not that."

The thesis was the essence of everything Khalif believed, I explained, and Khalif believed it for one simple reason: because Dr. Al-Siddiq had convinced him of it. Just as Al-Siddiq had later convinced Khalif to marry his youngest daughter. What's more, it was under Al-Siddiq's influence that Khalif had returned to al Qaeda in Iraq and persuaded the AQI leadership to distance themselves from bin Laden and then change their name to the Islamic State of Iraq and al-Sham—ISIS.

"Forget the couriers and forget the wives," I argued. "The person we should be looking for is Abdul Aziz Al-Siddiq. He isn't just Abu Khalif's father-in-law. He's Khalif's spiritual, political, and strategic mentor. And as we move closer and closer to the final battle and the cataclysmic End of Days—at least in Khalif's mind—who would he want at his side more than his professor, his mentor, his father? Find Al-Siddiq, and I guarantee you'll find Abu Khalif."

PART SIX

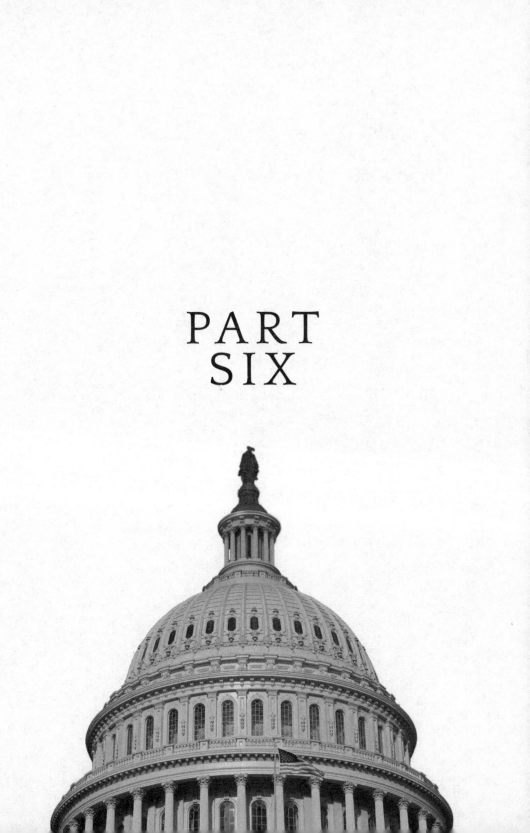

86

★ ★ ★

RAMAT DAVID AIR BASE, ISRAEL

To my surprise, I slept soundly for the first time in months.

When the alarm on my phone went off at 6 a.m., rather than roll over and rest for another thirty minutes or so, I got up, threw on a pair of jeans, a sweater, and some sneakers, and went for a long walk around the base.

Despite all that had happened the previous evening, despite all that Yael had said and how hurtful it had been, I wasn't angry or bitter. I felt oddly rested, strangely peaceful, and truly ready to get back to my family.

There was no need to pack my suitcase. I had never unpacked since arriving on the base. I couldn't watch television; the apartment I was using didn't have one. Nor a radio. Nor anything to read.

I guess I could have checked the headlines on my phone. That was certainly how I normally started my day, but on that morning I had no desire to hear more bad news. I knew what our entire team knew: more ISIS attacks inside the U.S. were not only coming, they were imminent. The pope was still heading to the U.S. any day. Despite the credible warnings the Mossad and other intelligence agencies were picking up, the Vatican refused to call off or even postpone the recently planned trip.

Meanwhile, large numbers of college students were heading south for spring break, even as the chatter concerning impending attacks inside the homeland—and particularly against resorts and theme parks and amusement centers—was growing exponentially. For all I knew, the attacks had already begun. If not, they would likely commence over the next few days. What was the point of torturing myself by tracking every threat in real time on Twitter or other social media? There was nothing I could do to stop the attacks. I'd been summarily removed from any such role. It had been made abundantly clear my services were no longer needed, and thus I was heading back to St. Thomas.

Hoping to pass the time and enjoy a final view of the Israeli countryside—as this was very likely the last time I would be here—I strolled the grounds of the base in the morning dew and fog. I watched several F-16s take off and bank toward the Syrian border. A number of Sikorsky helicopters also lifted off and headed northeast as well. I couldn't help but wonder if their pilots were embarking on training missions or routine patrols, or heading into harm's way. But there was no one around to ask, and no one would have told me anyway. I didn't exist. No one on the base outside of Yael's team knew my name. I was just "the new guy," and by tomorrow I wouldn't even be that.

Eventually I returned to the apartment and took a long, hot shower. I thought about shaving my head and getting rid of my beard as well, but didn't feel up to it. I'd let Matt get a good laugh and then shave it off next week. Instead, I toweled off, dressed in some clean khakis and a black polo shirt, and slumped in a chair.

I pulled up a Bible app on my phone but found I had no idea what to read. I had raced my way through the New Testament in the last few weeks and found all of it fascinating. I especially loved the verses that made it clear I'd go to heaven when I died.

Like when Jesus said, "Truly, truly, I say to you, he who hears My word, and believes Him who sent Me, has eternal life, and does not come into judgment, but has passed out of death into life."

Or when the apostle Paul wrote, "For I am convinced that neither death, nor life, nor angels, nor principalities, nor things present, nor things to come, nor powers, nor height, nor depth, nor any other created thing, will be able to separate us from the love of God, which is in Christ Jesus our Lord."

Or when the apostle John wrote, "He who has the Son has the life; he who does not have the Son of God does not have the life. These things I have written to you who believe in the name of the Son of God, so that you may know that you have eternal life."

Such verses had spoken powerfully to me in recent days. But now that I had read the New Testament, what was I supposed to do next? Plow my way through the Old Testament? That had little appeal. *The Garden? The Flood? The Law? Who begat whom?* I had no idea how any of that was relevant to me. But was I just going to skip it? Wasn't it important? Weren't there things in there God wanted me to know? I had so many questions, and I looked forward to sitting down with Matt. I knew he had answers, and I was fairly certain I wasn't likely to find them on my own.

In the end, I did finally dip into the Old Testament. After stumbling around for a while, I settled on the book of Psalms. I picked a random number and decided to read the ninth chapter. One passage particularly captured my attention.

My enemies retreated;
    they staggered and died when you appeared.
For you have judged in my favor;
    from your throne you have judged with fairness.
You have rebuked the nations and destroyed the wicked;
    you have erased their names forever.

The enemy is finished, in endless ruins;
the cities you uprooted are now forgotten.

How I wished this were true for me. It just wasn't. My enemies were not retreating. By all measures, they were advancing. They weren't staggering or dying. They weren't finished or in endless ruins. Abu Khalif and his men were still on a genocidal killing spree. And I was being kicked off the battlefield and sent into hiding. Where was the justice in that?

I glanced at my grandfather's pocket watch and realized it was time. So I grabbed my suitcase and briefcase, walked out of the room, and locked the apartment door behind me for the last time.

I suddenly found myself overwhelmed by a profound and pervasive sense of sadness. I was about to leave a team I had truly begun to respect and admire. I was leaving a job unfinished, and there were few things I hated more. And then there was Yael, who had tried to let me down gently but nonetheless had rejected me. I wasn't angry at her. To the contrary, I genuinely wanted her to be happy. But it stung, in part because of the suddenness of it all. I'd come to Israel imagining everything going so differently between us. It had never even occurred to me that she might be seeing someone else, much less falling for him, much less agreeing to marry him. Last night I'd been in shock. This morning I felt like I was grieving the loss of another friend.

We would not write. We would not call. We would not keep in touch. There would be no point. She had a new love and a new life ahead of her.

What exactly did I have in front of me?

87

★ ★ ★

It was nine o'clock exactly when I knocked on the conference room door.

A moment later, I heard Yael's voice through the intercom telling me to come in, and the electronic locks opened. I entered and found the entire team assembled with Ari Shalit at the head of the table. It was immediately apparent by their disheveled appearances and the empty coffee mugs that they had not just arrived. They'd been there much, if not all, of the night.

"Please, J. B., take a seat," Yael said.

There was a spot available next to her, but I chose not to take it. Instead, I walked over to Shalit and took the empty chair next to him and prepared myself for what was coming. Yael would undoubtedly thank me for being on the team, however briefly. She'd say I'd been helpful, and Ari would agree, and the team would nod, and I would say thank you, and they would clap, and that would be that. I'd already decided I wanted to leave on a positive note. I was grateful for these specialists, a unique breed with a high calling, and I desperately wanted—no, *needed*—them to succeed, so there was no point saying anything sour or critical. The entire little ceremony would be mercifully quick, and soon I'd be on a chopper bound for

Ben Gurion International Airport and then on a long flight back to the U.S. Virgin Islands.

Except the morning took an unexpected turn.

"The team and I have been here since just after midnight," Yael explained after I'd sat down.

"Why's that?" I asked. "What's wrong?"

"We've been testing your theory," she replied.

"What theory?"

"About Dr. Al-Siddiq."

"Okay," I said cautiously.

"The short version is that over the past few hours we've determined that Al-Siddiq hasn't left Saudi Arabia in four years," she continued. "He lectures. He writes. He's somewhat of a big shot. Runs seminars. Runs conferences. Islamic scholars from all over the world come to see him. But he doesn't travel."

"Go on." Did the team find my theory compelling or ridiculous? And if the latter, why bother telling me minutes before I departed?

"Two days ago, Al-Siddiq booked his first international flight in four years," Ari Shalit noted. "Want to take a guess where to?"

"I have no idea."

"Istanbul," Shalit said.

"Interesting."

"We thought so," Shalit added. "Is he going on vacation? Doing a little sightseeing for the first time in his life? Or is he going to meet with his daughter and with Khalif?"

"The fact is we don't know for certain," Yael said. "But everything you told me last night about Al-Siddiq checks out. We've been going over his life, his writings, his phone calls and e-mails, our databases—everything—double-checking your work. And you're right—he's a close friend and advisor to Khalif. He clearly loves his daughter, as does Khalif. Once we realized he'd just bought a ticket to Turkey, we found ourselves hoping this was the break we've needed."

Shalit noted that Al-Siddiq was booked on Turkish Airlines flight 109, which would depart Medina at 4:40 p.m. local time and land in Istanbul at 8:15 p.m. From there he had a connecting flight to Antalya, the Turkish resort city on the coast of the Mediterranean. Then came the kicker: Shalit was sending Yael, Dutch, and me to Istanbul.

"Me?"

"The mission is this: Find Al-Siddiq, follow him, and report back," Shalit said. "You leave in fifteen minutes. Any questions?"

Many, actually—but one thing was clear: I wasn't going home just yet after all.

★　★　★

We flew first to Rome on a Gulfstream IV.

I was excited, encouraged by the break. I had raised the question of why they were sending me back into the field now that Khalif had issued a fatwa calling for my murder. They'd made such a big deal about how I wasn't trained and it wouldn't be safe. Now their message seemed to have changed.

Shalit had simply responded that my instincts had consistently proven accurate. That was why he'd brought me onto the team in the first place, and they were too close to success to monkey with the formula. He needed me to help run Khalif to ground. With false documents and disguises and the like, they would do everything in their power to minimize the danger to me, but Shalit had certainly been honest and direct with me about the risks. "There is a very real chance you won't come back," he had said before I left.

I knew, and I said yes anyway. I wanted to see this thing done. Period. End of sentence.

Dutch, Yael, and I disembarked with our luggage and headed into the main terminal. There, we were to board a commercial flight to Istanbul. Turkish Airlines flight 1866 would be wheels up at 3:25 p.m.

local time and wheels down in the onetime capital of the Ottoman Empire—the former seat of the caliphate—just after seven that evening. This would be cutting it close. It would give us barely an hour before Dr. Al-Siddiq landed and entered the same airport. But Dutch insisted that the somewhat-convoluted route was the right way in. He had the most field experience in this type of operation, so Yael had appointed him ops leader for this mission.

Given the deeply strained relations between the Israeli and Turkish governments at the moment, a Mossad team couldn't simply jet into Istanbul directly from Israel these days without drawing a high degree of attention from the Turkish police and intelligence agencies. That would not do, especially now with the fatwa out there. The last thing we wanted was Turkish authorities focusing their attention on me, much less my Mossad colleagues. Far better, Dutch said, would be for us to all enter Istanbul on a commercial flight—on the country's national airline—through a long line at passport control with thousands of other tourists and businessmen.

He and Yael weren't particularly worried about getting into Turkey with their false papers. They were pros and did it all the time. But they were a little concerned about me. It wasn't just the Turkish border police we had to worry about. It was any Muslim who might have seen the photo ISIS was using—the one they were now spreading across the globe using all manner of social media—and who might notice me as I walked by. The good news was that the photo ISIS was using was one they'd pulled off the *New York Times* website. It was, therefore, somewhat dated. In it, I was bald. I was clean-shaven. I was wearing a Western suit and even a tie. What's more, it had been taken five or six years earlier.

Now I had a full head of hair. It was short, but it was growing, and along with my full beard, this changed my look fairly dramatically. In addition, Dutch insisted that Yael and I once again pose as a married Muslim couple, as we had in Dubai. Yael, therefore, was again wearing a black silk *abaya* and *niqab*, covering her head to foot, including her entire face. I, on the other hand, was not wearing the Zegna suit, Italian shoes, or gold Rolex watch I had worn in Dubai. Rather, I was wearing a crisp white cotton *thawb*, the full-length, long-sleeved, traditional tunic worn by men from the Gulf region. Dutch had also asked me to wear a *taqiyah*, a short, rounded skullcap commonly worn by Muslim men.

Had I been flying into Israel in such garb, I could have expected to be asked many questions by the Israeli border police about who I was, where I was coming from, why I was coming to Israel, whom I knew in the country, what other Muslim countries I had visited, and so forth. But just the opposite would be true flying into Turkey, especially given that I spoke Arabic reasonably well. Rather than standing out, I should blend right in. True, what Yael and I were wearing was distinctive to the Gulf, not Turkey, but Turkish airports had a steady stream of Gulf visitors and welcomed them without hassle and even without visas.

There was just one problem, and it had nothing to do with my appearance or my fake passport or my fake marriage to Yael. This was far more serious.

The plane was late.

88

★ ★ ★

ISTANBUL, TURKEY

Our arrival was delayed by nearly forty minutes.

By the time we touched down in rain-drenched Istanbul, cleared passport control, and linked up with the Mossad's station chief—a Turkish Jew in his midfifties who asked us to call him Mustafa—it was already 8:06 p.m. That gave us less than ten minutes before Al-Siddiq's flight from Medina was supposed to land.

From there, the news got worse. A quick glance at the arrivals board indicated that Al-Siddiq's flight had landed early. In fact, it was already disembarking, and it was on the other end of the terminal.

Yael and Dutch were calm, cool, and collected. They had been doing this sort of thing for a long time. But I was new and I was freaking out. We had no margin for error. This was our only known link to Abu Khalif. There was a very high likelihood that Al-Siddiq had been summoned by Khalif and could take us right to the ISIS emir. Losing him would be catastrophic, and I feared that's what was about to happen.

Mustafa tried to calm me down. He explained that he and his team had arrived and entered the airport three hours ago. He had four agents—two men and two women—stationed near the gate where Al-Siddiq's plane had arrived. He had other agents positioned along the corridors throughout the airport, allowing him to track the Saudi theological professor no matter what direction he chose to go. Furthermore, Mustafa had two teams of agents outside the airport, waiting in SUVs, ready to follow Al-Siddiq if he surprised us by leaving the airport instead of making his connecting flight to Antalya. If all that weren't enough, he had three agents on motorcycles positioned near the exit ramps to the main roads near the airport so that even if those driving Al-Siddiq somehow managed to elude Mustafa's two SUVs, he would still have eyes on the target until the others could catch up.

Mustafa's recommendation was that we head directly to the gate where our flight to Antalya would soon be boarding, and let his team take care of the rest. They were trained, experienced professionals. They knew this airport inside and out. They knew what they were doing, and they knew the stakes. Still, he said he was fairly confident that all these precautions weren't going to be needed anyway. His instincts told him Al-Siddiq was heading to Antalya.

"Get on the plane," he whispered. "And don't get caught."

Dutch agreed and we quickly split up and went our separate ways. Yael and I wheeled our luggage through the airport, then headed to a café across from our gate, purchased cups of Turkish coffee, found an empty table, and sat together, eyes peeled and hearts pounding. Dutch, meanwhile, disappeared for a while, then passed by without acknowledging us and headed for a newsstand not far from the gate. There he leafed through magazines and bought himself a pack of gum and a candy bar, occasionally checking his wristwatch and waiting for the announcement that it was time to board.

Mustafa was nowhere to be seen. Nor were any other Mossad agents—at least none that I could identify. No one I saw around me or near me looked Israeli. None even looked Jewish. But then again, Mustafa didn't either. His dark features and bushy mustache weren't tricks of the trade. He wasn't wearing a wig and makeup. He was the real deal. Yael said the Istanbul station chief and his family had made aliyah in 1982. They were all now true-blue Israeli citizens. They'd gone to Israeli schools and fought in the IDF and paid Israeli taxes and assimilated into Israeli society. But Mustafa still looked Turkish because he was Turkish. He spoke the language as a native and could read and write as a native and thus was ideally suited to serve the Israeli intelligence system in Turkey.

One of the curious and fascinating advantages the Mossad had gained from two thousand years of Jews living in exile was that with Jews coming back to the land of Israel from every nation on the earth, the intelligence agency had the unique ability to recruit Israeli citizens who looked, sounded, and acted like Arabs, Russians, Germans, Italians, Ethiopians, Yemenis, Brazilians, Koreans, and even Chinese. These agents didn't need to be taught how to blend into a foreign society. They didn't need to learn new languages or customs or idiosyncrasies before becoming spies. This thought should have calmed me somewhat, yet it did not.

Where was Al-Siddiq? Had he already deplaned? Was he really going to Antalya, or was that just a ruse? Who was traveling with him? How would we identify them? What if they identified us?

I grabbed my phone and opened the app that Dutch had briefed me on during the flight to Rome. Everyone on the team, myself included, was wearing glasses similar to the ones I'd been given in Dubai. But this version didn't simply have a built-in microphone. It also featured a high-resolution video camera. Every team member was thus transmitting to each other's smartphones live images of whatever we were seeing at the moment.

When the app loaded, my heart nearly stopped, for there, in front of me, was a real-time, if somewhat grainy, image of Abu Khalif's mentor. He was here. He was on the ground, in the airport, and on the move.

A text message now flashed across the bottom of the app. **No checked luggage. Just a carry-on. No companions. Seems to be alone.**

I didn't buy it. There was no way Al-Siddiq was going to the emir unaccompanied. I could believe he thought he was traveling alone, at least for the first leg of the journey. But I had no doubt Abu Khalif had ISIS operatives on that flight from Medina. I had no doubt they were in this airport. Watching their mark. Tracking his every movement. Just as we were. *So who were they? And why hadn't the Mossad guys identified them already?*

Heading to men's room, the next text read. **Six breaking off.**

Three, follow him, read a text from Mustafa.

Then came another: **One and two, reposition along the corridor.**

And a third: **Six, hold back in case he turns around. All others, hold your positions.**

Then came a message from Dutch. **Where are the trackers?** he asked, voicing my concerns precisely. **Tell me we've spotted them.**

I've got one, Yael texted. **At the gate to Antalya. Female, jeans, veiled.**

Startled, I instinctively popped my head up to look. I immediately saw an attractive Muslim woman in her late twenties. She was wearing designer jeans, a brightly colored blouse, and a *hijab*. At first glance, I was sure Yael was wrong. The woman looked like a college student, not a spy. But Yael quickly tapped my leg under the table with her foot. Her message was clear and emphatic: *Don't look. Turn away. Don't risk making eye contact.*

She was right, of course. I wasn't trained for surveillance. I wasn't supposed to be doing what everyone else was doing. For now, my job was to monitor the video feeds while keeping my head down and staying out of trouble.

Looking back at the app on my phone, I tapped the feed coming from Yael's glasses and studied the young Muslim more carefully. Now I knew Yael was right. The woman was pretending to read a magazine but she wasn't really reading. She was scanning the faces of every passenger in the lounge, and she was texting something. *But what? And to whom?*

She wasn't alone. That much was clear.

89

★ ★ ★

By the time we boarded, the team had identified no fewer than four ISIS operatives shadowing Al-Siddiq.

Dutch was sitting in first class and was among the first to board. That would allow him to study each passenger coming onto the plane after him and give us the opportunity to see each of them via the live images he was webcasting from the camera in his glasses. It would also give him the chance to "accidentally" bump into Al-Siddiq when the Saudi professor was boarding, enabling Dutch to slip a tiny tracking beacon into his pocket or his carry-on suitcase. Once we were back on the ground, we would be able to follow Al-Siddiq wherever he went.

Yael and I had been assigned seats in the very back of the plane—in the last row, actually, near the galley and the bathrooms—so we were among the last to board. This was a problem. Everyone else got to study us as we moved down the aisle. And since the release of Abu Khalif's fatwa, I was growing increasingly anxious, though I fought hard not to show it. Still, my heart was pounding. My palms were perspiring. I suddenly felt incredibly awkward and conspicuous in the garb of a Gulf Arab.

I immediately noticed the young woman with the *hijab*. She was sitting in first class, to my left as I boarded, in a window seat two rows behind Dutch, and she was eyeing me suspiciously, making me even more nervous. Five rows behind her were two large, burly Arab men sitting in aisle seats across from each other. They, too, had been identified by the team as likely ISIS operatives, and their cold, blank, soulless eyes sent chills down my spine as I passed them.

Two rows behind them, on my left, I spotted Al-Siddiq. I'd been studying photographs of him for days, and in the terminal I'd seen him from afar or via the video stream on my app. But to see him up close, face-to-face, made my blood run cold. This was the theological and ideological mentor to the man who'd killed my family.

It was disorienting how normal he looked. Unlike Khalif, who bore more than a passing resemblance to Charles Manson, Al-Siddiq looked more like a distinguished professor of English literature than a genocidal End Times psychopath. He had a somewhat oval face, a closely trimmed mustache and beard, a long, patrician nose, and bifocals in rather dated gold wire frames. Dressed in a light-blue oxford button-down shirt, a tweed blazer, tan slacks, and loafers, he was also sitting in an aisle seat, and it struck me that he was doing the exact opposite of what I was doing. He, a fanatic Muslim, was trying to look like a Westerner while I, a brand-new Christian, was trying to pass myself off as a devout Muslim. We were trying to fool each other and anyone else who was watching, trying not to be noticed until our missions were accomplished.

That said, Al-Siddiq didn't look any more comfortable in his disguise than I was in mine. He had a John le Carré spy thriller in his lap, but he wasn't reading it. Rather, he was nervously fidgeting with the air-conditioning system and mopping his brow with a handkerchief.

As I moved past him, he looked at me and our eyes locked for a moment. I forced a smile and nodded to him, then looked away. But as I did, I saw his eyes narrow and his brow furrow, and I suddenly realized that I was acting more like an American tourist than a fellow Sunni Muslim from the Gulf. Now I was truly worried. *Had he recognized me? Why had I been so foolish? Why had I let myself make eye contact?* Worse, everyone else on the team who was riveted to the images on the app on their phones had seen the mistake I'd just made, along with Al-Siddiq's uncomfortable reaction.

Still, there was nothing I could do about it now. I had to keep moving and keep praying. Coming up on my right, three rows into the economy cabin, was a handsome young Arab man that I surmised was in his midthirties. This was the fourth ISIS operative the team had identified, and I was careful not to look in his direction at all as I passed him. I already had his face tattooed in my mind's eye, and it was he who struck me as the most dangerous of all. He had dark, brooding eyes and a large, bushy black beard. His features suggested he was a Saudi. He was in excellent physical shape, and he looked smarter and far more cunning than the two heavies sitting several rows ahead. Mustafa had alerted us all by text message just before we'd boarded that this was likely the leader of the ISIS team shadowing Al-Siddiq. But he'd also reminded us that there could be other ISIS operatives on the flight that had not been identified, including one or more of the flight attendants.

As per the plan, Yael took her seat by the window in the final row on the right. I took my seat on the aisle. That made me more exposed to anyone coming back to use the bathroom, raising the risk that I could be seen and identified. But we didn't have a choice. A Muslim woman traveling with her husband, especially one wearing an *abaya*, would never be allowed to have the aisle seat. So I buckled up and said a silent prayer, and soon we were rumbling down the runway and up into the treacherous winter storm that was descending not just on Istanbul but on much of the northern Mediterranean region.

Twice during the short, bumpy flight, Al-Siddiq made his way down the aisle to the restroom. Both times he eyed me strangely, and as he did, my stress was off the charts. The first time, I buried my head in *Asharq Al-Awsat*, the London-based Arab daily newspaper. The second time, about thirty minutes later, the young Saudi followed him to the restroom. That time I pretended I was reading *Al-Hayat*, another Arab daily, as he stood directly at my side.

My imagination ran wild with what atrocities the ISIS killer beside me had committed and what atrocities he was preparing to commit next. Compounding those fears, Al-Siddiq was spending an unusually long time in the restroom. Why? Was the turbulence causing him airsickness? Was he ill for some other reason? Were his own anxieties causing him stomach problems? Or was he suspicious? Had the run-in with Dutch made him paranoid? Was he searching his clothing? Had he found the tracking beacon? Maybe he hadn't found it the first time, but could that be why he was back again?

As Al-Siddiq came out of the restroom the second time and prepared to pass the young Saudi, the plane was suddenly jolted by turbulence. Both men stumbled in the aisle. Al-Siddiq grabbed the headrest in front of me to stabilize himself. And in that moment, out of the corner of my eye, I saw the young Saudi slip a small note into the outside pocket of Al-Siddiq's blazer. It happened so fast, so smoothly, so professionally that for a few moments I doubted that I'd actually seen it. But as the young man stepped into the restroom and Al-Siddiq worked his way back up the aisle and took his seat, I saw him look around nervously to see if anyone was watching him. He even looked back down the aisle toward the rear of the plane. I made sure I was carefully hidden behind the newspaper. When I looked again, I saw him pull the note out of his pocket, read it, and then quickly put it away.

I immediately leaned over and whispered what I'd seen to Yael.

"So contact's been made," she whispered back. "Now let's see where they go."

90

★ ★ ★

ANTALYA, TURKEY

No sooner had we landed in Antalya than it became clear we weren't staying long.

Yael immediately received a call from Trotsky, informing her that someone had purchased a ticket for Al-Siddiq from Antalya to the Turkish city of Gaziantep on SunExpress Airlines. Flight 7646 would depart at 6:45 a.m. local time and was expected to land precisely at 8:00. What's more, Trotsky indicated that there were newly purchased tickets to the same city in the names of four additional passengers who had been on our flight from Istanbul.

This was a significant break. We had video and still images of the four ISIS operatives, but until now we didn't have their names. To be sure, the names on the passenger manifest were unlikely to be their real ones. But they could be cross-checked against the Mossad's databases as well as with Jordanian, Egyptian, UAE, and Saudi intelligence to put together a travel profile. We would soon know what cities they had been to in the last twelve months using these particular aliases and who their travel partners had been.

"We're on it," Trotsky told Yael.

As soon as Yael briefed us, Dutch called Mustafa. The Turkish station chief had arrived in Antalya with his team on a Learjet a mere twenty minutes before us. They were waiting for us with six rented sedans and SUVs, ready for us to follow Al-Siddiq and his handlers wherever they went. But now, with Al-Siddiq's revised itinerary, Dutch issued new orders. Three of Mustafa's men and one woman needed to purchase tickets and take the SunExpress flight to Gaziantep. That would put fresh eyes and new faces on the plane to watch Al-Siddiq's every move. The rest of us, Dutch said, needed to rush to the Learjet. Together we would head to Gaziantep with all haste.

★　★　★

Gaziantep was the last major Turkish city before the border with Syria.

It was almost eighty miles—close to a two-hour drive—south to Aleppo. Nearly every foreign fighter who wanted to join ISIS or the al-Nusra Front or one of the other rebel or jihadist groups battling for control of Syria found his or her way to Gaziantep. There they would hole up in a cheap hotel, make contact with a smuggler, and pay big money for someone to get them safely across the border.

Why the Turkish government was letting this happen was another matter altogether. The fact that a member of NATO—a longtime and stalwart ally of the United States—was now allowing blood-thirsty terrorists (aka "foreign fighters") to crisscross its territory and its borders absolutely infuriated me. But the geopolitics of the situation was another matter for another time.

As our Learjet touched down at Gaziantep Oğuzeli International Airport just before sunrise, it was easy to imagine that Al-Siddiq was, in fact, about to take such a journey into Syria and very possibly into Aleppo. Several members of Yael's team were now actively considering the theory that Khalif was hiding out in Aleppo. That would keep him inside the caliphate's territory, near his forces, in direct contact with his commanders throughout Syria, but not in Raqqa, where so many ISIS members were being targeted and killed in drone strikes.

If this were the case, Al-Siddiq wouldn't have to wait for days in a cheap hotel. He already had his contacts. He already had four ISIS operatives at his side. He had a deep and intimate and enduring friendship with Abu Khalif. Indeed, he was the father of Khalif's first wife. He had almost certainly been personally invited on this journey by Khalif. There seemed to be no other reason for Al-Siddiq to be traveling to Gaziantep when he hadn't traveled outside of Saudi Arabia for at least four years. Whether he was specifically heading toward Aleppo or not, I couldn't say. I still leaned toward Khalif being hunkered down in Turkey. But either way, something big was in motion. I could feel it. I just hoped nothing I did would blow it.

By the time Al-Siddiq and his entourage landed, we were all in position and ready for any move he might make. There was a fresh team inside the airport, ready to jump on a new connecting flight if Al-Siddiq and his men surprised us again. The rest of us, however, were positioned in various vehicles on or near the airport grounds. I was behind the wheel of a dark-blue Toyota RAV4 with Yael at my side. We were idling at a gas station on Highway D850, not far from the entrance to the airport parking lot. I'd changed into blue jeans, a black sweater, and my leather jacket, though I still had the traditional Muslim skullcap on. Yael, meanwhile, had changed out of the *abaya* and was wearing gray slacks, a maroon blouse, and a black fleece, though she was also wearing a headscarf. We now looked a bit more like Turkish Muslims than ones from the Gulf—all the better, we hoped, to blend in to our surroundings.

Suddenly Yael's satphone buzzed with a series of text messages from Dutch.

Al-Siddiq exiting airport.

With three men.

Woman has broken off from group.

Have separate team following her.

Al-Siddiq and group walking to parking lot.

Getting into van.

White.

VW Caravelle.

Pulling out.

Heading north.

I pulled onto the highway, gunning the engine and putting us a good distance ahead of the approaching VW van. I knew Dutch and the two agents with him would be tailing Al-Siddiq in a silver Audi. Mustafa and three more members of his team would bring up the rear in a black Ford Explorer.

Tracking system working, Dutch texted. **Signal five by five.**

That was a relief, since Al-Siddiq was heading into the heart of the largest city in Turkey's eastern provinces, a metropolis of some 1.5 million people. Without the tracker, the chance of losing the Caravelle in a dense, highly congested city few of us had any experience in—and in which Yael and I had *no* experience—was very high. Even with the tracker we needed to stay fairly close. The system had a range of up to five miles, and was accurate to within one hundred meters, but if Al-Siddiq or his men were to realize we were trailing them, they might just be good enough to escape and disappear into a city whose layout they knew well and we did not.

Suddenly Dutch's Audi surged past the Caravelle and then past me. Dutch instructed me to slow down a bit and let the Caravelle pass. I did as I was told—subtly, gradually—and a few minutes later the VW did roar past. A minute after that, the Explorer passed us too, and now Yael and I were the last in line, a good three to four miles behind the Caravelle and at least five to six miles behind the Audi, even as other cars on this busy highway wove in and out around us.

After another ten minutes, Dutch texted to say he was exiting off the main highway onto O-54. He wanted to give Al-Siddiq and his men a wide berth and no cause for concern.

The Caravelle did not exit. It stayed on D850 and thus so did Mustafa and I.

A moment later, however, Dutch told Mustafa to stop for gas at the next service station. Yael and I would then be tasked with following the Caravelle while Dutch found a road to intercept us and reenter the mix.

As we headed into the city, the morning rush hour was building. I had barely gotten through the last few yellow lights to keep up with Al-Siddiq and was worried he or the men with him would soon realize we were following them.

"We need someone to relieve us," I told Yael, who immediately agreed and texted Dutch.

A moment later, a motorcycle roared past us, followed by a message from Dutch ordering us to drop back.

"Is that guy with us?" I asked. "I didn't know we had someone on a motorcycle."

"Neither did I," Yael said. "Let me check."

She sent a text, and a few seconds later the phone buzzed in her hands. "You're not going to believe it," she said, reading the message.

"What?" I asked, coming to a stop at a red light.

"That's Pritchard," she said.

"Paul Pritchard?"

"Yeah."

"From Dubai?"

"The very same."

"What's he doing here?"

"Good question," she said. "Guess we're about to find out."

91

★ ★ ★

GAZIANTEP, TURKEY

I never would have imagined Gaziantep had a Holiday Inn.

But it did. It was right downtown, it was cheap—a mere thirty-five dollars a night—and it had plenty of vacancies, and that's where Al-Siddiq and the ISIS thugs stayed, in a suite with an adjoining room on either side.

Dutch and Mustafa rented the rooms directly above and directly below the suite and the two additional rooms. In these, they proceeded to attach listening devices onto the respective floors and ceilings, hoping to eavesdrop on private conversations and gain useful intelligence. Other members of the team took rooms on the same floor as Al-Siddiq's suite, specifically at either end near the elevators and stairwells. They discreetly set up small video cameras and motion sensors with silent alarms that would vibrate when any of the ISIS team left their suite or when anyone entered or exited the hallway. At the same time, they hacked into the hotel's Wi-Fi system and the local wireless phone network, hoping to intercept any e-mails or text messages.

We also rented a suite on the ground floor, which became our war room. Yael and I and two other agents—one male and one female—set up a bank of laptop computers, digital recording equipment, and various other devices allowing us to monitor everything that was happening in the rooms upstairs. We were far enough away that we could hold meetings and make calls back to the team at the Ramat David base without any risk of being overheard by the terrorists.

With the surveillance operation set up, Dutch, Mustafa, Yael, and I gathered in the war room with Paul Pritchard. I was eager to hear why Pritchard was there. So was Yael. And we were about to find out. The former CIA operative brought news. He explained that two of the three men now watching over Al-Siddiq were operatives who had personally worked for Abu Khalif in the past and were likely still closely connected to him.

"How do you know?" I asked.

"They were former residents of Abu Dhabi," Pritchard replied. "The Baqouba brothers recruited them into ISIS a few years ago, and Prince bin Zayed and his men have been tracking them ever since."

He handed us dossiers on both men, and I was struck by the level of detail. There were photos of the men and their parents and siblings along with fairly extensive bios and lists of their known associates. Perhaps most interestingly, there were transcripts of intercepted e-mail conversations between the men and Ahmed Baqouba from when they were first being recruited and didn't know they were being monitored.

"Why didn't the prince snatch these guys at the beginning?" Yael asked as she scanned the transcripts.

"That's on me," said Pritchard. "I advised him not to move too quickly. I was sure we could keep close tabs on these guys and that hopefully they would take us to the Baqoubas and then to Khalif himself. I was wrong. Less than two weeks after these e-mails were intercepted, both men gave us the slip. We've been hunting them ever since. When Ari Shalit sent stills of your suspects from Istanbul, Prince bin Zayed and I instantly recognized two of them. So here I am."

"Guess you're about to get a second bite at the apple," I said.

"That's the plan," Pritchard said.

"What about the third guy?" I asked.

"Sorry; I'm afraid we don't have anything on him," Pritchard admitted.

"Actually, we do," Yael said. "I just got an e-mail from the king in Amman. The moment Ari sent him the images from Istanbul, His Majesty called him to say he recognized one of the faces. The guy's a Jordanian. He was with Zarqawi from the earliest days of AQI. When Zarqawi was killed, he became loyal to Khalif. According to His Majesty, the guy is one of Khalif's personal bodyguards."

These were promising leads indeed. If all this was true, the evidence suggested some of Khalif's most loyal aides had been dispatched to pick up one of Khalif's most trusted friends. The chances we were getting closer to the emir had just grown exponentially.

Suddenly Dutch's phone rang. It was Nadia, the leader of the Mossad unit Dutch had assigned to track the young woman who had broken off from the others. About twenty minutes after Al-Siddiq and the team had departed the airport, she'd walked out of the terminal and gotten into a dusty old Chevy with an older woman who appeared to be in her fifties. Rather than heading north on D850 into Gaziantep, however, they'd taken a right onto D400 and headed east until they'd reached Nizip, a city of about a hundred thousand located about fifty kilometers east of where we were.

"Nizip? Why Nizip?" Dutch asked.

"We have no idea," Nadia replied.

"What are they doing now?"

"They've arrived at some sort of estate. It's a huge, sprawling compound."

"Like a hotel?"

"No, it's some sort of private home, I'd guess. The weird thing is, there aren't any men—just women and children."

"Give me the coordinates—we'll task a satellite over it."

"Sending them now."

"Good. Keep me posted."

"Will do."

Al-Siddiq wasn't taken to Aleppo or anywhere else that night. Instead, he and his handlers hunkered down in the hotel and did nothing. In fact, they did nothing for the next four days. No calls. No text messages. No e-mails. They barely even had any conversations. Nor did they leave the suite. Not once. They didn't go out to eat. They didn't go buy a newspaper. They did open the door once to get more towels from housekeeping, but that was it.

We could hear them eating every few hours. They munched on apples and cracked nuts, and we could smell fresh oranges on our casual walks past their closed doors. This suggested their suitcases and backpacks had been filled more with food than with clothes and other personal effects. It also suggested they had been anticipating hiding out in these hotel rooms for the better part of a week.

We, on the other hand, had not been anticipating doing nothing for so many days. We had to send members of the team out to restaurants and grocery stores to get supplies, even though we knew Al-Siddiq and his band could bolt at any hour of the day and we could get caught shorthanded. We also risked someone spotting us and getting suspicious, reporting us to the local police or to ISIS itself. Why were these guys—and the women in Nizip—sitting around doing nothing? Why weren't they moving? Why weren't they linking up with others? Why wasn't Al-Siddiq being taken to Khalif?

One possibility was that they were waiting to receive word that it was safe to take Al-Siddiq into Syria. That was quite plausible, we concluded.

Another possibility was that ISIS had a team in the hotel, possibly even among the hotel staff, watching to see if anyone was following Al-Siddiq. Pritchard even suggested there could be an ISIS team operating out of nearby hotels and apartment buildings, watching around the clock, trying to determine if there was anyone suspicious, anyone who might be a foreign agent. If this was true, the longer we stayed, the longer we left vehicles on nearby side streets ready to move at a moment's notice, the longer we sent people out to get takeout and groceries, the higher the risk we could be spotted and attacked.

The only reassuring news was that if we'd been spotted already, we would probably have already been attacked. The fact that we were still alive suggested we had not been spotted.

At least not yet.

92

★ ★ ★

At just after nine Thursday morning, one of our silent alarms went off.

It was our fifth day in Gaziantep. Someone had just opened the door of the suite and was headed down the hallway. Yael alerted the rest of the team. Mustafa was on duty on the first floor, buying a Pepsi from a machine in the lobby, when one of Al-Siddiq's men suddenly burst out of the stairwell, brushed by him, and headed to the parking lot behind the hotel. Mustafa immediately texted the team and our four drivers, all of whom were positioned on various streets many blocks away, having been ordered by Dutch to remain even farther away from the hotel after Pritchard had raised his concerns. Now they fired up their engines and prepared to roll.

Ten minutes later, Al-Siddiq and his two other men came down the elevator and bolted out the front door. When the VW Caravelle pulled up, they jumped in and roared off.

Dutch and his men went to work in the cars. Pritchard quickly caught up to them on his motorcycle. They were trailing the Caravelle visually and via the tracking beacon while carefully watching their backs to make sure they weren't being lured into a trap.

The team had briefly debated attaching an additional tracking beacon to the VW. In the end, however, Dutch had decided against it. He believed the van should be neither tampered with nor even approached, on the theory that it was likely being watched closely for just such a development. Pritchard agreed, and that was that.

Yael and I did not roll with the trackers. Rather, we joined Mustafa and two of his agents upstairs to break into the terrorists' suite and adjoining rooms before housekeeping could get to them. It was a risky move, especially if there were ISIS operatives still in the hotel watching the rooms. But Mustafa insisted it had to be done.

We spent the better part of an hour going over each room with a fine-tooth comb, but the men had left nothing useful behind. There was no luggage. No personal items. Not even any trash. If that weren't discouraging enough, the rooms had been wiped down so thoroughly that not a single fingerprint—even from previous guests—could be lifted. This suggested neither Al-Siddiq nor his handlers were planning on returning to the hotel. They were moving on. But where?

We went back downstairs to the war room and waited. We played cards and paced and drank instant coffee. We didn't hear from Dutch or his team for more than an hour, and with every minute that passed, Yael's and my anxiety grew. We didn't dare call or text the guys. They were in the midst of a high-stakes operation, and the last thing we wanted to do was distract them, even for a moment.

Then, just before noon, Yael received a call. But it was not Dutch. It was Ari Shalit, and he had news. President Mahfouz had just called Prime Minister Eitan. The Egyptians had been carefully reviewing the photos Shalit had sent them of the young woman in the *hijab* who had been traveling with Al-Siddiq. It had taken several days, but they now had a positive ID.

She was an Egyptian, born and raised in Alexandria, the daughter of a prominent leader of the Muslim Brotherhood who had been jailed and later executed after Mahfouz came to power. At that point, she and her three brothers had all become radicalized. Two had gone to Iraq to join ISIS and had blown themselves up in a joint martyrdom operation that killed 179 people at a church in Baghdad. Her remaining brother had died during the battle of Dabiq back in December. Now she was the only one left. According to Mahfouz, the young woman had been with ISIS rebels on the outskirts of Aleppo as recently as four weeks ago.

As Yael related the details to the rest of us, I couldn't help but be intrigued. Did these new tidbits suggest we might soon, in fact, be heading into Aleppo, however chaotic and dangerous the situation on the border?

But Shalit wasn't done. According to Israeli intelligence, the paramilitary forces of the Syrian Kurds had been engaged in heavy fighting with ISIS in recent days along the Syrian-Turkish border. By all accounts, the Kurds had gained the upper hand. They were taking significant swaths of territory from ISIS, and there were now only a few corridors between northwestern Syria and Turkey still under ISIS control. Shalit said his analysts were telling him it might no longer be possible for any ISIS personnel to get from Gaziantep into Syria or from Aleppo into Turkey. If Abu Khalif was in Aleppo, he might be stuck there.

Then, just as the sun was going down, Yael's satphone rang again. This time it was Dutch. He and his team had tracked the VW all day. There was no question Al-Siddiq's men were trying everything they could to spot and shake anyone trying to tail them. Their tradecraft was spectacular, he said, but with the tracking beacon in place, Dutch and Pritchard and the rest of the team had ultimately followed the men to a compound high up in a mountain range not far from Nizip.

"Is Khalif there?" Yael asked.

"I don't know," Dutch said. "Maybe."

"What do you mean, maybe?"

"We haven't seen him. But it's possible."

"Where are you guys exactly?"

"I'm hiding in a cave near the crest of a ridge. Pritchard is on another ridge, off to my right. The rest of the team is watching the cars and maintaining a perimeter."

"What can you see?"

"I'm looking down at a huge walled compound—huge. The whole thing is about the size of a soccer stadium. It looks like an ancient Ottoman fortress of some kind. Pritchard thinks it's from the sixteenth century. The walls have got to be fifteen or twenty feet high, and thick—two or three feet thick at least. There's an enormous mosque in the back left corner with a big marble dome and a stone minaret probably thirty, thirty-five feet high."

"What else?"

"There's a two-story row of stone buildings along the left side of the compound. I can see through some of the windows. It looks like classrooms. Could be a madrassa, though there aren't any kids around. On the right side of the compound, there's a similar two-story wing. Pritchard says from his angle it looks like a dormitory—bunk beds, dressers, lavatories, that kind of thing. In the middle there's a giant courtyard."

"Security?" Yael asked.

"Airtight," Dutch replied.

"How many men?"

"There've got to be at least two hundred ISIS fighters down there, maybe more if some are inside or downstairs—we've seen stairwells that seem to go to an underground level."

"You're sure they're ISIS?"

"Absolutely—the black flag is flying from the top of the minaret."

"In the middle of Turkey?"

"Well, I'd hardly call it the middle. We're 1,200 kilometers from Istanbul by road and a good 750 kilometers from Ankara. Believe me, this is the frontier—rural, rugged, and only ten or twenty miles north of the Syrian border."

"Would you hide an ISIS emir there?" I asked.

"I might," Dutch said.

"What are the men doing now?" Mustafa asked.

"Several dozen are patrolling the perimeter or hunkered outside the gates in huge APCs with a lot of weaponry. The rest are sitting in the courtyard, eating dinner."

"Who else is there?" I asked.

"What do you mean?"

"Do you see any women?"

"No."

"And you said no children?"

"Not any that I can see."

"What about elderly?"

"Not from my vantage point."

"So it's just young men?" I pressed.

"I don't see anyone older than forty—most look like they're in their twenties. Big. Strong. Good shape. Fighters. And they're Arab, not Turkish."

"All armed, I presume?"

"Heavily."

"Okay, so what's your gut tell you?"

"Well, there's no question Al-Siddiq is there, along with the three ISIS operatives who brought him."

"You can see the van?" Yael asked.

"Affirmative," Dutch replied. "And the tracking signal from Al-Siddiq is still strong and clear, but . . ."

His voice trailed off.

I was about to ask him to finish his sentence, but Yael held up her hand, motioning me to be quiet. She knew Dutch better than any of the rest of us. She knew how he thought, how he operated. She knew he'd speak when he was ready and not a moment before. And sure enough, a few seconds later, he finished his thought.

"But *if* Khalif is in there or if he's coming," he said, "we're going to need a lot more men."

93

★ ★ ★

As evening fell, we headed for Nizip.

Mustafa and the rest of his team brought food, water, blankets, more weapons, and additional ammunition to Dutch and his team up in the mountains. Yael and I, on the other hand, checked into a dusty, grungy old hotel, once again posing as a Muslim husband and wife, she in her *abaya* and me in my skullcap. The moment we found our floor and our chambers, we locked the door behind us and slid the dresser in front of the door. It would hardly stop jihadists from bursting into the room if they found us, but it might slow them down enough to give us a fighting chance.

Using the small desk in the room and the two nightstands on either side of the small double bed, we again set up a mini war room with our laptops, digital recording equipment, state-of-the-art headphones, and a slew of satellite phones and chargers. We kept two MP5 submachines always within reach.

Meanwhile, up in the mountains, Mustafa would soon be giving Dutch and Pritchard cases of sophisticated directional microphones and video cameras equipped with high-powered zoom lenses, night vision, thermal-imaging technology, and the ability to broadcast encrypted signals back to us. Our job was to pinpoint Al-Siddiq and listen to his conversations in the hopes that this might lead us to our prey.

By one in the morning, Mustafa had delivered the equipment, and Dutch and Pritchard had it all up and running. The encrypted signals were coming in. Yael and I were recording everything, and we'd located Al-Siddiq in the compound. He was not in the dormitory. He was in the other wing, in one of the classrooms located on the second floor of the madrassa. The shades were drawn, so we could not see him, but we could hear him, and we were stunned by what we were listening to.

Rather than being welcomed, the Saudi professor was being grilled. The interrogators—two of them—sounded significantly younger than Al-Siddiq, and they were asking questions in rapid fire, barely giving him time to answer. *Whom had he told that he was leaving Medina? Who else? What did his wife know? Who had booked his tickets? Why hadn't he followed the precise instructions he'd been sent? Whom had he spoken to on his journey? Why had he worn Western clothes? Didn't he understand that was forbidden? Had he been followed? How could he be sure? What precautions had he taken? Why hadn't he brought his laptop? Where was his laptop? Was it secure? Did his wife have access to it? Didn't he know the risks?*

The interrogation continued until just before 3 a.m. Then the men left, slammed and locked the door behind them, and all we could hear was heavy breathing and sobs and the sound of clanking metal, like chains.

What in the world was going on? Why was Al-Siddiq being treated like a spy, a traitor, a mole, rather than a guest of honor? Yael and I sent urgent flash text messages to Dutch and Pritchard and back to Ari— all encrypted, of course—telling them what we were hearing. They didn't get it either. I looked at Yael, stricken with the rapidly rising fear that this was not only a mistake but very well could be a diversion. Had Al-Siddiq been bait? Had he been cleverly dangled in front of us to distract from Khalif's real movements? The very thought sickened me. But for the moment, I could think of nothing else.

Yael texted our concerns to Shalit, who urged us not to give up hope.

Take a break, he wrote. **Try to get some sleep—a few hours at least. And we'll go back at it when the sun comes up.**

Yael and I looked at each other and then around the small, musty room and at the creaky double bed. This was hardly the five-star accommodations we'd had in Cairo or in Dubai, and we were both exhausted. For much of the past few weeks, we'd been operating off of sheer adrenaline. I had, anyway, and now it all seemed to have drained out of my system.

"I'll be out in a minute," Yael said, breaking the silence as she grabbed her MP5 and ducked into the tiny bathroom to change and brush her teeth.

I sat down on the bed, holding my MP5 and praying I'd never have to use it. I also prayed for something else, something far more important—the strength to let Yael go. We'd been spending an awful lot of time together, and though we weren't talking about personal things—and though we were often with the rest of our team, completely focused on our work—I was simply intoxicated to be in her presence. I'd never met anyone as strong and yet as sensitive, as funny and yet as intellectually stimulating. I loved watching her mind work. I loved seeing her process information, seeing her direct the team. And I also loved how she looked in every piece of clothing she put on. It was killing me to be so physically close to her, all day, every day, knowing she was engaged. She wasn't available. She'd chosen someone else. I'd lost my chance, before I'd even realized I had a competitor, before I'd even known I needed to fight for her.

I fumbled through my carry-on bag until I found my toothbrush and paste. Then I turned off the overhead light and the room was illuminated merely by the greenish glow of our electronic gear.

Just then, the bathroom door opened and Yael came out. I slid past her into the bathroom and took a cold shower. When I finally came out of the bathroom and clicked off the light, Yael was already in bed and under the covers. She just looked back at me and shrugged.

The room was tiny. There was nowhere else to lie down. If there'd been a full bathtub instead of a mere shower stall, at least I could have slept in the tub. Without another option, however, I reluctantly climbed into the bed and thought the entire hotel must be able to hear it creak. If I could have, I would have moved myself over to the very edge of the mattress, but there was literally no room to move at all. And so I lay there, trying not to move, listening to her breathing.

Sometime later, she turned over, and the bed made a terrible racket. Once she'd settled, her mouth was right by my left ear. "I'm sorry, J. B.," she whispered.

"For what?" I whispered back, surprised.

"For the way I treated you at first. And for not telling you sooner."

"Don't worry about it," I said. "I'm a big boy. I'll be okay. I'm glad you're happy."

"I'm not sure I'm the kind of girl that can do happy," she said.

"What is that supposed to mean?"

"You know what I do. You know what I see, what I know, where I am, where my job takes me. Not exactly conducive to being a happy person."

"Maybe it's time to stop."

"Maybe it is."

"*I'm* going to stop," I said.

"What do you mean?"

"When this is done, I'm going to put in my letter of resignation at the *Times*."

"Why? You're such a great reporter."

I didn't reply. I just lay there, staring at the ceiling, straining with every ounce of my being not to turn and kiss this woman.

"I don't know," I said finally, deciding I was better off talking than not. "I think I'm just through."

"Yeah," she said. "Maybe this is it for me, too."

"There's always the prime minister's office," I said, trying to be helpful.

"I can't," she whispered. "If I'm done, I need to be really done. I need to start a new life—a real life."

"Meaning what?"

"Being a wife. Being a mom. Taking my kids to the park, to the beach, to the mountains, teaching them to read, to write, to sing."

"You'll be good at that," I said.

"You think so?" she asked.

"I do."

And a few moments later, she nestled up next to me and fell sound asleep.

94

★ ★ ★

NIZIP, TURKEY

I didn't sleep that night.

I couldn't. For the next few hours, I just listened to the monotonous ticking of my grandfather's pocket watch on the nightstand beside me and prayed for strength and mercy. In my forty-some-odd years, I'd made a lot of mistakes, done a lot of things I wasn't proud of. But that was the past. That was behind me. I was on a new path now. I wanted to do the right thing. I wanted to honor my Lord. I just wasn't sure I was going to make it.

By God's grace, I made it through the night without kissing the beautiful and unavailable woman sleeping beside me. And in the morning, the new day brought very good news.

Yael grabbed the satphone off the floor on her side of the bed, beside her MP5, and took the call from Dutch. "You're kidding," she said. "That's incredible. Okay, we're on it."

"What?" I asked, suddenly feeling a jolt of adrenaline surge through my system.

"They think they may have found him."

"Who? Khalif?"

"They're not certain," she explained. "But a few minutes ago,

Al-Siddiq was let out of his cell. Someone apologized to him, told him they had to make sure he hadn't been compromised. Then— well, here, let's take a look."

She jumped out of bed, grabbed her laptop, and powered it up. In a moment we had our headphones on and were watching video footage transmitted from the mountain. The time stamp read, *07:12:36.*

At first, I didn't recognize Al-Siddiq. He was no longer wearing an oxford shirt and tweed blazer. Rather, he had on a traditional white *thawb* similar to the one I had worn entering Turkey. His head was covered in a red- and white-checked headdress known as a *ghutra,* secured to his head with a classic *igal,* a thick black cord that was worn doubled. He was strolling across the courtyard with another man, about his same height, also dressed in traditional white robes, though this one was wearing a ceremonial outer cloak known as a *bisht.* This man's *ghutra* completely obscured his face from anything but a direct, eye-to-eye view.

"Thank you for coming, father," the shrouded man said, speaking so softly we had to play it back several times to be sure.

"It is my honor," Al-Siddiq said.

"Ahmed and Faisal explained their procedures?"

"They did, and of course I fully understand."

"I hope you know they meant you no harm."

"Yes, yes, of course."

"We cannot be too careful."

"I know," Al-Siddiq said.

"You are my guest of honor."

"No, Your Excellency; it is my honor completely."

"So would you like to see her?"

"Is that possible?"

"It is surely possible."

"Then, yes, absolutely, I would love that."

"Good—she will be here in a matter of moments."

"She is coming? Here? Now?" Al-Siddiq asked.

"They are bringing her even as we speak."

The satphone rang. Yael answered it and motioned me to patch in through the app on my phone. It was Ari Shalit.

"Have you seen it?" Shalit asked, urgency thick in his voice.

"We're watching it now," she said.

"Both of you?"

"Yes."

"J. B. is with you?"

"Yes, of course."

"I'm here," I said.

"Good—so is it him?"

"Maybe," I said tentatively.

"It looks like him," Shalit said.

"I can't see his face," I said.

"Can you tell by his walk, his gait?"

"No, I'm sorry."

"But does it sound like him?"

"Hard to say," I confessed. "He's speaking low, almost mumbling. That's not like him. That's not how he was with me."

"Maybe he's different with his father-in-law," Shalit said.

"Maybe."

"But of what you could hear, does it sound like him—the style, the cadence, the air of authority?" Shalit pressed.

"Maybe—it's possible—it's a start," I replied. "We'll need more, but—"

Shalit cut me off. "No, no, you're not understanding the situation," he said. "I need an answer. I need to know now. The prime minister needs to know—not later, not tomorrow—we need to know right now, this second."

"Why? What's the rush?" I pushed back.

"If it is Khalif, how long do you think he's going to stay in that compound?" Shalit asked. "A few hours? A day? This is Abu Khalif. This is the emir of the Islamic State. He could leave in the middle of the night. He could leave in the middle of this conversation. This is the most wanted man on the planet. Just because we've found him—*if* we've found him—that doesn't mean we'll know where he is tomorrow."

Yael looked at me. I could see strain and fatigue in her eyes.

"You're the expert, Mr. Collins," Shalit pressed. "This is why you're here. No one in the West—no one outside his inner circle—has spent as much time with Abu Khalif as you have."

"Right now I'm looking at a man in a robe, with a shroud over his face, mumbling, practically talking under his breath, and you want a 100 percent positive ID?"

"It's not what *I* want," he shot back. "The prime minister and the entire security cabinet are assembled. They're in the Kirya, in the war room. They're waiting for an answer. Are we go or no go?"

"I need a few minutes," I said.

"You don't have a few minutes," Shalit warned me. "Right now there's a caravan of women and children heading toward the compound. As best we can tell, all four of Khalif's wives and all of his children have been staying in Nizip, and now they're headed to see Khalif—if it's him—and they're almost there. Dutch has a sniper rifle out. He's in position. He has this guy in his sights. He's ready to take the shot—and risk the consequences of two hundred ISIS fighters going crazy and storming up the mountain—but we need an answer, and we need it now."

95

★ ★ ★

My mind was racing and the pressure was enormous.

It *did* seem like Khalif, but could I be certain? If I was wrong, I'd be condemning an innocent man to death. Well, maybe not innocent. This was clearly a senior ISIS commander. He was surrounded by two hundred or more ISIS fighters. But was he the emir or not? For that, I needed more data. I needed more time. But Shalit wasn't going to give it to me.

So far, all the pieces of the puzzle were consistent with this being Khalif. The shrouded man had called Al-Siddiq "father," a term of honor, affection, respect. He'd apologized to Al-Siddiq for having his men interrogate him. And he had used the names Ahmed and Faisal—the first names of two of the Baqouba brothers. It would make sense they would be with Khalif, helping to protect him and vet his guests. What's more, Al-Siddiq seemed excited to see someone, a woman, and the shrouded man seemed to have planned ahead for Al-Saddiq to see her. Could it be Aisha, the professor's daughter, the emir's wife?

In almost every way, it added up. But there was a real risk. What I was seeing wasn't hard evidence. There could be other Ahmeds. There could be other Faisals. Al-Siddiq was Khalif's father-in-law, but he was the theological mentor of the entire Islamic State movement. There could be any number of other senior leaders who revered him as "father." And we hadn't actually heard any mention of a wife or a daughter, much less the name Aisha.

"Collins," Shalit pushed, "I need an answer."

"I'm sorry," I said. "But I can't. I don't have enough data."

"You've got all you're going to get."

"Then my answer is no—I can't say beyond a doubt that this is Khalif. I'm sorry."

"Yael, what do you say?" Shalit demanded.

"Don't ask me that," she replied.

"I'm not asking," Shalit said. "I'm ordering you to give me your assessment."

"You heard the expert," she demurred. "He spent hours with Khalif. He wants this guy as badly as any of us. But even he can't say for certain."

"Can you?" he asked.

Silence.

"You're the head of the unit tracking him," Shalit continued. "Collins doesn't work for us. You do."

"But *you* pulled him onto this team over my objections," she argued. "You didn't do it out of pity. You did it because he knows what he's talking about. He knows this guy. He's seen his face. He's heard his voice. He's the expert, and if he's not sure, then I'm not sure."

Shalit cursed.

Then Yael nudged me. She was staring at the live video feeds from the mountaintop positions. The women and children had arrived. They were pouring into the compound. Whatever chance we might have had was now lost, and suddenly the line went dead. The call was over. Shalit had hung up.

Yael just stood there, staring at the monitor, the satphone in her hand, not sure what to say or do. I didn't know either, and I felt sick.

I excused myself and headed into the bathroom and took a shower. By the time I came out, Yael was dressed in faded jeans and a gray sweatshirt and was sitting at the same desk, still watching the real-time video feed of the courtyard. As hundreds of armed men milled about at the edges of the compound, the children all gravitated to the shrouded man sitting under an archway, in the shadows, partially obscured from our view. Meanwhile, Al-Siddiq sat on the other side of the courtyard, beside a woman wearing a headscarf who appeared to be in her late thirties. They spoke in whispers. Our microphones weren't picking up any of it, but it certainly looked like a man and his married daughter catching up on old times.

Yael looked at me. "It was the right call, J. B. It was. The case was circumstantial. Ari was pushing you too hard, probably because he was being pushed too hard. For what it's worth, I'm proud of you."

"Thanks," I said, but Yael's encouragement didn't erase the gnawing feeling in my gut that I'd just made a very serious error in judgment.

Over the course of the next few hours, we picked up bits of audio—little snatches of sound—that gave me more and more confidence the man we were staring at so intently was, in fact, Abu Khalif. He finally used the name Aisha and then used it several more times. What's more, he asked Al-Siddiq for an update on the death toll from the attacks in America.

What sealed it for me was when the shrouded man asked for an update on the fatwa. And then came the moment that made my blood run cold.

"Has anyone found him yet?" he asked.

"Who?" Al-Siddiq pressed.

"Collins. Have we tracked him down? Has anyone gotten a lead on his surviving family? If one of our people find them, I don't want them killed. I want them alive. Make sure all our people know that. Especially James Bradley. I want him captured and brought to the site. I will take my vengeance out on him myself."

With that, the man I was now certain was Abu Khalif disappeared. He got up, left the courtyard, entered the front door of the mosque, and was completely obscured from our view. For the next three days, while the women and children remained in the compound and Al-Siddiq took a morning and evening stroll, often with his daughter, we did not see Khalif again, nor did we hear his voice.

Shalit was furious, and I couldn't blame him. The longer Dutch and Pritchard and the others were up on those mountains, the more likely they were going to get spotted and captured. If they were caught, they'd be beheaded, or burned alive, right before our eyes. We were out of options and out of time, and there was no way to sugarcoat it—this was my fault.

96

★ ★ ★

"What if the women and children leave?" I asked.

It was about three in the morning on the fourth day. Yael and I were drinking bad black coffee we'd heated in a tin pan on a small portable hot plate and watching the monitors so Dutch and Pritchard and the guys in the mountains could get a few hours of shut-eye.

"What do you mean?" she asked.

"I mean, let's say the wives and kids all get up and leave one morning; what's the plan? We haven't seen Khalif in days. We don't know where in the compound he actually is at this point. The last time we saw him, he went into the mosque. But he could be anywhere, underground or in one of the two wings. So what if Dutch or the other snipers never get another look at him?"

She looked at me, considering. Then she said, "Honestly? I don't think it matters whether we can see him or not. Khalif is never leaving that compound."

"What do you mean? Why do you say that?"

"Think about it. This is where Khalif has chosen to settle himself, his wives, his kids, and his senior leadership. He's safe here. He's in a NATO country, safe from air strikes by the U.S. or Israel. The

427

Turkish police aren't in sight. Neither is the military. He isn't going anywhere. He's essentially got carte blanche."

"Why?"

"Why is the president of Turkey—with his megalomaniacal dreams of becoming an all-powerful sultan and reviving the glories of the Ottoman Empire—allowing the emir of the Islamic State to reside in his territory? I have no idea."

"You think he knows?"

"Maybe yes, maybe no, but let's face it—the government in Ankara are a bunch of Islamists, and they're becoming more radicalized every day. Why else have they been letting foreign fighters cross their territory to go fight for ISIS? Should it really surprise us the head of ISIS is living right here?"

"So you guys have to storm the place, like how the Americans got bin Laden in that compound in Pakistan."

"With the force we've got?"

"Well, you'd obviously need more men."

"It's not going to happen."

"Why not?"

"Dutch has been begging for more manpower, heavier weapons—but the security cabinet says no."

"Because if a bunch of Israeli commandos get caught or killed on Turkish soil, you've just triggered a war with NATO?"

"Maybe," she said.

"What about the Jordanians? The Egyptians? The emirates? They all want to take out Khalif. They've all provided tremendous support. You've seen it. This is historic—Israelis and Arabs working so closely on a major intelligence and military operation? It might be unprecedented."

"But they're not going to risk being seen as invading a NATO ally either."

"So where does that leave us?" I asked.

"The Kurds," Yael replied.

"The Kurds?"

"The Syrian Kurdish rebels, to be precise. They now control most of the border with Turkey, and they hate ISIS with a passion. They also hate the Turks. They want their own country. They want to link up with the Turkish Kurds—between ten and twenty million people—and the Iraqi Kurds to create a unified Republic of Kurdistan."

"So how does that help us?"

"A few days ago, a squad of Syrian Kurdish rebels near Aleppo got into a firefight with Assad's forces. The Kurds won. The regime guys were slaughtered. In the process, the Kurds captured a Russian-made surface-to-surface missile launcher—the SS-21 Scarab C. It's got a range of about 115 miles, and it's equipped with a GPS-linked guidance system, so it's pretty accurate."

"And?"

"And let's just say the Mossad has pretty close ties to the Kurds. We don't see eye to eye on everything—don't get me wrong. But the enemy of my enemy is my friend, right? The Kurds are taking out ISIS forces. They're taking out Assad's forces. We try to help where we can. So Ari asked the security cabinet to authorize the Mossad to discreetly let the Kurdish rebel commanders know someone might have found Abu Khalif, and if that turns out to be true, would they be interested in taking him out. The cabinet agreed, and Ari set the plan into motion. Now everything's set. The moment the women and children leave the compound, Ari will give the Kurds the precise coordinates for the missiles, and three minutes later, it will all be over."

I was silent, processing this new information, as we kept our eyes on the monitors. All was quiet at the compound. Everyone except the guards on duty was sound asleep. Yael suggested that I try to get some sleep, after which she would do the same.

I tried, but I simply couldn't fall asleep. Too much was happening—or more precisely, not happening. We'd done it. We'd hunted down

Abu Khalif. We'd actually found him. We had him surrounded. Yet we couldn't take him out.

Meanwhile, out there in the rest of the world, innocent people were dying. ISIS was butchering, enslaving, and raping men, women, and children. And why? To hasten the coming of their messiah, to fulfill their ancient prophecies, and maybe for sheer pleasure. Yet however ghastly their killing spree had been so far, they were just ramping up. They had already come after my country. They had already come after my family. Soon they would be coming after me. The stakes could not be higher.

Yet as I lay there, staring at the ceiling, thinking of my mother and my nephew now in heaven and Matt and his family now in hiding, I was growing desperate. Our window to move was rapidly closing. Dutch and his men couldn't stay out there much longer. They were going to get noticed. They could very well get killed. We had to pinpoint Khalif's precise location and then we had to strike fast.

But how?

97

★ ★ ★

For well over an hour, I war-gamed every possible scenario I could think of.

I prayed for wisdom—no, actually, I begged God to show me what to do. But no answer seemed to come.

Then it was my turn to relieve Yael and let her close her eyes and get some rest. Bleary-eyed, I splashed cold water on my face. Then I made myself a fresh pot of bad coffee, sat down at the desk in front of our laptops, and donned my headphones while she collapsed in the bed and immediately fell asleep.

Just before dawn, the Muslim call to prayer rang out from the minaret. It wasn't a recording. Even through my headphones I could tell someone was actually in the tower, calling the faithful to their morning rituals. I remotely adjusted one of the cameras and zoomed in, hoping it might be the emir. But it was Al-Siddiq. Soon hundreds of foreign fighters came out of the dormitory and into the courtyard, each with a prayer rug. Then they all bowed down, facing Mecca, and began their prayers.

Before long, the sun began to rise, yet the compound—tucked into a small canyon and surrounded by mountain peaks—was still covered in long, dark shadows. The two dozen guards at the front gate were replaced by a new shift. Various other clumps of guards throughout the grounds were being relieved as well.

Eventually, as the first rays of sun splashed across the lawn in the courtyard, Al-Siddiq came out and went for a long, quiet, peaceful walk. No one was with him. Not his daughter. Not any of the fighters. He simply walked alone. And still, no sign of Khalif.

Why not? Where was he? Why wasn't he showing his face? He couldn't possibly sense we were watching him. If he had, his men would have attacked Dutch and Pritchard and their colleagues, and we'd be dealing with a bloodbath, not the prospect of another day of sitting around doing nothing.

At precisely eight o'clock, the courtyard was full of Arab fighters again. Now they were doing their morning exercises. By nine, I could see signs the wives and children were gathering in the various classrooms to begin their daily studies. All of this was pushing my frustration to the boiling point. I was watching a genocidal, apocalyptic terrorist community going about their day, business as usual, and I couldn't take much more of it.

When Yael eventually woke up, showered, and dressed, we spent several hours brainstorming ways to break the stalemate—but yet again we came up with nothing. At one point in the early afternoon, we got a call from Shalit. He wanted an update. We had little to tell him. He had little to tell us. The security cabinet was becoming divided. Several members were suggesting it might be time to pull us all out of Turkey. They understandably feared sparking a major confrontation with Ankara if Turkish authorities found us here. One member of the cabinet was urging Prime Minister Eitan to authorize the Kurds to simply decimate the entire compound immediately, even with Khalif's wives and children there. He argued that in the end it would be the Kurds who would get credit for taking out the ISIS emir and several hundred ISIS fighters, and they would take any blame for collateral damage as well.

However, the prime minister had strenuously objected to the suggestion. "The government of Israel does not target innocent women and children—*ever*—period, end of discussion," he'd said, and that was that.

For this I was immensely grateful and relieved. I hadn't signed up to kill innocents. I'd signed up to bring Abu Khalif to justice. I would never be party to an operation that would countenance the targeting of the wives and children of terrorists, no matter what some politicians back home or anywhere else in the world might advocate. I hadn't always lived by the morals and the ethics that my grandfather and my mom had modeled for me, but I had no doubt what they would say about purposefully killing innocents in pursuit of taking out a terrorist.

Some might argue that Khalif's wives and children weren't innocent. But I didn't buy the argument. So far as I was concerned, they were effectively hostages of Khalif and the demonic system he had built around himself. Under the Islamic system, no woman could refuse a marriage proposal by him. And regardless of what the women thought about Khalif, they had absolutely no say in his day-to-day affairs. The children? What choice did they have in being born to a genocidal father and raised in this sinister family? None whatsoever. Might some of them one day join ISIS and devote themselves to a life of violent jihad? Yes, I knew they might. I wasn't blind. I could see the path they were on. But did this condemn them to death by a Syrian missile before reaching their teenage years? Not in my mind. Besides, might they not choose other lives, especially if their father met his demise and they were free from his slavery? I couldn't say for sure, but they might, and even that sliver of hope was enough for me.

"Have you gotten any rest?" Yael asked by midafternoon.

"No, but I'm fine," I said.

"You don't look fine. Your eyes are bloodshot. You're getting dark rings under them. Why don't you try to lie down for a while?"

"How can I?" I asked her. "How can I sleep while Khalif is up there in the mountains, free and clear, planning some new horrific attack? We can't sit here anymore. We need to do something."

"I agree," she said. "But we've been over and over it, and we've come up with nothing."

I was about to throw my hands up in despair when suddenly a thought occurred to me. "How precise are those Syrian missiles—the ones the Kurds captured?" I asked.

"Quite."

"I mean, could they take out the mosque but leave the classrooms unaffected?" I asked.

Khalif's wives and children were sleeping in the madrassa, while Al-Siddiq and all the male fighters were sleeping on the bunk beds in the dormitory.

"I don't know about *unaffected*," Yael replied. "Those missiles pack some pretty powerful explosives. But yeah, given the size of the compound, I doubt anyone in the classrooms or the dorms would be killed if the Kurds hit the mosque. Injured maybe, but not killed. But why do you ask? I mean, we don't really know Khalif is in the mosque."

I ignored her question and asked another of my own. "What if Khalif was actually in the dormitory? Could one of the missiles take out the dormitory and not destroy the classrooms or kill those inside?"

"I think so."

"Can you find out for sure?"

"I could," she said, "but why? What good does it do if we don't have precise intel on where Khalif is?"

"Just find out," I whispered. "I have an idea."

98

★ ★ ★

It was almost midnight when Yael finally gave me some answers.

Yes, according to Shalit, the Mossad analysts, and the chief of staff of the Israeli Defense Forces, the Russian-built missile was that precise. Given the size of the compound, *if* we could actually find Khalif, and *if* he was actually in a part of the compound that was far enough away from the women and children, then yes, the Kurds could hit that section, and the women and children should survive.

But that was a lot of ifs. The brutal fact remained—we had no idea precisely where Khalif was, and without that specificity, the prime minister and his security cabinet were not going to authorize a strike.

I pressed Yael on the specifics. I asked dozens of questions about the technical details of the missiles, their size, their range, their speed. I pressed her on the design of the guidance system and on why Shalit and the IDF were so confident. To her credit, she really had done her homework. She had answers to all the questions I was asking and then some. In the end, I was satisfied.

And then she asked a question of her own. "Why are you asking all this? What are you thinking?"

I had wondered how I'd feel when this moment came. I feared I might be jittery, tense, equivocating. But instead I found myself speaking in a calm, firm, but gentle voice. "Yael, I'm going to that compound," I said. "Tonight."

"What are you talking about?"

"Khalif wants to find me, wants to kill me—fine, he can have me. I'm going to surrender," I told her.

"Are you crazy?"

"Not at all. Listen—the moment I arrive, Khalif will think he's won. But I'll be wearing a tracking beacon. I'll be wearing the glasses you guys gave me. You'll know exactly where I am and thus exactly where he is. The moment I'm in his presence, you can tell the Kurds to take the shot, and in three minutes, it'll all be over."

"But how will you get out?"

"I won't."

Yael's eyes went wide. "J. B., that's lunacy—no—absolutely not," she shot back and launched into a desperate attempt to dissuade me.

But I cut her off. "Yael, stop," I insisted. "My mind's made up. This is the only way, and you know it. Dutch and Pritchard can't stay up there indefinitely. They're going to be caught. They're going to be killed. And you said it yourself—Khalif isn't leaving that compound, and why would he? He's hiding behind the human shield of his wives and children. It's time to take him out. Tonight."

"J. B., come on. You're exhausted. You're not thinking rationally. There's another way, and we'll find it."

"No, there isn't. I wish there was—believe me—but there isn't, and you know it. I've been thinking and praying about this nonstop. And this is it. We're out of time. This is our only play."

"What about Matt? What about Annie and Katie?" she asked, a look of near panic in her eyes as she observed the resolution in mine.

"Why do you think I'm doing this?" I asked her. "Khalif has triggered a worldwide hunt for my family and me. The only way Matt and Annie and Katie come out of this alive, safe, and free to live without fear is if we take out Khalif right here, right now."

"So what are you going to do, walk up to the door and knock?"

"Why not?"

"Because it's *insane*."

"No, what would be insane is to keep sitting here doing nothing, to let him keep hunting my family, to let him continue his genocide without stopping him if I can."

"But what if the moment you're caught, he puts you in a cage in the middle of the courtyard and gathers his wives and children all around him?"

"That's why I have to go now, in the middle of the night, while his wives and children are sleeping."

"But what if he's sleeping with them?"

"Then his men will wake him, and he'll come to me."

"How do you know?"

"Because he won't be able to help himself," I replied. "He's a fanatical, apocalyptic Muslim. He believes he's ushering in the End of Days. He believes he's preparing for the coming of the Mahdi and the establishment of the global caliphate. He'll want to gloat. He'll lecture me. He'll go off on a bloodthirsty, demon-possessed rant, and while he does, the Kurds will push the button, and boom. It'll all be over before he knows it."

"You're really serious?" she said quietly. The look in her eyes was shifting. Gone was the shock. Gone, too, was the defiance. Now all I saw was sadness.

"I am," I said.

"And you're not scared to die." Her eyes were filling with tears.

"I used to be, Yael, but I'm not anymore."

"Why not?"

"Because I know where I'm going," I said.

I told her what I'd done. I told her how Matt had been trying to convince me about Jesus Christ for years. I told her how I'd been angry, how I'd completely rejected my brother, how I hadn't even talked to him for nearly a decade. But then I told her what had happened on the plane on the way to Dubai, how I'd finally received Christ as my Savior. "Everything's changed, Yael. *I'm* changed. I've made enough bad choices in my life. It's time to make a good one."

"But how could this possibly be good?" she asked, tears running down her cheeks.

"Because it's one of the first things I've ever done that isn't about me," I replied. "It's for Matt and Annie. It's for Katie. And for everyone else facing death at the hands of Abu Khalif."

Until that moment, I'd basically lived my entire life in utter self-centeredness. I'd ruined a marriage, become an alcoholic, and put countless friends and colleagues in harm's way. And for what? To get a good story? To win a Pulitzer or some other award? Was that really worth it? I'd concluded it wasn't. Not for me. Not anymore. It was time to do something for others. It was time to follow the example of my Savior.

"I told you about the letter Khachigian left me. Did I ever read it to you?"

"No, you just summarized it—that he was urging you to go after Khalif with everything you had. I don't think this is what he meant."

"Maybe not, but he did urge me to listen to Matt and give my life to Christ, like he finally did."

"Okay, fine, and you did that. But—"

"I know this doesn't make sense to you, Yael. And I'm sorry. But just listen to me for a moment. Khachigian closed the letter with a verse of Scripture, something Jesus said to his disciples. 'Greater love has no one than this, that one lay down his life for his friends.' Honestly, I'd never even heard of that verse until a few weeks ago. Then the pastor quoted it during the memorial service. I've been chewing on it ever since, but until this afternoon I never really understood it."

"And you think you do now?" she asked.

"Yeah, I do. Sometimes you don't get to win like they do in the movies. Sometimes, if you really love someone, you just have to lay down your own life so they can live. I know you think that's crazy. And for most of my life I would have agreed with you. But now I finally know where I'm going when I die. The moment I draw my last breath here, I'll draw my first breath in heaven with Christ. I'll get to see my mom and Josh again and be with them forever. Death isn't the end for me. It's just the beginning. I'm ready. I wasn't before, but now I am. And at least my death will mean something."

I reached for my carry-on bag and pulled out a few folded pieces of paper and handed them to her.

"What's that, your suicide note?" she asked.

"I'm not committing suicide, Yael."

"Of course you are."

"No, it's not suicide; it's called sacrifice."

"Same thing."

"Look, I don't want to die. I don't. But I'm willing to—for the right reason, at the right moment, and this is it."

"Okay," she said, wiping the tears from her eyes, though they just kept coming. "So what's that?"

"It's for Matt," I said. "Would you make sure he gets it?"

"What is it?"

"It's a letter explaining everything I just told you, with more details on how I finally came to trust in Jesus and how I came to conclude that this is the only way to keep him and his family safe. Don't worry—I left out anything that might be classified. I didn't mention you or Ari or any of the others. You can read it if you want. But will you take it to him personally? Will you promise me that?"

She nodded, and then she put her arms around me and began to sob.

99

★ ★ ★

The night was cold and quiet as I drove eastward along Highway O-52 toward the mountains.

I could still feel the sting from the tiny tracking beacon Yael had injected under my right armpit. In a final conference call with Yael and Shalit, Dutch had explained that this device, though minuscule, was designed to emit as strong a GPS signal as possible, even if I was taken underground.

I was touched by the last words Shalit and Dutch had said to me. They'd both told me I didn't have to do this. But when I'd insisted one last time, they'd said how grateful they were for my sacrifice, especially knowing that the entire plan rested on the Kurds taking all the credit. My name, I knew, would never be associated with this operation at all. I thanked them and said the last thing in the world I wanted was credit. The only way Matt and his family would ever be safe was if no one ever knew of my association with the plan to take down Abu Khalif once and for all.

Yael had said little on the call. Rather, she had just sat beside me, holding my hand and answering any logistical questions that came up. When the call was over, she'd given me a long hug. And then she'd watched me walk out of the hotel room for the last time.

Beside me, on the passenger seat, was a brand-new satellite phone. It had never been used before. It had no phone numbers for Shalit or Dutch or Yael or anyone else in the Mossad programmed into it. I was not expecting to receive any calls on the way to the compound, nor was I planning to make any. But Shalit had insisted that I take it. It would only ring, he said, if he believed there was a technical glitch that could prevent the Syrian Kurds from firing their missile at just the right moment.

I pulled off the main east-west highway onto a dirt road that headed up into the mountains. I was following coordinates Dutch had provided for the Toyota's GPS system, and with no traffic, I was making good time. I thought about the letter I'd written to Matt. I hoped I'd been clear enough about how grateful I was to him and how much I looked forward to seeing him on the other side. I thought, too, of the other thank-you notes I'd left in my carry-on bag—one for Yael, one for Ari, one for President Mahfouz, another for Prince bin Zayed, and the last one for King Abdullah II. Without this team and their courage, we would never have found the ISIS emir, and we could never have brought him to justice. I was sorry I'd never get to write the story of the unprecedented cooperation I'd witnessed between Israel and these Sunni Arab leaders. But I was grateful for the time I'd gotten to spend with them, for the insights and access they'd given me and the personal kindness they had shown me.

Finally I turned up a small, one-lane road. According to the map on my dashboard, I was less than half a mile from the compound. But suddenly I found myself approaching a guardhouse flying the black flag of ISIS and manned by armed fighters in black hoods. The guards, clearly stunned to see any unauthorized vehicle coming toward them, immediately pointed their AK-47s and began screaming at me in Arabic. I pulled to a stop, turned off the lights, and killed the engine. Then, as instructed, I got out of the car with my hands over my head. The screaming continued in full force. I was instructed to lie down on the ground, on my stomach, spread-eagle. Then I was promptly searched and then stripped. When I was pulled back to my feet, I was stark naked, surrounded by no fewer than six men pointing weapons at me.

"Who are you?" the leader shouted. "Why have you come?"

"My name is J. B. Collins," I said in Arabic. "I heard the emir was looking for me. I've come to talk to him. I work for the *New York Times*."

The expressions on their faces were priceless, and I hoped the video image being captured by my glasses was being transmitted back to Yael and the team crisp and clear. The men around me refused to believe me at first until they went through my wallet and found my driver's license.

"You're really J. B. Collins?" the leader said, astonished.

"I am," I said. "As I understand it, the emir has invited me to see him. I have a source that says he is staying in a mosque just up the road. Would you please take me there? I have a deadline."

Again, the men were nearly speechless.

"What source?" the leader finally asked.

"I really can't say."

"You must."

"I will tell the emir, but no one else. I'm sorry."

The next thing I knew, the leader was on a cell phone, presumably to his boss, and a few moments later, they ordered me to put my jeans and T-shirt back on. They did not return my shoes or socks, or my grandfather's watch or my leather jacket, and I was freezing in the night air.

It was barely three o'clock in the morning. The temperature was somewhere below fifty degrees. But this mattered little to me. So far, the plan was working. My hands and feet were bound tightly with rope, and I was shoved into the back of the Toyota. The leader and two of his henchmen drove me to the front gate.

By the time we arrived, so had a crowd of ISIS fighters. There had to have been forty or fifty. Word was spreading rapidly through the camp as I was hustled through the main gates, across the courtyard, and into the mosque.

The hatred in these men's eyes was unlike anything I had ever seen, yet it was mixed with a bizarre combination of curiosity and disbelief. I knew I should have been terrified. At any other time in my life, I would have been. But there was something surreal about the entire situation. It was almost as if I were outside my body, watching myself through the monitors back in the hotel in Nizip, as Yael was doing now.

And then, suddenly, I found myself standing face-to-face with Abu Khalif.

100

★ ★ ★

The predawn call to prayer wouldn't go forth for more than an hour.

It was obvious that Khalif had just been roused from sleep. His robe was rumpled and his eyes were bleary. I, on the other hand, was all too awake. I was seated, chained to a chair. I was cold. But I was not afraid.

At first Khalif did not say a word. He just walked around me and then stopped in front of me—maybe three or four feet away. He stared at me, completely baffled. The fact that I no longer looked like I did when he first saw me in Iraq—that I no longer looked like the photograph he'd released to the world, that I was no longer bald, that I was sporting a full beard—all of it confused him.

Ahmed Baqouba walked into the mosque with some two dozen fighters. I recognized him instantly, but he too looked baffled when he saw me. Baqouba had my wallet in his hands, and he looked down several times at my Virginia driver's license and then back at me. He handed the license to Khalif, who did the same. Finally Faisal Baqouba entered the mosque with quite an entourage around him, and now all three men were standing directly in front of me.

By God's mercy, the plan had worked. All three men were in the same place. I prayed the missile was already in the air.

444

But suddenly Ahmed surged toward me. He was seething with rage and as he approached, he slammed his fist into my face. I could hear the cartilage in my nose shatter. I could feel the blood gushing down my face. My glasses were crushed against my cheek. The pain nearly made me black out.

"Who are you?" Ahmed demanded.

"Collins," I said, willing myself to stay conscious despite the fact that my face felt like it was on fire. "James Bradley Collins."

"That's impossible!" the Baqouba brother roared. *"Tell me the truth."*

"I heard the emir wanted to see me," I continued, unable to see because of all the blood in my eyes. "So I came to see him. Perhaps he has something to tell the world."

"You're lying!"

Someone had grabbed me by the shoulders and was shaking me violently. But the voice was not the same. This was not Ahmed. Nor was it Faisal. Khalif himself was now standing in front of me, shouting.

"Who sent you? How did you know I was here?"

I tried to speak, but the pain was rapidly becoming unbearable. So I just kept silent and tried to focus my thoughts on what was coming. I could imagine the missile exploding from the mobile launcher near the Syrian border. I could picture it gaining altitude, stabilizing, arcing toward the compound.

I thought of Matt. I thought of Yael. I thought of the decision I'd made on the plane to finally accept what I already knew in my heart to be true. I thought of the verse about what true love looks like—laying down your life for others.

Khalif continued screaming at me. But I just kept imagining the inbound trajectory of the Syrian missile as it streaked across the Turkish plains at more than five times the speed of sound.

And then, suddenly, it arrived.

EPILOGUE

★ ★ ★

My cell phone rang just after noon local time.

I was at the hospital, visiting Annie and Katie, so I didn't answer it. Annie had just come out of a coma. She was groggy and in pain. She couldn't speak. But she recognized me. When I held her hand and asked her if I was a doctor or her husband, she squeezed my fingers twice. When I asked if I was her husband or J. B., she squeezed once. I was ecstatic. Katie had already been awake for several days. She was sitting up. She was talking—not much, but she was trying, and I was overjoyed.

So when my phone rang four more times in a row, I ignored it. There was no one I wanted to talk to right then, no one I was going to interrupt these moments of miracles for. But then I heard a commotion out in the hallway. And then a nurse burst in and told me in the accent of the islands to quickly turn on the television.

"No," I snapped. "Please, give us some privacy. We don't want to watch TV right now."

"But the news—it is so wonderful!"

"Why?" I asked. "What happened?"

"The leader of ISIS—they got him; they really got him!"

That, I admit, got my attention. I clicked on the television in Annie's room and found myself watching the breaking news coverage,

446

spellbound. All the broadcast networks and cable news networks were covering the story. I kept flipping from channel to channel. Details were sketchy so far, but the basic narrative was clear enough. After a two-month-long manhunt, Kurdish rebels, operating out of northern Syria, had hunted down and found Abu Khalif, the leader of the Islamic State, in a compound in eastern Turkey.

The missile strike had killed not only Khalif but two of his top deputies and at least a hundred of his most trusted fighters. The Turkish government denied knowing Khalif had been hiding on their territory and said they had police and military crews on the scene and a full investigation was under way. An anchor said the president of the United States was preparing to address the nation soon. Congratulations for the Kurds were pouring in from the leaders of Israel, Jordan, Egypt, the United Arab Emirates, and Saudi Arabia.

My thoughts immediately shifted to my brother. I pulled out my mobile phone, suddenly hoping it was J. B. who had called. Surely he knew the details. Very likely, he'd been right in the middle of the operation. But the number showed it wasn't J. B. It was FBI agent Art Harris instead.

I called back and after a single ring heard his voice.

"Is it true?" I asked. "Did they get him?"

"They did, Matt," Harris said. "The president will officially confirm it when he speaks to the nation at the top of the hour, but I can tell you we are certain. Abu Khalif has been killed."

"That's amazing—I can hardly believe it," I said, flooded with emotion. "And what about J. B.—did he call you? Is he okay?"

"What do you mean?" Harris asked. "Isn't J. B. there with you?"

"No, of course not. I thought he was working with you—or maybe with the CIA."

"Matt, what are you talking about?" Harris pressed. "You're saying J. B. isn't with you on St. Thomas?"

"No. J. B. left the same day you dropped us off here."

"He left? Where?"

"He said he was going to hunt down Abu Khalif. I was against it—fought him tooth and nail on it. But in the end I figured you two had cooked up some plot together."

Harris eventually convinced me he had no idea what this was all about, but he promised to look into it and get back to me.

Two days later, just after breakfast, there was a knock at the door of our home overlooking Magens Bay. I was alone in the house, preparing to go see Annie and Katie again. I went to the door and opened it, fully expecting to see Harris. Who else could it be?

Instead, I found a beautiful young woman wearing a pale-blue sundress and flats. She had a cast on her left arm and a number of fresh-looking scars on her face.

"May I help you?" I asked.

"I hope so," she said. "Are you Matt Collins?"

I just stood there, mouth agape, so caught off guard to hear my real name that I had no idea how to respond.

"I'm so sorry to bother you at home," the woman said, removing her sunglasses. "I realize you don't know me, and this must seem very strange. But my name is Yael Katzir. I was a friend of your brother."

"You're Yael?" I said, even more stunned.

Then she reached into her purse, pulled out several pages of a handwritten letter, and handed the pages to me. "I have this letter for you, Matt," she said. "It's from J. B.—a letter and a story . . ."

MOSCOW, RUSSIA

Louisa Sherbatov had just turned six, but she would never turn seven.

The whirling dervish had finally fallen asleep on the couch just before midnight, crashed from a sugar high, still wearing her new magenta dress and matching ribbon in her blonde tresses. Snuggled up on her father's lap, she looked so peaceful, so content as she hugged her favorite stuffed bear and lay surrounded by the dolls and books and sweaters and other gifts she'd received from all her aunts and uncles and grandparents and cousins as well as her friends from the elementary school just down the block at the end of Guryanova Street.

Strewn about her were string and tape and wads of brightly colored wrapping paper. The kitchen sink was stacked high with dirty plates and cups and silverware. The dining room table was still littered with empty bottles of wine and vodka and scraps of leftover birthday pie—strawberry, Louisa's favorite.

The flat was a mess. But the guests were gone and it was Thursday night and the weekend was upon them and honestly, her parents, Feodor and Irina, couldn't have cared less. Their little girl, the only child they had been able to bear after more than a decade and two heartbreaking miscarriages, was happy. Her friends were happy. Their parents were happy. They were happy. Everything else could wait.

Feodor stared down at the two precious women in his life and longed to stay. He had loved planning the party with them both, had loved helping shop for the food, loved helping Irina and her mother make all the preparations, loved seeing the sheer delight on Louisa's face when he'd given her a shiny blue bicycle, her first. But business was business. If he was going to make his flight to Tashkent, he had to leave quickly. So he gently kissed mother and daughter on their foreheads, picked up his suitcase, and slipped out as quietly as he could.

As he stepped out the front door of the apartment building, he was relieved to see the cab he'd ordered waiting for him as planned. He moved briskly to the car, shook hands with the driver, and gave the man his bag. The night air was crisp and fresh. The moon was full, and leaves were beginning to fall and swirl in the light breeze coming from the west. Summer was finally over, thought Feodor as he climbed into the backseat, and not a moment too soon. The sweltering heat. The stifling humidity. The gnawing guilt of not being able to afford even a simple air conditioner, much less a little dacha out in the country where he and Irina and Louisa and maybe his parents or hers could retreat now and again, somewhere in a forest with lots of shade and a sparkling lake for swimming or fishing.

"Thank God, autumn has arrived," he half mumbled to himself as the driver slammed the trunk shut and got back behind the wheel. Growing up, Feodor had always loved the cooler weather. The shorter days. Going back to school. Making new friends. Meeting new teachers. Taking new classes. Fall meant change, and change had always been good to him. Perhaps one day, if he continued to work very hard, he could save enough money to move his family away from 19 Guryanova Street, away from this noisy, dirty, run-down, depressing hovel on the south side of the capital and find some place really lovely and quaint and quiet. Some place worthy of raising a family. Some place with a bit of grass, maybe even a garden where he could till the soil with his own hands and grow his own vegetables.

As the cab began to pull away from the curb, Feodor leaned back in his seat. He closed his eyes and folded his hands on his chest. Yes, autumn had always been a time of new beginnings, and he wondered what this one might bring. He was not rich. He was not successful. But he was content, even hopeful, perhaps for the first time in his life.

He found himself reminiscing about the first time he'd laid eyes on Irina—the first day of middle school, twenty-two years ago. He was so caught up in his memories that he did not notice the car parked just down the street, a white Lada with its headlights off but its engine running. He didn't notice that the front license plate was covered with some sort of masking tape, revealing only the numbers 6 and 2. Nor did he notice the car's driver, nervously smoking a cigarette and tapping on the dashboard, or the two burly men, dressed in black leather jackets and black leather gloves, emerging from the basement of his own building. When the police would later ask about the men and the car, Feodor would be unable to provide any description at all.

What he did remember—what he could never possibly forget— was the deafening explosion behind him. He remembered the searing fireball. He remembered the taxi driver losing control and crashing into a lamppost not fifty meters up the street, and he remembered smashing his head against the plastic screen dividing the front seat from the back. He remembered the ghastly sensation of kicking open the back door of the cab, jumping out into the pavement, blood streaming down his face, heart pounding furiously, and looking up just in time to see his home, the twelve-story apartment building at 19 Guryanova Street, collapse in a blinding flash of fire and ash.

ACKNOWLEDGMENTS

★ ★ ★

One of the greatest joys of writing novels is seeing where they wind up being read and by whom.

Over the years, I have had the joy of meeting and hearing from readers of my books all over the world, from police officers to prisoners on death row, from rabbis and imams to pastors and priests, from students in high school and college to ministry and relief workers in remote tribal jungles, from senior government officials in world capitals to soldiers, sailors, airmen, and Marines on the front lines of the war on terror. I always love discovering how such varied people from such varied backgrounds hear about these books and what draws them to reading these stories when they have so many other matters pressing for their time and attention.

That said, however, I was in no way prepared for what happened last year. In January of 2016, my wife, Lynn, and I learned that Jordan's King Abdullah II had read *The First Hostage*, and rather than banning me from his kingdom, he invited Lynn and me to visit him in Amman. We had never met a king before, but we were both deeply grateful for the invitation and for the tremendous hospitality His Majesty showed us when we arrived. We had the honor of spending personal time with the king and a number of his generals and advisors. We observed a live-fire military exercise, visited a refugee camp, flew in the king's personal helicopter, visited several military bases and training centers, and saw some of the Hashemite Kingdom's most impressive archaeological treasures and biblical sites, from Mount Nebo to Petra.

Those five days in Jordan last spring were surreal, and they made me shake my head, yet again, that I really get to do what I do. Since I was eight years old, I have always had a passion to tell stories on paper and on film, to take people on adventures, to lead them on journeys and through experiences they otherwise would never go. What I hadn't understood when I was eight, however, was that as I wrote such stories I, too, would get to go on so many adventures and enter places previously inaccessible.

Along the way, I have had the great honor of meeting all kinds of readers, young and old, rich and poor, powerless and powerful. And I want to thank each and every one of you in the U.S., Canada, Israel, Jordan, and in dozens of countries all over the world where my books are translated and sold. Thank you for reading these thrillers. Thank you for all the kind and supportive messages you send me via e-mail, Facebook, Twitter, and good old-fashioned snail mail. Thank you for the constructive criticism and for reading my blog and for sharing it with others. Thanks, too, for constantly urging me to turn out these books faster and faster. Believe me, I'm doing my best!

I learned quickly in my writing career that dreaming up stories isn't enough. I knew I would need an extraordinary team of professionals to help me get these stories published, marketed, and publicized. By God's grace I have been blessed with just such a team and am deeply grateful for their passion for excellence and their personal kindness to me and my family.

Scott Miller is my literary agent, and he and his team at Trident Media Group have consistently proven to be the best in the business. Since my first novel, *The Last Jihad*, so many years ago, Scott has been a wise counselor and a true friend.

Mark Taylor, Jeff Johnson, Ron Beers, Karen Watson, and Jeremy

Taylor at Tyndale House have been an absolutely first-rate publishing group. All but two of my books have been published by them and I count it a tremendous joy and honor to work with such hardworking, creative and fun people. They not only do their best to help me do my best, but they have built a great team around them, including Jan Stob, Cheryl Kerwin, Dean Renninger, the entire sales forces, and all the other dedicated professionals that make the Tyndale brand shine.

June Meyers and Nancy Pierce work with me at November Communications, Inc., and they are beyond fantastic! Year in and year out they do an outstanding job helping me keep my head above water with everything from schedules to flights to finances and so much more—and they do so with great kindness, precision, and class.

I owe so much to my family and to Lynn's and am so thankful for their prayers, their patience, and their boundless encouragement.

I'm so thankful for the four wonderful sons the Lord has blessed us with: Caleb, Jacob, Jonah, and Noah—I love being on this remarkable journey with these boys, whatever the twists and turns and regardless of how much turbulence we encounter.

My parents, Leonard and Mary Jo Rosenberg, keep running the race with perseverance and for this I am so grateful.

Most of all I want to say thank you, thank you, thank you to my dear wife, Lynn. She continually blesses, inspires, and astounds me. She is such an amazing, creative, hardworking, and super encouraging friend and soul mate. I don't deserve you, Lynnie, but I will stick to you like glue!

ABOUT THE AUTHOR

★ ★ ★

Joel C. Rosenberg is a *New York Times* bestselling author with more than three million copies sold among his twelve novels (including *The Last Jihad*, *Damascus Countdown*, and *The Auschwitz Escape*), four nonfiction books (including *Epicenter* and *Inside the Revolution*), and a digital short (*Israel at War*). A front-page Sunday *New York Times* profile called him a "force in the capital." He has also been profiled by the *Washington Times* and the *Jerusalem Post* and has been interviewed on ABC's *Nightline*, CNN *Headline News*, FOX News Channel, The History Channel, MSNBC, *The Rush Limbaugh Show*, and *The Sean Hannity Show*.

You can follow him at www.joelrosenberg.com or on Twitter @joelcrosenberg and Facebook: www.facebook.com/JoelCRosenberg.

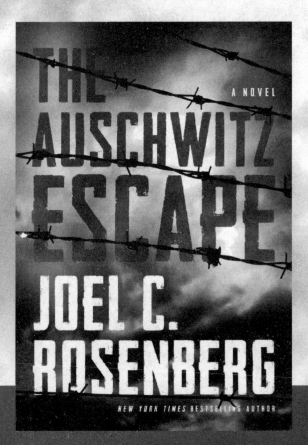

TYNDALE HOUSE PUBLISHERS IS CRAZY4FICTION!

Fiction that entertains and inspires

Get to know us! Become a member of the Crazy4Fiction community. Whether you read our blog, like us on Facebook, follow us on Twitter, or receive our e-newsletter, you're sure to get the latest news on the best in Christian fiction. You might even win something along the way!

JOIN IN THE FUN TODAY.

 www.crazy4fiction.com

 Crazy4Fiction

 @Crazy4Fiction